Harmony Black, Book Five

by Craig Schaefer

Publisher's Note: This is a work of fiction. Names, characters, places, and incidents are a product of the author's imagination. Locales and public names are sometimes used for atmospheric purposes. Any resemblance to actual people, living or dead, or to businesses, companies, events, institutions, or locales is completely coincidental.

Cover Design by James T. Egan of Bookfly Design LLC.
Author Photo ©2014 by Karen Forsythe Photography
Craig Schaefer / Right to the Kill
ISBN 978-1-944806-17-0

CONTENTS

The Story So Far

The Vigilant Lock program was created in the late 1960s, drawing upon consultants in the Federal Bureau of Investigation, local law enforcement, and the military. It operates without oversight or legal authority. Its mission is to track, hunt, and exterminate occult threats to the United States and its people.

It is also a lie.

On the trail of a dead man, Vigilant agents Jessie Temple and Harmony Black discovered the truth. Their organization was created by a conspiracy within the courts of hell. The courts of the East Coast, too weak for open warfare, created Vigilant Lock as a deniable weapon. They used human agents as proxies, sending them to destroy their rivals while keeping their own hands clean. Those who learned the truth were quietly eliminated.

Harmony, Jessie, and their team managed to turn the tables. They took over Vigilant from within, assassinated the demonic infiltrators, and sent a message to the occult underground: the lie just became real. Vigilant Lock is under new management, and no one is safe.

That was seven months ago. Vigilant Lock has been rebuilt from the ground up, recruiting new agents and establishing a secure network of contacts and safe houses. Their first real test was a trial by fire as they went head to head with an interdimensional syndicate called the Network, as part of the operation now known as the Wisdom's Grave incident.

Vigilant survived. And the courts of hell are waiting, pensive, wondering who their next target is going to be.

Tonight, they find out.

1.

The spire of Takahashi Tower rose above the Los Angeles skyline like a barbed spear, brutal and sleek. Its spike-tip pierced the veil of roiling yellow smog, gouging a bloodless wound, while its curved walls of mirror and chrome drank in the setting sun.

In the belly of the twenty-eighth floor, a span of cash-green carpet and Italian marble had become the staging ground for a feast. Caterers lined up tables and set out deep dishes with Sterno heaters; their blue flames kept a steady heat beneath under-spiced meatballs and vegetarian lasagna. Music was playing over the company PA system, a mix of the safest and most forgettable hits of the '90s, but the acoustic guitars struggled to ring out over the din of conversation as the minions of Mortensen, Keppner, & Burr LLP gathered for their mandatory reward. Some tugged at their ties as they sipped from plastic flutes of cheap champagne, waiting for the moment they could leave without raising any eyebrows. Others endured the party gamely, loading up on free food and coming back for seconds and thirds.

Harmony Black drifted through the crowd with a frozen smile on her face and a serving tray in her outstretched hands, offering fresh drinks and taking the empties. Her burgundy vest and ivory blouse marked her as a member of the catering crew; they mostly hired temps, so it was easy to get on the payroll in time for tonight's party. She'd had it easier than her partner Jessie, who had to earn her invitation the hard way: applying for an entry-level job and putting in the hours, three and a half weeks of on-site surveillance as she laid the groundwork for tonight's operation.

Jessie passed her in the other direction, sleek in a strategically low-cut emerald dress that clung to her rich dark skin like shimmering forest leaves. No eye contact, but a moment later the plastic bead nestled in Harmony's left ear thrummed with an annoyed sigh.

"You don't know how bad I want some of that champagne," Jessie said over the secured channel.

"You really don't," Harmony murmured. Her fake smile brightened as she passed out another glass. "This stuff is, like, three dollars a bottle."

"Nobody ever accused me of being a classy drinker. Tell me again why I had to spend a month in nine-to-five purgatory when you're the one with the accounting degree?"

Harmony slipped off to the side of the crowd. She whispered her response, her lips barely moving as she leaned over a recycling bin and off-loaded her empty plastic flutes.

"Because this was an infiltration op, and you're good with people. Besides, you made me do all your work anyway. Got eyes on the target?"

"She's hard to miss. Check behind you, seven o'clock."

Harmony chanced a look while she set out a round of fresh flutes on her tray. She grabbed a warm bottle from the small army concealed under a linen tablecloth and twisted the wire cage over the cork. Jessie was right: Dima Chakroun stood out from the crowd, dressed to impress in French couture and white lace. She had big, bright eyes and a runway stride, and vintage pearls cradled the olive hollow of her slender throat. A pack of hangers-on followed wherever she walked, hungry for her attention, for her smile, for anything she might offer them.

A couple of the men looked like they'd follow her, drooling, all the way to the gates of hell. They didn't know how close they were.

* * *

"Dima Chakroun," Harmony had said at the briefing. "French-Lebanese, multiple degrees in accounting and finance from Villanova University, senior partner at MK&B—"

"And a clinical psychopath," Jessie added. "Who, at the tender age of fourteen, cut her boyfriend's heart out and offered it up to Satan. She's gotten more ambitious since then."

A humming projector clicked. The slide changed, painting a new woman's face on the glowing square of the briefing-room wall. A golden bob of hair, deep blue eyes, and a mean little smile. Harmony gestured to the photograph.

"Chakroun is currently the personal accountant for this woman. Calls herself Nadine, previously Nadine Ashton; she burned that identity and the charity foundation it was attached to, but not fast enough to stop us from getting a foot in the intel door. A couple of stray emails led us to Chakroun's doorstep."

"Can't overstate this enough," Jessie said. "Nadine is an incarnate demon. If you see her in the field you do not, under any circumstances, engage. She's not as combat-oriented as some of her kin, but that doesn't mean she can't rip your throat out without breaking a sweat. Also, she's previously demonstrated mind-control abilities. All she has to do is get her hands on your exposed skin, and you belong to her. So, don't get close and don't get seen. Harmony and I went toe-to-toe with her once before, and we're damn lucky to still be here in one piece."

"We're not hunting heads on this op," Harmony said. "We're following the money. Access to Nadine's financial trail could expose a vast amount of infernal activity all across the Midwest. Targets we can flip or take down one by one."

A member of the support team, a fresh recruit straight out of Quantico, raised his hand.

"So what's the plan?" he asked. "Snatch the accountant and put the squeeze on her?"

Jessie shook her head. "Interrogation—even enhanced interrogation—is worthless on a true believer. Dima Chakroun actually wants to go to hell when she dies. Not much we can threaten her with. We can't flip her to our side, either. She's damned, so no matter what happens here on earth, the second she kicks the bucket she's going to be standing down in Nadine's throne room to answer for her sins. Nadine tortures her own people for fun. You don't want to know what she does to her enemies."

"And she scours her trail every time she thinks she's been compromised," Harmony said. "So we won't give her the courtesy of a heads-up this time. Our objective is to penetrate Dima Chakroun's office, gain access to her accounting files, steal a copy, and exfiltrate without being detected. We leave the accountant in play. If we do this right, we walk away with a map of Nadine's dirty money, everybody who's paying her and everybody she's paying, and nobody ever knows we were there."

* * *

Champagne splashed into a plastic flute. Droplets clung to the sides and glittered like diamonds under the hard office lights. The dregs of the bottle filled the last glass three-quarters of the way. Harmony set it aside, keeping Dima and her pack in her peripheral vision.

"Kevin?" she murmured. "Are you in position?"

The young man's voice crackled over the ear bead, soft and faintly surly.

"Over by the break room, boss. Damn, these catering outfits are itchy. This shirt is more starch than...shirt. I think I'm getting a rash."

"You're the one who wanted more field assignments," Jessie said. "Welcome to the glamorous life of a spy. Harmony, I'm ready to move as soon as you are."

Harmony's hand hovered over one of the plastic flutes at the edge of her tray. She wore a ring on one finger, a Victorian-styled design with seed pearls and pewter, small and unobtrusive.

Her hand turned as her thumb slid between her fingers and pushed open a clasp. The ring's face dangled open on a concealed hinge, and tiny grains, like golden sand, rained down into the champagne. She gave her hand a practiced flick, closing the secret compartment before anyone noticed.

"Ready," she said. "Initiate phase two, green light."

Harmony picked up her tray of drinks, put on a smile, and went hunting.

* * *

On the other side of the party, Jessie had a target of her own. She'd spent most of her sojourn at MK&B learning the lay of the land, playing the role of a fresh-faced new recruit looking to make a name for herself in the accounting big leagues. All the while, studying her coworkers, learning their weaknesses, how to bend them. How to hurt them if she needed to. The work came naturally to her. Jessie Temple had the eyes of an apex predator; she kept them concealed behind custom-made contact lenses, turning their inhuman turquoise tint to a muted amber.

Egon Bakowski was dead ahead, invading one of his interns' personal space as he maneuvered her between his cologne-drenched bulk and the wall. Jessie had pointed him out to Harmony when he arrived. Making sure he was over-served to the point of slurring his speech was easy; she kept feeding him fresh glasses, swooping in to swap out his empties every fifteen minutes or so. He'd just progressed past the "photocopying his butt" stage of office-party intoxication and was headed straight for "fistfight the boss" territory. Right where Jessie wanted him.

She slipped in between him and the intern. Her fingers curled, making a shooing motion. The intern vanished with a look of gratitude.

"Egon," Jessie purred, reaching up to smooth the rumpled lapel of his jacket. "Just the guy I've been looking for."

He gave her a bloodshot leer, primed by two weeks of careful and subtle flirting. He was too unsteady on his feet, rocking like a sailor in a gale-force storm, to handle subtle tonight. The man was a walking human-resources violation when he was stone cold sober, which—along with his managerial position in the IT department—was exactly why Jessie had picked him.

"Hey, brown sugar," he mumbled. Jessie had found it was easy to keep a smile on her face by imagining what his head would look like torn off and impaled on a stick.

It was one of her favorite coping mechanisms. She sidled closer to him, hips swaying like she was slow-dancing to the music, a little body language to get his clammy hand on her waist. His eye-watering cologne clung to a thin film of sweat odor, like he'd decided to bathe in Drakkar Noir instead of taking a shower.

"I was thinking," she said, "we should get to know each other a little better."

"I *like* that idea," he said.

Bet you do, asshole. She put her hand on his hip and leaned close to whisper in his ear.

"Not here, people are watching. Someplace...private. How about that broom closet, near the print shop? Meet me there? Ten minutes."

As she whispered, her fingers dipped into his pocket. He always kept his key card in the left front side, on top of his wallet; she'd watched him take it out and put it away for days. Her fingertips curled against the glossy plastic rectangle and snaked it into her palm.

"Baby," he said, "I'm gonna rock your world."

She watched him trundle off. With any luck, he'd fall asleep in the broom closet, making the world a little safer for interns everywhere. And come tomorrow morning, by the time he noticed his card was missing, he wouldn't have a clue where or how he'd lost it. She kept it palmed as she prowled between knots of conversation. Kevin was dead ahead, a string bean of a twenty-year-old with ruffled hair and a hangdog look on his face, draped in a catering outfit with sleeves half an inch too long. Jessie moved close and reached for a flute of champagne. She slid the stolen card onto his tray and took the glass in one smooth motion, walking away without a word.

"All right," she said under her breath, "you're up at bat."

* * *

Kevin took the long way around the room, trading full glasses for empties, invisible in his caterer's uniform. He made his way to the lip of an open hallway.

"How do I look?" he whispered, gripping his tray tight.

Harmony had moved to the left of the hallway's mouth, Jessie to the right, both of them checking the crowd. They watched for turned faces, anyone looking in Kevin's direction.

"Wait for it," Harmony said over his ear bead. "Wait for it, and...*now*. Go, go, go."

He slipped up the hall and out of sight, leaving the party behind. His brisk stride carried him to the security door of the IT department, nothing but dark shadows beyond the glass. He whisked the stolen card across the little black reader; it chimed, flashed a green light, and the door clicked.

He couldn't risk turning on the lights. Jessie's recon work had yielded a floor plan, and they rebuilt it at headquarters using folding chairs and card tables to mimic the tall cubicle walls. She made him run the gauntlet again and again, first in the dark and finally blindfolded, until he could cross the department floor at full speed without bumping anything or making a sound. Every second counted. He could feel them draining away as he navigated to a windowless door in the back. The second key reader chimed, the door surrendered, and he made his way into the icy blue glow of the server room.

Kevin crouched down and unloaded his tray, racking up champagne flutes in a row at his side. He flipped the tray over. A thin tablet, fixed to the underside with angled strips of duct tape, lit up with two sharp taps and cast his face in hard-edged shadows. A mini-USB plug jutted from one side of the tablet; he gave it a tug and it unspooled on a tether of retractable black cord.

He found the server he was looking for, plugged in his tablet, and got to work. He'd finished ninety-five percent of the hack days ago, commandeering the office's systems—and most of Takahashi Tower's while he was at it—with the help of Jessie's inside connections. The final five percent needed him to be on-site. He ran intrusion protocols, slipped around barricades, his fingers dancing a flamenco across the tablet's face.

A flood of scrolling text erupted into a spread of camera feeds. He found the one he needed, tapped it twice and made it blossom to fill the tablet screen, and executed his custom patch. The camera was fixed on an empty corridor, overhead lights gleaming off polished Italian marble, and lines of closed doors adorned with brass nameplates.

"Three, two, one, and…you're good," he said. "I'm feeding a static five-second loop of footage to the security monitors. The executive wing is officially blind."

"One more door in the way," Jessie whispered. "Harmony?"

"My turn," she said.

2.

Magicians called it a force. The art of giving someone freedom of choice while staying in near-total control, guaranteeing they picked the choice you wanted them to make all along. Harmony's force began with a bit of subtle feng shui, arranging her serving tray so that one particular flute was right at the front, easy to grab, while the others were pushed back and nuzzled up against some strategically placed empties to make them less appetizing.

She infiltrated a knot of conversation, zeroed in on Dima Chakroun, and offered her a drink. The fashion plate favored her with a smile and a slight lift of her flute as she took it in her slender hand. Harmony inclined her head, subservient, and passed out drinks to her party of hangers-on. Then she faded back to the sidelines.

This part wouldn't take long. Dealing with supernaturals was touch and go, but Dima was just a human with friends in low places. Part of operational planning involved stealing the results of her most recent medical checkup; they had her blood work, allergies, body mass, and weight, everything the chemists in the Basement needed to whip up a custom-made devil's brew.

There it was. Harmony watched from a safe distance as the smile died on Dima's lips, blood draining from her cheeks. A thin sheen of sweat glistened on her brow as she set her flute down and said her apologies, extricating herself from the pack.

"Shit," Jessie breathed, "think she's headed for the—"

"Already there," Harmony said.

She'd anticipated that problem. Dima was making a beeline for the employee washroom, just off the lobby. She got there to find Harmony standing in her path, all apologies.

"I'm *so* sorry, the ladies' room is closed for cleaning. Someone had a"—Harmony dropped her voice to a conspiratorial whisper—"an *accident* in there. It's all over the walls and you can't imagine the *smell*—"

Dima clapped a hand over her mouth in mid-turn, her skin waxy and wet, and headed the other way. Her heels rapped out a rapid-fire Morse code distress call on the marble floor.

There was more than one flavor of a magician's force. Sometimes you could get the job done by taking away every choice except for the right one.

"There she goes," Harmony murmured. "Jessie?"

"Ready."

* * *

Jessie watched Dima steam right past her, taking a hard left with her palm squeezed against her lips and tears welling in her eyes.

"Almost feel bad for her," Jessie said, moving in pursuit.

"She's a satanic serial killer." Harmony's voice crackled in her ear.

"That's why I said 'almost.'"

Dima broke away from the party and headed off down the western corridor, aiming for the executive suites. Jessie followed at a distance. She prowled under the blinded eye of a security camera. Around the corner,

Dima's key jiggled in the knob of her office door. She stumbled through the doorway, running now, no time to close it behind her, and Jessie froze until she heard the door of her private bathroom slamming shut.

Jessie slipped off her heels. She curled her finger around the ankle straps and let them dangle as she crept into Dima's office, circling her ornate hand-carved desk and flipping up the lid of the accountant's laptop. The screen lit up at the press of a button, and the welcoming chime of the operating system was muffled by gagging, splashing sounds from the far side of the bathroom door.

* * *

At the briefing, Kevin had handled the technical end, running down the electronic obstacles in their path.

"MK&B doesn't just crunch numbers for hell's aristocracy," he explained. "They deal with banks, big pharma, oil companies, super-sensitive accounting records. As a basic security protocol, every partner's personal computer is air gapped. That means no Internet connection. No Ethernet, no Wi-Fi, nothing. You can't hack what you can't connect to."

"So we have to get you into Chakroun's office," Jessie said.

He shook his head and brandished a slender matte-black USB stick.

"I call it an ice pick. Slot it when you boot her system up, and it'll automatically run through four different encryption cracks, from dictionary attacks to most-used-password lists. On top of that, thanks to the background intel you've gathered, we know every important name and date in her life: every friend she's had since grade school, every pet she's ever owned, birthdays. You know, the stuff that people shouldn't use for passwords but usually do anyway. I'm putting together a custom list just for her."

* * *

The ice pick slid into an open port. A window blossomed in the bottom left corner of the screen. Tight rainbow lines of text scrolled past, too fast to read, as the attack began. Jessie kept one eye on the office doorway. Judging from the agonized, wet noises behind the bathroom door, Dima wouldn't be a problem for a while.

Seven more seconds and the ice pick struck gold. It typed out Dima's password under a shroud of asterisks and the system welcomed Jessie inside. The firm had a standard system for naming QuickBooks files, arranging them under client numbers for anonymity, and Dima followed the rules. Jessie found Nadine's work folder and slid it between windows with a click of her fingertip, starting the slow process of copying over twenty gigabytes of data onto a memory stick.

"Got it," she whispered. "Couple more minutes, I'll be back at the party, and Dima will never know she just got her financials jacked. Still wish we could have taken her down."

"Once we start acting on that data," Harmony said, "Nadine's eventually going to figure out what happened. Neutralizing Chakroun ourselves would probably be a mercy compared to what Nadine will do to her. She's got a zero-tolerance policy when it comes to failure. Kevin, are you clear?"

"All clear, boss. Locked up behind me, wiped down the key card and dropped it into a recycling bin in the break room. I'm ready to take off."

"Not until the end of the party. Jessie heads out first. We clean up and leave with the rest of the catering crew.

No room for mistakes tonight. If my hunch is right, we just got our hands on the ammunition to bring down Nadine's entire network."

The progress bar inched its way along the screen. Jessie bounced on her stockinged feet, toes curling, counting under her breath as she watched it work.

Kevin's voice whispered in her ear, tight as a tourniquet.

"We have a problem. We have a *big* problem."

"Talk to me," Jessie said.

"Party crashers," he said. "Nadine just showed up."

* * *

On the far side of the room, concealed behind a small mob of hungry partygoers at the row of catering trays, Harmony craned her neck to follow Kevin's wide-eyed line of sight.

Nadine was here. Draped in Prada, stiletto heels clicking, flanked by a pair of gorillas in tailored suits as she sauntered into the room like she owned it. Harmony's catering getup was barely a disguise; one glance and Nadine would recognize her in a heartbeat. One glance was all it would take to burn this operation to the ground. Harmony turned, ducking her head, moving to stay on the edges of Nadine's periphery. She had to get away from the party, out of sight, and fast. The closest exit was the one Jessie had left by, the corridor to the executive wing.

"Coming your way," Harmony said. "Files?"

"Almost done," Jessie said. "Thirty seconds, forty tops."

"We can still salvage this. All we have to do is get out without being seen. Kevin, you okay?"

"Yeah," he breathed. "I mean, she knows you and Jessie,

but she's never seen my face. I mean, I don't *think* she has. I'm safe as long as she doesn't suspect anything."

"Hold it together. Slip away as soon as you can, get some privacy, and find us an exfil route. We're not going home empty-handed."

* * *

Hold it together, Kevin thought. *Yeah. Easy. Just pretend I'm not standing ten feet away from a face-eating torture demon who looks like Taylor Swift.*

Nadine was arguing—more like dictating terms—with a red-faced executive with a bad suit and a comb-over. He was trying to tell her that it was after office hours, and certainly they held themselves to the very highest standards of customer service, but—

"But," Nadine said, "despite wanting to confirm an extremely important transaction with my accountant, you're telling me to come back in the morning. Is this an elite financial-services firm or a strip-mall bank?"

"The highest—highest possible standards, but as I said, this is well past office hours—"

Nadine reached out and curled her fingers beneath his chin. Gentle, holding him fast, her eyes locked and unblinking. The tip of her thumb slowly stroked his jawline.

"I'm a hands-on manager," she said. "And I expect to be obeyed, without question, by those who serve me. Now...are we going to have a problem here?"

The fire in his eyes sputtered and died. His breathing slowed, his jaw going slack.

"No," he said softly. "No problem here."

She let go of him.

"Good. Now then, where is Dima Chakroun?"

"She, ah—" The man swallowed hard, eyes glazed as he

gestured behind him. "She went back to her office. She wasn't looking good, think it was the food."

Nadine's eyes narrowed at the catering spread. Her pert nose wrinkled.

"If she ate any of that pig slop, my faith in her good judgment is going to be sorely tested." She reached up and curled her fingers around her thugs' shoulders. "Boys? Go and fetch Dima for me, would you please? I'll wait."

As the two men turned toward the executive wing—they'd clearly visited in person more than once—Kevin stepped to one side. He had to get distance, whisper out a warning. A half-drunk executive with a marinara-stained tie got in his way, deliberating over Kevin's tray of drinks as if they weren't all exactly the same. He kept his cover intact, stood still despite his feet wanting to walk on their own, and moved along as soon as the guy picked a glass. He pivoted toward the edge of the crowd—and found himself standing face-to-face with Nadine.

You flinch, you die.

He poured the rush of nervous energy into a big, bright smile, scooped a flute of champagne from his tray, and offered it to her.

"Would you care for a drink, ma'am?"

"Well," she said, smug as a cat with a saucer of milk. "Such courtesy. Someone at this party has proper etiquette. Too bad it isn't an actual employee."

As she took the flute, her silky-soft fingertips brushed over his. A ripple of raw pleasure snaked along his arm. He felt like he was slipping into a warm bath, his head wreathed with steam, his muscles unclenching and all his anxiety draining away.

"I might have to take you with me when I leave," she

said with a wink. She sipped from her glass, grimaced, and put it back on the tray. "And that…is dire. Darling, would you do something for me? I want you to find the nearest sink and empty every single one of these glasses down the drain. Just pour them all out, so no one else has to suffer drinking that plonk. Can you do that? For me?"

Of course he could. That was more than reasonable.

* * *

The progress bar inched toward its final destination, copying the river of evidence onto Jessie's USB stick. Ten seconds remaining, nine—

Harmony appeared in the doorway. She nodded up the hall. Jessie held up eight fingers, then seven, counting down. Dima had mostly gone quiet in the bathroom.

"Shit, sorry," Kevin's voice said in their ear beads. "You've got company. Two of Nadine's guys coming your way, looking for Dima."

Transfer complete. Jessie snatched the USB stick, powered down Dima's laptop, and shut the lid, snuffing the rectangle of light. Harmony crouched down. She pulled up one leg of her slacks and plucked a palm-sized .22 from her ankle holster. Her other ankle had a custom rig for a vital accessory: the stubby black tube of a sound suppressor. She screwed it onto the gun's barrel, fingers finding the thread and working in a practiced rhythm while she watched the hall at her back.

"What's our route?" she whispered.

"I—*shit,* sorry. Sorry, I've been pouring out this champagne—"

"Did she touch you?"

"She just brushed my hand. I had no idea. I didn't even realize she *did* anything."

Harmony's eyes narrowed to slits.

"That's how she works," she said. "Breathe. Focus. It's a psychic neurotoxin, but it wears off fast. Right now, you need to find us a way off this floor."

Jessie hustled around the desk and out into the hallway, slipping her heels back on. She hadn't left a trace behind. Dima was still in the bathroom, and if they made it out without raising any alarms, they were home free.

"Bad news," Kevin said. "That wing dead-ends another two hundred feet past Dima's office. Your way out is your way in."

Harmony hid her gun behind her back. She looked to Jessie. "Bluff."

As Nadine's men rounded the corner, walking side by side, Jessie leaned against Harmony and threw her arms around her shoulders.

"Oh God," she drawled, "he left me, Becky. My man did me wrooong."

Harmony gave the men an apologetic smile as she pulled Jessie along, step by stumbling step. "My friend, uh, had a little too much to drink. Don't tell anyone we're back here, okay? I'm just trying to sober her up before we go back to the party."

"Try coffee," one of the men grunted, barely giving them a second glance.

The other froze in his tracks. He stared at Harmony, rusted gears turning behind his piggish eyes until something clicked.

3.

Everything happened in the space of a second.

The thug with the broad shoulders and beady little eyes knew Harmony's face. Maybe he'd been with Nadine's posse—the few who survived—last time they squared off. Maybe he'd just been smart enough to pay attention to his briefings. No matter how he knew, he knew. His mouth opened to shout as Harmony's free hand poked the small of Jessie's back, three quick taps to warn her. Jessie broke left, and Harmony's gun hand swung up to take aim.

He was faster than he looked. He lunged in, swatted her weapon aside, and hooked his arm around her throat, spinning Harmony around and squeezing her neck like a python. His buddy had barely registered that something was wrong, coattails flaring as he turned, just in time to meet the heel of Jessie's shoe. She leaped up, snapped out a kick, and hit him square in the belly, slamming him back against the mahogany wall.

Harmony strained for breath, black spots blossoming in her vision as the arm squeezed tighter against her windpipe. She drove her elbow into his gut, then again, hearing him grunt and finally he buckled as he lost his grip on her. She spun and grabbed the lapel of his coat, yanking him close, and put the tube of the sound suppressor against the base of his chin.

She pulled the trigger. The .22 let out a pair of muffled pops. The crumpled slugs lodged somewhere inside his brain. He twitched and shook, eyes rolling back until there was nothing but bloodshot white, and crimson syrup guttered from his gaping mouth.

Jessie didn't give his partner time to recover. She threw sledgehammer punches into his chest, her otherworldly blood driving her muscles harder than a heavyweight champion. His ribs shattered, jagged shreds of bone puncturing his lungs. His body rattled against the wall then slowly slumped to the marble floor. She grabbed hold of his neck as Harmony shoved her own opponent down, bracing her gun and stepping over his body.

"No witnesses," she said. Jessie nodded. She wrenched the other thug's neck to one side, sharp and fast, snapping his spine.

"Are you guys okay?" Kevin whispered over the comm line. "What just happened?"

"Mission just went south on us." Jessie looked to Harmony. "Scrub it, cut our losses? I'll kick that door in and take Dima out right now. Nadine'll burn her financial trail when she sees the carnage, but it'll take her a while to get her operations back up and running, and without her favorite accountant to help."

"No," Harmony said. She stared at the bodies, then to the open office door. Dima still hadn't found the strength to leave the security of her private bathroom, and the party was far enough away, the music covering the sounds of impact, that nobody was running to investigate.

They still had an intact cover. What they didn't have was an excuse for a couple of dead shooters. As soon as Nadine found her men's bodies, she'd put two and two together and know she'd been compromised.

For a moment, everything went quiet.

Harmony's mind shifted inside itself. The rhythm of her pounding heart, the rush of blood-pulse in her ears, all faded to a distant drumbeat as her emotions receded like waves and turned into a wintery flatline. The hallway, the bodies, the building became a wash of data points. She saw the world in mathematical equations. Alchemical formulas. This interaction plus this interaction equals mission failure. She ran through the possibilities one by one, tossing aside the failure points, until she found the equation that fit.

"April. Are you on the line?"

April Cassidy's warm Irish brogue gusted into her ear. "On overwatch as always. How can I help?"

"Kevin, leave the party, find some privacy, and get us an evac route. April, there's one way we can salvage this operation. One reason for an outbreak of random violence that doesn't connect to Dima Chakroun or Nadine's financials."

Harmony looked to her partner, her eyes gleaming with a flash of insight.

"We're turning this into a heist. A heist that just went violently, tragically wrong, and these men were in the wrong place at the wrong time. April, find us something to steal."

* * *

Kevin abandoned his post and his drinks. He kept the tray, cradling it close to his chest with the concealed tablet still taped to its underbelly. He barged into the men's room, locked himself in the farthest stall, and squatted on the toilet seat with the tray balanced on his knees. The tablet glowed under his fingertips. He swiped through blue neon schematics, floor plans and maintenance specs drawn in trails of light.

"Might have something," April mused. "Two floors directly above you. There's a small office belonging to a firm called Hollywood Memories; they authenticate and sell film and sports memorabilia. Among other recent catches, two days ago they posted an ad for the upcoming auction of a baseball autographed by Ty Cobb. Bidding is expected to open in the low five figures."

Jessie's low whistle carried over the comm line. "I'd steal that. Kevin?"

Outside the stall, a urinal flushed. Kevin scrambled, fingers tapping, calling up a new window and activating a back door he'd implanted over a week ago. Someone was humming, washing his hands. Kevin didn't speak until the bathroom door swung shut again.

"Okay. Found a way. Harmony, Jessie, take a left and get into the third office from the end. That puts you directly under Hollywood Memories."

"And?" Harmony asked.

He punched a subroutine into action. Remote systems, turned into traitors, whirred to life at his command.

"I'm sending a ride."

* * *

Wood splintered under Jessie's shoulder and a door swung on a twisted hinge. The yawning doorway shed an oblong of light across a gloomy executive office.

On the far side of a wall of floor-to-ceiling windows, Kevin's ride descended. An unmanned window-washing rig, the narrow platform dangling from steel cables.

"You're kidding me," Harmony said.

"Hey, if you'd like to head back to the party and take your chances with Nadine, go for it. As for me—"

Jessie crossed the room in three brisk steps, swept up the leather-backed chair, and rammed it casters-first against the closest window. The window buckled, shuddering in its frame. The second hit smashed a hole through its heart. The tempered glass, treated for safety and strength, shattered in chunks instead of shards. Rounded, lumpy fractures framed the gaping hole, and hot summer wind whistled in, sending loose files flying in a paper cyclone. A city-smoke stench rode on the current, carrying the tang of ozone and diesel fumes.

The metal grille rattled, wobbly under Harmony's shoes as she stepped out onto the platform. Jessie was right behind her and the city was below, twenty-eight stories straight down to the gridlocked street. Distant sirens wailed up through the canyons of concrete and glass. Harmony's hands curled on the safety rail, squeezing tight.

"All aboard," Jessie said. "Kevin? Take us up."

The platform groaned, steel cables squealing, and the rig lurched as it began to climb. Higher and higher, stretching the dizzying drop, and every gust of wind making the steel tremble like it could slip out from under their feet at any second. Tendrils of smog gusted past them, a yellow bank of fog that left a stinging residue in the back of Harmony's throat.

The rig groaned to a stop and they faced a fresh wall of mirrored glass. Jessie tugged off one of her high-heeled shoes and slipped it over her right hand, wearing it like a climber's spike.

"Hold *tight*," she said.

Harmony gripped the rail while Jessie studied the glass like a sculptor with a fresh block of stone. Then she drew her hand back and struck. The spike of her heel slammed the middle of the glass, the pane shuddering but holding fast, and the platform swayed on its cable tether. She hit it again, and again, precision blows delivered with short, sharp hisses of breath while the platform jolted as if it was trying to buck them off.

One more time, and the window broke. The heel gouged a fist-sized hole and rained a shower of broken glass. Jessie worked her way around the break, aiming for the weakened spots, chiseling the tempered glass away one rounded chunk at a time until she'd carved a gap big enough to wriggle through.

They touched down on soft beige carpet, fallen glass glittering in the dark and the wind whistling at their backs. There wasn't much to Hollywood Memories: just a couple of desks, a small reception area—and a tall black-iron safe, half Harmony's height, standing beside a dusty display cabinet.

"Tear it up," Harmony said. "We need to make it look like we ransacked the place."

Jessie obliged, tugging out desk drawers and dumping a flurry of papers onto the carpet, while Harmony gravitated to the safe. She crouched down, studying the dial, the hinges. A file folder crumpled under Jessie's heel as she stood behind her.

"Can we get it open?" she asked.

Harmony rubbed her chin. "No. But we don't have to. We're staging the scene as an attempted robbery; a failed heist is just as good as a successful one. If we were doing this for real and had the right equipment with us, how would you crack this thing?"

"Thermal lance?"

"My thought exactly. We don't have one, but we can fake it. Stand back."

Jessie eased away as Harmony rose. She clasped her

hands before her, spreading her feet and squaring her footing, and took a deep breath.

Harmony's mind went blank. Her one thought, her sole desire, was a freight train on a straight-arrow track. A pulse of glowing sigils spelling out words in a forgotten tongue. The track became a roller coaster and her impulses spiraled, dove, twisted into a cursive loop, and now the train of words spelled out other words, glyphs layered upon glyphs. They shimmered with inner light, deep under her skin. Her blood ignited.

Earth, air, water, fire, she thought. Her mental finger curled around the mnemonic trigger. *Garb me in your raiment. Arm me with your weapons.*

She pulled the trigger.

Blue fire bloomed from her clasped hands and streaked through the air, splashing across the face of the ironclad safe. Her body was a forge, a bellows, sucking in oxygen, converting it with alien alchemy, and spitting it back out as flame. She held the fire steady, searing, her skin breaking out in beads of clammy sweat as she channeled the inferno's glory.

Her breath ran out and took her strength with it. The last of the fire sputtered, falling, hitting the carpet and setting it ablaze. Her knees buckled and she collapsed to the office floor. The magic wasn't free. Payment came due with short, raspy breaths, a burning ache behind her eyes, and cramps that twisted her gut in knots.

Jessie's arm was under her shoulder, helping her up, pulling her back from the spreading flames. The shrill whine of an alarm jolted her back to her senses.

"Whatever you guys just did," Kevin said in her ear, "this whole place just went nuts. They're herding everybody to the fire exits and locking the elevators down."

"Good," Harmony said, leaning on Jessie and fighting against the cramps. "Don't blow your cover. Leave with the crowd, then evac just the way we rehearsed it."

"What about you two?"

"We'll be fine. *Go*. We'll meet you back at HQ."

Harmony had her second wind by the time they shoved through the emergency stairwell door. The alarm was squalling, a constant klaxon whine, and two floors down the exodus from the office party was an angry and confused stream of stumbling people. Harmony and Jessie hung back, watching the flow, until they saw Nadine's blond bob in the heart of the crowd. They waited for a silent ten count, giving her time to get ahead of them.

Then they casually walked down the steps, joined the parade, and evacuated the building as two more anonymous faces in the crowd.

By the time they made it down to the lobby there was already a cordon of emergency vehicles out front, red and blue lights strobing across the mirrored tower, paramedics rushing to deliver triage and firefighters preparing for their ascent. Nobody noticed Harmony and Jessie or even looked their way as they slipped from the chaos, vanishing into the labyrinth of Los Angeles.

They ended up in a late-night diner out in Fairfax. It was a coffee, bacon, and eggs kind of midnight. Harmony checked her phone; it pinged as April forwarded her the first headline. "*...news of a dramatic robbery gone bad, as thieves used an office party to commandeer a window washer's rig, penetrating the offices of a Hollywood memorabilia* *collector two floors above. The theft was thwarted when a fire, presumably caused by an equipment malfunction..."*

Jessie came back from the restroom and dropped into the blue vinyl booth across from her. "What's the word?"

Harmony showed her the screen.

"They're reporting it. The way we want them to report it."

"They usually do," Jessie said. "April's probably in full spin-doctor mode right now."

"No mention of the bodies. Either Nadine works faster than we do, or the cops are sitting on that detail."

"Even odds." The waitress came by, laying out two steaming cups of coffee. Jessie shook a pair of yellow sugar packets between her fingers. "The story should hold. Only thing that worries me is the fact that dead men *do* tell tales sometimes. Figure those two shooters' souls are on an express elevator to hell as we speak. If Nadine catches up with them and asks what happened..."

Harmony raised her cup. She took her coffee straight, strong and rich, a bullet of clarity to keep her exhaustion at bay.

"Look at it this way. As far as we know, we're the only humans to stand face-to-face with Nadine, blow her plans, and live to tell the tale. More than once. Do you think there's anyone on this planet she hates more than the two of us?"

"Probably not," Jessie said. "What about it?"

"Put yourself in their shoes. Would *you* tell Nadine that you had a chance to catch us, but you blew it and got killed?"

"I'd lie like a cheap rug," Jessie said.

"Bingo. We might have to deal with demons and sorcerers and worse, but we've got one advantage. The one thing that never changes." Harmony eyed Jessie over her mug. "Human nature. So. Ready to call it?"

Jessie held the slender jet-black USB stick between her fingertip and thumb. It caught the diner lights, glistening, keeping its digital treasure safe inside.

They had taken Vigilant Lock back from the forces that corrupted it, shedding sweat and blood—too much blood, too many good operatives lost in the fight—just to begin rebuilding from the rubble. Tonight meant more than a harvest of concrete intelligence, a win they could act on. Tonight meant something they'd needed for a long time. A spark of hope.

"Mission accomplished," Jessie said. "Let's go home. No time for celebrations, we've got a lot of work to do."

4.

Kevin rendezvoused on an airstrip with April and rode home on the company plane. Harmony and Jessie had to fly coach. They staggered their departure times for safety. Harmony was the last to leave, flying out of Los Angeles on a red-eye bound for Washington.

Morning found her in the back of a cab in Bethesda, Maryland. The heart of town had become a hub of high-rises, corporate towers mingling with shopping promenades. Her destination was a little south of the action, an unassuming one-story brick of beige on Arlington Road at the tail of a shady parking lot. The sign out front, professional and bland, read Delaware Mutual Insurance.

The receptionist in the lobby greeted her with a nod. Her hands stayed under the desk, out of sight. The door behind her clicked softly at Harmony's approach, unlocked by remote as she passed under the watchful eye of a security camera.

Down a linoleum hallway, past an open office floor lined with cloth cubicle walls, she took a left and ended up in the file-storage room. Tall beige metal racks on automatic tracks rumbled as they circulated at the press of a button, rotating shelves packed with numbered folders and three-ring binders. One shelf stayed motionless, frozen on its chain-driven track. Harmony stepped into its shadow, out of sight, and reached for one particular binder. Five rows up, three to the right, with a sticky-tape label marked "93/93."

She yanked the binder down, then shoved it back into place. There was a mechanical rumble, and the floor shuddered beneath her feet.

With a soft click, a panel of buttery wooden wall at her back cracked open. She pushed it the rest of the way, stepping into the cage of an elevator, then closed the concealed door behind her. She stood at the heart of the cage, hands clasped behind her back and chin high, catching her blurry reflection in the stainless-steel walls.

"Identify," a voice commanded, the word carried on a crackle of electronic distortion.

"Special Agent Harmony Black. This week's recognition code is Oscar. Romeo. Vendetta. The color of the day is saffron."

A scarlet iris opened above the elevator door. She held still as a slice of blood-red light swept over her, shimmering from head to toe, pausing on her eyes for a retinal scan. The light winked out.

"Thank you, Agent Black."

With an unsteady jolt, the elevator lurched into motion, grumbling its way downward.

Liberating Vigilant Lock meant saying goodbye to the past. Their safe houses, their secure caches, everything down to basic methods and passwords had been so thoroughly compromised by the courts of hell that none of it was safe anymore. None of it ever had been. Upon taking formal command, Jessie's first order of business was finding a new base of operations. They'd bought up a vacant office building on the cheap through a shell company, recruited a skeleton crew of trustworthy engineers and contractors, and started carving out their new home turf. It was an intelligence hub nestled like a spider beneath the streets of Bethesda; Harmony wasn't sure who first called it the Basement, but the name had stuck.

At the bottom of the shaft, a grille of steel barred the way ahead. The elevator stopped with a chime and the grille rumbled aside to let her through.

The Basement was a labyrinth of drywall and dangling work lights strung along on bright orange extension cord. The smell of sawdust and industrial antiseptic hung in the air. Harmony skirted a pallet bearing dusty fifty-pound sacks of Quikrete and held back while a pair of workmen eased a stack of two-by-fours through a narrow doorway.

It was a work in progress. Under the circumstances, security had to come first, utility second, and comfort was not even an afterthought. *But it's ours,* Harmony thought. *This belongs to us.*

Kevin poked his head from an archway up ahead. He'd traded his catering uniform for ratty jeans and a World of Warcraft T-shirt. He looked her up and down. "You're still wearing that?"

"I just *landed,*" Harmony said. She kept walking and he fell into step at her side. "Some of us didn't get to ride home in a C-130. I flew Delta. Change of clothes can wait; is everybody here?"

"Here, and the briefing's already started."

She shot him a sidelong glance. "Without me?"

"Jessie wanted to wait. Our Commercial Sponsors are getting restless."

Understandable. The cabal of law-enforcement executives, military operators, and members of Congress who kept Vigilant funded and functional had been running scared for months. They'd been just as deceived as the rank and file, tricked into throwing their weight behind an infernal false-flag operation. Then they witnessed the purge from within, kicked off by the execution of a Kentucky senator at point-blank range. Over the course of three blood-soaked weeks, Vigilant's numbers were decimated as every last traitor and demonic loyalist found their reward in a shallow grave.

Jessie had done most of the killing herself. She was making a point.

Harmony heard April's voice drift from a doorway ahead. "...just beginning our forensic examination, but initial results are promising. The files are intact, and the details that line up with what we already know confirm the truth: we have Nadine's financial files. All of them. Disbursements, payroll for her human servants, investments across the Midwest."

A gruff voice echoed over a speaker. "So we can move on them. What are we waiting for?"

April turned in her wheelchair, spotting Harmony, beckoning her over. Jessie was at her side, standing at parade rest, and she'd changed from her party dress into a dark, professional pantsuit. She bathed in the glow of a bank of wall-mounted screens. Twelve in all, but four, scattered across the grid, were dark and silent. The other eight screens offered high-definition webcam views of the attendees, reporting in from across the country. Some sat in high-backed chairs in plush and sunlit offices; others were drenched in deliberate shadow, nothing but their hazy outlines to betray their identity.

"We move when the time is right," Jessie said. "Nadine is a high-value target with considerable reach and influence. I'm not authorizing any follow-up operations until we've studied and dissected every scrap of those records."

"Records which could be going stale by the second," said the woman on the top left corner screen. The distant spire of the Washington Monument rose up through a window at her shoulder. "Nadine has covered her tracks before."

"Which is why we covered ours, too, and left her accountant in play. She doesn't know she's been compromised."

Harmony cleared her throat, stepping up to stand at Jessie's side.

"When the Bureau trained me in close-quarters combat," Harmony said, "I was taught a very important saying: 'Slow is smooth, smooth is fast.'"

One of the shadowed figures, brass glinting on his lapel in the dark, gave her a nod and a faint grunt of agreement. The spindly man on the screen beside him frowned, brow furrowing.

"And that means what, exactly?"

"Charging into a fight gets people killed, sir. Operators and innocent bystanders. When you're going through doors, the right way is to move with intelligence on your side and a solid, methodical plan. Tactical movement may look slow to an outsider, but it's a deliberate and steady pace driven by purpose. And that's exactly how we'll deal with this data. We will study, we will plan…and we will execute."

Jessie flashed her a smile. She'd taken her contact lenses off, showing her natural turquoise eyes, too blue to be real. Or human. In the darkened room, they took on a soft, radioactive glow. She always made the Sponsors look her in the eye during these meetings. She wanted them to remember who they were dealing with.

"Let's table the discussion and go high-level for a minute," said another shadow, her voice modulated with a layer of electronic distortion. "I don't know about the rest of you, but given...recent events, I would appreciate an up-to-date threat assessment."

"Can do," Jessie said. "In addition to the usual assortment of stray monsters, renegade sorcerers, and psychic anomalies stirring up trouble—"

"And psychotic ghost clowns," Kevin muttered. "It was only that one time, but *still*."

"—the United States faces occult attacks from three primary vectors. First, obviously, are the courts of hell. A handful of demonic princes have laid claim to territory here: the biggest claims are on the West Coast and in the Midwest, while a scattering of much smaller, quasi-allied courts—and Vigilant Lock's secret creators—are scattered along the eastern seaboard. Seizing control of Vigilant and exposing the truth has left the eastern courts *severely* embarrassed. They're hot for payback."

"But they can't kill what they can't catch," Harmony said. "This is submarine warfare. They know we're in these waters, somewhere, and vice versa. Our best bet is to keep moving, run silent, and fire torpedoes before they do. We can also continue to play on the courts' antipathy for one another and occasionally benefit from mutual goals."

"You're not talking about an alliance," said the woman from DC.

"No. Not a formal one. But Caitlin Brody, the enforcer for the demon prince of the West Coast, has already proved herself willing to help if we're mucking up her competition's territory. For instance, once we realized Nadine's accountant was in Los Angeles, and she was moving truckloads of money through the city without permission—and without paying tribute—Caitlin granted us her blessing to operate in the city unimpeded so long as her name stayed out of it."

"Wait," the woman said. "You *notified* a representative of hell that we were moving against one of their own?"

April lifted her palms from the arms of her chair. She spread them gracefully.

"Politics, Senator. Hell is not a monolith. If anything, it's considerably more fractured, and has more infighting than, well...Congress."

"If it helps," Jessie said, "think of 'em as mafia families. Which brings us to threat vector number two: the Network. The *actual* occult mafia, with outposts on at least a dozen parallel Earths, probably more, and led by alien entities calling themselves the Kings of Man."

The man in the shadows, with brass on his lapel, coughed into his microphone.

"I've been reading this report about the Wisdom's Grave incident. You're certain about your conclusions?"

"One hundred percent," Harmony said. "Jessie and I were there, along with multiple assault teams. The creature formerly identified as the King of Rust is a confirmed kill. The kings *can* be hurt. And they can be destroyed. We know it now, and so do they."

"From what we're picking up on signals chatter," Jessie added, "the Network is scared shitless. Their big boss, Adam, is missing, and whatever else went down that night, it cut off their ability to communicate and get around like they used to. April, what was that metaphor you used?"

April kept her gaze on the screens, cool and steady, reading every expression as she spoke.

"Hercules and the Hydra. We've cut off the heads, but in this case, it was the Network's body that died. The Hydra's heads are still alive, still intact and extremely dangerous, but uncoordinated and biting in all directions."

"What about these civilian contacts?" asked the woman from DC. "And the multiple disappearances in the days after? Marie Reinhart—"

"Leave it alone," Harmony said.

The room fell silent.

"Excuse me?" the woman replied.

"Senator, with all due respect...leave it alone."

"What I think my partner means," Jessie said, "is Reinhart isn't a danger to us. And if the day comes when she wants us to know where she disappeared to, we *will* know. Let's move on. Our third and final primary threat vector: Robert Marius Diehl, technical and occult prodigy, closeted psychopath, terrorist, and Nazi fetishist, and *former* CEO of Diehl Innovations."

"Bobby is on the run," Harmony said, "and not just from us. The FBI wants him, and the IRS wants anything that's left over when they're finished. He's fled to an offshore haven called 'Xanadu.' As yet, we have not been able to determine its location."

"Doesn't sound like much of a risk," said the woman from DC. "He's a fugitive, his assets are frozen, and he can't set foot on American soil without risking arrest or elimination, depending on who catches him first. I'd say he's been dealt with."

Harmony and Jessie shared a quiet glance. Harmony turned back to the screens.

"I wish I shared your confidence, Senator, but we've crossed swords with Bobby Diehl and his operatives on multiple occasions. The man tried to spark an occult apocalypse. He's caused horrific civilian casualties, including a chemical attack on a small town, with absolutely no hesitation or regret. Yes, he looks like a cornered rat from where we're standing, but that's when a rat is most dangerous. He needs to stay a priority target until we've put a bullet in the bastard's head, verified his DNA, burned his corpse, and scattered the ashes just to be certain."

Harmony caught the vehemence in her voice, the anger burbling to the surface and spilling free, but she couldn't stop it. She caught her breath and dug her short-cropped fingernails into her palms, digging half-moon welts.

"Strong words, Agent Black."

Harmony fixed her gaze on the screen. She spoke slowly now, firmly, her rage a dragon on a short leash.

"Talbot Cove was my hometown, ma'am. I was the target of that attack. I was at ground zero when the gas bombs went off. So, yes. This is extremely personal to me. I won't pretend otherwise."

* * *

After the briefing, after the bank of video screens flickered and died one by one, winking out as the Sponsors went their separate ways, Harmony felt a tug on her sleeve.

"Have a minute?" April asked her.

Hammering echoed down the drafty hallways. And in the distance, the rumbling roar of a jackhammer as contractors dug out new territory. April gave her wheels a shove, rolling off to the side of the briefing room, and Harmony followed her.

"You should take some time off," April said.

The idea was bizarre. She might as well have told Harmony she should start wearing a fish on her head.

"We don't get time off," Harmony said.

"Of course you do. I've been Vigilant's in-house psychologist for years, Harmony. I've sent agents on mandatory recuperation leave more times than I can count."

"That was before. Before—" Harmony waved a hand, taking in the bare drywall, the exposed wooden timbers. "This. Before the truth. Before we burned everything down and started to rebuild. There's too much going on, too many operations in play. I'm needed here."

"Yes. We do need you. We need you effective and at peak levels of performance. You've...taken some hits in the last year or so."

Harmony folded her arms and turned her gaze. She stared at the dead video wall.

"Taking hits is part of the job. We take them so civilians don't have to."

"Bobby Diehl," April said, "isn't our only adversary who you have a personal vendetta against."

She let that hang in the air between them. Harmony didn't respond.

"Have you had a single night's sleep since we began the operation against Nadine's accountant?"

"I'll sleep now," Harmony said.

April eyed her over the rims of her bifocals. "Will you?"

"We're one step closer."

"To Nadine."

"To *ending* Nadine."

"You know," April said, "what she did to you, in

Chicago…your medical record affirms that the physical effects wore off some time ago."

"The record says it, so it must be true."

"But no one, especially not me, expects that the emotional effects did," April said. "You were traumatized—"

Harmony turned to face her, eyes flashing.

"I was not *traumatized*. I was injured on a mission. It happens."

"You were assaulted."

Harmony flung up her hands, pacing, pouring her nervous energy out before it twisted up something inside her.

"Assaulted," she echoed. "Facing violent altercations is part of the job."

"That's not what I'm saying, and you know it."

Harmony patted her left shoulder. "I have burn scars on most of this shoulder. On my hip? Facing off with the Ballard Ripper left me with twenty-eight stitches. My ribs have been broken multiple times, and I stopped counting the scars on my back and arms years ago. There's a reason I never wear short sleeves. I have been *shot*—"

"Not the same thing," April said.

"Shot, in the line of duty, and you want me to act like what Nadine did to me was any different."

April met Harmony's anger with a wall of steely calm.

"Because it was, and you know that it was. You need to acknowledge it."

"I need—" Harmony's shoulders slumped. Deflated. She glanced at her phone. No bars down here, she just needed to check the time. "I need to get going. Appointment. I'm…I've been doing the float thing, like you suggested."

"It's a start," April said.

5.

The first time Harmony laid eyes on a sensory-deprivation tank, she couldn't shake how much it looked like a coffin.

She had already been dubious. The owner of the "clinic"—converted from a guesthouse in the Bethesda suburbs—was a neo-hippie who kept a wicker dream catcher dangling over her cash register and burned sage to ward off bad intentions. Still, April recommended her, and she trusted April. The tank sat in a small tiled room, industrially scrubbed and smelling of mingled antiseptic and incense. Off to one side there was a row of wall pegs and a bench for changing, next to a boxy little shower for before and after the float.

"And it's just…water?" she had asked on her first visit.

The lid opened with a rustle. Pattie, the owner, gestured to the motionless fluid within.

"Water saturated with Epsom salt, for buoyancy, and heated to skin temperature. The idea is to make you as weightless as possible."

Weightless was a good word for it. This was Harmony's third visit, and now the process was routine. She locked the door and stripped off her catering uniform at long last. Her change of clothes was sheathed under dry-cleaning plastic, dangling from a peg on the wall. She showered, trying not to look at her quilt of scars or think about her argument with April, and approached the tank.

She stepped up, and in, and sank into the warm salty broth. Then she closed the lid of the tank and sealed herself in absolute darkness.

She floated.

There was no sound. Not at first. Then a distant thrumming, like drums on the horizon, their beats tinged with an electrical crackle. It was her pulse. Her blood pumping through her veins, singing out as she gradually lost awareness of her skin and muscles and bones. She simply *was*, a disembodied and weightless spirit drifting through the moonless dark.

The tangled chaos of her thoughts smoothed out, melting in the water's warmth. She found herself in the moment before the magic, out on a vast plain of perfectly even grid lines, the world reduced to neon graph paper. She was alone here.

She wasn't alone here.

On the far horizon, the lines of her perfect mind-grid went askew. A cold front crept in, ice frosting over the pure neon and cracking it. Lines sputtered and flickered out. With the cold came the first pangs of gnawing hunger. The hunger dug deep inside her, rummaging in her guts, and wrenched out flashes of memory to throw in her face.

* * *

They'd had her. Nadine was cornered, trapped in the bullet-riddled ruins of an underground nightclub, surrounded by the corpses of her hired help. Nadine had taken hostages. Harmony and Jessie had taken precautions; then they'd gone tactical. They thought they knew what the demon was capable of.

"I told you," Nadine had purred. "I'm a lover, not a fighter."

She put her hands on Harmony's body. Then her mouth. Then her magic, pouring into her as she took an ice pick to Harmony's walls and invaded her body and her soul at the same time. She didn't remember much in the aftermath. She had helped Nadine escape. Tried to kill her own team. Jessie had to choke her out.

She mostly remembered sitting in the carnage, feeling…dirty.

Someone tried to touch her, a reassuring hand on her arm. She flinched.

"Babe," Jessie said, "you're not okay. And that's okay, you get me?"

"I didn't want that. I didn't…want her to do that to me. I didn't want it."

Of course not, they told her. Nobody thought she did.

But she thought she did.

That was the most insidious trick of all, the core of a succubus's power. It wasn't enough that they could light you up with a single kiss, igniting every neuron in your brain, a rush of pleasure stronger than any drug known to man. It wasn't enough that you knew, coming down, that as long as you lived you would never ever feel that good again. It wasn't enough that they could stir their fingers in your brain and scramble you around, turn mortal enemies into lovers and your best friend into a threat.

The most insidious thing of all was that, in the heat of the moment, they could convince you that you were asking for it. And in the aftermath, when your senses returned, when you could look back with clarity and understand what had been done to you, that lingering doubt remained. That maybe you really did want it. Maybe you were guilty. Maybe you really were just as dirty as you felt, and you'd never feel clean again.

And with the dirtiness came the hunger. The full rush of a succubus's curse was a drug. And like a drug, once you had a hit, you wanted more. You needed more.

The next time they crossed paths with Nadine, it was at a Washington, DC, fundraiser. They were both there on a mission. Harmony had to keep her cover, and so did Nadine; instead of open warfare, they had to settle for passing glances and veiled threats. Nadine didn't miss a chance to slip close, putting her lips to Harmony's ear, and twist the knife.

"I feel…close to you now," she whispered. "After all, I've been *inside* you. I carved my initials in you. That's forever."

* * *

Focus. Breathe. Focus. Breathe.

Harmony floated.

She latched on to the distant drumbeat throb of her pulse. Sinking into the sound and pushing back the ragged knots at the edges of her serenity. She calmly smoothed the graph-paper lines, arranged them, brought order to the disarray.

A moment later they began curling and twisting back into knots. The cold was moving closer now, spreading tendrils of frost over her heart and turning the blood in her veins to icy sludge.

For a normal human, a succubus's curse meant addiction. For a magician, it meant loss. Loss of her connection to the universe, as the hunger strangled her inner strength. The first time it set in, her powers had sputtered out right when she needed them most; her command of the elements, her rapport with fire and air, was gone.

She'd found a cure. A cure named Romeo. He was a

cambion—demon-blooded, and the son of an incubus, with some of his father's touch. A touch that satisfied Harmony's aches and pains, made the hunger go away, and brought her magic back.

For a little while, anyway.

* * *

It had been a month since she last saw Romeo. They'd just finished a mission in Jersey City, running down the last of the traitors inside Vigilant Lock and performing a magic trick, making a body disappear. Jessie had wanted to go out drinking. Harmony said she had a headache and wanted to call it an early night. She waited until the coast was clear. Then she hopped in the back of a battered taxicab, shock absorbers squealing as they rocked across pothole-strewn streets.

A summer rain was pouring down, steaming off the pavement, washing the grime of the city off faded brick walls and down the crack-shot sidewalks. She found her sanctuary under a red neon sign, in a hotel that rented rooms by the hour. Romeo was waiting in room 19. Rain battered the window at his back, glazing the glass under rivulets of dirty water, lightning-flicker in the distance. Dust bunnies clung to the paper shade of a bedside lamp, and the weak bulb cast the room in long and dismal shadows.

"Hey," he said. He loosened his silk tie with the curl of a finger.

"Hey." Harmony's eyes shot to the open bathroom door, to the rickety wardrobe, to the underbelly of the floral-quilted bed.

"What?"

"You tell me," she said. "You look nervous."

He forced a chuckle. "Gosh, can't imagine why. You

know there's a price on your head, right? Not just one. Every court on the East Coast wants you dead or alive. Nadine wants you alive, and not for anything good."

"I know," she said. "You could make a lot of money, selling me out. Setting me up."

He raised his open hands.

"Hey. I'm not like that. You know I'm not like that. I'm not like *them*. I'm just sayin', not for nothing, I could get in serious trouble if anyone found out I was seeing you."

"And I couldn't?" she asked.

"I know, you got a…a situation. Hey, c'mon, let me take your jacket. And your hair's all wet. Hold on, I got a towel. Not their towels, this place is a dump, I brought my own. Here, sit, relax. I'll put some music on."

"Why?"

He fumbled for an answer.

"Just…trying to set the mood, that's all."

"I'm not here for the mood," Harmony said.

She took an envelope from her inside breast pocket and flicked it open with her finger. A stack of green nested inside, three hundred dollars in bank-fresh twenties. She tossed it onto the mattress. His gaze dropped.

"Why do you have to be like that?"

"Like what?" she asked. "Do you *not* sleep with women for money? Because last I checked—"

"I sell romance. Fantasies. I make lonely women happy for a while." He met her eyes, indignant now. "You don't have to make me feel bad about it."

"Not trying to." She paused. "I respect what you do. Everybody has to earn a living. Nothing wrong with it."

She raised her hand. Her fingers waved, vague, at the side of her head.

"I'm not good at…people," she said. "Emotions, facial

cues, sometimes I can't read them right. So I upset people, and I don't mean to."

He set his phone on the bedside table. He tapped the screen and music welled up, soft, romantic, Italian maybe.

"There we go. Music makes everything a little nicer." He gave her a sidelong glance, contemplative. "You just seem so angry. And you're angrier every time I see you."

"It's not you I'm angry at."

"That's not the only thing. I don't know a lot about this magic stuff. What I've got, I was born with it. It's just...innate, you know? Like flexing a muscle. You're my only client who does the magic stuff."

"And?"

"And you're...changing," he said. "At first I got tired after we got together. Last time, I was sick for two days. Like you're pulling something out of me. Siphoning it out."

"Not on purpose."

"No. I'm just saying, it doesn't seem healthy."

Harmony took off her jacket. She opened the wardrobe. A pair of mismatched plastic hangers dangled on a dented brass rod.

"If it's any consolation, I had a word with Caitlin. Prince Sitri's right hand, out in Vegas."

Romeo's eyebrows lifted. "Yeah?"

"Yeah." She hung her jacket up. "She says if I don't stop doing this, feeding on demonic energy, it's going to kill me."

He took a step back.

"Wait. What?"

"Yeah." She let out a bitter little chuckle. "But here's the thing. If I don't feed, the hunger comes back. And when the hunger gets bad enough, I can't do magic anymore.

And if I can't do magic anymore, I'm worthless in the field and innocent people get hurt. And innocent people die. So that's my choice. I can keep feeding my habit and save lives out there, or I can save myself and let the monsters win."

She gestured to the envelope of cash.

"So are we going to do this or not?"

* * *

Color erupted in the darkness. A tiny orange glow just above her face, winking on and off in a metronome strobe.

Harmony pushed back the lid of the sensory-deprivation tank and squinted as electric light flooded her eyes. She sat up, the salty brine roiling around her body. It didn't feel like she'd been floating for anywhere near an hour, but then again, a sense of time was one of the first things the tank took away.

A soft rapping echoed at the door.

"Harmony?" Pattie called out from the other side. "I'm *so* sorry to pull you out early, but Dr. Cassidy just called me. She said there's an emergency at your office, and she needs you to call your partner right away."

Harmony's salt-encrusted feet touched down on a tangerine bathmat. She padded carefully across the warm ivory tiles, grabbing a towel to dry her hands, and scooped up her phone from the bench beside the shower.

"I'm here," she said when Jessie picked up. "Sorry, I was doing that—that therapy thing I was telling you about."

"We've got a situation. You know how we left Agent Cooper embedded at Diehl Innovations?"

"Sure."

Cooper had been their prime conduit into Bobby Diehl's operations. She'd worked her way into his confidence, becoming his administrative assistant and a firsthand witness to the dark underbelly of his empire. They'd jumped through hoops—even arresting her at one point—to keep her cover intact. With Diehl ousted from his own company and on the run, it looked like her mission was over, but Jessie decided to keep her in place a little longer. Just in case.

"Bobby did just what I hoped he would," Jessie said. "He reached out for help."

Harmony's damp fingers curled tight around her phone. "Do we have a location?"

"No. He sent her on an errand down in Florida. Picking up some kind of package for him. She brought a minder with her to provide overwatch, and they were supposed to report in as soon as they got the goods."

"And?"

"They've gone dark," Jessie said. "We didn't just lose Bobby's trail. We lost two agents."

"We're going after them," Harmony said. It wasn't a question.

"Meet us at the hangar. Kevin's grabbing our gear, and Linder's going to brief us in the air. We go wheels-up in one hour."

The hot pulse of the shower drove Harmony's mind into gear. It sluiced the salt from her glistening skin, crystals glittering like diamonds around her feet. She felt the first pangs of hunger, distant, gnawing, but she could hold it at bay. She could hold it together long enough to get the job done.

The last of the water trickled down. She toweled off and tugged the plastic dry-cleaner wrapper away from her new outfit, freshly laundered and pressed. Black slacks. A crisp white button-down dress shirt. A shoulder holster. A man's double-breasted jacket. She slipped on a pair of black leather shoes, polished to a shine.

April was wrong. She didn't need time off, or to rest. This was the only time Harmony truly felt alive: when she was on a mission.

She reached for the final piece. A salmon-pink necktie, coiling around her throat with motions ingrained in her muscle memory. A loop, a twist, a knot. She drew the tie tight and flipped her collar down. She caught a glimpse of herself in the mirror, on her way out the door, and nodded. There she was.

Ready for battle.

6.

While the Basement was Vigilant Lock's fortress beneath the city streets, the *Imperator* was their eye in the sky. It was a C-130 Hercules, a four-engine turboprop built for moving troops and military cargo in and out of hostile territory. The plane was a workhorse made for rough weather and rougher landings, making it the perfect mobile command center. One side of the cavernous cargo bay, big enough to stack three armored vehicles from end to end and still have space left over, was given to a bank of video screens and a master console. The screens brought in real-time telemetry, news feeds, and status updates from teams in the field.

The bare metal deck shuddered under Harmony's feet. She stood at April's shoulder, Jessie at her side, as the central screen flickered to life. The man on the screen had a placid, almost painfully anonymous face, the kind of look that slid off peoples' eyes and out of their memory five seconds after they saw him.

Linder was the last of the old guard. The former commander of Vigilant Lock, with the consent of his demonic masters. He'd been fully aware of the true nature of the agency, but he'd stayed the course—and tried to minimize casualties, slipping subtle warnings to his people whenever he could risk it—with the conviction that America was safer that way. He'd landed in the top slot on Jessie's hit list when the truth came to light, but then he'd earned a stay of execution.

Linder was a covert-operations veteran, a man who'd spent his entire life moving between the alphabet agencies, cultivating contacts and racking up favors owed. He argued that they needed him if they were going to go rogue and take command of Vigilant, and in the end, they had to agree.

For the time being, at least. He was on thin ice and he knew it, but they gave him a better deal than his former employers in the courts of hell ever would. Defection was a one-way trip.

"Talk to us," Jessie said.

"At eleven hundred hours yesterday, I received an encrypted burst communication from Agent Cooper. I think it speaks for itself. Patching it through to your feed now."

Linder's image shrank to a picture inside a picture, gliding to the far corner of the screen. Now they were looking at a frozen image of Agent Cooper. Brunette, a long face, hard steel-blue eyes. The image lurched to life, wavering like it was being recorded on a camera phone.

"Cooper here. Tell Agent Temple I owe her twenty bucks; she was right about keeping me embedded. Bobby just pinged me on Skype. Couldn't trace the connection—didn't expect I'd be able to, but I gave it a shot—but we've finally got a lead on the bastard. Check this out."

The image shifted to an eggshell-white wall, no art, no windows, nothing to give a clue as to where it was shot. Bobby was pacing. Back and forth in front of a stationary camera, and the angle made Harmony think he was being filmed by a laptop on a desk. He looked worse than the last time they'd seen him, when they dropped the boom and took him from a billionaire to a bankrupt fugitive in a single afternoon. His normally immaculate hair was fraying, the French cuffs of his dress shirt dangled undone, and the baggage under his eyes showed how little sleep he was getting. He faced the camera and gave a desperate smile, a shadow of his old car-salesman act.

"Cooper. *Cooper*. Who's my number-one girl? You are."

"Mr. Diehl?" Cooper's voice echoed over the recording. "Where are you? They're saying you fled the country—"

"And I should have taken you with me. I know. I know, I must look so disloyal. World's worst boss, am I right?" He let out an off-kilter giggle. "Here's the thing. I had a suspicion I might need a little outside help. And I was right."

He hauled over an office chair, an ergonomic model with a chrome frame, and dropped into it. He ran an awkward hand through his mussy hair.

"The cavalry isn't coming," he said.

"Sir?" Cooper asked.

"The Network. The goddamn *Network*. After all I've done for them. I was supposed to be their golden boy, Cooper. I was supposed to be the herald of a new age. They were going to fix this. They were going to fix everything." He raised his open palm, snatched at the air, and curled it into a fist. "They aren't answering my phone calls. Adam is gone. I have no idea what's going on over there, but they aren't holding up their end of the bargain and it is *unacceptable*."

"Sir," Cooper said, "I don't—I don't know what you're talking about."

"I'm having a cash-flow problem, okay? And considering I hired a team of hard-core killers to watch my back, one of whom *eats people,* I really can't be having a cash-flow problem right now. So. Plan B. That's you. I already made the deal. I just need you to be the human interface. Get on a plane. You're headed for the Florida coast. Tampa."

"And I'll be meeting you there?"

Bobby wiped his nose on the sleeve of his five-hundred-dollar shirt, leaving a glistening trail, and snorted like he was coked to the gills.

"You'll be meeting my contact. Go to a dive bar called the Rusty Nail. Eleven, that's p.m., that's *tonight,* so you need to move fast. The contact is going to give you a briefcase. Do not, under any circumstances, open it. Treat it like it's full of nitroglycerin. Treat it like if you even look at it cross-eyed, it's going to explode and kill you and your family and anyone you've ever loved."

"Mr. Diehl," Cooper said, "you're…scaring me a little."

He went manic, leaning into the camera as his bloodshot eyes bulged.

"We're all a little fucking scared right now, Cooper!" He flopped back in his chair and took a deep breath. "Sorry. Sorry. No, look, it's okay. Everything is going to be great. I'm texting you a contact number. Once you have the case, call it, and the Concierge will arrange transport for you. You, and the case, will be brought to me at Xanadu. I'll do a little razzle-dazzle, a little song and dance, turn that case into solid gold, and then we are all leaving."

"Leaving?" Cooper asked.

"Leaving." Bobby made a walking motion with his fingers. "Going away. Starting fresh, in a place with no extradition treaties. I built an empire once. I can do it again."

Harmony tilted her head, studying the disheveled man

as she sifted through his words. That didn't make sense. Plenty of countries didn't have an extradition treaty with the United States—Libya, Morocco, Saudi Arabia, Mozambique—and a few might even welcome him with open arms if he managed to unfreeze some of his cash somehow, but that would only protect him from the FBI. Changing his address, even if he cozied up with some hostile government, wouldn't erase him from Vigilant Lock's kill list. He knew that.

"Trust the plan." Bobby stared into the camera, suddenly calm and collected. Looking at Cooper, but now it seemed like he was locked eye to eye with Harmony. Daring her to come after him. "Understand this. This…situation…is nothing but a temporary setback. When all is said and done, when the dust settles and the smoke clears, I'm going to be the last man standing."

"I'll head for the airport," Cooper said.

He flashed his pearly smile. "You're my number one, Cooper. My absolute number one."

The image went dark. The corner window blossomed, bringing Linder back onto the screen.

"Of course," Linder said, "I wasn't sending her alone."

A smaller window opened at his side. Static photographs, front and profile, of an olive-skinned man with a sharp chin, a thin black mustache, and a soul patch.

"Agent Ramon Dominguez, one of our newer recruits."

"Approved him myself." Jessie rubbed her chin. "Solid profile. Former Ranger, background in surveillance and long-range recon, good hand with a rifle. Popped his cherry when his element ran into a demon out in Afghanistan. He was the only survivor. Little drinking problem, but let's be honest, ninety percent of Vigilant field operatives have a drinking problem and the other ten are probably in denial or hooked on something worse. He was a solid choice for backup."

"My thought as well," Linder said. "He was instructed to shadow and protect her from a distance. Separate flights, and at no point were they to make direct contact, in case Cooper was being watched upon her arrival. He would only intervene if she was in immediate danger."

"And did he?" Harmony asked.

"I wish I knew. Cooper was instructed to make the rendezvous at the bar, acquire the case and find a safe location to inspect its contents, then notify me at once so we could decide on our next move. She never made contact. Neither did Agent Dominguez. They've both gone completely dark. It's been over twenty-four hours since last contact, so we have to assume the mission went wrong."

"We don't even know if Dominguez made it to Florida," Jessie said. "If the op was compromised somehow, he could have gotten jacked before he even got on the plane."

"Or upon his arrival. In any case, my primary concern—" He caught himself. "Besides the safety of our agents, of course—"

"Of course," April murmured under her breath.

"—is the package that Agent Cooper was supposed to acquire. It sounds like Diehl cashed in a favor. And unfortunately, given his past history, we know that he had friends in both occult-underground circles and among certain...hostile foreign actors."

"And it's something he can turn into a quick and dirty bundle of cash, a big enough bundle to let him disappear for good." Jessie glanced sidelong at Harmony. "You're thinking what I'm thinking."

Harmony was back on Main Street in Talbot Cove,

watching the gas bombs go off. Seeing people she'd known her entire life fall to the street, choking, dying, *changing*, as the mutagen turned their bones to rubber and melted their skin like candle wax.

"It's a weapon," she said.

"Could be biological, chemical, supernatural…" Jessie looked back to the screen. "But we know Bobby would set off a nuke if he thought it'd get him what he wanted. No question he'd *sell* one."

This used to be the part where Linder would give them their marching orders. Instead, he held his silence, deferring to Jessie. It was her call now. She stepped back, addressing Harmony and April.

"Okay. We land, we follow Cooper's trail, we find out what kind of trouble she and Dominguez got into, and we pull them out. Then we get our hands on that mystery briefcase before any bad guys run off with it."

Harmony looked to the screen. "That number Bobby said he was going to text her. Do we have it?"

Linder nodded. "It goes to a gas-station pay phone a few miles outside of Tucson, Arizona. It's either under constant surveillance or some kind of routing system's been installed on the line."

Either was possible. The Concierge was an underworld legend, a professional smuggler who worked through a network of cutouts and intermediaries, moving people and contraband like ghosts through the nation's arteries. Nobody had ever seen their face—not knowingly, at least.

"We've got one more objective," Harmony said. "If Bobby isn't responsible for whatever went wrong down there, he may not even know about it yet. Which means the Concierge is still waiting for Cooper to call for a pickup."

Jessie smiled. “And waiting to take her and the case straight to Bobby’s doorstep. Think we can hitch a ride?”

7.

Aselia Boulanger drifted out of the cockpit. The Creole woman stifled a yawn behind her hand, then gestured over her shoulder with her thumb.

"Linder's got me shuttlin' y'all down to retirement country. Now, here's the thing. I got us a hangar; the *Imperator* is registered as a Ulysses Shipping cargo transport, usual cover, and the hangar rental's good for two days. I already made arrangements for ground transport, gonna have a car waiting when we land. Civilian sedan, but I can't guarantee the make and model, that okay?"

Aselia was their own Concierge, a survivor of Vigilant Lock's last incarnation. When she'd had to go underground, she turned from a pilot to a smuggler, mostly running weed across the Louisiana bayou. She'd boasted there wasn't a vehicle—land, water, or air—she couldn't pilot, and Harmony believed her. Just as importantly, she'd been rebuilding her old network of contacts since Jessie recruited her, giving Vigilant's teams the power to move right under their hunters' noses.

"If it has four wheels and doesn't die on us, that's just fine," Jessie said. "Wait. Aselia? Who's flying the plane?"

"Marco."

Jessie shot a glance at the cockpit door.

"Is he...allowed to do that?"

"Marco's a good pilot. I mean, maybe not takeoffs and

landings, but he can keep her level. And it's not like he's going to try and disassemble the plane while we're airborne." Aselia paused. "Anymore. It was just the one time, and we had a discussion about it."

Kevin had been standing at the tail end of the cargo bay, rummaging through a jumble of lashed-down crates. Now a loose wheel squeaked on one corner of a rolling cart as he pushed it over to the command console. White linen draped the lumpy bottom shelves, concealing their bounty.

"I was still prepping up until a minute before takeoff," he said, "but it's amazing what you can do with an actual, functional organization backing you up."

April turned her chair toward the cart. "As opposed to being set up to fail by the demons using us as deniable weapons?"

"That's a bingo. Standard protocol was to shred ninety-five percent of the mission reports, to make sure Vigilant's teams didn't work too closely together or figure out anything useful. When we opened up the artifact vaults in the *Wunderkammer* to relocate all our stuff, most of it was long gone: the eastern courts stole anything that might come in handy."

"At least they left the hazardous-containment unit untouched," Harmony said. "Most of the bottled-up spirits in there are sworn enemies of the eastern courts; they don't want those monsters getting out any more than we do."

"We've verified the inventory?" April asked.

Harmony narrowed her eyes. She looked to the rolling cart.

"Verified it personally," she said. "Among other delightful inmates, we've got the trapped soul of a fifteenth-century serial killer in there. I wasn't taking any chances."

"The lost intel hurts more than the lost stuff," Kevin said, "but we're doing our best to catch up. I hereby bring you the bounty of Vigilant Lock's all-new support division, under the direction of yours truly. The Print Shop is turning out top-notch paper, the Skunkworks is refining your field arsenal, and Occult-Tactical is...doing some really freaky stuff. Last time I was down there, they had a goat. An actual live goat."

"I authorized the goat," Jessie said.

"Everybody's working on folding card tables and pulling all-nighters while we get the Basement up and running, but I think you're going to be happy with the results. First up: new civilian cover identities, for when you don't want to flash your FBI badges around."

Kevin laid a pair of black leather portfolios, like sheaths for a check at a fancy restaurant, out on the cart. Harmony opened hers, running a fingertip along nestled pockets. Her face stared back from a weathered Maryland driver's license, but the name was "Helena West" and listed her address as an apartment in the Bethesda suburbs. Business cards, crisp black on cream with careful creasing as if they'd been carried around in a wallet for a few months, proclaimed her the manager of accounting for Delaware Mutual Insurance.

"I sell insurance?" Jessie said, holding up one of her own cards. "Really?"

"*Director* of sales," Kevin said. "Setting up Delaware Mutual was our first priority, once we picked out a new HQ. It's a solid cover and a verifiable, legitimate company on every level. Except for, you know, not actually having any customers. You *do* have company credit cards. You also have a good reason to be poking around in Tampa."

"What's our story?" Harmony asked.

"Annual gathering of the American Associated Insurance Vendors' Lobby, being held at the Tampa East Holiday Inn. It was last minute, but by the time we land you should have attendee credentials and a reserved room waiting."

"You're making us stay at the Holiday Inn," Jessie said, her voice flat.

"With any luck we won't be here that long," Harmony said. "We get in, we get the job done, we go home."

She couldn't tell them about the faint, nagging gnaw in her gut, like she'd been fasting for most of a day but the real hunger hadn't set in yet. And with any luck, they'd be done here—and she'd be on her way for a rendezvous with Romeo—before it did. She focused on the paper, committing details to memory. A new address, a new birthday, the sketched outline of an imaginary life. The Print Shop hadn't skimped on details; they'd even given her a little pocket litter to carry around, a monthly rail pass and a rumpled receipt from a meal at an Italian restaurant near the office, dabbed with an artful blotch of dried marinara sauce.

Kevin leaned under the cart and carefully picked up his next offerings, laying them on the top shelf: a pair of buttery calfskin shoulder holsters and twin pistols, with matte-black grips and barrels the color of desert sand.

"Courtesy of Aselia's buddy in New Orleans, meet your new backup: the Sig Sauer P320. This is the X-Series model. Chambered for nine-millimeter, you've got Viking Tactics day and night sights for around-the-clock violence, and Skunkworks made a few modifications.

Namely, they machined a threaded barrel for"—Kevin reached under the cart and held up a pair of storm-gray tubes, almost longer than the guns—"new suppressors. These babies are grade-nine titanium, but light as a feather."

Jessie scooped up one of the pistols, holding it low as she eyed the sights, lining up a trio of luminous green dots. Harmony gave Aselia an uncertain glance. She didn't have to say a word.

"I know," she said, "you don't like people messing with your weapons."

"Not if my life might depend on them," Harmony said.

"I ran a box of rounds through both of those guns personally, with and without the cans, and I cleaned and oiled 'em when I was finished. They check out."

Harmony shrugged off her jacket and reached for the shoulder holster. "*You* I trust."

"Skunkworks wanted to set you up with something smaller, like a P225 designed for concealed carry, but considering we don't know what you're walking into and Bobby Diehl's got a track record of using unconventional troops—"

"Like zombie Terminators," Kevin muttered.

"—I want you packing as much punch as possible. To that end, sending you out with three magazines each. One is loaded with Freedom Munitions HUSH rounds. Subsonic ammunition. Combine those with the cans, you can take out the trash without raising too much of a ruckus. If you need to get loud and nasty, the other two mags are carrying RIP."

Aselia held up a single bullet for their inspection. The bright copper tip was ridged like the serrated blades of a saw.

"That's RIP as in 'Radically Invasive Projectile,'" she said, "and there is truth in that advertising. They penetrate deep, explode into fragments of twisted metal, and dig wounds like trenches on a battlefield. Against a human or a cambion target, it's going to ruin their day. Against an incarnate demon, at the very least it'll hurt like a mother and slow them down."

Jessie whistled. "You do not mess around."

"When it comes to my team? I do not. I thought I was going to spend the rest of my life playing possum in Des Allemands, working charms and smuggling reefer to make ends meet. You didn't just pull me out, you gave me a shot at payback." Aselia shot a glance at the silent, dark video wall. "Still think we should have put two bullets in the back of Linder's head, but he's held up his end of the bargain. For now."

Harmony was navigating the labyrinth of her new weapon. Checking the sights, judging the weight, sliding a magazine home and popping it out again, getting a feel for the gun. Having something mechanical in her hands helped her focus. She split herself in half; while her surface mind had a task, something to practice, hands in constant motion, her deeper thoughts took on sharpness and form. A weapon in their own right, poised to attack the problem ahead of them.

"I've got one other thing for you," Kevin said. "Back in LA, I didn't like how you almost got stuck out on the side of the building."

"Says the man who told us to get onto a window-washing rig," Jessie replied.

"Hey, the plan worked. But only because you were able to get through the glass, and it could have been a real big problem. Got me thinking that you need some kind of multi-tool in the field. A general-purpose escape kit."

"That *would* be nice," she said. "Old Vigilant was never big on giving us useful gear. Cheaper to recruit new humans than it was to keep the ones they had alive."

"I talked to Skunkworks. They already had an unrelated project underway and I thought we could merge ideas, whip up a quick-and-dirty prototype."

He pulled back another layer of cloth and unveiled the results. A pair of fountain pens nestled on white linen. Their chrome bodies were just a little too fat, a little too long, and the clip on the cap had an unnatural bulge. They'd pass muster at a glance, but anyone giving them a thorough look would realize there was something off about them.

"We put our heads together and, well, this is the very rough alpha." He picked up one of the pens to demonstrate. "It doesn't actually write, which should be a baseline goal for a secret spy pen. We're working on it."

"So what *does* it do?" Harmony asked.

He shoved his finger under the clip. It ratcheted upward. A concealed curve of steel glinted beneath.

"For starters, the clip has a tempered and serrated blade. It's small, but sharper than a Ginsu; it'll saw through rope, thick nylon, you name it. It will cut glass, we tested, but you'll need time and a lot of elbow grease."

"Could be useful," Harmony said.

He tapped the belly of the pen. "Ultimately there's going to be a hollow compartment in here. So, for instance, Jessie could use it to tote her lockpicks around."

"But there isn't one yet," Jessie said.

"Hey, R&D takes time. Like I said, it's an alpha. Right

now the body of the pen is taken up by a very high-powered, single-shot canister of highly compressed air."

"And we want that because?"

Kevin pointed to the base of the pen. The chromed steel was shaped like a circus tent, coming to a hard-angled point.

"Skunkworks was already developing an updated ballistic-mace weapon. This reinforced tip is designed for maximum penetration."

Jessie smothered a snicker behind her hand, passing it off as a sudden cough.

"*Anyway,* you can use it as a punching tool if you need to break something open, like so." He gripped the pen in his fist and pantomimed a thrust. "Focused energy means less force to get the job done."

"Definitely useful," Harmony said. "I can think of a few times when a tool like that would have saved us a lot of trouble."

"I haven't gotten to the best part. Okay, so, first take hold of the shaft. Make sure the tip is pointed away from your face—" Kevin paused. His shoulders slumped as he turned to Jessie. "Go ahead."

"What?" she asked, the picture of wide-eyed innocence.

"Really? No commentary?"

"There comes a time," she said, "when a man dunks on himself so hard that no further dunking is required. Please, proceed."

"Okay, so. You pull back the slicing clip all the way, like so." He tugged it back on the concealed hinge. "Then put your thumb at the base of the clip, just under the blade, and—"

The pen let out a car-crash *crunch* and bucked in his hand hard enough to jerk his elbow back. The chromed tip lanced across the plane, fast as a bullet, and slammed into the bulkhead on the far side of the consoles, burying itself in a bed of crumpled steel.

His arm slowly dropped to his side. They stared at the impact crater, no sound but the thrum of the turboprop engines.

"You shot my plane," Aselia said.

"I, uh…thought the trigger press was stiffer than that," Kevin told her.

"You *shot* my *plane*."

"I mean, technically it's Vigilant Lock's plane—"

"I'm going to kill him," Aselia said. Harmony got between them fast.

"So, uh, you can see the"—Kevin backpedaled as he talked, slipping around the cart—"the practical applications in the field. It's a one-shot tool, for now, but if you need to break into something fast, or break out of something, it'll get the job done. And hopefully you won't need to, but you can use it as an improvised weapon in a pinch."

"It's got potential," Harmony said. She juked left, staving off Aselia's slow and murderous advance. "And we all appreciate your hard work."

"Jessie," Aselia said, "tell your partner that Kevin has to die now. He shot my plane, and he has to die."

"Anyway, if you could bring these two"—Kevin stared at the discharged pen, set it down, and swapped it for the intact one—"this one prototype into the field with you, we could really use your feedback to improve the next iteration."

Harmony took the pen.

8.

The side door of the C-130 swung wide and let in the Florida summer. Hot, muggy air washed over Harmony's face, so thick she could drink it, and her skin was going clammy before she'd finished walking down the four-step ramp. At the edge of the cavernous hangar, an anonymous blue Nissan sat abandoned on the tarmac.

"There's your wheels," Aselia said. "Keys should be in the glove box, papers are clean, please return it as undamaged as possible. I'm working on a more permanent solution for ground transport, so we don't have to rely on the locals wherever we go. Well, Marco's mostly working on it—but it's not ready just yet."

"Should I be worried?" Jessie asked.

"I talked him out of the ejector seats. I think. I mean, we'll find out."

Insects trilled, their high-pitched drone a constant undercurrent beneath the rumble and roar of jet engines. Kevin hustled along, trying to match Harmony's long strides.

"You should take me with you," he said. "I'm useful in the field!"

Behind them, Aselia folded her arms. "Oh, no. I've got a special project that needs attention back here. Just me and you."

"Aselia," Jessie said, "do not beat up Kevin. That's my job."

"We can make it a group project."

"Let's keep the inter-staff assaults to a minimum," Harmony said.

She opened the driver's-side door of the Nissan. A wave of trapped heat boiled out, washing over her like the backdraft from a furnace door. She hovered, waiting for the inferno to die down. Jessie circled around to the other side.

"I'm talking to Human Resources about this," Kevin said.

"Harmony?" Jessie asked. "Do we *have* an HR department?"

Harmony took a deep breath.

"At the moment, I'm pretty sure that's me. So please, everyone, for the sake of my sanity, play nice. Kevin, get patched into the local signals traffic; I want police band, EMS, the works. If anything weird happens in a fifty-mile radius, I want to know about it."

Kevin snapped her a salute. She got into the car, wincing as she patted the steering wheel. The Florida sun had turned it into a branding iron. She fired up the engine, put the air-conditioning on full blast—though it ruffled her short-cropped hair with a gust barely cooler than the outside air—and reached for her seatbelt.

"With any luck, we'll get this wrapped up by tonight."

"Ever the optimist," Jessie said, slipping into the passenger seat beside her.

"More hope than optimism. Cooper and Dominguez wouldn't have gone dark on their own. That leaves two possibilities."

"Dead or taken," Jessie said.

"And if they've been taken by friends of Bobby Diehl's,

every second counts. If we don't find them and get them back fast, we might not get them back at all."

They had landed in St. Petersburg. A curving ribbon of sun-drenched highway led them east, across the endless span of the Howard Frankland Bridge as the road followed the coast and then swung out over the glittering crystal waters of Tampa Bay. The sun was a bright and shining hourglass.

"We're headed for the east side of the city," Jessie said, navigating. "Orient Park, just south of MLK Boulevard."

Tampa was a jumble. Harmony was used to cities with clean districts, clear lines of navigation. The street grid felt like a web woven by a spider on meth. The social lay of the land was even harder to read; they passed walled estates and salmon-roofed Spanish houses that looked like celebrity compounds, and two blocks down they hit a snag of traffic along a graffiti-drenched boulevard where all the stores had barred windows and rolling security shutters. Two more blocks and they were prowling through a suburban tract for retirees. Lincolns and bug-flecked Oldsmobiles gathered dust in front of tiny seventies-era bungalows.

All of the lawns were yellow, scraggly, balding like a Casanova past his prime. *Watering Ban in Effect,* read a flyer nailed to a leaning wooden utility pole. *$1000 Fine.* The nicer parts of town were lush and green. Harmony wondered if they were too rich to be subject to the law, or if they just wrote a check in advance.

She turned south along a neck of barren lots, the dead turf blistered with clapboard shacks and tract housing. The biggest two businesses along this stretch of road were a bail bondsman and a liquor store, their barred windows standing side by side with competing neon lights. The Rusty Nail was a little farther down. Bobby had described the place to Cooper as a dive bar, and he didn't lie; the bar was as gritty as the humidity on the dank, muggy air, the edge of the stone porch caked with the remnants of somebody's last binge. At least they'd staggered outside before heaving it up. This looked like the kind of place where drinking was a professional's pursuit, and a solo one at that.

Their wheels rumbled across a strip of gravel parking lot. The engine went silent and the air-conditioning gusted its last breath, replaced by the endless trill of cicadas.

"Approach?" Harmony asked.

Jessie slid her dark glasses on, a shield of emotionless onyx over her turquoise eyes.

"Figure we give 'em the official credentials," Jessie said. "No reason to think anyone here is working directly for Bobby or his mystery friend, and they might need a little persuasion to talk."

That worked fine for her. Harmony took the lead, pushing through the swinging screen door and stepping into the bar. The only relief from the heat came from a pair of overhead wicker fans, their blades wobbling as they ineffectually slapped at the air. Another fan, an old aluminum-clad model, perched on the edge of the bar and swiveled its face from side to side with a rattling whine. A television above the bar was tuned to Fox News. The clientele mostly watched their drinks instead, old men huddled low and staring into the amber depths like they could read their futures there. Harmony could, too. There wasn't any magic in knowing they'd be right back here tomorrow, trading their pension checks and their livers for a few hours' solace.

The bartender was a college kid, his tank top soaked in a river of sweat as he made his way up and down the bar. He looked like he'd rather be anywhere but here. He brightened up a little as Harmony and Jessie stepped up; they were the only women in the near-empty taproom, and Harmony suspected that wouldn't change much when the nighttime regulars arrived. His tentative smile turned to a frozen, uneasy mask when they flashed their FBI credentials.

"Special Agent Black, Special Agent Temple," Harmony said. "And you are?"

"Dave?" he said, like he wasn't entirely sure.

Jessie gave him a casual smile. "Hey, Dave. First things first, you aren't in any trouble. We're not here about that baggie of pot in your pocket."

His cheek muscles rippled through contortions. He was riding in the front seat of a roller coaster now, soaring high and diving low in the space of a sentence. Harmony gave Jessie a sidelong glance. She didn't even see a bulge on his hip. Jessie caught her question and subtly tapped the side of her nose.

Jessie's father had raised his little girl to follow in his footsteps. He'd taught her the essentials, from wilderness survival to hunting and fishing to the best methods of smuggling a naked, bloody victim across state lines. He had inducted her into his one-man cult, his service to the alien King of Wolves, and ritual ordeals left Jessie with the turquoise eyes that only hinted at the corruption burbling in her toxic blood. Her transformation had given her a nose sharp enough to smell fear—or, for that matter, a stray baggie of cheap weed—perfect night vision, and her constant companion: a craving for brutal violence, along with the muscles and speed to inflict it.

The Dixie Butcher was dead, but part of him would always be with her.

"It's…I'm just holding it for my roommate," the bartender said. "It's not really mine—"

"Were you working here last night?" Harmony asked.

His head bobbed. "Yeah, till two. Usual night guy called in sick, so I had to pull a double shift. I closed up."

Jessie had her phone out. She'd pulled up a pair of pictures: candid, everyday shots of Cooper and Dominguez, tight on their faces.

"Did you see either of these people in the bar?"

He studied the photos, rubbing his chin.

"The guy, no," he said. "I mean, maybe? But I don't think so. It was a quiet night, and he's definitely not one of my regulars. Now, her, she was definitely here. That was the only interesting thing that happened all night."

"Interesting how?" Jessie asked.

The bartender pointed to the far end of the room, where a clutter of sad-looking tables stood shoved to the wall under a long strip of dirty mirrors.

"She came in around ten, grabbed a chair in the back. Ordered a club soda, nothing else. That's not too weird, you know, we get some twelve-steppers who come in to meet their friends sometimes. But she stood out, younger than the usual crowd. A couple of guys, they weren't regulars either, hovered over her table and talked to her for maybe ten minutes."

"Don't suppose you have security cameras in here?" Harmony asked.

His response was an incredulous stare and a wave of his hands, inviting her to spot anything worth stealing.

"What'd they look like?" Jessie asked.

"Maybe in their mid-twenties, one white guy, one

Latino. The white guy was all tatted up, full sleeves. Cheap ink, too. He came over, said he and his buddy needed to take her out the back, and was that okay."

"And you let them?" Harmony said.

The bartender shot a look at the screen door and dropped his voice, like he had some hot gossip to dish out.

"Way he explained it," he said, "his buddy had a thing going on with the lady. The lady's *husband* was in his pickup out front, waiting for them to come outside so he could catch 'em in the act."

"Photographs for the divorce lawyer?" Jessie asked.

"A shotgun," the bartender said. "Way he explained it, the husband had a jealous streak, a violent temper, and a loaded weapon. I'd love to say nothing like that has ever happened here, but they weren't the first couple who ever left by the back door. I don't need my bar turning into a country-western song."

"And the woman?" Harmony asked. "She went along with that story?"

He shrugged. "I didn't talk to her. Just the guy with the tats. But I looked right at her, made eye contact, and she didn't seem worried or like she was having any kind of problem. She walked right along with 'em, totally chill."

And a civilian bartender, Harmony thought, *already stressed and tired from pulling a double shift, wouldn't notice if the "totally chill" lady had the barrel of a gun pressed to her back*. Something occurred to her, another possibility.

"Did either of the men have a case with them?" she asked. "A briefcase, suitcase, rolling luggage? Anything like that?"

He shook his head. "Nah, not that I saw, anyway."

Harmony and Jessie shared a glance.

"We're going to need to take a look out back," Jessie said.

9.

There was nothing behind the Rusty Nail but a desolate patch of scrub and gravel looking out across more vacant lots. Tract houses and bungalows squatted in the near distance, on the far side of a tangled chain-link fence. The gravel strip curled around the side of the bar, meeting up with the lonely road. A generator chugged along, making wet coughing sounds, and a dirt-encrusted sedan with two flat tires and a broken back window rusted away under a vinyl overhang.

"So they didn't bring the goods," Jessie said. She took her sunglasses off. Her nose wrinkled as she tasted the stagnant air.

"Two possibilities," Harmony said, studying the gravel.

"I'm all ears."

"They knew ahead of time that Cooper was a double agent. They didn't bring the case because there was never going to be a handoff. They showed her a gun, walked her out back, shoved her into a car, and left."

"And the other?" Jessie asked.

"They didn't bring it. They told her—truthfully or not—that it was somewhere else. Either out here or a short ride away."

Jessie's eyes glinted, her brows tight. "Motive?"

"Whatever is in that case, it's most likely a weapon and definitely dangerous. They might not have been comfortable walking around with it. Especially if they thought there was any chance things weren't on the up-and-up."

Jessie stood at the edge of the gravel, looking out across the vacant lot. A stray, hot wind picked up a scrap of crumpled newspaper. It rolled like a tumbleweed along the yellowed grass.

"Where the hell was Dominguez?" she said. "He had *one job*."

"We don't know if he made it this far. If Cooper's cover was blown, they could have picked him off anywhere. For that matter, they might have spotted him."

"The 'jealous husband with a shotgun,'" Jessie said.

"Sure. So they hustle Cooper out the back, where Dominguez can't see, and slip out right under his nose. But that doesn't explain why he hasn't reported in. No. We have to assume somebody snatched him, which brings us back to the blown cover theory."

Harmony was seeing ghosts. They walked out the back door, luminous and blue in her mind's eye, as she reconstructed the scene of the crime. The two men flanked Agent Cooper, staying close, walking her to a car that shifted and rippled with static—not enough data to picture it clearly.

Fresh tire streaks, black and thick, curved where the gravel met the pavement of the road and veered sharp north. Recent. They left in a hurry. They hadn't been hurried inside the bar, though, taking their time to talk to Cooper and ease her out back.

"What changed?" Harmony murmured.

She crouched low to get a new perspective. Jessie was midway across the lot, studying divots in the gravel.

"Got some blood here," Jessie said.

She showed Harmony the spatter. Rusty flecks, a small rain of dried crimson in a short, hard flurry.

"Fresh?"

Jessie's nose twitched. "Recent."

Sunshine glinted off crumpled metal, halfway buried under a mound of stray gravel. Haphazard, like it hadn't been deliberately concealed; more likely it had been kicked aside under a sliding shoe. Harmony took a pen from her breast pocket and nudged aside the stray rocks until it came loose.

"Spent brass," Jessie mused. "Twenty-two. Small gun."

"Even without a suppressor, a twenty-two can sound like a lot of things. Do me a favor—pop your head in and ask that bartender if he heard something like—"

"Like a car backfiring, a minute or two after they took Cooper out back," Jessie said. "On it."

Harmony studied the spatter, how it ended right against the sunken impression of tires. *The rest of the blood ended up on your car*, she thought. *But how did it get there? Who had the gun, and who took the bullet?*

In the right hands, a .22 could be a hitman's tool. She stood up and stepped back. In her mind's eye, the blue ghosts forced Agent Cooper to her knees. One leveled a handgun, pressed it to the back of her head, and pulled the trigger. Luminous blood guttered from the pencil-sized wound in Cooper's skull as her body crumpled to the—

No. Rewind.

The blood would have pooled where she landed, not arced, the slug trapped in her brain with no exit wound on the other side. She backed the ghosts up, a murder in reverse as the bullet slid back into the glowing muzzle of the .22.

Was it Cooper's gun? She played it out again. Cooper's ghost drew the .22 this time, putting it to the back of the man in front of her, opening fire—

No. That didn't make any sense. Cooper was a highly trained agent. She never would have fired just *once*. She would have double-tapped, turned and dropped low, and taken out the man behind her before he could react. Harmony could see it play out, but what she saw didn't match the evidence.

Rewind.

She took a couple of steps left, under the shade of the dirty vinyl overhang, trying to get a better angle. Her hip bumped the battered old sedan, and broken safety glass crunched under her shoe.

She paused, measuring the distance between the glass and the blood spatter. Jessie came back outside. She squinted up at the sun.

"Got a hit," Jessie said. "He heard the gunshot, maybe a minute after they stepped outside. He thought somebody blew a tire out on the road."

Maybe a minute. That scanned. Harmony watched the ghosts leave the bar, passing through Jessie's body. Their lips moved in silence.

"She knew," Harmony said. "Cooper knew it was a setup. They lured her out, promising the case was stashed somewhere close, but they came on too strong or they played their hand too soon. She wasn't about to get into that car; she knew it was a one-way trip."

"They killed her?"

"No."

Harmony paced, following the motions of the imaginary phantoms. She reached out just the way she pictured Cooper doing it.

"The guy in front of her had the gun on his belt. She snaked it away from him."

Cooper's ghost grabbed the .22. She fired. A phantom bullet punched into the small of the thug's back and painted the gravel in bright scarlet.

"The one behind," Harmony said, pantomiming a grab. "He got her arm, wrenched it back before she could finish the job."

Cooper's ghost struggled as he pinned her. The one in front turned, still on his feet and bleeding, yanked the pistol from her hand. His buddy hauled her around and shoved her, hard. Cooper flew back and Harmony heard the abandoned car's window shatter against her shoulders. Cooper collapsed to the gravel, out cold in a puddle of safety glass.

"She went down here," Harmony said, pointing with her toe. "Not dead. She didn't die here. They took her. Fast, because one of them was wounded."

A phantom car, icy blue, kicked up a storm of gravel—burying the spent brass—and left black smears on the road as it turned a hard left and squealed out of sight.

Jessie was already on her phone, pacing as fast as she talked.

"April. Hey. Need you to check all the area hospitals. Looks like Cooper might have shot somebody. Check to see if anybody reported admitting a GSW victim after eleven last night. The vic is male, mid-twenties, either a Latino or a white guy with full tattoo sleeves."

* * *

April toiled in the belly of the *Imperator,* mechanical keyboard rattling as she took in the wall of screens. She sat back in her wheelchair, glowing light glinting in her bifocals, and studied the constant streams of data. The parked plane was a sauna; they'd lowered the cargo ramp to let fresh air inside, but it wasn't helping much.

Jessie's voice piped in through her headset. April nodded. "On it. One thing we can't discount: he would likely know that hospitals are legally obligated to report gunshot wounds. He might have gone to an off-the-books surgeon instead."

"If he knows one," Jessie said. "It's worth a look. Call it due diligence."

Kevin was stationed at April's side, a few feet down the bank of consoles. He was hunched over his screen, studying dispatch feeds as he flipped between broadcast channels, listening in with a pair of big, bulky headphones. His chair rattled as he sat up with a jerk. He looked to April, waving his hand.

"Is that Jessie? Patch me in, quick!"

April tapped a couple of keys and brought Kevin in on the call. His voice, suddenly breathless, gusted over the line.

"Boss?" he said. "You need to hear this. Chatter on the police band."

"Is it Cooper?" Jessie asked.

April studied the young man. He'd gone pale, bloodless from whatever he'd overheard.

"Jesus," he said, "I hope not."

10.

They weren't dressed for the beach. Harmony's stiff shoes sank into white sand and the sun continued its brutal percussion beat, drenching her blouse with sweat under the black shroud of her jacket. Jessie strode at her side, dark glasses on, her lips pursed in a tight and stony line.

There was a crowd up ahead. Beach bunnies squeezed in alongside men with bronzed skin and beer guts dangling over their swim trunks, all craning their necks and standing on tiptoe to see over the police cordon. Uniformed officers held the line. Evidence techs swarmed at their backs, down on the water's edge. Harmony looked for the man with the most brass on his crisp blue shirt. She flashed her badge.

"Feds?" he said, looking between Harmony's face and her ID photo. "Who called you?"

Harmony sidestepped his question. "We have reason to believe this situation could be connected to an ongoing investigation."

Jessie pointed behind him. "May we?"

The cop gave an uneasy glance over his shoulder. Someone had set up a makeshift canopy, white sheets on stakes driven into the wet sand, to shield the evidence while the technicians snapped photos and took measurements. A couple of grim-faced EMTs stood at the cordon's edge with a stretcher, waiting for permission to take everything away.

"Sure, just, ah...prepare yourselves, okay?"

"Not our first crime scene." Jessie snapped her credentials shut and brushed past him.

The evidence. That was how Harmony tried to think of a dead body. There was no person there, no soul lingering behind. They were gone, wherever souls went, and only meat remained. That made it easier to take. No matter what condition the body was in, no matter what they'd suffered before the light went out behind their eyes, it wasn't a person anymore. It was evidence. Evidence meant clues, and clues meant a hope for justice.

This time, she couldn't do that.

Agent Cooper lay where she'd washed up on the beach. Down on her belly in a wet furrow, where a foamy wave lapped against her matted hair. Her bloodless face was turned to one side, glassy gaze fixed upon some distant and unknowable horizon. Her empty eyes captured the sun's glow, illuminated; she had learned secrets that only the dead know.

One arm splayed out, broken, ligature bruises on her wrist and something deeper, sharper, like a predator had sawed into her flesh in a hunger to get at the marrow in her bones. Something that left long, gaping gashes from her shoulders and all the way down her naked back, gouging her skin in thin, long tears, wounds upon wounds.

Her waist was where she ended. There was nothing underneath but hamburger flesh and jutting, broken bone. *Bisected*— Harmony thought, then stopped herself. Too clinical. Agent Cooper had been ripped in half.

They'd seen bodies like that before. Vigilant Lock had a database of monsters capable of inflicting that kind of damage, tearing their victims to pieces with mad brute force. This was more than brutality. Harmony couldn't see Jessie's eyes behind her glasses, but she knew her partner was drawn to the same detail she was. The mutilation of Cooper's back wasn't random. The cuts were precise. Layered. Deliberate. Harmony's gaze flicked to the wounds on the dead woman's wrists, where she'd bruised and skinned them raw struggling to get free.

"Jessie—"

"They tortured her," Jessie said.

* * *

"There was no briefcase."

Jessie had been riding at Harmony's side in sullen silence. Her hands clenched into fists, eager to pour out her frustration, but there was no one to use them on. No target, just the image of Cooper's dead eyes, seared into the skin of her memory.

"At the bar?" Harmony asked. She glanced to the red light up ahead and flicked the Nissan's turn signal.

"At *all*. Bobby knew he had an informant in his company."

"We kept her safe," Harmony said. "Jessie, we jumped through burning hoops to keep her cover intact."

"He knew there was an informant, and you know what he does to people who cross him. He can't leave his rathole, but that doesn't mean he can't drop a few bucks on a hired gun or two. He lured Cooper out, he set her up, and he had her killed."

"What logical reason—"

"He doesn't *need* one," Jessie snapped. "You know how he operates. He'd do it out of sheer spite. Payback for the betrayal and one last 'fuck you' from him to us before he disappears for good."

Harmony thought about that. She turned the wheel, checking street signs. The cop had told them where to go. They'd already called ahead and made an appointment with the medical examiner.

"If that's true," Harmony said, "then he just made a very bad mistake. If he paid those men to kill Cooper—and presumably Dominguez, too—there's a trail. And if there's a trail, we can find him."

Jessie folded her arms.

"Goddamn right," she said.

"We shouldn't jump to conclusions, though. There's at least one other possibility."

Jessie gave her a sidelong glance. "Which is?"

"That Bobby was telling the truth and thought he had more control here than he did. Look, his empire is going down in flames, his own company gave him the boot, he's a wanted fugitive. He is not a good or safe person to be close to right now, agreed?"

"Sure," Jessie said.

"Say you're Bobby's friend. He contacts you through a back channel, says hey, you owe him a favor and he's cashing in." Harmony paused. "If you're anything like he is, you might be wondering how much he can hurt you, on purpose or by accident. Can he drag you down with him? *Will* he drag you down, if you hand over the goods and he gets caught red-handed? Maybe trade you in for a lighter sentence?"

Jessie nodded slowly, following her train of thought. "He can't do anything to help *me* out, not with his life turning into a slow-motion Hindenburg crash. All he can do is flail his burning arms and spread his chaos around. And whatever shady business I'm in, that kind of chaos isn't good. I might start thinking that I'd be better off with Bobby dead."

"So you pretend to agree," Harmony said. "You wait for his emissary, and you grab her."

"And you squeeze her until she tells you how to find Bobby."

Jessie leaned her head back. She closed her eyes.

"Once I took over Vigilant, I read her files. The things she had to do, the shit she had to endure to win Bobby's confidence...the sacrifices she had to make." Jessie's arms squeezed tighter across her chest. "I promised her. I promised her that if it was possible, if there was any way I could make it happen, she'd be there when we took Bobby down once and for all. She *earned* the right to pull that trigger, Harmony. More than anyone, she earned the right to the kill."

"You know this wasn't your fault."

"I kept her embedded," Jessie said. "I kept her undercover, just in case Bobby poked his head up. Well...he did. And now she's dead."

"Operatives die, Jessie. That's a risk we all take when we go into the field, and we all know it. Cooper knew it better than most of us. She saw the risks, she knew the odds, and she did it anyway. She went out there, time and time again, putting her neck on the line. Because it was *worth* it."

The address was just up ahead. It was a long funeral slab of a building behind a curling fence, dun brick with horizontal stripes of sandy tan. Tall letters to the right of the door read Hillsborough Medical Examiner.

"One other thing we all know," Harmony said.

"What's that?"

"Nobody retires from Vigilant Lock. It's not that kind

of job. We fight the monsters until the monsters get lucky. And on the day that they do, the rest of us, the ones still standing and fighting, make a promise."

Harmony pulled into a parking spot. The engine rattled and fell silent. She turned in her seat, looking Jessie in the eye.

"We promise that we'll find the monster responsible. We will hunt them, we will find them, and we will make them pay. Whatever Cooper went through, in her final moments she would have known this. She would have known that we'd come looking for her. And that we'd do the exact same thing she would have done for us."

She opened her door. A hot and murky wind gusted in smelling of raw soil and dead grass, a boneyard in high summer.

"We made a promise to avenge her," Harmony said. "Now we have to keep it."

* * *

Cooper's body became an art piece under the hard lights of the morgue. The seaweed and sand had been washed away, the gristle of her wounds bloodless and glistening. She lay contorted on the steel slab, muscles locked in rigor mortis; her shoulders were bent, one arm hooked like a crab claw, partially lifting her off the metal. Her milky eyes shone.

The cop had seen worse, but only once. His dress shirt, stiff with starch, hugged his beer gut like a cardboard sleeve. He lingered by the wall of mortuary lockers, beefy arms crossed, watching the medical examiner work. The air curdled with the warring odors of industrial antiseptic and meat-rot.

"You don't say one word to them unless I'm present and give the okay," he said.

"Understood," the ME said, focused on his studies. He was a fastidious man, with the hands of a clocksmith.

"Not one word."

"As you've said."

"This isn't right," the cop said. "No idea why the Feebs are poking around here, but it isn't right."

The morgue-room doors swung open, and Harmony and Jessie came in on the heels of his complaint.

"Because the victim is a witness to multiple federal crimes," Harmony said.

"About that," the cop told her. "You know we got a field office here in Tampa, right? I had a word with the agent in charge. He's never heard of you."

Harmony flipped open her glossy ID folder, presenting her bona fides. Jessie did the same.

"We're not with the Tampa office," Harmony said. "We're with CIRG, the Critical Incident Response Group. We provide special support nationwide, wherever and whenever we're needed. I'd be happy to refer you to our supervisor in the Crisis Management Unit, SAC Walburgh, and she'll provide whatever information you need."

He could try, anyway. SAC Walburgh was a voicemail box in an empty office. They'd showed their credentials, so he showed his, flashing a silver shield.

"Lieutenant Briggs," he said. "So this is what, some kind of gangland hit?"

"That's our working theory."

Briggs turned back to the medical examiner. "Right now, I've got one and only one question: what happened to the bottom half of her body? Because it looks like something ate her."

The ME was hunched low, nudging at the ragged folds

of Cooper's torso with a magnifying glass and some kind of stainless-steel probe. Unraveling the jigsaw puzzle of her flesh, one millimeter at a time.

"The wounds are suggestive of an animal attack," he murmured.

"Shark?" Briggs asked.

"I'm lining up the cleaner bites with tooth samples," the medical examiner explained. "That will help us narrow down a specific match."

Briggs took a deep breath.

"Look, I just need to know if I should close that beach or not. I'm not going to be the asshole from *Jaws* who lets tourists get chomped on. If there's a man-eater out in those waters—"

"Time, Lieutenant. Precision work takes time."

"What else can you tell us?" Jessie asked.

"If you've noticed her wrists—"

"The ligature marks," Jessie said, her voice tight. "She was restrained."

"Not just that."

The examiner gestured with his probe, pointing to a line inside a line, cutting a deep channel through a pool of black bruises.

"She was restrained *twice*. This was a second restraint, used only on her left wrist and after the initial injuries there. My working theory is that she was tied to something, a weight—a cinder block, for example—intended to hold her corpse underwater. They used cheap rope or simply mis-tied the knot; it came loose, and the tide brought her remains to shore."

Jessie looked to the cop. "You got a boat? Something you can use to trawl the waters out there?"

"You think there's a dumping ground? More vics?"

"Possible," she said. "She had a companion who may or may not have also been abducted; we can't find him to verify. We also believe that one of her assailants suffered a gunshot wound. Small chance he died from it. If these people are using Tampa Bay as a body dump, he might have been buried at sea along with her."

"I've got boats," Briggs said.

Harmony had fallen silent, gears turning behind her eyes, sifting through the pieces.

"What about the wounds on her back?" she asked.

"Can't even begin to speculate," the examiner said. "Haven't gotten that far yet. And…hmm. It looks like I've found a match here. I think I can confirm that the death was caused by a shark attack."

"So I close the beach?" Briggs said.

"Not necessarily."

He raised a pair of tweezers. His test sample, a triangle of razor ivory, glistened under the overhead lights.

"Your victim appears to have been attacked by an oceanic whitetip. Most sharks aren't dangerous to humans at all. The majority of attacks are accidental or occur when the animal feels threatened, but the whitetip is considered an aggressive species."

"So I close the beach."

"The oceanic whitetip is a *deepwater* shark," the examiner said. "Not found in Tampa Bay. Unless someone managed to unleash one far from its natural habitat—and you'd have to talk to a marine biologist about that, I don't know if it would even be able to survive the experience—your victim was only dumped here. She died out at sea."

11.

Jessie took the wheel. Harmony was somewhere inside herself, assembling puzzle pieces with mental fingertips, sliding the evidence around until it fit.

"The rope was around her wrist," she finally said.

Jessie shot a glance into the rearview mirror, pulling out of the parking spot. They'd finished up with the cop, giving him Cooper's civilian cover and a few details, mostly calculated lies, to help his investigation along. His next move was rounding up a few fishing boats and trawling the waters off the beach, hunting for bodies. He said he'd call if he found anything.

"Yeah?"

"So she would have been upside down underwater. People don't normally do that. Think about the clichés, mobsters 'fitting people for cement shoes.' When murder victims are submerged, they're usually bound by the ankles."

"Where are we going with this?" Jessie asked.

"Theoretically, they could have done it in deep water. Take her out on a speedboat, chum the ocean to draw a school of whitetips, and toss her in." Harmony's brow furrowed. "But then the job's done. If they're deep enough for whitetips, they're deep enough to leave her remains behind. Taking her closer to shore before dumping the body would have been an unnecessary risk. Better chance of her washing up, which she did. And the rope was around her wrist. Around her wrist because it happened *after* the attack. She didn't have ankles to bind."

"So they didn't throw her in," Jessie said. "They dangled her in, maybe dragged her behind the boat. Fed half of her to the sharks and kept the rest."

"Again. If they were equipped to weigh her remains down, safer to do it in deep water. The methodology works. The decisions don't. Irrational at best."

"If criminals were rational people, they probably wouldn't be criminals."

Harmony reached for her phone.

"I don't think Agent Cooper was murdered in deep water," she said. "I think it happened here. On land. Yes, Kevin? I need you to run a search on marine facilities in Tampa and the outlying area. Aquatic shows, aquariums and zoo exhibits, anywhere with exotic animals. Find out if anybody has a permit to keep oceanic whitetips."

* * *

Nautilus Conservation Research had a permit. And a receipt for two mature oceanic whitetips, bought a year ago from a dodgy wildlife merchant who mostly worked with foreign zoos. At 4:00 p.m. on the dot, two days a week, they offered free tours to the public.

Their HQ was a big box of wavy sheet metal painted a pale blue, perched on the edge of Cockroach Bay. There were boat ramps along the shore and mangrove islands in the distance, dots of lush green in the placid waters. The cicada drone was as unrelenting as the muggy afternoon heat. A barn-style door stood open on the edge of the narrow parking lot, and a small crowd was gathering out front. Jessie ducked low, swapping her dark glasses for her amber contact lenses.

"How do you want to play it?" Harmony asked.

Jessie looked up, eyelashes fluttering over perfectly forgettable irises.

"Let's pretend to be normal," she said.

They hovered at the edge of the pack, maybe ten people in all, a mix of elderly locals and soggy T-shirted tourists looking for anything with the word "free" in the title. Beyond the barn door, the main floor of the research center was an aquarium in miniature. Tall oval tanks dotted a concrete floor marred by faded water stains. Workstations on sleek glass desks parsed a stream of running data from the tanks, tethered by slinky bundles of bright orange cable.

A woman came out to greet them, sheathed in a water-spotted lab coat and clutching a clipboard to her chest. She had a sunbather's tan, golden hair, and more bubbly effervescence than a glass of sparkling wine.

"Welcome, welcome everybody!" She flashed a perfect smile. "Welcome to Nautilus. I'm Dr. Joy, the facility manager, and I'm *so* glad you could all join us this afternoon."

She ushered them inside and held court at the edge of a low round pool ringed by faded brick. Stingrays flitted through the shallow water, their wings ruffling up clouds of pristine sand. Inside, Harmony got a better look at the layout. It really was just a big metal box, fans churning the humid air between long bars of lighting almost thirty feet up. Pathways and cables wound between the tanks, and a pair of open staircases in the back led the way to a raised platform with more workstations and a server rack.

In one corner, near the doorway, the gray nozzle of a security camera framed them in its sights. Harmony glanced up to the platform. No security guards or monitoring station in view. *So where is it feeding to?*

"We're a think tank—and a fish tank," their tour guide said, offering a dramatic wave to one of the six oval tanks, "coordinating with pharmaceutical and cosmetic companies across the globe. Our goal is to find more respectful, sustainable, and healthy ways to use the ocean's bounty to benefit all of humanity."

Harmony had all of her eyes open now. She called to her second sight, and it painted the salt-tinged air in shades of shimmering violet. Psychic pulses pinged out like sonar, searching for a hard surface to bounce off of. They faded instead, echoing into the blue. The only supernatural presence in the room was her and Jessie.

Jellyfish rippled in one of the tanks, their tendrils waving as they flowed through the water. Dr. Joy walked the tour group over to the glass, explaining the jellyfish's niche in the financial ecosystem. Collagen for cosmetics, mucus for experimental biofilters.

"Jellyfish research could even pave the way to improved methods of filtering plastic trash, which is being dumped into the ocean at an unsustainable rate." Dr. Joy gestured to the tank. "Besides, I think these plump little guys are kinda cute. You just can't pet 'em. Now let me introduce you to the stars of our facility…"

She led them to the shark tank. A pair of oceanic whitetips shimmered beyond the glass, stony gray and eight feet long from nose to tail. Their sleek fins sliced the water like razor-edged wings. Harmony's stomach went tight. She searched the clean, clear water for any trace of blood, any sign that Agent Cooper might have spent her last agonizing minutes in this room. Nothing.

But one of the steel rafters ran directly above the tank. Perfect for dangling a shark's dinner into the water.

"Meet Buster and Keaton," Dr. Joy said. "These two

gentlemen—and don't let the scary teeth fool you, they really are perfect gentlemen—are oceanic whitetips. And the whitetip, sad to say, is on the endangered species list. They're hunted across the world for their meat, their hides, their cartilage, and most of all, their fins."

"What are their fins good for?" Jessie asked.

Joy's enthusiasm dampened as she looked to the gliding sharks.

"Very little, I'm afraid. Shark fin soup is a traditional part of Chinese cuisine, and many people believe—with no scientific basis—that it's a form of natural medicine. This led to the practice of 'finning,' where sharks are captured, their fins are chopped off, and the sharks are then dumped back into the ocean. Which, since sharks use their fins to process oxygen, generally leads to their slow death by asphyxiation. Thousands of pounds of shark fins are harvested every year, often illegally."

She paused, letting that sink in. A flicker of her smile returned.

"The good news is, the practice is on the decline, but whitetips are still heavily overfished. Here at Nautilus, we're investigating ways of artificially reproducing some of their most valuable gifts. For instance, shark cartilage is in high demand for medical research. We're making strides toward creating a lab-cultured substitute, offering the same chemical properties but without the need to harm a single shark to get it. Speaking of medical research, in our next tank we have a much smaller and possibly surprising guest: the tilapia fish!"

As the tour went on, Harmony and Jessie lingered at the back. Jessie leaned close, murmuring under her breath.

"Been scoping the staff."

"Anything?" Harmony said.

A tiny shake of her head. One of the scientists cut across their path, a man with silver hair and a tablet that streamed pages of fresh data.

"Nobody matching the perps at the bar. Five employees plus Dr. Joy, three women, two men, and both of the guys are in their late forties at least. Witch senses tingling?"

"Nothing," Harmony said.

"Dead end?"

Harmony's lips pursed. Nautilus Research checked out, at least on the surface level. Her gut was nagging her, telling her the water was deeper than it looked. Her gaze flicked to the security camera—one of four, by her count, capturing the tanks and balcony from every angle. The one above the entrance had moved again. It wasn't stationary: the nozzle had tracked the tour group since they arrived, following their movements across the floor.

"Camera at three o'clock," she breathed. "Don't stare."

"Yeah?" Jessie asked.

"There's no security station. Who's on the other side?"

Jessie glanced up to the balcony, gaze drifting across the monitors, double-checking. No camera feeds in sight.

"You see a hatch?" Jessie said. "Anything that looks like a basement?"

"Nothing. Could be off-site."

"Or hidden for a reason," Jessie said.

"Whoever's controlling that camera is either bored enough to watch a guided tour—"

"Or checking out anybody who shows up," Jessie said, "because they fed somebody to their pet sharks the other day and they're afraid someone might follow Cooper's trail."

The tour was wrapping up. Dr. Joy led the pack back

toward the open barn door as she answered questions from a tourist with a thick French accent. Harmony felt a decision weighing down on her. She could walk away empty-handed or take a chance.

"Got an idea," she murmured to Jessie. "Could be dangerous, though."

Jessie gave her a nudge. "That's my favorite kind of idea. Go for it. I'll follow your lead."

Harmony's fingers glided over her microbead earpiece as she eased it from her pocket. She turned it on as she palmed it and slipped it into her left ear, covering the move by scratching an imaginary itch. She was transmitting now, her voice bouncing back to Kevin and April at the *Imperator*. She didn't speak, not yet, but they'd see her feed go live. No time to fill them in on the plan; she'd just have to trust that they'd pick up on her intentions and follow through on their end.

As the tourists drifted out, she and Jessie stayed behind. Dr. Joy gave Harmony a small, almost shy-looking smile. Not the first time—she'd drawn the researcher's full attention more than once during the tour, feeling like they were having a one-sided conversation.

"Thank you for the tour," Harmony said. "I have to say, that was entertaining and educational."

"That's what we aim for." Dr. Joy held Harmony's gaze like she was caressing it in her hand. "Are you…local, or—"

"We're from out of town. Actually, we're in the process of scouting out some new investment opportunities for our firm."

Harmony held out her hand.

"The name's West," she said. "Helena West. I work for Diehl Innovations."

12.

On board the plane, Kevin sat up so fast his chair rattled. He turned to April, eyes wide as Harmony's voice echoed in his bulky headphones.

"What is she *doing?*"

April sipped her tea, her voice dry.

"Her job," she said.

"No, I'm saying, that's not her cover. They're supposed to be insurance-company reps. Why the hell would she say she works for Bobby Diehl?"

"She patched us in for a reason," April mused. "Clearly, she expects us to figure it out. And quickly."

* * *

Dr. Joy's smile lingered, but some of the bubbly enthusiasm drained from her eyes.

"You folks have been in the news a lot lately," she said.

"And not for the right reasons, I know," Harmony said. "The public still associates us with the…misdeeds of our former CEO. Hopefully, our upcoming rebranding will help, once we take his name out of it. That's part of why we were brought on. My coworker—"

"Madeline," Jessie said, stepping in for a quick handshake.

"Madeline and I were just hired last week, as part of the changeover initiative. Our team has been tasked with carving out new footholds, now that our cell-phone business...well, let's just say consumer confidence in our product has slipped a little. We're looking to diversify."

* * *

"I don't get it," Kevin said. "Their insurance-company cover was bulletproof. You know how much work we put into that? Why is she tossing it all out the window?"

"She's improvising in the field," April said. She inhaled the steam wafting from her tea, camphor and fragrant herbs unlocking passages in her mind, pointing her toward the unwritten plan.

April had an impossible job. She wasn't the head of Vigilant Lock's psychology department: she *was* the psychology department. The reborn organization had the reach to find and recruit operatives, the resources to send them into battle with the powers of hell and worse, but not the staff to put them together again when they came back broken.

Arguably, impossible or not, she was the best woman for the task. She'd honed her skills in the FBI's Behavioral Analysis Unit, putting her doctorate to work unraveling the minds of human monsters. Handy, when duty called her to provide insight into the inhuman variety. But April considered her talent as a profiler secondary to the task of keeping her team mentally healthy and whole. To do that, she had to know how they thought. She had to anticipate Harmony and Jessie's moves and have support ready before they needed it.

"She's baiting them. Hired one week ago. That's significant. Bobby has been on the run for months, with no hand in his former company's operations."

"Yeah, but baiting them *why?*" Kevin said.

"She suspects these people were involved in Agent Cooper's death. Consider the possibilities. If Bobby penetrated Cooper's cover and set her up to be killed, a pair of Cooper's coworkers showing up will draw immediate attention. If Cooper was murdered by Bobby's traitorous 'friend,' who would rather see Bobby dead than hand over whatever they'd promised him, same outcome. This is a deliberate provocation."

"They're gonna get found out. All these people have to do is put in a call to Diehl's HR department, and they'll find out nobody named 'Helena West' even works for—wait." Kevin spun his chair around, facing front, huddling over his keyboard as he rattled off a machine-gun streak of commands. "That's why she patched us in."

"Insight?" April asked.

"Cooper was Bobby's right-hand woman—for his legal, *non*-shady shit—which meant she had access to the whole Diehl Innovations company database. And in about five minutes, I'm going to have her login password. The company doesn't know she's dead yet, no reason they'd revoke her permissions. I'll slip in, alter the human-resources registry to add a couple of freshly hired employees, and cover my tracks on the way out."

April was in motion at her own console, listening to Kevin while her fingers dialed up a direct line to Bethesda. She swiveled down the microphone arm on her headset.

"Print Shop? This is Dr. Cassidy, authorization nineteen-seven. We need a rush revision of the business cards you prepared for Agents Temple and Black. Same cover names, new company and titles. No time for a delivery from headquarters. I'll transmit the specifications and once you design them, we'll put in a rush order at a local civilian printer so I can deliver them personally."

* * *

Dr. Joy was playing with her hair.

It was a tiny tic, a gesture of habit as she curled a stray golden lock around her fingertip, mostly with her eyes on Harmony. They stood in the shadow of the security camera, the lens tracking their every move.

"So, Doctor—" Harmony was saying.

"Please. Call me Neptune." She chuckled. "I know, right? I was doomed from birth. Get a name like Neptune and you basically either have to become a marine biologist or join NASA. To be honest, I think my parents were hoping for NASA, but they pretend not to be disappointed when we get together for Thanksgiving dinner."

"Neptune," Harmony said, trying to mirror the scientist's easy smile. "We think that Nautilus Conservation Research might be an excellent investment opportunity for us. That is, if you're in the market for new sponsors."

"Well, it's not my decision to make, but—" Neptune paused. Five feet to her right, an office phone perched on the edge of a sleek glass desk began to trill. She checked the caller ID and scooped it up. "Sir? Of course. Yes, absolutely."

Harmony and Jessie lingered on the edge of a mostly one-sided conversation. Eventually Neptune finished agreeing and hung up the phone.

"*Always watching*," the scientist breathed, in a tone that showed just how little she enjoyed it. She shot a split-second glance at the camera before turning back to them. "Speaking of decision-makers, that was Dr. Cranston, our president and founder. He asked me to say he'd be pleased if you'd be able to join him for dinner tonight. Say around seven? He'd like to hear more about your company and what you might be able to offer."

Harmony read the look in her partner's eye. She nodded. "We'd love to. Which restaurant?"

"His home," Neptune said. "Dr. Cranston prefers to entertain guests at his home. It's in Parkland Estates; I'll give you directions. Can I walk you out?"

They stepped through the open barn-style door, into the muggy haze of the parking lot. The canopy of the summer sky was just starting to fade but still glowing, like an azure gem flecked with soot. Neptune stayed close at Harmony's side as she rattled off a long list of streets and turns by memory. Clearly, she'd made the drive more than once.

"I mostly get a T-shirt and flip-flop crowd on these tours," Neptune told her. "Not a lot of women in suits and ties. It's a distinctive style."

Harmony blinked at her. "Oh. Well. It's just...me."

"Do you do sports?" Neptune gestured at her head. "I mean, the short hair. It's a sporty look."

"I try to stay active."

The scientist watched them go, falling back to the open doorway as they got into the car. Jessie tossed Harmony the keys, belted in on the passenger side, and slipped her earpiece in. Her lips were pursed like she was about to burst out laughing.

"What?" Harmony said, throwing the car into reverse. She swung it around, aiming for the open road, with Neptune silhouetted in the rearview mirror.

"You are unbelievable."

"What?"

"You didn't catch that, did you? At all."

"I don't know which 'that' you're referring to," Harmony said, "so obviously not."

"She was *hitting on you.*"

Harmony pursed her lips, like she was doing math in her head. Long division.

"Are you sure?"

"Oh my God," Jessie said, grinning. "She was all over you from the second we walked in. I was getting *jealous* back there. And I don't normally get jealous, because I'm a goddamn sexual tyrannosaurus. But nope, I barely got a handshake out of her. She was all about the sweet, sweet Harmony."

Harmony squirmed in her seat. "I…I don't think she was. I mean, are you really sure?"

"You've got to be kidding me. And what did you think that was all about, her commenting on your suit and your hair? She was trying to figure out if you're gay."

"I think we're *all* trying to figure that out," Kevin's voice said in Harmony's left ear. "Oh, shit. Forgot my mic was turned on. Sorry."

"Wow." Jessie slid back in her seat and whistled. "Slick moves, champ."

"Uh. Anyway. Reason my mic is on: I've got good news. We've got you covered, or at least as covered as you can get, under the circumstances. I slipped your new identities into the roster at Diehl Innovations. If anyone calls to check up on your story, they'll verify you were both hired last week. Only problem is there's no way to insert you into the phone registry from off-site, so if they try to call you there, they'll find out you don't actually have an office."

"Not worried," Harmony said, happy for a change of subject. "If they check up on us, odds are they'll call HR and use the employment-verification trick, just like we do. Easiest way to find out where somebody works."

April's voice chimed in over the line. "We've also upgraded your accommodations to better maintain your new personae. Insurance agents stay at the Holiday Inn. Six-figure corporate negotiators stay at the Vinoy Renaissance Hotel."

"*Yes,*" Jessie whispered, pumping her fist.

"I'll need to rendezvous with you, to provide reservation details and your freshly printed business cards."

Harmony glanced at the dashboard clock.

"We can swing by the hangar on our way to dinner," she said. "We'll be there as soon as we can."

They disconnected the line and pocketed their earpieces.

"I have clearly failed you as a partner," Jessie said.

"What?" Harmony squinted at her. "Why would you say that?"

"Because you have no game. It is my responsibility to impart game unto you, and I have not lived up to my natural and moral obligations. This is a proverbial 'give a woman a fish, she eats for a day' situation. See, I thought I wanted to get you laid. In truth, I need to teach you how to get *yourself* laid."

"We don't need to have this conversation," Harmony said.

"You're overlooking the advantages of interpersonal skills," Jessie said. "If these people are shady, Neptune's a valuable source of intel. You might have to pump her for information. Vigorously. For hours on end. All night long, if need be."

Harmony half smiled, half grimaced. "Stop. And I don't

overlook the advantages. I just know you're better at it than I am. You're the people person, I do investigation and tactics."

"You know," Jessie said, "sometimes it's smart to stick with what you're good at."

"But," Harmony said, anticipating it.

"But sometimes that can be a crutch, to keep you in your comfort zone. And a comfort zone is nothing but a cage with nice furniture. So, what's that tactical mind of yours telling you about this dinner invitation?"

"It's telling me that either Nautilus Research is hurting for capital, or this Dr. Cranston—who is creepily fixated on watching tour groups—is way too eager to meet a couple of random out-of-town businesspeople."

"You think he's Bobby's guy? The man with the mystery briefcase?"

"I'd say there's an excellent chance," Harmony said.

"If I was in his shoes," Jessie said, "I'd be thinking we were probably more of Bobby's people, coming to find out why Cooper hasn't brought back the goods yet."

"Agreed."

Harmony drummed her fingers on the steering wheel.

"Which means," Harmony said, "there's also an excellent chance that he's going to try and kill us tonight."

13.

If Cranston was short on cash, all he needed to do was sell his house.

He lived in a millionaire's playground on a street lined with palm trees. He made his nest in a stone cathedral the color of white beach sand, with an ink-black scalloped rooftop, Spanish windows, and a four-car garage, secluded behind a ring of wrought-iron fencing. Two cars sat in the kidney-shaped driveway: a polished storm-gray BMW coupe and, incongruously, a battered Jetta with a Greenpeace bumper sticker. Harmony parked next to the Jetta.

Cold metal fluttered against Harmony's breastbone. She wore an ancient, tarnished coin on a slender chain under her dress shirt, ringed with a faded Greek inscription. Mostly for good luck. It had been passed down from her great-great-grandmother, first witch of her family line, who claimed it once belonged to the Oracle of Delphi.

Probably not. Great-great-grandma was a bit of a huckster. All the same, the coin got jumpy in places where reality had gone thin around the edges. Harmony thumped her finger against her salmon-pink necktie, quieting the coin with a tap, and slid into her second sight. Her vision painted the house and the shady, quiet street in glimmering azure, but nothing stood out, no signal in the mundane noise. Jessie asked a question with her eyes.

"Not sure," Harmony said. "Coin's acting up."

"Magic on the premises?"

Harmony shoved open the car door.

"Sometimes it just goes off. Reacts to stray bits of weirdness, scraps of random cosmic energy."

"Or?" Jessie asked.

"Or something's here from someplace else."

The doorbell chimed, echoing and dour, like an invitation to Sunday mass. The woman who answered it wore a maid's uniform in funeral black, a white bonnet adorning her long, straight hair, hands sheathed in satin gloves. She had a wide mouth with thick, wormy lips, and leaden-lidded eyes that made Harmony think of a swamp toad.

"We're—" Jessie started to say.

"The dinner guests," the maid responded, as if announcing a medical prognosis. "Yes. You will follow me."

She turned without a word, trudging through a foyer lined in pristine alabaster. They trailed in her wake, eyes sharp. Not just for a potential ambush, though the risk was never far from Harmony's mind: beyond getting justice for Cooper, they still had to figure out what happened to Agent Dominguez and recover the mystery briefcase, if it even existed. Too many questions to go in with guns blazing. They'd get their answers, and then they'd deal with Cooper's killer.

High windows invited the last shreds of dying sunlight into the mansion, painting long streaks along gleaming ice-white tile. The air was museum cold, not a speck of dust, and a grand piano perched at the edge of a sitting room. Cranston's tastes ran to ivory velvet and polished glass. Fragile, and clean like a surgical theater waiting for the first patient of the day.

The maid hauled aside a wooden door, rattling on a recessed track, and sullenly waved them into the parlor beyond. The room was half library and half aquarium. Bookshelves, full from floor to ceiling, alternated space with panels of glass and murky water. The tank partitions were built behind the bookcases, giving the impression of one vast watery enclosure all around them. Schools of neon goby, tiny and bright electric blue, fluttered between musty hardcovers. Jellyfish pulsed their way, tendrils wavering, alongside marine biology textbooks, while striped Siamese tigerfish stood guard over Chaucer and Proust.

Their host was waiting.

He was squat and wide, built like an engine block in a tailored suit, silk cravat artfully wrapped around his broad neck. His jowls drooped, and his frog mouth and heavy-lidded eyes made him look like a relative to the maid in the hall. He wore his silver hair in a disheveled mop.

"Ladies." He raised a glass of white wine. His sonorous voice was at odds with his brutish looks, a gentleman squeezed into a barbarian's body. "Judah Cranston, at your service. So pleased you could join me on such short notice."

Neptune stood beside him. *Explains the Jetta out front,* Harmony thought. She'd traded her lab coat for a ribbed dress in bright aquamarine, delicate earrings, and high heels with elaborate golden straps. Her gaze locked onto Harmony like a heat-seeking missile.

"The pleasure's ours," Jessie said.

He swapped his wine glass from his right hand to his left, freeing it up for a handshake as Jessie stepped forward. The gesture drew Harmony's eye. Halfway up to the first knuckle, Judah Cranston's fingers were joined by a webbing of saggy skin. He caught her looking just a second too long, and his thick lips curled in a smile.

"It's quite all right. I'm accustomed to being stared at." He held up his open hand. "It's called syndactyly. When I was a child, my mother told me I was part fish. Not true, alas. It's nothing but a birth defect, bit of a genetic quirk, but that pleasing lie sparked a lifelong passion."

"And here we are today," Neptune said. She gestured to a rolling glass cart. A bottle of wine, freshly uncorked, nestled in a silver ice bucket amid a clutter of crystal glasses. "Drinks?"

"Please," Jessie said. She turned to Judah. "Your aquarium is impressive. The one here and the one at your…would you call it a laboratory?"

Jessie's small talk bought Harmony time to concentrate. The coin fluttered against her breastbone again, insistent. There was something here. Her second sight painted the room; the neon goby were living sparklers in the water, the jellyfish blooms of pulsing flesh, as her senses pinged out like sonar. Life energy, nothing unusual, nothing unexpected. Neptune Joy was as mundane as the white zinfandel she was pouring.

Judah wasn't. A faint web of deep violet energy clung to him, shimmering under his skin like a map of his veins. Harmony had seen that before. It was residual magic, the lingering power that clung to a magician after hours—or years—of dedicated ritual work. No telling what he used it for, but their host knew his way around a pentacle.

"Laboratory, research facility." Judah sipped his wine

with a careless shrug. "I like to think of it as a place for building a sustainable future, but that's more of a mouthful."

Neptune passed a pair of glasses to Jessie and Harmony. Her fingers lingered over Harmony's for a fleeting moment, longer than they needed to. Then she retreated, looking almost bashful as she took her station by the drink cart. Harmony wondered if her boss had invited her, or if she'd invited herself.

A bell chimed. Judah looked to the parlor door with a broad smile.

"Ah. Supper's ready. Please, ladies, follow me? We'll continue this meeting—and this wine, excellent choice, Neptune, your palate is superior as always—in the dining room."

They followed him down alabaster halls, chasing the ghostly echo of the bell. Jessie paused, pointing past a pair of open double doors. The room beyond was lined with tatami mats, the far walls shrouded behind tall white paper screens. Another wall sported a small arsenal in lacquered wood, blunt swords and staves for training.

"You've got a dojo," Jessie said. "In your house. That's pretty cool."

Judah chuckled. "Why go to the gym, when you can bring the gym to you? The syndactyly wasn't my only flaw; I was a sickly child, and the doctors expressed doubt that I'd live. My father wasn't having it. He set me onto a vigorous regimen of exercise to strengthen my body, and I've adhered to it ever since."

"I noticed the swords," Harmony said. "Do you practice kendo?"

"I dabble. My chosen art, though, is escrima. I ended up in the Philippines as a young man and found myself utterly fascinated by the style." He glanced sidelong at her as they walked, as if seeing her for the first time. "You have a certain…reserved discipline in your movements. Very calculated. Very spare. I'm betting you're a martial artist yourself."

"Aikido," Harmony said.

The heavy folds of his eyes lifted. "I'm going to have to be careful around you."

"Oh? Why's that?"

"It's one thing to face an opponent who comes armed with powerful strikes. Quite another to face one who plans to turn your own momentum against you."

"I hope we're not opponents," Harmony replied.

He had an amused twinkle in his eyes. "As do I. But we should spar sometime. Just a bit of friendly competition; you don't really know someone until you've tested each other's skills."

Candlelight danced at the heart of the dining room table, tall and slender blue sticks burning in silver holders. The wax almost matched the deep sapphire hue of the walls. Tall, arched windows looked out over a groomed lawn, palm trees shivering in a hot evening wind. Judah took his seat at the head of the table.

"I assume seafood's not on the menu," Jessie said, sliding into a chair at Harmony's side.

"Never, in my house," their host replied. "Though I certainly had more than my share as a boy. My family comes from the sea. Well, we *all* come from the sea, on a long enough scale, but we were New Englanders. The Cranstons were a fishing family, back to the days of Melville."

"How did you move from fishing to oceanic science?" Harmony asked.

“We didn’t move. The fish did. Once the big commercial interests sailed in, they harvested the water to the breaking point and beyond, until there was nothing left to catch.” His eyes darkened. “As they do. As we always do. We take and take, until nothing remains.”

The maid wheeled in a cart, pulling back a silver lid to unveil a gust of steam carrying the scents of roasted meat and sea salt. She spooned a puff pastry onto Harmony’s china plate. A faint trail of scarlet leaked from a crack in the flaky skin.

“Beef Wellington,” Judah said. “It may be hypocritical of me to eschew fish while happily dining on cows, but it’s a delicious hypocrisy. Call it my revenge on the land.”

Their host didn’t skimp on the side dishes, either. Winter greens, gently wilted, joined their plates along with roasted fingerling potatoes, their skins adorned with pale green herbs. The delicate pastry crumbled as Harmony sawed into her Wellington, the meat beneath bloody rare. The flavors mingled on her tongue, buttery breading and tenderloin, simple but rich and strong.

“Revenge?” Jessie asked.

“I’m being melodramatic, but I won’t deny a certain anger drives my work. The demise of my family’s business was simply a symptom of a much greater problem. More than seventy percent of our world is ocean. Think about that. There’s more water than dry land. Even calling it ‘Earth’ is an unconscious sign of humanity’s arrogance; we can’t live in the ocean, so we don’t acknowledge it at all.”

“It’s ungrateful,” Neptune chimed in, scooping up a forkful of greens. She was the only one at the table without a beef Wellington, doubling up on the vegetables instead. "Human life came from the oceans in the first place."

Judah lifted his wineglass to her. "Ungrateful. Perfect word for it. The ocean is our mother. She gives us food, medicine, *miracles* of science. Tell me, my new friends: do you know how much garbage is dumped into the ocean every single year?"

"I'm guessing it's a lot," Jessie said.

"Eighteen. Billion. Pounds. Over a million pounds an hour, all day, every day. She gives us her bounty, and we feed her our filth. Chemical runoff. Untreated sewage. Plastic. We have created entire spans of ocean, dead zones, where no marine life can survive."

"And there's no backup plan," Neptune added. "Beyond the damage we're doing to the entire ecosystem, we need clean water to live, and that's a simple fact. Once we kill the oceans, humanity dies with them."

"An entire species," Judah muttered, "gifted with intelligence but no vision, driven to slow-motion suicide."

He set his fork down.

"But I do go on. Forgive me."

"Nothing to forgive," Harmony said. "You're both passionate about this. That's what drew our attention in the first place."

"Yes," Judah said, "we should talk about business, shouldn't we? You have my interest, to say the least. Did you know that you're not the first representatives from Diehl Innovations to approach me about a potential investment?"

Harmony and Jessie shared a glance.

"Really," Harmony said.

He dabbed at the corner of his mouth with a cloth napkin, utterly casual.

"Yes. There was another, about a month ago. Oh, help me out, Neptune. What was her name?"

Neptune gazed into Harmony's eyes.

"Natalie Cooper," she said.

"Cooper." Judah snapped his fingers. "That was it. Do you ladies know her?"

14.

Harmony had a natural poker face. Sometimes she was thankful for it. Like right now, with Judah waiting for her reaction and Neptune staring like she could read her thoughts.

After Bobby fled, with their stock value plunging and their investments in ruins, Diehl Innovations was left scrambling to survive. While the board of directors grappled with chaos, Agent Cooper had fallen into a murky professional limbo; she was an administrative assistant with more reach than most senior executives, stationed at a desk outside an empty office with no duties and nobody to report to.

Nobody but her real employers, anyway, and she sent Jessie regular dispatches as she kept her ear to the ground, hoping for some clue to Bobby's whereabouts. Mostly she sat at her desk and played solitaire, collecting a paycheck. She wasn't heading up Diehl's new investment initiative, because Harmony had made the entire thing up two hours ago. And she absolutely wasn't flying around the country a month ago, reaching out to random marine-biology labs.

Judah and Neptune were lying. And if they knew Cooper at all, it was from last night. When they had her murdered.

Dropping her name was the opening move in a game of shadow-chess. Was it just to test Harmony's reaction? A probe, to find out if they really were who they claimed to be? Or did Judah *want* her to know he was lying, an open challenge to confront him over it?

"Cooper," Harmony echoed. She looked to Jessie. "Wasn't—wasn't she Bobby Diehl's admin before he left the company?"

Jessie pretended to think about it. "Think so. I figured they'd have either reassigned her or let her go."

Harmony turned back to Judah. "Yeah, she's not in our department. I'm kind of surprised she contacted you, to be honest. That's not her kind of work."

"Well," Judah said. "Maybe Bobby sent her."

There was a dare in his eyes. She declined it. Her cover story was a wall between them, holding fast.

"A month ago, you said?" Harmony shook her head. "Couldn't have been, he's been gone longer than that."

"Curious," Judah replied. "Well. I'm sure we'll get to the bottom of it."

Neptune had been watching the back-and-forth like a spectator at a tennis match. Harmony gave her a moment's eye contact as she reached for her glass of wine. She didn't have any of her boss's cool confidence. *She looks confused,* Harmony thought. *Or worried.*

"You didn't say," Jessie said to Judah.

"Hmm?"

"If anything came of it."

"Oh. Oh, no, just an initial call, we never set up a formal meeting. Not for lack of interest on my part. As I'm sure you can imagine, an organization like ours is quite expensive to maintain."

"That fish-food budget's got to be a killer," Jessie said.

"Or acquiring the fish in the first place," Harmony said. "Like those sharks of yours. Come to think of it, I was curious about that. Of all the species to collect, why an endangered species like oceanic whitetips?"

Judah didn't blink. "Precisely because they are endangered. If we master a means of synthetically and cheaply replicating the materials they're being hunted for—their cartilage, their fins—we can save them from extinction."

"But aren't they dangerous?"

Neptune seemed happy to be back in her wheelhouse. That, and she'd been drinking wine for the last couple of minutes like it was water in a desert oasis. The liquor colored her cheeks.

"Oh, not our babies," she said. "They're sweethearts. Trust me, I hand-feed them myself. Shark attacks are rare in the wild. For one thing, believe it or not, we're as scary to them as they are to us. For another, well, humans are a lousy meal. We're all stringy muscle and hard bones. Compare that to a nice yummy invertebrate or a fish they can gobble up in one bite, and there's no reason for a shark to try and eat us."

"But accidents do happen," Judah said, his eyes locked with Harmony's.

Jessie set her napkin down.

Harmony caught her body language. It was time to go. He'd shown his hand, they'd flashed theirs, each daring the other side to make the first move. Now they needed to fall back and give him room to make a mistake.

"Thank you for dinner," she said, easing her chair back. "And your time. Can I hope we'll be hearing from you?"

Now he was all warmth again, rising with them.

"I guarantee it. I'll be reaching out to you soon, to talk about details. With any fortune, this will blossom into a long and mutually prosperous relationship."

Harmony gave him one of her freshly printed business cards. Since Kevin couldn't slip her cover identity into Diehl Innovations' actual phone system, the number on the card was a decoy. It had a Los Angeles area code to match the company's office tower, but it would automatically bounce to a voicemail box with a prerecorded out-of-the-office message. Just like the rest of her thrown-together story, it was sturdy enough to stand up to a stiff wind, but it would buckle under a storm.

Neptune walked them out. She hovered close to Harmony, not too close, wobbling a little as she walked. Harmony wasn't sure if it was the wine or if she just didn't wear high heels very often. She wasn't sure about Neptune at all. She'd dropped Cooper's name, shared in her boss's blatant lie, but everything after that seemed to leave her confused. As off-balance in the conversation as she was in her shoes.

Harmony thought about what Jessie had said. Not about getting her laid, that was the last thing on her mind right now, but about stepping out of her comfort zone. Either Neptune was in on the plot to kill Cooper, or her boss was playing her for a pawn. If the latter, she probably knew more than she realized. And she wanted to talk. Harmony slowed down. Jessie picked up on her intentions; she lengthened her stride, making a gap between them as she headed for the car.

What do I say? Harmony thought. This was frustrating. Give her an interrogation room and a folder of evidence, and she could make any suspect crack. Move the scene to a warm Florida night, the breeze kissed by the faint flowery scent of Neptune's perfume, and everything went fuzzy around the edges. There wasn't any structure out here to keep Harmony safe. Interrogations had rules; seductions didn't.

"I'm...glad you were here tonight," she said. "It was nice to see you again."

Neptune's cheeks dimpled. "You too. So, are you headed back to LA?"

If she was in on the murder, she and Judah would probably take a shot at Harmony next. That was fine. The entire point of coming here was to provoke a response and force Cooper's killers to show their faces. If she was innocent, she was still useful. Either way, it was time to take more of a risk and roll the dice.

"We're in town for a couple of days," Harmony said. "We're staying at the Vinoy Renaissance Hotel."

The toe of Neptune's shoe dug a nervous divot in the driveway.

"So I could...find you there?" she asked.

"You could," Harmony replied. "If you look in room 215."

* * *

"You *dog*." Jessie's fist lightly punched Harmony's shoulder. Harmony glowered at her.

"Drive."

They pulled out, headlights sweeping across iron fences and the long, palm-tree-studded stretch of the boulevard. Harmony checked her phone. She had one message from April and one from the medical examiner's office.

"You heard the man," Harmony said. "Judah was all but bragging, trying to get a reaction out of us. The way I figure it, he doesn't know what to make of us; we could be Bobby's shooters, or we could be undercover cops. All he knows for sure is that we're not who we say we are, and he's smart enough to play it safe."

"So, Judah was his buddy with that mystery briefcase Bobby wants so badly. Bobby called his favor due, and Judah—or the guys who grabbed Cooper at the bar, working for him—took Cooper out instead of paying up."

"That's my theory," Harmony said.

"What about Neptune?"

"Gave her my room number. Either she'll show up to talk or show up with a gun."

"Which do you think?"

"I think something's wrong here," Harmony said. "She backed Judah up. We know for an absolute fact that they didn't meet Cooper last month, and she sure didn't approach them on behalf of Diehl Innovations. It's a straight-up lie, and not only did she back him up, she was the first person to say Cooper's name."

"But," Jessie said.

"But while her boss was delivering veiled threats and all but daring me to call him a liar, Neptune looked like she wasn't following a word of it." Harmony set her phone to speaker mode and tapped April's name on the speed-dial list. "She'll show up to talk, or she'll show up with a gun."

"You sound comfortable with that," Jessie said.

"I am. Odds are, now that we've all sniffed each other out, Judah's next move is to try and *take* us out. If an attack is coming, I want it on the battleground of my choice."

The phone purred. Harmony listened to it ring, waiting.

"Maybe we should get a jump on that," Jessie said, "circle back and put a few bullets in him."

"Can't. Not until we find out if that briefcase Bobby's

expecting really exists and what's inside it. I'm not leaving a possible weapon of mass destruction floating around out there, up for grabs."

April picked up the phone. "Harmony. Everything all right at dinner?"

"Besides, Agent Dominguez is still missing." She turned to the phone. "We have some leads. What did we miss?"

"Just an update from forensics. They've started cracking into Nadine's financials."

"Anything good?" Jessie asked.

"'Good' isn't the word I'd use," April said. "'Significant,' perhaps. When she arrived at that office party, Nadine mentioned she wanted to double-check an important transaction, correct?"

"Something like that," Jessie said.

"That morning, her accountant did authorize a sizable transfer of U.S. currency."

"How sizable and to who?" Harmony asked.

"Five million dollars," April replied. "It was sent to an escrow account at a bank in the Cayman Islands. No indication of what it was for, and we don't have more information than that—not yet, anyway. The Caymans are a British territory, also a lucrative tax haven for less scrupulous American investors."

Jessie whistled. "That...is money. Escrow account?"

"A third party," Harmony said. "Sometimes a safeguard for a sketchy deal. Say I offer to pay you to do something for me, but I'm not a hundred percent sure you'll get the job done, and you're not sure I'll pay up. So I put the money in an escrow account that neither of us controls. That's proof that the money's real. Once you show proof that you upheld your end of the bargain, the escrow holder sends you the cash."

"So nobody gets screwed."

"Exactly," Harmony said. "Nadine's not a bastion of trust, and anyone who deals with her knows she can't *be* trusted. Probably not the first time she's used a system like this."

"Five mil, though? She's a demon who can mess with people's minds. Also, she has her own cult of assassins. What does she need to spend that kind of money on?"

"As soon as we know, I'll pass the word along," April said.

Harmony thanked her and broke the connection. Her next call was to the medical examiner.

"It's Agent Black," she said. "I hope I'm not calling too late."

"Not at all, we tend to burn the midnight oil around here. I wanted to let you know that we started preliminary blood work on your shark-attack victim. Found something a little strange. I'm going to run more tests—"

"What did you find?"

"An enzyme called 5'-nucleotidase. Also, heightened levels of serotonin."

"Serotonin?" Jessie said. "Isn't that the happy chemical your brain makes? Like when you fall in love or look at cat pictures on the Internet?"

"Normally, yes. Serotonin in the brain creates positive neural feedback. But when it enters the bloodstream, the effects are quite different and…much less pleasant. A victim can lose control of their muscles, even go into violent seizures."

Harmony's lips tightened in a thin line. They knew Cooper had been tortured. They thought—hoped—that the brutal cuts marring every inch of her back had been the extent of it.

"Serotonin, in combination with that enzyme," the medical examiner said, "is only found in one source I'm aware of. Stingray venom."

"She was stung by a stingray?" Harmony said.

"That's why I'm rerunning the tests. Because looking at these results, factoring in the falloff over time...it looks to me like she was stung *repeatedly,* over a course of at least three hours. And stingrays only attack when they feel threatened. It doesn't make sense."

"Thank you," Harmony said, her voice flat. "Please call me as soon as you know more."

She ended the call. She looked over at Jessie.

"We know one spot with sharks *and* stingrays," Jessie said, "and Judah Cranston owns the place."

"We didn't see anything unusual the first time."

"Yeah, well, some places look a little different after dark. What do you say we break in and organize our own private tour?"

15.

They weren't the first to arrive.

The big wavy sheet-metal box looked like a melting ice cube in the Tampa dark. Above the barn doors, *Nautilus Conservation Research* was painted on a plank of weathered driftwood; with no lights in the parking lot, the faded script became untraceable glyphs, wet and foreign.

The door was open, just a crack.

Jessie killed the headlights. She pulled into the parking lot at the far edge, silenced the engine, and pointed.

"Either somebody forgot to lock up when they left, making this the luckiest and easiest break-in we've ever committed, or—"

Harmony unbuckled her seatbelt. "We're never that lucky and things are never that easy."

"Agreed."

Jessie reached up and tapped the dome light, making sure it wouldn't turn on when they opened the car doors. Light was the enemy now. She bent forward and carefully touched her eyes, taking out her amber contact lenses. Her true color, wolf-turquoise, gleamed like smoldering sapphires.

They moved in silence, gently opening the car doors, not shutting them all the way as they stepped out into the lot. Harmony took point, crouched low, skirting the long way around so that anyone inside the building wouldn't catch a glimpse of movement through the cracked barn door. At the corner of the wavy steel box, Harmony paused. She pointed two fingers in the other direction, toward the long and windowless side of the building. Jessie nodded.

They hadn't seen any other ways in or out on the tour, but that didn't mean they didn't exist. While Jessie held her post out front, watching the door, Harmony jogged a long circuit along the research lab's outer wall. Her shoes were light on loose dirt and gravel, rustling soft as the hot night winds.

No side doors. No back doors either. Nautilus was a killing box with a single point of entry. She didn't like that. They'd have to open the door wide enough to get through. That meant making noise and giving whoever was inside one, maybe two seconds of advance warning. She could empty her gun in two seconds. Any competent shooter could.

She circled around and met up with Jessie, flanking the barn door. Jessie crouched and leaned in, squinting; her eyes let her see in the dark as well as any natural-born predator. She waved the flat of her hand from side to side. No movement. Then again, with the bulky tanks taking up most of the research lab floor, someone could still be in there. Either they'd already left or they were lying low, lurking behind cover.

A flurry of hand signals laid out the order of battle. Harmony grabbed hold of the barn door with both hands, fingers curling around the warm metal, as Jessie's pistol slithered from its calfskin holster. Three. Two.

One. The door groaned on its unoiled track as Harmony hauled it backward. It shuddered to a stop and Jessie was already moving, charging inside and darting left, Harmony on her heels but hooking around to go right. The doorway was a perfect shooter's alley illuminated by moonlight, and their silhouettes were moving targets. First priority was getting clear and grabbing cover.

Harmony ran and slid, her shoes hissing on the water-spotted concrete as she dropped, landing on one knee with her head down behind the rounded brick of the stingray pool. She turned into a statue, gun braced in a two-hand grip, ears perked.

Water rippled, languid as the stingrays glided sleepily through their sandy pool. A generator thrummed softly in the dark.

She poked her head up, just a fraction of an inch.

Gentle beacons of light dotted the laboratory floor. Monitors on the sleek glass workstations, processing data from the tanks through the night, pumped out feedback in scrolling neon graphs. The tall glass tanks caught the light and tossed it between themselves and multiplied it, turning the chamber into an inky hall of mirrors. One of the sharks swam close to the glass, transformed by the darkness, a blurry and alien behemoth.

Harmony stepped out, slow and easy. Jessie was ten feet away, hunkered down behind a workstation, using an office chair for flimsy cover. She pointed upward. Harmony followed her line of sight to the security camera over the entrance. The camera dangled from its mounting, plastic box shattered and leaking its guts on a tattered wire. Crude, but effective. Higher up on the wall, over to the left, it looked like another camera had gotten the same treatment courtesy of a bullet.

Harmony moved in, circling the first tanks, trying to

stay clear of the monitor screens and keep her profile turned so anyone hiding would have less to shoot at. Jessie's waving hand snagged her attention. She'd spotted the intruder.

They weren't hiding at all. They were just distracted.

Up on the balcony at the back of the lab, where the server racks and biggest workstations were kept safely away from the water below, a figure stood hunched over one of the monitors. The intruder was dressed for a race, face hidden behind the opaque shroud of a motorcycle helmet, form sheathed in a full black leather bodysuit with armored joints and lime-green piping. The biker's gloved hands whispered out keyboard commands. Then they plucked a USB stick from the system's tower, making it vanish.

The twin open staircases to the top were bare metal. No chance of sneaking up on the intruder without being heard. Instead they fanned out, Harmony blocking the left staircase, Jessie taking the right. Then Jessie cleared her throat.

"No doubt about it," she said. "Something fishy is going on here."

"Show us your hands," Harmony called out. "Step back from the computer, and keep your hands raised and empty."

As the biker obeyed, leather gloves tentatively going up, Harmony shot Jessie a sidelong glance.

"'Something fishy'? Really?"

"Hey, I've been wanting to say that since we *got* here. You should be amazed I showed that much restraint."

The biker turned, standing on the balcony above. Harmony saw herself and Jessie reflected as featureless blobs in the helmet's visor.

"Now come downstairs." Harmony framed the biker in her sights. "Toward me."

The biker paused, helmet slightly tilted, as if making a decision.

Then the biker charged. Straight toward the balcony railing, flipping up and over and plummeting twelve feet down to the concrete floor. They hit the ground, tucked and rolled, then sprang to their feet. Harmony's finger brushed her trigger. No shot. The biker had landed squarely between her and Jessie, making sure neither would open fire.

Metal flashed between the biker's fingers. Not a gun. A brass disk, about the size of a soup-can lid. It trailed a hot-pink neon glow as it whipped downward in the figure's grip. The biker's other hand was bent back, baring a little skin between their glove and the wrist of their bodysuit. The edge of the disk ripped across the exposed flesh, slicing like a razor, spattering blood onto their boots.

The intruder threw the disk like a ninja star, straight down at the water-stained concrete.

Everything went white. Harmony felt herself falling back, landing hard as an explosion washed out the world with a *crump* of raw sound like a concert speaker blowing out. All she could hear after that was the ringing of an endless bell.

Her vision swam back, blurry, images overlapping and sliding in and out of focus. Jessie was pushing herself to her feet. She shouted something. Harmony shook her head, couldn't hear a word. She got up, stumbling, following in Jessie's wake.

The biker was on the run, charging out the barn door. Their twin was out in the parking lot: another rider in black leather, straddling a revved-up motorbike. The runner jumped into the saddle behind the pilot, slapped his shoulder, and the bike lurched into action. It shot across the parking lot like a bullet, bounced as it hit a rough patch of gravel and swung out into the street, rocketing out of sight behind a line of swaying palm trees.

Jessie leaned with one palm against the barn door, catching her breath. Harmony staggered up behind her. Jessie said something. She almost caught it, her hearing coming back to her in throbbing waves as the impact faded, but she couldn't make it out.

"What?" Harmony asked, louder than she meant to.

"I said I've got an ongoing list of people who need their asses kicked," Jessie snarled, turning, "and it just got longer. C'mon, let's check the balcony and see if we can figure out what kind of data they were after. Might tell us who they are."

* * *

"Shipping records," Kevin said, hunched over his terminal in the belly of the *Imperator*. The biker had left the balcony workstation unlocked when they were interrupted, and Jessie fired over a full rundown of every file accessed after the break-in.

Harmony's voice echoed over his headphones. "For the research lab?"

"Yeah, going back about a year. Everything that's been shipped to and from...wait a second."

"What is it?" Harmony asked.

He clicked his mouse, highlighting a few isolated lines in neon yellow.

"Not just the lab. A few of these shipments—a couple of new centrifuges, a Unisys mainframe—were directed to Judah Cranston's *house*. Also, I don't know if this is weird, but they make a lot of purchases from chemical companies—"

"It's a research facility."

"Yeah, but..." Kevin frowned at the screen. He started copying and pasting, rearranging the data into a new picture. "A *lot* of companies. Small orders with a lot of overlap, placed on different days, and these aren't super-specialized firms; just one company could probably provide ninety percent of whatever they need."

No response. A pensive silence filled his headset.

"Boss?"

"They're spreading the purchases out," Harmony said. "Makes it harder to build a paper trail. We've seen that before. Do we know what they ordered? Specific chemicals and quantities?"

"Not from this. But the records do tell us exactly who they do business with. Tomorrow morning I can make some calls, do a little social engineering. Are you looking for anything in particular?"

"Find out what they bought from different suppliers, and how those chemicals potentially interact," Harmony said. "Like I said, we've seen that kind of purchasing pattern before, mostly from people trying to stay under ATF's radar. Terrorist cells."

"You think Judah's building a bomb?" Kevin asked.

"I think we need to find out for certain. You've done all you can for tonight. Tell everybody to pack it in, go to the hotel, and get a good night's sleep. Tomorrow's going to be a busy day."

"What about you and Jessie?"

"We've got a little more work to do," she said.

16.

Harmony had recovered the brass disk from the scene of the crime. It nestled in a plastic baggie, one razored edge still flecked with the biker's blood. Both sides were carefully engraved with a jagged seven-pointed star, its angles uneven and twisted glyphs etched between each of its points. Before the magical weapon went off, it had gleamed in the dark. Now the metal was tarnished, sooty like a burned-out light bulb.

"We've seen this before, too," she said to Jessie.

They'd taken the mystery back to the hotel. The pink Mediterranean tower of the Vinoy Renaissance loomed over the oceanside, where sleeping yachts and ivory sailboats bobbed in the resort's private marina. They ended up at a cozy side table in Marchand's Bar and Grill. The hotel's rococo flair and quiet elegance spread from the central bar, crimson upholstery under dangling glass-dome chandeliers, to the tall, thin windows framed in geometric leading.

Harmony carefully slipped the wrapped-up disk into her breast pocket as a waiter in a trim vest swung by. Jessie glanced up from her menu.

"I'll have...ooh. A Black Manhattan."

"We're still working," Harmony said.

"Two Black Manhattans."

"Seriously," Harmony said as the waiter swooped away.

"There's a chance Neptune might show up looking for me tonight. I need a clear head."

"You need to relax. Especially if your new girlfriend shows up. One drink."

"We've seen this disk before," Harmony said, steering the subject into a more comfortable lane.

"The Bogeyman case," Jessie said. "When we faced off with the Gresham brothers, they dropped one of those on us."

"One of the many, *many* occult relics that wandered away from our evidence vaults twenty minutes after we turned it in."

"You think it's the same disk?"

Harmony shook her head. "No. You saw the before-and-after. It burned itself out after it went off; this is a one-shot deal. They might have been crafted by the same magician, though. The Gresham brothers were working for Fontaine."

"Our favorite demonic bounty hunter."

"He supplied them their gear. Now he gets *his* gear from all over the place—"

"But we saw that biker take a twelve-foot fall like it was nothing," Jessie said. "No pure-blooded human can pull that off."

"And they were armed with demon tech. Somebody from the courts of hell is nosing around Judah Cranston's business."

"Not sure who that complicates things for: us or him. Might be able to use that, if we can figure out what their angle is. Tell you one thing I know for certain."

The waiter returned. He set down a pair of Old Fashioned glasses, filled with an inky black cocktail. Harmony reluctantly sniffed hers, then took a sip. The barrel-aged whiskey had a robust, rough, burnt-wood flavor as it seared down her throat, tinged with sweet caramel from a splash of Averna liqueur.

"Oh, that's good," she had to admit. "And what do you know?"

"That it's great to have an artifact vault that isn't being robbed blind on a daily basis by our former bosses. I want to get that disk back to HQ and have the weirdos in Occult-Tactical take a crack at reverse-engineering it. I wouldn't mind having a magical flashbang in our arsenal."

Harmony took another sip. She contemplated her drink, rolling the glass in her fingers.

"When I think about how much we lost over the years," she said. "All the field data they deliberately erased, the captured relics that went right back into demonic hands. We were treading water, never making an inch of progress—"

"Hey," Jessie said. "It's a whole new ball game. So what's your plan for when Neptune shows up?"

Harmony thought about that. She spoke her answer to her glass.

"Watch her hands, expect an ambush, and shoot first."

Jessie slumped back in her chair, staring at her.

"Goddamn," she said. "You're *hoping* she's coming to try and kill you."

"I wouldn't say hoping."

"No. You are. You'd rather stare down a gun than a bouquet of roses."

"I doubt she's bringing roses," Harmony said.

"Metaphor. I use metaphors sometimes. And you know exactly what I mean."

"FBI training doesn't incorporate seduction as an authorized field technique," Harmony said.

Jessie rolled her eyes. "You know, all you have to do is flip her to our side; you don't have to seal the deal if you don't want to. But assuming she's Judah's pawn and not his partner, she might be the best source of inside intel we've got."

"I know."

"And if you do want to seal the deal—I'm not saying you do or you should, I'm saying if, then I'm the last person on God's green earth who's going to pass any judgment. You haven't dated anybody since Cody."

"The last time I saw Cody," Harmony said, "we were pointing guns at each other. Which nicely sums up my aptitude for romance."

"As long as you keep telling yourself that."

"It's easy for you," Harmony said. She shrugged, shifting in her seat. "You're...you're hot, and you're funny, and you're not...awkward around people."

Jessie laughed. "And I drink too much and drive too fast, and I have a penchant for incredibly sketchy hookups, where I indulge in weird and extremely rough sex. I am nobody's role model."

"I'm just saying, you're the kind of person that people want to be with."

"Yeah, well...I'm not necessarily looking for somebody like me."

"How do you mean?" Harmony asked.

Jessie stretched, languid, rolling her shoulders.

"I mean," she said, "as much as I love living *la vida loca,* if I was looking for something serious—something that lasts, something real—I'd want somebody...stable. A woman with a good head on her shoulders and her feet on the ground."

"Somebody boring," Harmony said.

Jessie stared at her, silent for a moment, contemplative.

"Nah," she said. "Not boring."

The waiter came by. He set a fresh glass in front of Jessie, the new cocktail a deep, rich shade of chocolate brown.

"What's this?" Jessie asked.

"The 'Espresso Yourself,'" the waiter said. "Espresso, vanilla vodka, and Kahlua."

"Okay," Jessie said. "*Why* is this?"

"Compliments of the lady at the bar."

The lady at the bar sat alone, wrapped in a short purple dress that belonged on a Fashion Week runway. Or she did, at least. She had high cheekbones, deep olive skin, and big bright eyes, eyes that only got brighter as she raised her own identical cocktail in a salute and flashed a sly smile.

"This is exactly what I'm talking about," Harmony said.

Jessie mirrored the woman's smile, but it faltered on her lips as she looked back at Harmony.

"I'll send it back."

"Go," Harmony said. "Seriously. It's late, Neptune's probably not coming, and I'd have to handle it on my own even if she did. Absolutely no reason one of us shouldn't have some fun tonight."

"You sure?"

"Positive. Go. Get weird. Name the baby after me."

Jessie started to rise, then paused.

"Harmony, you…do know how babies are made, right? Do we need to talk about the birds and the bees?"

Harmony shooed her with her hands and blurted out a laugh. "*Go* already. For crying out loud."

* * *

Jessie carried her drink toward the bar, prowling, a

panther on the hunt. A challenge gleamed in the stranger's eyes.

"An espresso cocktail?" Jessie asked. "Trying to keep me up all night?"

"Sleep is for the weak and the dead." Gold hoops dangled from her slender wrist as she held out her hand. "Coraline."

"Jessie."

Jessie gave her hand a gentle squeeze and slid onto the stool beside her. The plush crimson upholstery rustled.

"You know," Jessie said. "Kudos. It's rare that somebody makes a play so ballsy that it even impresses me."

"What? The drink? I clocked you the second you walked in. Might as well have a rainbow following you around."

"Not that." Jessie nodded back over her shoulder. "You're not concerned you might have just tried to cut in on my girlfriend?"

Coraline had a giddy, crystalline chuckle. "She's not your girlfriend."

"And you know because?"

"Well, you came over to sit down, not throw that drink in my face. There's a clue. But I already knew. Lips lie, body language doesn't. So what brings you to this muggy little paradise?"

"Insurance company convention," Jessie said.

"There is no way you sell insurance for a living." Coraline inclined her head toward Harmony, who was finishing her drink alone. "Her, I can see it."

"I'm in marketing."

"Me too! Cosmetics. In town to ink a contract, sort of thing I thought computers made obsolete. I landed at five this morning, the signing took twenty minutes, and my flight out isn't until ten a.m. tomorrow. Total waste of time."

Jessie sipped her espresso. Strands of vanilla vodka feathered the warm coffee.

"Might not be a total waste. We'll have to see, won't we?"

"That we shall," Coraline replied.

"Nice choice of cocktails, by the way. This is tasty."

Coraline clinked her glass against Jessie's.

"Maybe I do want to keep you up all night," she said.

"Maybe I'll let you," Jessie replied.

* * *

"Lost your wingman, huh?"

Harmony glanced up from her phone. She'd been finishing her drink one careful sip at a time, checking her email, occasionally glancing over at the bar to keep an eye on Jessie. She hadn't noticed the new arrival. He hovered a few feet away, carefully outside of her personal space.

He was in his thirties, slender and trim, wearing a houndstooth vest over his beige dress shirt. He fiddled with his glasses as she turned to face him.

"Sorry. My friend keeps telling me I should actually try to talk to people, and I said I'm great at talking to people, just...saying all the dumbest things." He glanced back over his shoulder. "And...he's gone."

"I've been there," Harmony said.

"We're in town for an insurance company convention. Which, now that I think about it, is probably the saddest way I could introduce myself. That's maybe one step above 'Hi, I do card tricks.'"

"You might be surprised. I know a guy who does some pretty impressive card tricks. And if you're talking about the American Associated Insurance Vendors' convention, I'm here for the same reason."

"We lucked out, huh?" He gave the lounge a wave, taking it in. "A lot nicer than the Holiday Inn."

He took a half step toward the table then paused, catching himself.

"Do you mind if I, uh, sit down? I mean, if you're busy, I'll go away, it's no big deal."

Harmony glanced to her dwindling drink, to the darkened window. Her instinct was to make an excuse and retreat, fading back to the privacy and security of her hotel room. Back to her comfort zone.

Jessie's words came back to her. *A comfort zone is nothing but a cage with nice furniture.*

"Sure," she said.

"I'm Ethan," he said, smiling anxiously as he slid into Jessie's empty chair.

"So are you in sales or…?"

"Accounting. I'm not sure if that makes me more or less interesting than being an insurance salesman. I figure it's about even."

She slid one of her business cards—the originals, with her Delaware Mutual identity emblazoned in black on cream—across the table. He scooped it up and his smile grew.

"Helena West, Manager of Accounting," he read aloud. He met her gaze and flipped the card around. "It's a pleasure to meet you, Ms. West, and I'll be hanging onto this. Just be warned: if I call you on Monday, it's probably because I'm looking for a new job."

"Oh? Why?"

"Well, I've been butting heads with the VP of Finance over quarterly projections. He's…nuts. His projection completely ignores our tax liability, he forgot to include distributions to the partners, it's a mess. So I sent the CFO two versions, his and mine, so he could compare and decide which was more accurate."

"Sounds fair," Harmony said.

"Well, the CFO called me this morning from the home office, demanding to know why our numbers are so different. I told him first and foremost, the VP doesn't know his butt from a hole in the ground, and the entire Finance department can't figure out why he hasn't been fired yet."

Ethan leaned back in his chair. His gaze drifted to the ceiling as his fingers tugged at his starched collar.

"I didn't realize it was a teleconference. And he was patched into the call."

Harmony cringed. "Oh God."

"Yup. We have a Meeting, with a capital M, first thing when I get back. So I'm determined to enjoy myself tonight, before I face the firing squad."

The waiter came by. He asked if they needed anything. Harmony glanced to her empty glass. This was her chance to ask for the check, pay her tab, and retreat into solitude. She looked at Ethan.

"You know what?" she said. "I think we both deserve another drink."

17.

"She's a squeaker," Coraline muttered into her glass. The bartender had just come over to bring another round of drinks. They'd switched to sangria. Coraline's gaze lingered on the bartender's back until she stepped out of earshot.

"A what now?" Jessie said.

"Oh, I play this little game sometimes. I look at somebody, I listen to her voice, the way she talks…and I try to guess what she sounds like when she comes." Coraline nodded at the bartender. "Her? She lets out high-pitched squeaking noises. I guarantee it."

Jessie furrowed her brow. She thought about it as she lifted her glass.

"I can hear it."

"Right? You always know a squeaker when you see one."

"Fun game," Jessie said. "What about me?"

Coraline studied her, fingers to her chin, eyes narrowed, appraising Jessie like a work of art.

"I'm hearing…breathiness. Almost like you're hyperventilating. Muscles taut, struggling to keep control. You won't cry out, no matter how good it feels. That's too much like surrender. See, you don't want to *have* sex, you want to *win* at sex."

"I might have a tiny competitive streak," Jessie said. "Can I play this game?"

"Please. Do me."

"You're expressive." Jessie sipped her sangria. "Performatively expressive. You want to make absolutely sure your lovers know what you like, what feels good, so they keep doing it. You want to be pampered in bed. Adored. Worshiped."

"Oh, you make it sound one-sided," Coraline said, serving up a playful pout. "I give as good as I get."

"So you say, but I don't have any proof."

"Well," Coraline said, "I do have an idea."

She leaned in. Her breath was a warm puff of air against Jessie's earlobe.

"How about we go up to my room, and I make you come so hard that you spontaneously scream out my name?"

* * *

"So she insisted, absolutely insisted," Ethan was saying, "on trying to deduct her hairdresser, the gowns she wears on stage—"

"What, on her Schedule A?" Harmony said. "That deduction specifically applies to mandatory work uniforms."

"Exactly. But wait for it. She got breast implants. Told me she wanted to deduct the operation under cost of goods."

Harmony blinked at him. "That...makes no sense."

"That's what I said, albeit in a more diplomatic fashion. She stood up, just like this"—Ethan straightened his back, lifted his chin, and swept his hand across his chest—"and said, 'Honey, *these* are the goods.'"

Harmony nearly dropped her glass. Her laughter fed his, and his energy brushed warm against hers, a moment shared, winding between them like an invisible thread.

This was all right. She still felt awkward, certain every other word out of her mouth was wrong, feeling her attempts at humor fall like a brick to the floor at her feet. He was awkward too, though, in all the same ways, and he still laughed at her jokes and it didn't seem like he was pretending.

This was all right.

Jessie had left twenty minutes ago, around the last time she and Ethan ordered another round of drinks. Hand in hand with Coraline, shooting a sly glance in Harmony's direction and giving her an approving thumbs-up behind Ethan's back.

Eventually they hit a lull in the conversation. The room was emptying out, the hour late. Ethan contemplated his empty glass.

"I was going to say…God, this could be creepy. I don't want to be creepy—"

"Say it," Harmony told him.

He took a deep breath, steeling himself like he was about to ask a cheerleader to the prom.

"Met one of my clients at the convention, and he gave me a bottle of wine, 2014 Silver Oak Cabernet Sauvignon. I mean, this is an eighty-dollar bottle of wine."

"Nice."

"Yeah, well, I only brought a carry-on bag. I can't check it, and I can't take it with me on the plane, so either I drink it tonight or I leave it for housekeeping. And you know, the housekeepers here are good, but not eighty-dollar-wine good."

He eyed her, bashful.

"Are you asking me up to your room?" Harmony said.

"I am." He held up his open hands. "I mean, just conversation and wine, that's all. No strings attached.

And if you're not comfortable with that, you know, that's totally understandable and cool—"

"Yes," Harmony said, the word racing to her lips. Her anxiety chased it, a looming threat in the distance, but her desire was too fast for rational thought.

"Yes?" he said, like he wasn't sure he'd heard her right.

"Yes."

* * *

His room was on the third floor, a twin to hers. Queen bed draped in ivory, pushed against a lime-green accent wall, marble-topped end tables and oval lamps that bore an odd resemblance to Life Savers candies. A low, round table tucked against the sheer drapes with a pair of low-backed chairs, and a long credenza with a mirror and a wide-screen TV. All the comforts of life on the road. Through the window Harmony could see the sleepy waters of the marina. Sailboat masts, their canvas furled, rocked listlessly from side to side.

She stood by the window, gazing out to the bay, while Ethan wrestled with a folding corkscrew. He'd failed at wrangling wineglasses, so they were using the tumblers that flanked the room's ice bucket.

"This is…not optimal glassware," he said, "and some connoisseur somewhere is going to be very mad at us."

"We won't tell," Harmony replied.

He was so nervous it almost put her at ease.

"Is it too cold in here? I can adjust the thermostat. Or you can, I mean, it's right there on the wall—"

Harmony smiled. "It's fine. Honest."

He had his back to her, finally getting the cork free with a hollow *pop*, pouring the wine. Something about the movement of his hands caught her eye. He'd been almost comical with the corkscrew, nearly falling over as he wrestled with it. Now his voice was still jittery, but his hands moved like a trained bartender, like this was something he'd practiced in the mirror a hundred times to get it right.

She knew because she'd practiced it a hundred times too, getting ready for her last mission.

That was how she knew to watch the reflection of the room in the mirror, where she could see the tumblers. That was how she knew to watch for the drop. For the thumb of his left hand, clenched against his palm, to subtly relax and let a tiny tablet fall into one of the glasses. It fizzed and dissolved in seconds.

He'd roofied her drink.

Her smile died on her lips. In a breath she rode out a flurry of emotions. Shock. Sadness. Then a cold anger that spread out from her heart, turning her veins to ice. She was an idiot. She'd believed his nice-guy routine, taken a chance, stepped out of her comfort zone, and this was what she got for it.

He turned, beaming, holding up the two glasses with the tainted one slightly forward. Magician's choice, pushing her to take the poisoned wine.

"Shall we?" he asked.

"One thing you should know," she told him.

He must have caught something in her tone. He tilted his head, uncertain.

"What's that?"

"I lied. My name isn't Helena West. My name is Special Agent Black, FBI. And you're under arrest."

He set one of the tumblers down. His entire demeanor changed. His awkward smile sagged, his shoulders slumped. Something behind his eyes shifted as he abandoned his mask.

“Well, damn,” he said.

“Put the other glass down, turn around, and place your hands behind your back.”

“Actually, there’s something you should know too,” he said.

“Oh?”

“I know exactly who you are, Harmony.”

His eyes rolled in their sockets. Their color ran from white to bloodshot to pus-yellow, like two rancid eggs burbling in a dirty skillet.

“And now I have to do this the hard way.”

He flung the glass in her face, tainted wine splashing her eyes. Then he came at her.

* * *

The second the elevator doors closed, Coraline attacked. Not like Ethan. She came at Jessie with her hands and her mouth, throwing her against the back of the mirrored cage, kissing her like she’d been poisoned and the antidote was on Jessie’s lips. Jessie’s shoulders thumped against the glass and she responded with a feral hiss and a smile.

“Let’s get something straight,” Coraline whispered in her ear, punctuating it with a flick of her tongue. “You’re a one-night stand. I’m going to fucking destroy you tonight, and I’m not even going to give you my phone number in the morning. You’re going to spend the rest of your life pining for me.”

Jessie laughed. “Oh, is *that* how you want it?”

She swung Coraline around, slammed her against the mirror, and pinned her there, their tongues twining until the elevator rumbled to a stop. She broke away and grabbed her hand, almost yanking her off her feet.

“Your room,” Jessie said.

She was just down the hall. Coraline didn't turn the lights on. She strode into the shadowy room, shoved Jessie toward the bed, and turned to the credenza.

"I'm losing my buzz. One second. Got a bottle of wine at the contract signing."

"We could have stayed down in the bar if we wanted to drink."

Coraline popped the cork on the wine. The bright silver label gleamed in the dark, and blood-red cabernet splashed into a pair of glasses.

"Not with our clothes off," Coraline said. She glanced over her shoulder. "Like I said, losing my buzz, and I'm not fucking you sober. Strip."

"I'm a present," Jessie said. "You have to unwrap me."

Coraline turned and thrust a glass at her. "Planning on it."

They clinked glasses. They drank, deep, pounding down the bittersweet wine.

"Delish," Coraline said.

Jessie started to respond, then paused. Blinking, squinting, uncertain, like her thoughts had suddenly slowed to a molasses drip. Coraline plucked the empty glass from her hand and set it on the credenza.

"Aw," she said, "what's wrong?"

"Feel…dizzy." Jessie's voice slurred.

"You should lie down."

Coraline gently guided her backward, Jessie unsteady on her feet, and pushed her onto the mattress. Jessie's eyes rolled back and her lashes fluttered as her lids fell shut. Coraline stood there a moment, studying her, watching the slow rise and fall of her chest.

"Damn shame," she murmured. "Missed opportunity. Would have been fun. Another life, another time, you and me would have gotten on like a house on fire. But duty calls…"

She turned back to the credenza. Her phone glowed in her hands, a slender rectangle of light. She tapped out a text message.

Temple is neutralized, she wrote. *Confirm when you have—*

Coraline looked to the mirror and froze.

Jessie was standing right behind her. She'd slipped her amber contacts out. Her eyes glowed ice-blue in the shadows.

"That dosage would have worked fine on somebody with human blood," Jessie told her. "By the way, I can see in the dark. Saw you drop the tablet in. Whoever briefed you about me did a lousy job."

Coraline set her phone down.

"Well," she said. "Damn."

"Yeah."

Jessie cracked her knuckles.

"I hope you weren't lying when you said you like it rough," Jessie told her. "Because we are *absolutely* about to get rough."

18.

The world was a blur, Harmony's eyes washed in red wine, as Ethan lunged at her. She sidestepped his punch, trained reflexes kicking in. Her hand latched on to his wrist. She twisted it, her other hand grabbing his shoulder, forcing him into an arm bar and turning his momentum into a weapon. He kept going, propelled past her, and crashed into the table.

She wiped at her eyes as he grabbed the empty tumbler. He swung it against the credenza. It shattered, half the glass turning to jagged shark-tooth shards, a makeshift weapon in his fist. Harmony jumped back as he thrust it at her chest, then again. Her leg hit the edge of the bed and she fell onto the mattress. She rolled as he dived at her, falling off the edge and tumbling onto the floor. The broken glass ripped a furrow in the mattress and sent puffs of white cotton dancing in the air.

She rose in a crouch and drew her gun. Ethan shot out a whistling kick. His polished shoe slammed against her hand hard enough to send a lance of pain jolting up her arm. Her fingers went slack. The gun fell, clattering to the carpet, spinning out of reach.

He threw the glass aside. Then he threw himself, landing on her, cracking the back of her head against the carpet as he straddled her arms and wrapped his hands around her throat. His thumbs dug in, cutting off her air supply, starving her. Ethan leaned close, his sweaty face twisted in a grimace.

"Could have been *so* easy, but no, you had to make me work for it."

Spots bloomed in Harmony's vision. She couldn't breathe, couldn't exhale, worthless air trapped in her swollen chest and scorching like lit gasoline. She twisted her wrists, struggling to get a hand free. She wrenched her right loose and tactics riffled through her mind like playing cards. She could go for his eyes, his nose, his neck—she calculated angles and distance, hunting for the option that would inflict maximum damage with a single strike.

Her body decided for her. In the space between seconds, as time slowed to a crawl and her vision burned away like a movie reel on fire, the world devoured by celluloid cigarette wounds, an alien hunger surged inside her.

For a moment, she was back in that seedy hotel room in Jersey City, talking to Romeo.

"And you're...changing. At first I got tired after we got together. Last time, I was sick for two days."

Her open palm clamped against Ethan's chest, right over his heart.

"Like you're pulling something out of me," Romeo had told her. *"Siphoning it out."*

Harmony *pulled*.

Ethan's hands froze around her throat. His jaw dropped. His muscles went rigid, his entire body trembling. Harmony latched on to something inside him and yanked it like she was fishing, the catch of the day fighting on the end of her hook. Her addiction, the core of aching hunger Nadine had forced inside her, unfurled Venus flytrap petals.

She drank him in. His psychic energy, the demonic taint in his blood, his power. She drank it down and devoured him from the inside. Her hunger became ravenous, out of control, and she knew she wouldn't stop until he was dead. She couldn't stop.

She didn't want to stop.

He yanked his hands away and shoved himself backward, off her and onto the hotel carpet. He scrambled back on his hands to get away from her. His eyes were human again, wide with terror.

"The fuck did you *do* to me?" he gasped, panting. He forced himself up, getting to his feet and running, stumbling, for the door.

Harmony rose. The stolen power surged inside her, a wildfire in her veins. She held out one cupped hand. His power was hers, a rush of raw magic converted in the reactor of her heart. A sphere of blue-hot flame erupted in the palm of her hand. Effortless.

Ethan ripped the door open. As he looked back at her over his shoulder, she saw that a streak of his hair had turned skunk-tail white.

The door swung shut. Harmony curled her hand into a fist and snuffed out the flame. She wasn't letting him get away. She took one step and nearly fell, knee buckling. Her spirit was burning but her flesh was weak, exhausted from the fight. She grabbed her fallen gun off the floor. Then she forced herself to move. Across the room, out the door, just in time to see Ethan lunging into the elevator cage and hammering the buttons. The door glided shut between them and the lit numbers above slowly counted down.

She hit the stairwell, clinging to the bare metal railing as she staggered down concrete steps lined with yellow paint. Curling around and around again, down to the bottom, holstering her weapon before pushing out into the lobby.

The elevator rattled open. Empty. Ethan had gotten off on the second floor, looking for another way out. She was about to turn and fight her way back up the stairs when a voice turned her around.

"Helena?"

It was Neptune, still wearing her ribbed aquamarine dress from dinner, a slender silver purse cradled in the nook of her curled arm. She stood in the heart of the empty lobby.

"Are you...okay?" Neptune said. She took a tentative step closer. "You don't look okay."

Harmony caught a glimpse of herself in a mirrored strip along the wall. Her hair was a mess, her tie dangling at a crooked angle, her face ruddy and glistening with sweat. Red smears marred the skin of her neck, the imprints of Ethan's murderous thumbs.

Jessie, she thought.

* * *

Jessie flew backward and the hotel-room mirror fractured against her shoulders, filling the shadowy suite with the shrill crackle of broken glass. Coraline threw a punch. Jessie dodged left and Coraline's knuckles slammed into the mirror, raining razor-edged shards and spatters of blood. Neither of them was pretending to be human anymore. Coraline's demon blood came out to play, her eyes egg-yolk yellow and her face a twisted road map of veins that glowed like ultraviolet paint under a black light.

Jessie snapped out her foot and kicked Coraline in the hip. The assassin fell back, stumbling. She grabbed one of the chairs and swept it up, thrusting it at Jessie like a lion tamer. Jessie grabbed onto the chair legs and charged, shoving it forward, using it to slam Coraline up against the wall. Coraline went low, sweeping out one leg and knocking Jessie off her feet.

The chair came down and shattered against Jessie's back. She slumped, pushing herself on one arm, dazed but still moving.

"Why don't you just stay down," Coraline hissed. She held on to the broken chair leg, brandishing it like a club.

"I was about to *go* down, until you tried to poison me." Jessie grabbed Coraline's ankle and yanked hard. "Your loss, bitch."

Coraline's ankle turned. She fell, thumping to the carpet. The chair leg whistled through the air. Jessie caught it and they wrestled for the club, kicking at each other as their bodies twisted.

"You wouldn't be able to handle me in the sack," Coraline said through gritted teeth. "You know what this is for me? Foreplay."

She had both hands on the chair leg. She wrenched it away just as Jessie's fist plowed into her gut, knocking the wind out of her.

"More like a perfect Friday night," Jessie said.

She grunted as Coraline swung the leg, cracking it against her shoulder. She grabbed Coraline's wrist and jerked it down, pinning her arm behind her back.

They froze for a second, down on the hotel-room carpet, eye to eye in the dark.

Then their lips met. Coraline's fingers went slack. She

dropped the chair leg. Her free arm curled around Jessie's waist, tight, as Jessie's knee slid between her thighs.

* * *

Down in the lobby, Harmony shoved herself away from the wall and staggered toward the elevator. Her mind was a tempest and she couldn't hold on to a single thought; they fluttered around her like butterflies. She had to get upstairs, had to find Jessie. Hopefully, she'd taken the woman from the bar back to her room. Otherwise she had no idea where to start looking—

"Helena?" Neptune said. Still standing there, ten feet away, anxious.

"Sorry," Harmony said. "Need to find my partner."

"Partner?" She blinked. Her head turned and dipped, just a bit. "Oh. I…I didn't know you had someone."

"No, not that kind of—" Harmony sighed. "I mean my coworker. I mean, we're so close, I think of her as my partner, but we don't have that kind of—I mean, I'm single."

A little spark came back to Neptune's eyes.

"Oh." She paused. "*Oh*. Your nose is bleeding."

Harmony felt a warm trickle on her upper lip. She put her hand to it, her fingers coming away sticky and red. Neptune opened her silver purse, rummaging fast.

"I've got some tissues—"

The elevator chimed. Harmony waved a shaky hand at the door as it opened.

"Neptune, I…it's not you, okay? I'm glad you came, but I'm not doing too good right now—"

"Let me help. Please?"

She came close, wadded-up tissue in her hand, and gently pressed it to Harmony's nose.

"Tilt your head back. Look, I didn't…I didn't come here

expecting anything. Okay? I just wanted to talk. Still want to."

She looked Harmony in the eye.

"I lied to you tonight. And I feel bad about it. Something is very wrong here, and I want to make it right. Will you let me?"

She needed to find Jessie, to make sure her partner, her *friend,* was all right. But Neptune had information. Information that might stop something terrible from happening. *Stash her in my room,* she thought, *make her safe, then go hunt for Jessie. Neptune will keep.*

"Let's go upstairs," she said.

Neptune eased her onto the elevator. The tissue was almost soaked through, ivory turned to cherry red. She dug out another one and tilted Harmony's head farther back.

"Do you get nosebleeds a lot?" she asked.

No. Then again, she didn't siphon the magic from an unwilling demon-blooded assassin a lot either. She still wasn't sure how she'd done it. It had come naturally to her, as easy as riding a bike. Ethan's stolen power ran riot in her veins, throbbing, aching for an outlet.

"I think it's the climate," Harmony said. "The heat, the humidity. Florida is kind of a lot."

Neptune giggled. "I think 'Florida is kind of a lot' should be our new tourism slogan."

As they got off the elevator, Harmony's phone began to buzz. She lowered her head just enough to check the screen.

"Gotta take this." She carefully put it to her ear, keeping the screen away from the bloody tissue.

"Hey," Jessie said before she could get a word out,

sounding breathless. "Are you alone? Are you somewhere you can talk freely?"

"I'm with Neptune," she said. "Ethan turned out to be a real jerk, by the way."

She hoped Jessie could read between the lines. As always, her partner didn't let her down.

"Yeah, my date turned out a little different than expected."

"Are you okay?" Harmony asked.

"Oh, I'm good," Jessie said. "I've got company for the night."

In the background, a furious voice shouted, "*Untie* me, you fucking *bitch*!"

At her side, Neptune's eyebrows lifted. She'd heard that.

"What room are you in?" Harmony asked. "I'll be right there—"

"Nooo," Jessie said. "No, I need to conduct a very vigorous interrogation here. My methods will be deeply unorthodox. Unorthodox, inventive, and invasive. I wouldn't want to scar your delicate psyche by allowing you to witness them."

"If you're sure," Harmony said.

"Give me…four or five hours? Actually, you know what? Just wait until I call you back."

Jessie hung up.

"Your friend is…" Neptune's voice trailed off when she couldn't settle on a word.

"Adventurous," Harmony replied.

19.

Harmony sat in the chair by the window, head back, filling the trash basket at her feet with a growing collection of bloody tissues. The stream had faded to a tiny trickle. She felt shaky, drained, her skin flushed with heat even as the room's air-conditioning pumped out a steady gust of cold air against her pale cheeks.

"I'm gross," she said. "I'm sorry I'm gross."

Neptune perched on the edge of the bed, watching her, wringing her hands.

"You're not gross," she said. "I work with marine life all day. Believe me, I know gross when I see it. I'm lucky if I can get through the day without being covered in slime. That and uninjured."

"Uninjured?"

"I work with *special* marine life. I've nearly been impaled by a stingray. I've been stung by jellyfish more times than I can count—"

"But you hand-feed the sharks," Harmony said.

"Oh, they're sweeties." Neptune studied her. "That's not the first time you've asked me about the sharks."

Harmony blotted her face with a clean tissue. No more blood, only the rusty smear on her hands and her upper lip. She tossed the tissue into the wastebasket, got up, and ambled into the bathroom. Neptune hovered in the doorway while she washed up.

"You had something to tell me," Harmony said.

She soaked a hand towel in warm water and reached for the soap. She let Neptune take her time. The woman was either afraid, ashamed, or just wanting to get the words right before she spoke them. From the look on her face, eyes down and cheeks tight, it was some combination of all three.

"Before you arrived, Dr. Cranston took me aside. He said that at some point during dinner he was going to pretend he'd forgotten a name. And I was supposed to say 'Natalie Cooper.' He made me repeat it, like, five times, just to make absolutely certain I remembered."

The smear on Harmony's lip vanished under the towel. The wet white cotton turned the shade of cherry blossoms. She glanced at Neptune.

"You have no idea who that is, do you?"

Neptune shook her head. "No. And the thing about being contacted by someone from Diehl Innovations before you? That's a lie. I've reviewed our financials with Dr. Cranston, so I know that's a lie."

Harmony ran her hands under the tap, massaging the bloodstains away. So Neptune was a pawn after all, roped in as part of Cranston's scheme to rattle her and Jessie.

Or she was his partner, and she'd come here tonight with a sob story to worm her way into Harmony's good graces.

She wanted to trust Neptune. She was aching to trust somebody tonight. But after Ethan, she couldn't let herself lower those iron walls again so soon.

"Did he tell you why?"

"I asked," Neptune said. "After you left. He said it was just business. He said I didn't need to worry about it. He said you were being...dealt with."

"Dealt with," Harmony echoed.

Her head bobbed. "Those exact words. I asked what he meant. He changed the subject, said I was doing a great job on our new research projects and that he was putting a bonus in my next paycheck."

Dealt with, Harmony thought. Like sending a couple of demon-blooded killers to their hotel? One flaw in that theory. They'd faced another pair of supernatural operatives tonight, the bikers who broke into Nautilus Research. And they clearly weren't on Cranston's side.

Either there were *two* demonic couples out there—the data thieves and Cranston's shooters—or Cranston hadn't made his move yet.

She reached for a dry towel. Neptune reached for something else to say. Harmony could hear it in her pensive silence. She gave her room to let it out.

"Something is wrong," Neptune said. "Something has *been* wrong, for a while now, and I've been keeping my head in the sand and ignoring it."

"With Nautilus Research?"

"With Dr. Cranston," she said. "He's working on something, a side project all his own, and he froze me and the rest of the staff out. He's got us making deliveries to his house, he's brought on extra staff who report directly to him—"

"Extra staff," Harmony said. "Two men? In their twenties, one a Latino, the other a white guy with a lot of tattoos?"

"That's them. I don't know who they are, they just pick up orders that get shipped to the research lab to take back to him. They give me the creeps. They're not scientists, I know that much. They come off like...well, thugs. One time I heard them joking about how the research center reminded them of the fish sticks at Hillsborough."

"Hillsborough?"

"County jail," Neptune said. "I don't know why a man like Dr. Cranston would hire people like that."

Harmony dried her hands. No more blood, not the kind anyone could see.

"Helena? Could I ask you something?" Neptune said.

"Of course."

"In the hall, when you had your head back and you answered your phone, I…I saw your jacket fall open." Neptune eyed her, uneasy. "Why do you have a gun?"

"A lot of people carry weapons when they travel."

"And when I saw you in the lobby," Neptune said, "why did you look like you'd just been in a fight? Your throat—"

She gestured. Harmony glanced in the bathroom mirror. *Bruising. Damn.*

Neptune was afraid. That, or a hell of an actress. Harmony had to decide which. Keep her walls up or open a tiny gap, just big enough to set Neptune's fears at ease. She had the look of a woman who was done letting things slide. Good chance, if she froze her out, Neptune would go poking around on her own. If she did that, odds were she'd learn more about her boss than she ever wanted to.

Neptune stared into Harmony's eyes, searching for something.

"He's dangerous, isn't he?"

"Yes," Harmony said. "He is."

"Who is Natalie Cooper?"

Harmony weighed her answers. She settled on the truth.

"A friend of mine."

"And…she's dead, isn't she?"

"Yes," Harmony said. "She is."

Neptune took a halting step backward. Through the

shock, clarity. She wasn't stupid. Harmony knew she wasn't telling her anything she didn't already know.

"I need you to do something for me," Harmony said, "and it's very important."

"Name it," Neptune whispered.

"Nothing. Nothing out of the ordinary. You go to work, you do your job, you don't even hint that you're aware of *any* of this. Keep your head down and let us handle it."

"But I can be helpful—"

Harmony stepped close to her, intimate, holding Neptune's gaze.

"He's dangerous. I can keep you safe. I am *going* to keep you safe; that's my job. But if you draw his attention, I can't protect you. Understand?"

Her head bobbed once.

"Let us handle this. It'll all be over soon."

"How will I know when it's over?" Neptune asked.

"I'll tell you myself. And I won't be able to tell you everything, but I'll answer whatever questions I can. That's a promise. Okay?"

Her hands rested soft on Neptune's shoulders. Neptune let her turn her around, ease her toward the hotel-room door. She hovered on the threshold, though. She wanted something. Harmony understood. Neptune wanted the same thing she did tonight: some firm ground under her feet and someone she could trust.

"Harmony," she told her. "My real name is Harmony."

Neptune gave her a faint smile and stepped into the hall. Now she had something she could take home with her.

Harmony locked the door, flipped the bolt, and hooked a finger around the knot of her tie. She undressed on her way to the bed, snuffing out the lights. She was asleep thirty seconds after her head hit the pillow.

* * *

The trill of her phone pulled Harmony from the depths of sleep. It felt like she'd only been gone for seconds, but the first rays of sunlight filtered into her room through the gossamer curtains.

"Hey," Jessie said, "can you swing on by? I need you to guard the prisoner while I take a shower."

The prisoner in question was tied to the bedposts with sheets twisted into ropes. Jessie had tossed a shower towel over her naked body. She glared, sullen, as Harmony walked into the room.

"Harmony, Coraline. Coraline, Harmony. Careful, there's some broken glass by…what's left of the credenza."

"She's tied to the bed," Harmony said.

"Yeah, well, sometimes I like to be tied up, sometimes I do the tying up." Jessie shrugged. "It's called being a switch. Deal with it."

Jessie picked her way across the wreckage, dressed in a hotel bathrobe and flip-flops. She yanked the curtains open and let sunlight stream into the room. Coraline winced at the light.

"*Damn* it. Warn me before you do that." She turned her head away from the window and locked eyes with Harmony. "Did you kill him?"

"Who? Ethan? No. He ran away."

"Ugh. Typical. Also, note that he did *not* come to rescue me. Also typical."

"Friend of yours?" Harmony asked.

"My kid brother. Did you beat his ass?"

"Pretty much."

"Good," Coraline said. "He's had it coming for a while, so don't feel bad."

"I don't."

"We actually met our new friend earlier last night," Jessie said. "She was the one who hit us with the magic flash-bang. Ethan was driving the motorbike."

"So you don't work for Cranston," Harmony said.

Coraline pursed her lips in sullen silence.

Jessie strolled from the window. She leaned in, putting her hands on the edge of the mattress.

"Our new friend here—"

"We are *not* friends," Coraline said.

"Works for the Court of Windswept Razors."

New York. The Razors were one of the smallest courts of hell, with less territory than the rest, but they were also one of the wealthiest. Ruling Manhattan meant ruling Wall Street; some of the biggest movers and shakers in the city had signed their employment contracts in blood.

"New management's taking over," Coraline said. "The old hound is out—'out' as in shredded and splattered all over his office—and Ariel is in."

Harmony rolled her eyes. "Of course she calls herself Ariel."

Jessie shook her head, not following. Harmony looked across the bed at her.

"Really?" Harmony said. "Ariel. Because the last Razors boss called himself Prospero."

"You lost me," Jessie said.

"Shakespeare. *The Tempest.* Jessie, do you read *any* of the stuff I suggest?"

"Hey, Jess," Coraline stage-whispered. "Your partner is a nerd."

Harmony gestured to the woman on the mattress. "And she's here why?"

"Because I'm amazing in bed," Jessie said.

"Barely adequate," Coraline shot back.

"You weren't saying that an hour ago—"

Harmony crossed her arms. "*Not* what I meant."

"We're here for the same reason you are," Coraline said. "Bobby Diehl. We've been hunting down Network operatives in New York, a task made considerably easier by their high command all vanishing on the same night. The ones we've captured and interrogated have no damn idea what's going on; all their comms are dead, and nobody's handing down marching orders. Diehl's a loose end, and Ariel wants him snipped."

"He lives in Los Angeles," Harmony said. "Why is that your problem?"

"Because his *money* lives in New York. Some of it, anyway. The streams we've been able to trace. He's got a private account that's been making regular payouts to Nautilus Research for a couple of years now. He's basically keeping them in business as a shadow investor."

"So you figured Cranston could tell you where Bobby is hiding, same as us."

"Tell her the rest," Jessie said.

Coraline rolled her head back on the pillow and stared at the ceiling.

"Prometheus Chemical," she said. "New Jersey company, does specialty manufacturing jobs. We have an inside line there, and that's all I'm going to say about that. Judah Cranston contacted them through a back channel asking about a special purchase order. And they shipped him what he wanted before we could put a quash on it."

Harmony's thoughts went to the shipping records. The

diversified purchases, spread out to keep them under the federal radar.

"What did he buy? Chemicals?"

"Machine parts," Coraline said. "A specialized delivery mechanism, custom-made to his specifications. Nice and compact, about the size of a briefcase."

"Delivery," Harmony echoed.

"For a compressed aerosol spray. Just set a timer and walk away. When it goes off, everyone and everything within a hundred yards gets a lungful of the payload."

Judah wasn't building a bomb for Bobby Diehl. He was building a chemical weapon.

"He had some bullshit about how it was for dispensing antibiotics for endangered marine life," Coraline said. "Even produced a patent for it, to back his story up. But you take all those puzzle pieces and click 'em together..."

Jessie ticked them off on her fingers. "The spread-out chemical purchases, the equipment being shipped to his house, the thugs on his private payroll, not to mention Bobby Diehl being his shadow partner—"

"Exactly. Whatever Dr. Frankenstein is cooking up, we want it stopped, same as you."

Harmony squinted at her. "Still not seeing your angle here."

"Hello? New York City is already the prime target for every pissed-off militant with a grudge. Bobby Diehl is a stone-cold lunatic, he's cornered, and his time's running out. If he's preparing his big middle finger to the world, aiming to rack up an epic body count before he goes to hell, we figure there's only two places he'd pick."

"Los Angeles or New York," Harmony said.

"Ariel wants this shit dealt with before he plays mad bomber on our doorstep. You two were a bonus grab.

Once we told Ariel a couple of Vigilant's head honchos were on site, she told us to drop everything and snatch you both. Snatch you, not hurt you, so she could have a chat under 'controlled conditions.' She was very specific about that. Didn't work out according to plan."

"At least you tried," Jessie said.

A phone lay abandoned in the wreckage of the room, over in the far corner. Its screen lit up, a call incoming with a FaceTime request, and a melodic chime filled the room. The caller ID simply read "*Her*."

"Oh shit," Coraline sighed. "Speaking of the boss."

20.

The melodic chime demanded attention.

"What happens if you don't answer?" Harmony asked. Jessie scooped up the phone.

"Depends on whether my reject of a brother reported in yet, and what kind of excuse he made up. The East Coast courts are all allied, so if she wanted to fly a tactical team down here and get all shooty, she can arrange that."

Jessie and Harmony shared a glance.

"She already knows we're here," Harmony said.

Jessie answered the phone.

She moved over to Harmony's side, turning the screen so they could both see the woman on the other end. She was pale, prim, her lips frosted pink. Her black sun hat and cat-eyed glasses reminded Harmony of Audrey Hepburn in *Breakfast at Tiffany's*.

"We're sorry," Jessie said, "Coraline can't come to the phone right now."

Ariel spoke fast, breezy as her stride, walking down a city sidewalk as she held her phone in front of her. Her other hand gripped a grande Starbucks coffee in a cardboard sheath.

"This is not how I wanted our introduction to go. Lemons, lemonade, moving on. Is Coraline dead?"

"She's fine," Jessie said. "We've got her wrapped up for safekeeping."

"Proof of life, please."

Jessie tilted the screen toward the woman on the mattress.

"Hey, boss," Coraline said. She waggled one of her bound hands in a half-hearted wave.

"This," Ariel replied, "is going to come up at your next performance review."

Jessie turned the phone around.

"Ms. Black, Ms. Temple. I just left my seven o'clock and I'm on my way to my seven fifteen, so we have a very small window to articulate our actionables. First off, congratulations on assuming control of Vigilant Lock. From one upward mover to another, kudos."

"Doesn't seem like a thing you'd be happy about," Harmony said, "considering the East Coast courts—including yours—created the scam behind Vigilant in the first place."

"My *predecessor* worked on that." Ariel's sunglasses rose as her nose wrinkled. "I considered it a gross waste of resources and an unacceptable level of risk. But he's dead now and I have the corner office, metaphorically speaking. Nothing says 'I was right' like standing on the corpse of my former manager. I'd like to convene at some point to discuss a formal nonaggression treaty."

"Nonaggression?" Jessie asked. "You know what our job is, right?"

"As I understand it, your self-directed mission is to protect humanity from assault by supernatural elements."

"Like demons," Harmony said.

"My prince has charged me with seeing to the security of his territory. To keep the status quo, and most importantly, to keep the money flowing. We're a very small court, and we live or die based on the integrity of the markets. The rogue monsters you hunt—Bobby

Diehl, case in point—are a threat to that integrity. So long as you don't come after me or my people, ultimately your organization is good for my bottom line."

Harmony held her silence, but she knew Ariel had a point. They'd already forged an uneasy alliance with her counterpart on the West Coast. With stakes this high, and the reborn Vigilant struggling to find its footing in a world teeming with occult threats, they had to pick their battles.

"I would like you to consider releasing my employee," Ariel said, "as a gesture of future goodwill."

"And what do we get out of that?" Jessie said.

Ariel sipped her coffee.

"Field support and no interference. Let's face it, this is a 'too many cooks' situation. I'll pull Coraline and Ethan out and let you handle the on-the-ground investigation. Meanwhile, I will retask my operatives with running background on Judah Cranston and forward all pertinents to you."

Jessie and Harmony shared a sidelong glance. Harmony knew what her partner was thinking. "Let you handle" was a nice way of saying "let you take all the risks." Once they cut Coraline loose, there was no telling if Ariel would even hold up her end of the deal. For that matter, there was no guarantee Coraline and Ethan wouldn't turn right around and take another shot at them.

There had to be a way to get more out of this bargain and put Ariel's overtures of peace to the test. Harmony shuffled the pieces in her mind's eye, stringing people and places together like programming code—a stream of luminous blue if-then-else statements running combinations and probabilities.

Then she saw it.

"What's your opinion on Nadine?" Harmony asked.

Ariel's eyebrows lifted. "*Najidanere?* She's unprofessional, erratic, untrustworthy—on a level above and beyond most of my kind, and that's saying something. Her greatest ambition is to become the queen of flyover country, which is just...kind of sad. Also, relations between our court and the Midwest have never been rosy; with the revelation that we'd been using Vigilant Lock to jab at them as a deniable proxy, well. You can imagine."

"Just because Vigilant is under new management," Harmony said, laying her gambit, "that sort of thing doesn't necessarily have to end."

Ariel paused in mid-sip. She lowered her coffee.

"You have my attention."

"We flipped Nadine's accountant. Dima Chakroun is working for us now. She notified us that Nadine authorized a five-million-dollar payment into an escrow account."

"Five million?" Ariel said. "I didn't know she had that kind of liquid capital. For what?"

"That's what we'd like to know. You have reach with the banks that we don't. If you happened to find out and slipped us the intel under the table so we could act on it...well, we can keep a secret if you can."

"This account. It's in New York?"

"The Caymans," Harmony said, "but it was routed through a Manhattan bank."

Ariel pursed her frosted lips.

"It's a big ask. Not impossible, but it's a big ask."

"So is letting your agent go," Harmony pointed out.

"She tries to kidnap us, and we let her go without so much as a spanking—"

"Oh, she got a spanking," Jessie said.

"Bitch," Coraline hissed. Ariel rolled her eyes.

"What I *mean* is," Harmony said, shooting Jessie a look, "I don't think it's out of line to ask for a little sweetener on this deal. One that could help you as much as it helps us."

"I like the way you think, Ms. Black. 'Mutually' and 'beneficial' are two of my favorite words. All right, no promises on results, but send me the details and I'll make it a line item on my day planner. We can circle around after this Tampa situation is resolved and schedule a meeting vis-à-vis discussing our long-term operative paradigms. We'll do lunch. Ciao."

The screen went dead.

"Is she always like that?" Jessie asked.

"Oh, you think she was kidding about the performance review?" Coraline said. "We have to fill out a self-assessment questionnaire and everything. Still, better than the old boss. I'll take anal over crazy any day of the week."

Jessie untied the knotted bedsheets. Coraline sprang up, tossed the towel aside, and brushed past her, snatching her phone out of Harmony's hand. She grabbed her dress off the floor and shimmied into it, scanning the wrecked furniture.

"Where the hell is my thong? No, you know what? You can keep it. Souvenir of the best night of your life, and the best you'll ever have."

"Until next time," Jessie said.

"There is no next time. Zip me up."

Jessie zipped up the back of her dress. They murmured

back and forth, rapid-fire whispers, as she guided Coraline to the door.

She saw her out, closed the door, turned, and looked at Harmony.

"What?"

"Nothing," Harmony said.

"No, that's a 'something.' You're giving me a 'something' look."

"I'm still not used to this."

"If you're not used to me getting freaky by now—"

"Not that." Harmony sat down on the corner of the mattress. Frowning, trying to work it through in her head. "Compromise."

Jessie stood close to her. Close, but giving her room, giving her time to sort her thoughts.

"When I started out," Harmony said, "I thought it was simple. Good guys, bad guys. No shades of gray. No wiggle room."

"Life's a little more complicated than that," Jessie said.

"I didn't *want* it to be more complicated than that. Conveniently overlooking the fact that life doesn't care what I want. When I started out, the idea that someday I'd be making alliances with monsters to catch *worse* monsters...I wouldn't have even been able to parse that. Then-me would have called now-me some kind of traitor."

"Way I see it," Jessie said, "what matters at the end of the day is results. We're saving lives. Doing our job. And if it takes shaking hands with someone like Caitlin or Ariel to stop somebody like Bobby Diehl, I'd say that's a fair trade."

"It's just weird. Weirder, after everything that's happened over the last year. If someone told me that one day I would give Daniel Faust my phone number—willingly—I'd say they were crazy."

"Is he still doing that...thing?"

Harmony took her phone out, scrolled through her text messages, and showed Jessie the screen.

"*Still want my car back,*" read one.

She scrolled down. "*We made a great team. Know what would make us a greater team? My car.*"

She scrolled down again. "*Lost: my car. If found, please return it.*"

"We are *not* a team," Jessie said.

"That's what I told him."

"So, I'm curious. That bit back on the call, about Nadine?"

"Sorry about that," Harmony said. "I would have run it by you first, but under the circumstances—"

"Hey, you had to make a play. I trust you, you know that. It just felt like you were fishing for more than free intel. Why'd you tell her we flipped Nadine's accountant?"

"So we can get a little hard proof of Ariel's intentions," Harmony said. "If she follows through, now that we've set her operative free and we've got nothing to hold over her, it shows she's serious about playing nice. Doesn't mean we can trust her, but it means she wasn't just blowing hot air to get Coraline out of custody."

"With you so far."

"On the other hand, there's a chance Ariel wants to kiss and make up with the other courts. Handing us to Nadine on a plate would be a great start."

"The thought did occur to me," Jessie said.

"If Ariel was lying, then most likely, right this minute, she's on the phone with Nadine."

A grin blossomed on Jessie's face. "Passing on a warning along with the bogus source. And we'll know, because if she does that, well...Nadine's gonna Nadine, and *her* next move will be tearing her accountant's guts out. The second Dima Chakroun turns up dead, we'll know Ariel snitched. Nice one, partner."

"Thanks. So, uh—" Harmony nodded to the door. "You and Coraline?"

"I don't know if she's girlfriend material, but next time we're in New York I'm going to need a night off. Maybe two. How'd things go with Neptune?"

"She's clean," Harmony said. "She had no idea who Cooper was; Cranston told her to drop the name on cue, so he could see our reaction. He's definitely trying to figure out if Bobby sent us. She also confirmed the two men who grabbed Cooper at the bar are working for Cranston. Still no word on—"

Her phone buzzed in her hand. Tampa PD.

"Special Agent Black speaking."

"Agent, it's Lieutenant Briggs. We met at the medical examiner's office."

"Of course," Harmony said. "How can I help?"

"Got something for you to take a look at. We rounded up some boats and trawled the waters off the beach where the first victim washed up."

"You found something?"

"Another body," he said. "What's left of him, anyway."

21.

The medical examiner's details were sparse: male, mid-twenties, his remains bound to a cinder block to keep him weighted down. Unlike Cooper's rope, his didn't come loose.

He also didn't have a face.

His naked, broken skull stared up at the hard morgue lights, scalp clinging on by thin strips of sinew. His bottom jaw was fractured, teeth reduced to chips and jagged shards of porcelain. The sharks had also taken one of his arms, along with his left leg up to the kneecap. The dead man's skin was mottled and slug-white, his remains laid out on a stainless-steel slab.

"It's not Agent Dominguez," Jessie said.

Harmony stood at her side, gazing down at the ravaged corpse.

"How can you tell?"

Jessie pointed to his surviving arm. "Dominguez had a memorial tattoo, from his days in the Rangers. Names of the buddies he lost. This guy doesn't."

His ink was on his collarbone. Solid black, the Roman numerals XIV with a pair of crossed swords behind it. Jessie's pointed finger glided down along the slab. Toward the bloodless wound in the dead man's abdomen.

"What does that look like? A .22?"

This had to be the thug Cooper shot outside the bar

when she wrestled for his gun. It looked like he'd taken it in the gut. Not a fast way to die.

"So you know who he isn't," Briggs said. "Any idea who he is?"

They knew he was on Judah Cranston's payroll, but they weren't going to share that with the police. Harmony weighed how much she could afford to give him. Too much and Briggs might poke his nose into their investigation. Too little and they'd look like they were holding back, which might mean *he* held back next time he found a lead.

"We think there was an altercation when the first victim was abducted," she said. "One of the kidnappers was shot with his own weapon."

Briggs nodded at the gunshot wound.

"So he dies from the bullet, they toss his body to the sharks to make it harder to identify, and weigh 'em down side by side. Makes sense."

"Except for one problem," the medical examiner said. "Submersion in water is a highly effective counter-forensic measure. Given enough time, water damage to a corpse can conceal any multitude of sins. That said, the body was found quickly enough that I can still issue some preliminary observations based on tissue composition, the quantity of water in the lungs, internal gases—"

Briggs hooked his thumbs in his belt loops. "Cut to the chase, doc."

"The bullet wound wasn't fatal. If he'd been taken to a hospital or attended to by a private physician with the right equipment, he almost certainly would have survived."

The medical examiner gestured to the corpse.

"He either died from drowning or severe trauma from

the shark attack. He was *alive* when he went into the water."

* * *

Harmony was thinking about a case. Not one of hers. She'd learned about it at Quantico, a side mention in a seminar about the psychology of criminal gangs. A drug mule, who had been loyal and reliable up to that point, claimed he had to dump over five thousand dollars' worth of cocaine to escape a police search. His superiors had a suspicion that he'd sold it himself and kept the money.

"What'd they do?" Kevin asked, sitting at his console in the belly of the *Imperator*. "Kill him?"

She paced behind him, chin cupped in her hand as she worked at the problem.

"No," she murmured. "They told him not to do it again."

"Organized crime is a trust game," Jessie said. "You bring somebody into an illegal conspiracy, you're handing them the chance to burn you, so you only bring in people you think you can rely on. More importantly, you treat 'em right. 'You failed your mission, so prepare to die' is comic-book stuff. Not that it doesn't happen, but it's a bad idea. Start offing your employees, you send a message to the rest."

April turned the wheels of her chair, swiveling around to face them.

"And not," she said, "the message one desires to deliver. It's not 'obey or die' so much as 'find a good lawyer and turn state's evidence before your neck is next on the chopping block.'"

"This guy didn't even fail," Kevin said. He rattled a few keys and brought the morgue photos up on the video wall. Five screens showed the dead man from every angle.

"Timeline," Harmony said. "This man and his partner

pick up Agent Cooper at the bar. They coerce her into going out the back door. She goes for the weapon, shoots him, his partner incapacitates her. Cooper is tortured, presumably interrogated about Bobby Diehl's intentions and whereabouts, and fed to the sharks. He's fed to them alongside her, both bodies are submerged, but Cooper's comes untethered and washes up on shore."

Jessie walked past her in the other direction. "Where the hell is Agent Dominguez? He hasn't reported in, and his body wasn't out there."

"Cranston keeping him prisoner?" Kevin asked.

"Best explanation," Jessie said, "but why?"

Harmony pointed to the screens.

"I keep going back to this. He had a survivable wound. Cranston had him murdered instead of saving him."

"Survivable in a hospital," April pointed out, "and hospitals report gunshot wounds. If Cranston doesn't know any underground doctors and taking him to the hospital was the only alternative, killing him might have seemed safer than risking police attention."

"Right." Harmony's fingertip bobbed at the screens. "And how do you think his partner feels about that?"

"Seems they were tight," Jessie said. "Neptune told us they always ran in a pair. Sounded like they did time together."

"You know what I'm thinking," Harmony said.

"You're thinking," Jessie said, "that right about now he's scared and angry, and wondering how much longer it'll be before Cranston uses him as shark bait."

"We can flip him. But first we need to find him. Best way to do that is by identifying the victim."

There were plenty of ways to identify a murder victim. Sometimes it was as simple as matching up the body with a missing-persons report. Eventually the Tampa police would learn the name of the man on the slab. "Eventually" wasn't good enough.

"Can't run a facial recognition scan without a face," Kevin said. "Fingerprints?"

"Water damaged," Harmony said. "Water is a nightmare for forensics. Soft tissue is the first to go."

"DNA?"

"Takes too long." Jessie stood at Harmony's side. Her eyes glinted as she stared up at the screens. "Got to be something here we can use."

Harmony saw it. She pointed to the third screen, a photograph capturing the victim's shattered jaw, his bite-ravaged and waterlogged chest. They'd taken it to study the bullet wound, but something more important jumped out at her. The black ink tattoo on his collarbone, a Roman-numeral XIV adorned with crossed swords.

"That ink looks...standardized, like a logo, military maybe. Kevin, run it through the Bureau's tattoo recognition database, see if we get a hit."'

He fired up Photoshop on his monitor. He cropped the photo, adjusting focus and contrast, singling out the tattoo and sharpening the image.

"Kind of a long shot, boss."

"Right now," she said, "I'll take what I can get."

The database went to work, numbers piling upon numbers as the system hunted for a match. The XIV held steady on the left side of Kevin's screen, a fixed image, while the right side flickered like a storm of flash cards.

April held up a finger. "Payroll records. They work for Nautilus Research; Cranston would have to report their wages for tax purposes."

"According to Neptune, they're not officially

employees," Harmony said. "I suspect they're getting paid under the table."

"Professional thuggery is a cash business," Jessie added.

"And we're certain we can take Neptune at her word?" April asked.

She said "we," but her focus was all on Harmony. Harmony was sure, then she wasn't. She thought about that until she landed on firm ground again.

"She's scared," Harmony said. "I didn't tell her anything she didn't already know, deep down inside. She knew something was wrong with her boss, and she doesn't want to get caught up in it."

"Little late for that," Jessie said.

"We'll keep her safe."

Kevin pointed to the screen. The dead man's tattoo had found a twin.

"Got a hit."

Harmony leaned over his shoulder. "Military?"

"Prison. XIV with a couple of swords means you're repping Familia 14. It's a prison gang"—he scrolled through a database, highlighting chunks of text with a click—"offshoot of a California gang called Nuestra Familia. A former Nuestra member got out of lockup, flew coast to coast to get a new shot at a life of crime, failed hard, landed in the Cross City Correctional Institution, and started up his own version of the franchise."

"How widespread is it?" Harmony asked.

"Not. Far as I can tell, it only exists at Cross City Correctional."

"Which is where?"

"Dixie County, about two and a half hours north of Tampa." He looked over his shoulder. "It also has over a thousand prisoners at any given time, and we have no idea when this guy was inside, so please tell me you're not going to ask me to start searching through mug shots."

"No," Harmony said. "The only identifying mark we have is that tattoo, and he got it in prison; he wouldn't have had it when he was booked."

"So, dead end?"

Harmony was thinking about Neptune. Going back over their conversation, hunting for anything she could use. Neptune's words drifted back to her. *One time I heard them joking about how the research center reminded them of the fish sticks at Hillsborough.*

"Dig back...let's say ten years. Cross-index prisoners who have been incarcerated at Cross City Correctional and at the Hillsborough County jail."

She stood perfectly still while he worked, frozen with her eyes on the morgue photographs.

"More than I expected. Sixty-seven."

Harmony nodded. "Now for those sixty-seven, toss out anyone who doesn't currently have a registered address within twenty miles of Tampa. Check probation records; parolees have to disclose where they're staying."

"They don't have to tell the truth," Jessie pointed out.

"No, but they've got to live reasonably close to whatever address they give, at least if they want to make their regular check-ins with their probation officer."

"Down to twelve," Kevin said.

"Bring 'em up on the screens."

One by one, mug shots blossomed over the dead man's body. Five of them were black; Kevin ruled those out right away. What remained on the video wall were seven scowling convicts and a faceless corpse.

"Guy on the upper left is way too big," Jessie said. "He's

pushing three hundred pounds, easy, and that mug shot is from two months ago. This other one's out, too. Beyond being tacky as hell, the tattoo on his forehead disqualifies him."

Kevin furrowed his brow. "How? Our body doesn't have a face."

"Double thunderbolts," Jessie said. "You can join the Familia 14 or you can join the Aryan Brotherhood, but not both. That'd be confusing for everybody involved."

One mug shot caught Harmony's eye. Olive skin, dark hair, glowering at the camera. He was wearing a shabby polo shirt, neckline just low enough to flash a hint of black ink. No telling if it was the same tattoo, but he definitely had some work done.

"This one," she said. "Pull up his rap sheet."

"Oscar Espina," Kevin said. "Spent four years in Cross City for sexual assault. Other than that, he looks like a Tampa native, given how many times he's been in and out of Hillsborough. Mostly petty stuff: burglaries, trying to move stolen goods, a couple of assaults that look like bar fights. He's kept his nose clean for the last eight months, or at least he hasn't gotten caught again."

"Parole?" Harmony asked.

"For another four months. Says he hasn't missed a single check-in." Kevin glanced to the screen. "Well. I mean, if this is the guy, he's about to. His registered address was a men's shelter in Beymont; now he's at a transient motel."

"Looking for employment is a requirement of probation," Harmony said. "What's he claiming?"

"TampaFast Courier Services. Says he's a driver."

Before Harmony could say another word, April swiveled back to her keyboard.

"Already on it," she said. "Let's see what the IRS has to say about Mr. Espina's employer."

22.

The IRS had a lot to say about TampaFast Courier Services. No one was the slightest bit surprised to see Judah Cranston's name as the registrant, or his home address listed as the principal place of business.

"It's a real company on paper, registered as a DBA," April said. "Albeit a nearly dormant one, and it has no actual presence beyond that. No website, no clients, no evidence that they do anything at all. There's nothing suspicious about that from an outsider's perspective; thousands of new startups pop up and fail every single year. Some people register sole proprietorships for businesses they *might* run and never get around to doing anything beyond the initial paperwork. In all the venues where the government pays attention—annual filings, for instance—Cranston is meticulous."

Spreadsheets and notarized applications replaced the mug shots up on the video wall. Harmony studied them, eyes narrow, following the money trail.

"DBA means the company is entangled with Cranston's personal finances," Harmony murmured. "No separation from a tax standpoint, and he's keeping TampaFast afloat with the money he makes from Nautilus Research. How about W-2 forms? Who's on the company payroll?"

Two names: Oscar Espina and Randy Hern. Both were on file as professional couriers, each pulling down fifty thousand dollars a year.

"Not bad, for a courier service that doesn't make deliveries," Jessie said. "Fifty K, though? That's not living extra large, but it's not transient motel money either. Why was Espina living in a shithole like that?"

"Drugs?" Kevin guessed.

He was already on the move, anticipating Harmony's next request. Two minutes later he had Randy Hern's rap sheet and latest mug shot up on the main screen.

"And here's Oscar's fish-stick eating buddy," Kevin said. "They did time together last year, a three-month stretch at Hillsborough. Looks like Oscar got hired first, then Randy joined the crew a couple of weeks later."

The curly-haired ginger leering at the camera had freckles and a bad sunburn. He wore a muscle shirt cut to show off his full tattoo sleeves, an ocean of cheap prison ink that looked like a bored teenager had spent a year doodling on his arms.

"A Latino and a white guy with full sleeves," Jessie said. "Perfect match for the bartender's description."

Harmony stared at the mug shot, burning his face into her memory.

"Give us an address."

* * *

Randy Hern's address on record was a trailer park, not far from the Tampa fairgrounds. Palmetto bugs, fat roaches the size of Harmony's thumb, skittered lazily through the weeds in a "recreation area" one step removed from a vacant lot. Most of the trailers looked like they hadn't moved since the mid-seventies and had come out in a losing fight with a storm or two along the way.

Randy's screened windows were open. Harmony stood on her tiptoes, taking a look. There wasn't much to see inside but scattered clothes, an overflowing ashtray, and a portable TV. She caught the faint odor of cheap cannabis. It didn't look like anyone was here, but Jessie knocked anyway. They waited, listening to the hot wind rustle through the palm trees.

"Let ourselves in?" Jessie asked.

"Doubt we'll find a signed confession in there. We need to talk to Randy two-on-one. Don't want to spook him; let's find a spot to watch and wait, and we'll corner him when he comes home."

They were turning away when one of his neighbors, a plump woman in a Tweety Bird T-shirt and sweatpants, looked up from the plastic-box garden she was watering.

"You lookin' for Randy?" she called over.

"Yes, ma'am," Harmony said.

"What is it, 'round noon? Most days about this time, if he's not smoking up in there, he's grabbing lunch over at Babes. But you didn't hear that from me."

* * *

"Oh," Harmony said, staring up at the dirty marquee at the edge of the near-empty parking lot. A woman's silhouette, with a bust size not found in nature, reclined atop the name of the club.

Jessie turned to look at her. "What kind of place did you think it was?"

"I wasn't sure. I thought she meant 'Babe's' with an apostrophe *s*, as in 'a place that belongs to a person named Babe.' But instead it's Babes in the plural. Multiple babes."

Jessie unbuckled her seatbelt.

"Your mind," she said, "both awes and frightens me."

Harmony wondered what kind of person went to a strip club for lunch. She got her answer on the other side of a windowless door and a black curtain. A few locals had shown up for the $5.99 steak and fries special, sawing at gristle-and-shoe-leather fillets while a DJ spoke in a bored monotone.

"Wasn't that great? Yay. And now, put those hands together for Tanqueray. Foxy, foxy, Tanqueray."

A Rihanna song thumped on the speakers while a woman in a schoolgirl outfit wandered out on stage, took hold of the pole, and strolled in a languid, aimless circle. An old man looked up from his plastic plate and held out a dollar bill like it was an obligation.

"This job takes us to the classiest places," Jessie said.

They spotted Randy by his mop of ginger hair. He sat at a small round table near the back of the club, more focused on his food than the show. He didn't look up until Harmony's and Jessie's shadows fell over his plate.

"Not looking for a lap dance," he said.

Harmony showed him her badge. His eyes flicked in dangerous directions. First to her, then to the knife in his hand, then to the door of the club.

"That idea you're having," Jessie said, "is a bad one."

He set the knife down.

"I didn't do nothin'," he mumbled with his mouth full.

"Careful," Jessie said, "my partner's a grammarian."

He swallowed his steak. "Don't know what that is."

"Do you know what kidnapping is? How about conspiracy to commit murder?" Harmony asked.

"It's not fish sticks at Hillsborough," Jessie said. "More like you go to Coleman for twenty to life. The food's even worse there. If you're a bad boy, they serve you Nutraloaf. You ever eat the loaf, Randy?"

He squirmed in his seat like he'd been pinned with a needle.

"The good news is," Harmony said, "there might be a

way out. One that doesn't end up with you dead like your buddy Oscar."

Randy's dull eyes stopped roaming the club. He squinted at her.

"What are you talking about? Oscar's not dead."

Harmony thought this situation looked wrong from the start. "Honor among thieves" was usually nothing but an opportunistic lie, but Randy and Oscar had done time together, worked together—finding Randy enjoying his lunch without a care in the world seemed out of character for a man whose partner had just been fed to the sharks.

He wasn't putting up a front. He had no idea. Harmony and Jessie shared a glance and a wordless understanding.

"Let's save some time," Jessie said. "I'm going to tell you what we already know. Judah Cranston, your boss, told you and Oscar to go to the Rusty Nail and abduct a woman named Natalie Cooper. Cooper was expecting a handoff. You probably told her the briefcase wasn't with you, that you had to drive her to where you'd stashed it."

"But out back," Harmony added, "she smelled a rat. She shot Oscar."

"Yeah, but—" Randy froze. Two little blurted words, a confession he couldn't take back.

Jessie leaned in, looming over his table.

"'Yeah, but' it was a piddly little .22. A gutshot. But hospitals report gunshot wounds. So, once you were done with Cooper, you threw your buddy Oscar to the sharks right alongside her."

Harmony saw where she was headed. They'd caught Randy off-balance and they needed to keep him there, holding his feet to the fire. He hadn't been the one who murdered Oscar, but the more trouble they could pile on his shoulders, the more desperate he'd be to make a deal.

"Your own jail buddy," Harmony said, feigning disgust. "And you killed him, to keep him from snitching on you."

"*No*. That didn't—" He pressed his palms to the table. "You got it all wrong. That's not what went down. Oscar isn't dead. Yeah, the bitch shot him with his own piece. But like you said, it wasn't a big deal. Hell, I got him bandaged up. He was barely even bleeding when I dropped him off."

"Dropped him off?" Harmony asked.

He took a deep breath, struggling to hold on to the last of his cards.

"You're going down for this," Jessie told him, "unless you give us somebody to go down in your place. You know what they're going to do to you behind bars when they find out you offed your own partner? Hey, Harmony, you think we could pull some strings, get our boy here a cell at Cross City? I bet Oscar's old buddies in the Familia 14 would love a little quality time with the man who fed him to the sharks."

"I think we can arrange that," Harmony said.

Randy was neck-deep in denial. "You're wrong. You're both so wrong, you don't even know. Oscar was gonna be fine. The doc said he was gonna bring in a patch-up guy—you know, a medical doctor, not a fish doctor—and take care of him."

"And you didn't stick around, why?" Jessie asked.

"Doc was worried somebody might have seen the snatch go down. He told me to get my ass someplace public that was nowhere near the Rusty Nail. Get receipts, try to build an alibi in case I got picked up for questioning. He said he was going to handle everything."

"Oh, he handled it, all right." Jessie gave Harmony a sidelong glance. "Show him."

Harmony pulled up one of the morgue shots on her phone. He flinched when she turned the screen around. Randy didn't have much of a poker face; they watched him race through every argument he could think of, each one crumbling before it hit his lips.

"Cranston doesn't know any patch-up men," Harmony told him. "That or he weighed the cost of a house call against the value of your buddy's life and decided on the cheaper option."

"Son of a bitch," Randy breathed.

"If I were in your shoes," Jessie said, "I'd be wondering how long it'll be before I'm next on the menu. I mean, he let you believe Oscar was going to be just peachy, and obviously that's not a sustainable lie."

"Sounds to me like he's cutting loose ends," Harmony added.

"Swear to God," Randy said, still reeling. "I just…I just dropped them off, Oscar and the chick we were supposed to grab. That's all I did."

"At Nautilus Research," Harmony said.

"No. No, it was at the doc's mansion." He stared at her, looking for some kind of a lifeline in her eyes. "He's got a second lab, down in his basement, behind a secret door. I've never been allowed inside, but me and Oscar bring…brought deliveries there all the time. Anyway, he's…"

Randy stopped talking. He bit his bottom lip and tried to disappear into his chair.

"Bad time for the silent treatment," Jessie told him. "You're fighting for your life right now, you feel me? Speak now, give us something good, or forever hold your peace. Once the cuffs go on, all deals are off the table."

"He didn't use the sharks at the research center, okay?

He doesn't do it there. He's got his own, in a tank in his lab. Like I said, never seen them, but I know he has 'em."

"You know," Harmony said, "because this isn't the first time you've done this."

"Like I said. We made deliveries. Usually science-geek stuff, machines, barrels of chemicals. Sometimes people. People nobody would miss. Oscar handled that. He used a shelter as long as he could get away with it. Then he moved into a transient motel. Lots of interstate drifters, and nobody bats an eyelash when one goes missing. That's what drifters do."

"He had you kidnapping bums," Jessie said, "to feed to his pet sharks."

"I figured it was like dogfighting, you know? Most dogs don't want to fight. You got to condition them, give 'em a taste for blood."

He sank lower in his chair.

"They got a taste."

"Don't you move a goddamn muscle," Jessie told him.

She tugged the sleeve of Harmony's jacket, pulling her back a couple of feet. Her voice was a hard-edged growl.

"We got an obligation to Cooper. Promises to keep. I'm going to take this scumbag around back and find a dumpster to leave his body in. I know you don't like killing cold, so if you want to go bring the car around while I finish the job, that's fine by me."

Some parts of this job went down bitter. Harmony had started out in the Bureau. The FBI had rules to follow. Laws to uphold. Vigilant Lock had been born into a world where those rules didn't always apply. Laws went out the window when the killer was possessed by a body-hopping demon, and prisons couldn't hold a sorcerer capable of turning into a living shadow. More often than not, Vigilant operatives went for the terminal solution.

Randy Hern was nothing but a low-rent thug. He could fill a prison cell just fine, and the justice system wouldn't have any problem handling him. The part of Harmony that still wore a badge recoiled at the idea of a summary execution.

There were bigger issues in play, though. Even beyond the promise—that if and when a Vigilant operative went down fighting, they could trust they'd be avenged—was the need for the reborn organization to put its foot down. The occult underground was watching, waiting to see if they had a bite to match their bark.

She was about to swallow her reluctance and give Jessie the go-ahead. Then something else gave her pause. No connection to her ethical qualms.

"Stay of execution," she said. "There's something we can use him for first."

They stepped back to the table. Randy's hands were frozen, his gristly steak and undercooked fries going cold in front of him. It was a sorry excuse for a final meal.

"There's a way out of this for you," Harmony said.

It was a lie, but the look on his face said he'd do anything she told him.

"Cranston's laboratory," she said. "Not the public one, the one under his house. Can you get us inside? More importantly, can you get us in without him finding out about it?"

"Yeah, totally!" He nodded like a bobblehead doll. "Easy, we can do it right now if you want. I've never been in there, but I've seen him punch the key code in a dozen times."

"We'll need an excuse to get Cranston out of the house," Jessie said to Harmony.

"Nah, you're all good," Randy said. "The doc's gone."

"Gone?"

"At least that's what he told me. He called me this morning, said...well, he said Oscar was doing fine and I'd hear from him soon. Also said he was going to visit his family for a couple of days, so I should just take it easy and lie low."

"What about his maid?" Harmony asked, thinking back to the dinner. "Any other staff on the grounds?"

"Just her and the lawn guys who come in once a week, but they always work Thursdays. She's probably gone; she usually travels with the doc whenever he leaves town. I never asked, but I kinda think they're cousins or something. Got that same frog-face look, know what I mean?"

Jessie drummed her fingers on her hip pocket, making her decision.

"All right," she said. "Let's go."

23.

"Hey, Neptune. It's Harmony. Can you talk?"

The gust of breath on the other end of the phone raced ahead of her voice. Harmony was standing on the sidewalk halfway down the block from Cranston's place, while Jessie kept an eye on their prisoner in the car. She'd been watching the windows, checking for any glimmer of movement beyond the ruffled curtains before they made their move. The kidney-shaped driveway out front was empty.

"Are you okay?" Neptune asked. No preamble.

"I'm fine. Just needed to ask you something: did Cranston tell you he was leaving town?"

"What? No. I mean, he doesn't come into the lab every single day, so if he took a short trip I wouldn't necessarily know about it. Did he?"

Harmony stared at the front windows.

"I'm trying to find out if he's home. Can you do me a favor? Text him. Say you've got some promising test results and ask if he wants you to run them over to his house. *Don't* actually go, just let me know what he says."

"Sure, give me two minutes."

It only took her one and a half. She called Harmony right back.

"He just said 'out on business, be back soon.' Want me to ask where he went?"

"Would you normally press him for details?" Harmony asked.

"No, I'd just wait for him to get back."

"Then don't. Just do what you normally would."

"Do you want me to come over there?" Neptune said. "I've been to his house plenty of times. I can help—"

"No." Harmony caught herself. Too brusque. She could do better than that. "I mean, no, but thank you. It could be dangerous. I appreciate the offer."

Men in handcuffs tended to draw attention; Randy's hands swung free at his sides as he led the way across the sleepy suburban street. Jessie had patted him down before they got in the car and now she stayed right with him, one hand clamped firm on his shoulder. He didn't try anything. Then again, he seemed to believe he was going to walk away after being an accessory to multiple murders—Harmony had muttered reassuring words like "witness protection program" on the drive over—so he had an incentive to cooperate.

"We can go in through the garage," he said. "He always has us lug the heavy stuff through the garage."

Randy punched in an entry code next to one of the broad bay doors. An engine rumbled and the ivory slats rolled upward. The garage was as empty as the driveway outside. Hermetically clean, not a single stray oil spot on the concrete, and paint cans on a utility shelf stood arranged in perfect symmetry.

The door between the garage and the house was locked. Randy looked at the unmoving knob like it had just ruined his entire imaginary plea bargain. Jessie sighed and stepped around him.

"Harmony, watch him."

She unfolded a black velveteen envelope. A row of

lockpicks nested inside. She chose a pick and a tension rake, crouched on one knee, and got to work.

Cold air gusted over them as the door swung wide. Cranston kept the AC on even when he wasn't at home, turning the pristine house into a tomb. Jessie held up a hand. She stood on the threshold, ears perked, hunting for any sign of movement. Once the silence satisfied her, she let Randy take the lead. They wound through the icy halls, past Cranston's personal dojo and the aquarium library, toward a stubby hall just off the kitchen. The hall bloomed into a pantry lined with metal shelves, stocked with enough staple goods—sacks of flour, sacks of rice—to hold out against a siege.

He nudged one of the flour sacks aside. It had been carefully placed to conceal a keypad.

"This is as far as I've ever been," he said. "The man's very particular about who he lets inside."

He tapped four buttons. The pad responded with a high-pitched beep. The shelving unit beside it popped loose, along with a chunk of the wall. Randy grabbed a shelf and hauled it back, turning the whole unit on a concealed hinge. Beyond was a plunging stairwell, frost-white and smelling of bleach. Randy dusted his hands off.

"Voilà," he said. "So, how does this work? Can I go now? We cool?"

Jessie and Harmony shared a wordless conversation. Harmony knew Jessie would have been just fine with blowing his brains across the wall of oatmeal canisters behind him, but they might need to cover their tracks and lay a trap for Cranston when he got home. A dead body would spoil that. Besides, as she pointed out with a tiny incline of her head, they had no idea what was up ahead. Cranston might have set traps of his own.

"Inside," Jessie told him. "You go first."

"Like I said, I've never been down there. I can't help with that—"

She grabbed his shoulder and gave him a shove.

"Do it anyway," she said.

The stairwell turned, doubling back twice and still diving, aiming for the heart of the house. And in that cold and bleached heart, beneath the distant thrum of a generator, stood Cranston's laboratory.

It was a close cousin to his public front at Nautilus Research, but sized down for the work of a single man. Ultrawide monitors perched on glass workstations along one wall, next to a server rack. There were storage shelves bearing sealed canisters, most of them in hazard orange or venom green, and benches laden with testing equipment. All of it pristine, not a speck of dust permitted in Judah Cranston's inner sanctum. Stark light streamed down from operating-room fixtures, spaced between the metal rafters.

And there was a tank.

Just one, eight feet tall and maybe ten across, and the antiseptic air took on a salty tang from the murky water within. Harmony tasted it as she breathed, standing frozen, transfixed by the sight before her. Cranston didn't keep sharks down here.

There was a woman in the tank.

She floated in the water, sinuous arms rippling, completely submerged. A mane of golden hair flowed behind her like a bridal train. She was naked, her skin alabaster, her face a motionless mask of serenity as if she were some classic statue brought to life. Just below her navel, bare skin became a coat of coppery scales. Instead of legs, her body ended in a tail with glittering metallic fins.

"That ain't real," Randy whispered.

"That's a mermaid," Jessie said. "Cranston has a mermaid."

"That ain't real."

Harmony took a step toward the glass. The mermaid turned to follow her movements, eyes curious. The ancient coin Harmony wore as a necklace, her family relic, began to thrum and shiver against her breastbone.

"Where the hell did he find a mermaid?" Randy said.

"Not here." Harmony's fingertip thumped the knot of her tie. The coin fell still, for the moment. "I don't think she's from this world."

"You mean...she's an *alien* mermaid? Like, from Mars or something?"

Behind her, Jessie was on her phone. "Just who I wanted to...really? What's his excuse? Okay. I mean, we're going to have words, but...right. Give him Cranston's address. I want him here in ten. Tell him to go through the garage and look for a pantry off the kitchen with a stairway going down. We'll be in the basement."

Harmony drifted across the lab, like the mermaid's gaze was tugging at her feet.

"What's going on?" she asked.

"That was April," Jessie said. "Agent Dominguez just reported in, and he's on his way. Apparently, he was covering the front of the Rusty Nail when they were taking Cooper out the back. He didn't want to admit how badly he fucked up, so he's been on the ground here running his own investigation, trying to get some results so he wouldn't be coming back empty-handed."

"That's not how we do things."

"And he's going to hear that from me, but apparently he's got something big for us."

Not this big, whatever it was. The mermaid held Harmony's gaze, her expression frozen and unreadable as her tail gently swayed in the brine. Her hands beckoned, undulating like a belly dancer in slow motion.

Harmony stood before the glass. On the other side, the mermaid swam close, hovering almost nose-to-nose.

Then she erupted. The mermaid's face split open, ripping into four strips of muscle and flesh that unfurled like the petals of a lethal flower. There was no skull underneath, just a gaping red and hungry maw, and the underbellies of the creature's flesh-tendrils were lined with hundreds of shark teeth. The teeth slapped at the wall of the tank, desperate and flailing.

Randy staggered back with a strangled curse on his lips. Harmony held her ground, motionless, watching. The creature's frenzy ended as quickly as it began. The torn petals of her face folded back together, putting her human disguise in place. She lifted her alabaster chin at Harmony, a silent pout, then shifted her attention to the others.

"I don't know how we're going to move this tank," Jessie muttered. She crouched to study the foundation, a strip of chrome that ringed the glass base. "How did he get her down here in the first place? Summoning? Is it some kind of demon?"

Harmony shook her head. "My coin doesn't react to demons. This is interdimensional."

"Think Cranston's hooked up with the Network? Or what's left of it anyway?"

"Maybe." She heard the doubt in her own voice. This felt different. Just an intuitive nudge.

Jessie stood up and propped a hand on her hip. The mermaid stared at her. Her arms began to sway once more, beckoning her closer.

"Bitch," Jessie said, "I don't think so."

The mermaid crossed her arms over her breasts and glowered at her.

"You can understand us, can't you?" Harmony murmured.

The mermaid glanced her way.

"You're sentient. Why is Cranston keeping you here? Are you his prisoner or something else?"

"I'm more curious about why he's been feeding people to her," Jessie said.

"That might be the only thing she can eat. Look. Her face isn't her face, it's camouflage."

One of the face-petals peeled back in the water, just left of her nose, revealing the glint of shark teeth.

"Some animals, even some carnivorous plants, evolve scents and lures designed to mimic their prey. To draw them close, keep them off guard until they attack. Wherever she's from, it's a place where mermaids are at least one step higher than humans on the food chain."

"Jesus," Randy said. "You mean this is the thing that ate Oscar? I'm gonna be sick."

Jessie's hand eased toward her blazer. And the shoulder holster underneath.

"And it's the thing that ate our friend Cooper. Which reminds me, we've got a little unfinished business—"

"Agents?" called a voice from above, lightly tinged with a Spanish accent. "Dominguez here. Is it clear?"

"Come on down," Harmony called back.

Resonating *thumps* echoed his footsteps in the stairwell. Dominguez was tall and lean, with slicked-back hair the color of charcoal and a snake charmer's smile. He pulled a hand truck behind him, the source of the thumping, using it to tote a hefty steamer trunk with brass fittings. He laid the trunk down while he talked.

"I knew you'd want to see this right away," he said.

"What I wanted," Jessie said, "was for you to *report in*. We had no idea if you were dead or alive."

"Hey," Dominguez said, "you knew my background when you recruited me. Long-range reconnaissance patrol is what I do. I'm used to going dark for months at a time."

"That's not how we do things."

"I'll make it up to you," he said.

He flipped up the lid of the trunk. Harmony's eyes narrowed. His story—that he'd been covering the bar from a distance, expecting Cooper to come out the front—was consistent with his orders. Going dark on the spur of the moment and playing cowboy was consistent with his background. That was as far as she could follow him; from there, everything about this situation felt wrong, a smooth solid line dissolving into fractal chaos.

"No comment?" she asked him.

"About?"

Harmony gestured to the tank.

"There's a mermaid three feet to my right, and you haven't said a word. Either you're staggeringly imperceptive, or you should be playing poker for a living."

"I'm pretty good at poker," he said, flashing her a smile. "But nah, I've been down here already. Ran an infiltration op yesterday afternoon, when Cranston was out running errands. Seriously, I'm ten steps ahead of you two. You ought to be thankful I'm here to bring you up to speed."

Randy had been staring, silent. Now he jabbed an uncertain finger at Dominguez.

"I know you."

The smile disappeared. "You don't know me, pal."

"No, I've *seen* you. The night Oscar got shot. The doc told me to get lost, to go build up an alibi. When I was pulling out of the driveway, you were pulling in—"

Dominguez's hand appeared from behind the trunk lid, gripping a matte-black pistol. The tube of a sound suppressor spat twice. One bullet caught Randy in the shoulder. The other punched through his cheek and spattered blood and bone against the glass of the tank. Harmony was reaching for her gun when he trained his sights on her.

"I wouldn't," he said. "Seen you on the range, Black. You're fast, damn fast. But I can empty my magazine before you clear your holster, and you know it."

She froze. So did Jessie, standing at her side. Randy's slack-jawed corpse slumped to the laboratory floor.

"So much for doing this the smooth and easy way," Dominguez said. "No problem, though. Like I said, I'm ten steps ahead of you two. By the way, Bobby Diehl sends his regards."

24.

Inside the tank, the mermaid hovered over the bloody smear from Randy's ruptured skull. Her face-petals split wide, and two greedy, sinuous tongues lapped at the glass as if she could taste the blood from the other side.

"You're a traitor," Harmony said.

"I'm a realist," Dominguez replied. "I thought I knew what I was signing up for when I joined Vigilant Lock. I thought I knew what hell looked like."

"You're definitely going to find out," Jessie muttered.

"I was at Vandemere Zoo, the night of the Wisdom's Grave op. I thought I was ready. The shit I saw...we took down a whole squad of Network shooters, and the fuckers *got back up again*. We chopped 'em into ground beef and they were still moving. And that wasn't the worst of it. These...dog-things, they dragged one of my guys down and ate him alive, right in front of me. I saw dead men walking, with armored plates bolted into their skin."

"We were there," Jessie said. "What, you pissed off because nobody gave you a medal afterward?"

"I'm pissed off because I didn't realize signing up for this outfit was *suicide*. I'm all for doing my patriotic bid, but you people are insane. You've got this one tiny shadow operation, working out of a goddamn basement, barely able to keep the lights on, and you think you're going to...what? Fight something like *that*? It's not just the occasional monster here or there or some nutcase who learns real magic. There is an army of those things, *worlds* full of stark raving nightmares, and we're nothing but a lit match in the wind. Look at that thing in the tank."

"What?" Jessie said. "Big tough guy like you afraid of a fish?"

"Oh, fuck you, Temple. That thing is from another dimension, and somehow it evolved to *eat humans*. What does that tell you about the nature of the universe, huh? What does that tell you about humanity?"

"It tells us that humanity needs to be protected," Harmony said. "No matter what. That's the job. That's the mission you signed up for."

"Yeah, when I thought there was a chance. We're not 'fighting the good fight' or whatever Pollyanna bullshit you want to preach at me. We're just waiting to get eaten. Well, not me. I started shopping for a better offer."

Jessie arched an eyebrow. "Bobby Diehl? That's your idea of a better offer? Maybe you haven't noticed, but he's a cornered rat."

"Bobby's the man with the plan. See, he figured it out. It was after he went on the run and left everything behind, but eventually he figured out Cooper was your mole inside his company. He wasn't going to let that slide. Meanwhile, he had his deal with Cranston, so he figured he'd kill two birds with one big fucking rock. Me. He's paying me six figures to kill Cooper—the slower the better, and I think that worked out just fine—and bring him the package Cranston promised him."

"Wait a second," Harmony said. "We thought Cranston murdered Cooper because he was backing out of the deal with Bobby. So why are you still breathing?"

"Because the minute I landed in Tampa, I went to see

Cranston alone. Cooper had no idea; I mean, the whole plan was that I'd trail her and keep hidden, so she didn't know I was never watching her back at all. I 'confessed' to Cranston that Cooper was an assassin. Bobby had sent her to kill him. Then I said, you know, I'd be happy to be his bodyguard for some financial consideration."

"You're not a double agent," Jessie said. "You're a triple."

"It worked like a charm. Cranston's thugs grabbed Cooper, the doc vigorously interrogated her for a few hours about an assassination plot that didn't even exist, and then he fed what was left of her to the mermaid. Know what I love about paranoid people? *So* easy to manipulate. I got it all on video for Bobby's viewing entertainment. The guy's crazy about snuff movies. And here's the best part."

He kept his eyes on them but nodded sideways, toward one of the workstations. A digital timer counted down on the screen of a laptop, twenty-six hours on the clock, next to a softly whirring industrial centrifuge. A briefcase on the nearby table stood open, exposing mechanical guts and test-tube-sized indentations. The delivery mechanism.

"Obviously, the deal's off. Cranston's taking his toy—I don't know what it is, some kind of bioweapon—and going into hiding. He's just got to finish synthesizing it. Automated process. Once that timer runs down, he's going to package it all up and hit the road."

"And you're his new best friend," Harmony said. "So you'll be right beside him."

"In the perfect place to stab him in the back. Or shoot him, whichever works. I call the Concierge, get a pickup, and fly to Xanadu to deliver Bobby the snuff footage and the weapon. I got paid by you, I got paid by Cranston, and next I'm getting paid by Bobby, all for one trip. Not bad, huh?"

"You're forgetting something," Jessie said.

"Oh? What's that?"

"You're forgetting the part where we track Bobby down and bury him in a hole deeper than the Mariana Trench. His fifteen minutes are just about up. You really want to go down with him? In his best-case scenario, he decides to go out with a bang and takes everybody he can with him. Which includes you, champ."

"You know, he was worried. Thought you people might have some vague idea of what he's got planned. Can't wait to tell him how clueless you are."

"You're bringing him a bioweapon," Harmony said. "It isn't hard to guess."

"You're thinking way too small. Now do me a favor. Take out your pieces, nice and slow, holding them between your thumb and your index finger. Then put them down on the floor."

Harmony rankled at giving up her weapon, but framed in the traitor's sights, she didn't have a choice. She could draw her gun along with her magic, conjure a shield of air thick enough to stop bullets—but she couldn't do any of it faster than he could squeeze that trigger. Her hand inched along, gingerly plucking her pistol from the shoulder holster, her other hand open and out as she laid the gun down on the tile floor. At her side, Jessie did the same.

He hadn't gunned them down the second he got here, which meant he had a reason—at least for now—to keep them alive. That meant they still had a chance.

"What about us?" Harmony asked.

"Well, first of all, kick your guns my way. C'mon, send

'em over." He waited until the pistols clattered along the frost-white tiles. He reached behind his belt with his free hand, produced a pair of handcuffs, and gave them a rattle. "Temple. Catch."

He tossed them underhand. She snatched them out of the air.

"Now cuff your partner's hands."

Harmony felt a flicker of hope, even as she turned and put her wrists behind her back. That meant he'd have to cuff Jessie himself. Dumb move. He'd have to get close, inside her reach. The cuffs ratcheted around her wrists, not tight, but tight enough to hold her.

"Got a pair for me?" Jessie asked.

Dominguez chuckled. "You think I'm stupid, Temple?"

"Is that a rhetorical question?"

"I don't know what the deal is with your freaky-ass eyes, but I know you're not human. I've seen you in the gym; you're strong enough to *break* cuffs."

He pointed to the steamer trunk, the supposed big discovery he'd been claiming to deliver, and swiveled it around with his boot. It was empty.

"Brought this just for you. Get in the trunk."

"Yeah," Jessie said, "I'm not doing that."

"Don't be a pussy. I drilled air holes. Killing you isn't on my agenda. I just don't want you busting loose and ripping my throat out while I'm trying to get shit done."

"When it happens, I won't be starting with your throat."

"Get in the trunk," Dominguez said, "or pick a kneecap."

"You're going to shoot me?" Jessie asked.

"No." He sighted down the barrel. "I'm going to shoot your partner and make you watch. You ever see somebody get kneecapped, Temple? They scream like you wouldn't believe. Or you can save all of us a lot of aggravation and just get in the damn trunk. *Now.*"

Jessie looked in Harmony's eyes. Harmony gave her an almost imperceptible nod. "It's okay," she said.

She wasn't sure if she was trying to reassure Jessie or herself. Jessie crossed the laboratory floor, careful and slow, and stepped into the trunk. Dominguez had done his homework: as she knelt down inside, it was just big enough to hold her. She had to ball her knees up to her chest, tight, and clench her arms against her sides to fit.

"Hope you're not claustrophobic," Dominguez said. "Not that I really care all that much. Hey, Black, turn and face the mermaid. You're making me nervous."

She turned toward the tank. The mermaid watched her, silent and curious. In the polished glass she watched her partner disappear. Dominguez shut the lid and threaded the finger-thick band of a padlock through the clasp. It locked with a coffin-lid snap.

He approached her from behind, gun trained on the small of her back.

"Where are you taking us?" Harmony asked.

"You? Nowhere. Funny thing: I didn't even know you two were in town, until Cranston showed me the security-camera footage from your dinner together. He was afraid you were more of Bobby's hired guns. Of course, I told him that's exactly what you were. Also told him I'd handle the situation."

"You're his new best friend."

"That's right. Naturally, I started thinking about how I could make the most of things. Killing you two would be easy. I'm already going to be on Vigilant's hit list once they figure out what I did, so adding another couple of bodies to the pile is no big deal."

"We're still breathing," Harmony said.

"Yeah, well, then I called Bobby, since I know you have history. He offered to pay me to murder both of you. Bonus if I do it slow and nasty and get it all on video. He's a real sick guy, you know that?"

"We're aware."

In the glass, Dominguez's blurry reflection gave her a shrug.

"Then I found out Nadine's got a bounty on you two. Strictly a live bounty."

"She wants to kill us herself," Harmony said. "She's been fairly outspoken on that subject."

"Then I'm thinking, well, I promised Cranston I'd liquidate you two. And I don't know how much longer I'm going to have to play the loyal bodyguard. Giving him a body would go a long way toward keeping me in his good graces, at least until I'm ready to take him out."

"What a predicament," Harmony said, her voice flat.

"I'm not going to kill your partner. I'm going to sell her. Already made contact with Nadine's people and they're just pleased as punch. A little irked that a human pulled off what a posse of demons couldn't, but they can grumble all they want as long as they pay me in cash."

Harmony had to smile. "Nadine's people? You'll be lucky if they pay you at all. Between her and Bobby, you're getting in bed with rattlesnakes."

"Meanwhile, here's the scenario: you broke into Cranston's lab, looking to assassinate him. Thankfully, I was on the scene, watching out for the doctor's interests."

"How are you going to explain the dead body on the floor? Randy worked for him. You can't pretend he was on Bobby's payroll, too."

"I'll figure something out. I'm good at improv. As for you, you're going to feed the fishes."

The blurry reflection of his arm swung up and then whipped down, whistling through the air. Harmony felt the barrel of his gun crack across the back of her skull in a burning shock wave. Then the laboratory floor was racing up to meet her, and her vision faded to black.

25.

Harmony woke to a world of pain.

The back of her head throbbed, and she could feel her hair matted like wet straw to her scalp. Warm blood trickled down the nape of her neck. Her arms were burning, shoulders twisted and strained. Her hands were numb and her wrists felt like she'd thrust them into a nest of fire ants.

Concentrate, she commanded herself, the word a mental slap across her face. She forced her eyes open. The world spun, hard lights stabbing at her as her vision reeled into focus.

She was hanging from the laboratory rafters. A length of rough hempen rope leashed her wrists; it ran over a steel rafter and then downward, to a winch on the far side of the room. Another loop of rope bound her ankles tight.

The tank was directly under her, the restless waters eight feet beneath her bare toes. The mermaid gazed up at her. One by one, the shark-toothed petals of her face unfurled to bare the raw red pit of her mouth.

The winch rattled and the rope dropped. Just an inch, a heart-dropping fall followed by a muscle-wrenching jolt. Harmony winced, her teeth gritting as a fresh lance of fire shot along her back.

Her shoes and jacket lay discarded on one of the workstation tables, along with her shoulder holster and her gun. A bulky camera stood on a tripod, aimed at the heart of the room. The steady red glow of the recording light told her why she wasn't dead yet. Dominguez wanted to get paid. He'd set the winch on a timer, designed to lower her into the tank one slow inch at a time. The mermaid was going to eat her alive, starting with her feet and working her way up.

This was how Cooper had died. With the camera recording every second of it, for Bobby Diehl's viewing pleasure.

The winch rattled. The rope dropped. The waters lapped against the glass as the mermaid slapped her tail, eager to be fed.

Harmony bit back a surge of panic. In a crisis, panic killed faster than a bullet. Words from her training blanketed her rising fear. *Assess the situation. Evaluate resources. Act with intent.*

Resources. The pen. He'd taken her obvious weapon, her pistol, but Dominguez had been in too much of a hurry to pat her down properly. Kevin's prototype from the mission briefing, the ballistic pen, was sitting snug in her pocket. Freeing her wrists was step one. For that, she had magic.

Magic needed serenity. Discipline. Above all, focus. Fear was the death of magic. She closed her eyes. She tried to ignore the pain, the danger, turning inward and taking deep breaths. As her chest swelled with air, the muscles of her back burned. A trickle of blood ran down her left arm, welling from where the rope had rubbed her wrist raw.

The winch rattled. The rope dropped, then jolted, wrenching her shoulders back. Her naked toes curled as the water frothed, sloshing around the hungry monster below.

She tried harder. Trying harder just made the magic slip away, dancing around her extended fingertips, like a snatch of a dream she couldn't quite recall. This wasn't working. *Focus.*

She thought about Jessie.

Right now, Jessie was locked in a trunk, under the gun, being delivered to Nadine's agents. Jessie needed her.

A connection sparked inside Harmony's heart. A pathway ignited along a ragged strip of nerve endings, glowing in the shape of a sigil. The pattern needed fuel. She found it in the stray bits of raw essence she'd stolen from Ethan. She transformed it like a Renaissance alchemist, transmuting his demonic energy to elemental power.

She smelled the tang of hickory smoke. She looked up as the rope leashing her wrists began to smolder. Gray smoke trickled up to the laboratory lights. Harmony concentrated, directing the flow of power to one focused point, tight as a laser beam.

The rope ignited. Then it broke loose and let go.

For a heartbeat, she was weightless. Then she was falling free. She lurched and shot up her hands to snatch the dangling rope. One hand missed. The other grabbed hold, tight, the rope twisting and spinning her around in a dizzying circle. Her free hand dove into her pocket. She tugged out the ballistic pen and flipped the clip back. One shot. She aimed for the tank, one inch above the waterline, squinting as she struggled to keep her trembling arm steady. Her strength was running out, the smoldering rope slipping from her sweaty grip.

She pressed the clip and fired. The chromed steel tip of the pen blasted into the wall of the tank and punched straight through it, jagged cracks spider-webbing in every direction. Then it burst. With a tidal-wave roar, the tank collapsed into broken sheets of glass and sent saltwater billowing across the frost-white tiles. The mermaid fell in its wake, tail thrashing, toothed flesh-petals flapping wildly.

The winch dropped and the sudden jolt stole Harmony's grip. She plummeted to the laboratory floor, landing hard on her shoulder as a slice of glass carved through her sleeve. She rolled on the slick tile, ankles still bound, struggling to get away from the flailing monster.

It pursued her. The mermaid dragged herself across the broken glass, tail slapping the wet floor. Her twin tongues licked the air and her petals slammed open and shut, desperate to kill one last time. Harmony pulled herself along the tile on her forearms, shards of glass clinking as she shoved them out of her way. The workstation was just ahead, and one sleeve of her jacket draped over the table's edge.

The mermaid was faster than she was. Harmony had to be careful on the slick tile, picking through the wreckage of the tank. The creature didn't care. She ripped herself open on the glass, leaving a trail of black blood that mingled with the cold puddles and became oil-slick rainbows.

Every pull of Harmony's forearms meant another searing yank of her shoulders. She fought through the pain, focused on the race as the mermaid closed in on her bare feet. With one last burst of strength, Harmony shoved herself up on one hand and lunged for the jacket sleeve with the other.

She fell, pulling the jacket down with her. And the holster that was resting on top of it. Harmony rolled onto her back as she yanked the pistol free. The mermaid reared over her, petals wide, ready to feast—and Harmony opened fire.

Radical-invasive rounds plowed into the mermaid's open maw. One bullet after another tore into the dying beast's gullet, punching holes through her body, spitting torn flesh and black blood in glittering arcs. Harmony squeezed the trigger again and again until the hammer slammed down on an empty chamber.

The mermaid crashed to the laboratory floor, motionless. Trails of black-rainbow blood leeched out from beneath her corpse like rivers on a map of hell.

Harmony lay still, waiting for the world to stop spinning.

"Oh my God," Neptune said. "Oh my *God*."

Harmony wasn't sure which 'oh my God' was directed at her and which one was about the dead monster on the floor. Neptune raced over to her side, glass crunching under her tennis shoes.

"Harmony! Are you okay? Oh God, you're bleeding."

Harmony groaned as she pushed herself up, sitting with her back to the table.

"Told you not to come," she managed to rasp.

"You did, and, well, I didn't listen. I thought you might not even be here, but I heard the gunshots and followed the sound." Neptune held Harmony's shoulder, eyeing the cut on her arm. "I didn't even know this was down here. And what…what is *that*?"

"Ideally, something you never would have found out existed," Harmony said. She reached down, tugging at the knotted rope around her ankles. "Grab my shoes and socks off the table? Don't know how much time I've got, can't stop moving."

"Harmony, *please*. Tell me what's going on. Tell me and maybe I can help."

She couldn't stop. She did anyway. Harmony looked into Neptune's eyes, feeling the waves of worry washing off her.

"That's a mermaid," Harmony said.

"Like some kind of medical experiment? Did Judah operate on a woman and turn her into that thing, or—?"

"No. It's an actual mermaid." Harmony took a deep breath. This was going to hurt. She reached up, grabbed hold of the table's edge, and winced as she forced herself to stand. "I don't really work for Diehl Innovations."

"Well, yes," Neptune said. "I figured that much."

Harmony held her gaze. Time was a weight on her burning shoulders. The window of opportunity for getting Jessie back was shrinking by the second.

"I'm part of an organization that hunts and eliminates supernatural threats"—Harmony waved a shaky hand at the dead mermaid—"threats like these, so they can't prey on people like you. One of our own turned traitor and kidnapped my partner. He's taking her somewhere...bad. Really bad, and if I don't get her back, and fast, she's going to die."

Neptune's eyes went wide. "Wait. Oh God, was she locked in a trunk?"

"What did you see?"

"When I first got here." Neptune pointed upward, tracing it back in her memory. "I parked up the block, to be safe. I saw a guy lugging a trunk out through the garage with a hand truck. He looked a little sketchy and I've never seen him at the house before, so I held back until I was sure he was gone. He really strained, wrestling it into the back of his pickup, like it weighed at least a hundred pounds."

Harmony felt a surge of hope. "Did you get a license-plate number?"

"No, but I remember the make."

"Good enough."

She snatched her phone from the table and hit the speed dial. Kevin picked up after one ring.

"Yeah, boss?"

"We need to move fast. Is April on the line?"

"Right here," April said. "Harmony? What's wrong?"

"Dominguez screwed us. He's working for Bobby Diehl. He took Jessie and he's going to sell her to Nadine for the bounty money."

"What can we do?" Kevin asked.

Harmony looked to Neptune. "Tell me about the truck."

"It was a pickup, silver—" Neptune squeezed her eyes shut, fighting to remember. "A long one, the kind with a back seat. It was a GMC…no. No, it was a Toyota. I'm sure of it. I remember the emblem on the back."

"Okay, good, you're doing great. Now picture the back bumper. Did it have any kind of sticker, like from a rental agency?"

Neptune shook her head. "No. No bumper stickers. It was dirty, though. A lot of spattered mud, like it had gone off-roading."

Harmony put the phone back to her ear.

"You get that?" she said. "It wasn't an airport rental. Now, Dominguez isn't a local. Not his car, no local resources, so—"

"He stole it," Kevin said.

"Hit the police reports, look for any mention of a stolen Toyota pickup. We're going to find that vehicle, we're going to find Dominguez, and we're going to get my partner back."

26.

Neptune scurried upstairs. She knew Cranston kept a first-aid kit in his bathroom, and the cut on Harmony's arm was still leaking. The torn sleeve of her dress shirt had turned cherry red, and droplets spattered onto the saltwater-slick floor at her feet.

"Found a hit," Kevin said. "Silver 2015 Toyota Tacoma, stolen from a construction site four hours ago. I've got a plate number."

"Good. I'm pretty sure I saw a couple of cameras on light posts while we were driving around. Does Tampa have a traffic monitoring system?"

April checked. "Privately owned. Red-light cameras. A civilian contractor operates them for the city; they watch for traffic violations and send tickets by mail."

"Kevin, can you—"

"Already working on it, boss."

* * *

Side by side at their consoles, April and Kevin worked in concert. Twin pianists, keystrokes yielding up a symphony of data. As she passed him the details on the camera vendor, separating the wheat from the chaff and shooting the essentials to his screen, he shifted to a second phone line and adjusted his headset.

Nationwide company with multiple branches. Good. Tampa was a satellite office. Even better. April sent him a link for their public-facing website, complete with staff lists. People hated red-light cameras; the company was trying to wage a charm offensive, putting on a human face and giving out too much information in the process.

They also outsourced their camera-monitoring software to a third-party vendor, who bragged about it in a press release. The press release led to a white paper; the company had proposed bringing their program to Cincinnati, and city rules mandated making all bids public. Nothing confidential inside, but it had all the technical details Kevin needed.

"Hey there, pal," he said, taking a disaffected-IT-guy tone of voice and slouching back in his chair for extra effect. "It's Tom Nelson, from the home office. Hey, I'm seeing that you guys haven't installed the new patch on your Apache servers."

"I...didn't hear about a patch," said the confused voice on the other end.

"Typical, they probably didn't pass the memo down. Yeah, they're rolling out the new XL-4 camera modules next month. I think you guys are...third on the upgrade list? You've got to have this update installed or they'll just conk right out. I'll tell you what, why don't we get this fixed right now so you can get on with your day? I'm just going to need you to let me remote connect and mirror your screen..."

* * *

Harmony held out her wounded arm, her soggy and torn sleeve rolled up to her shoulder, while Neptune dabbed her cut with ointment.

"Sorry," Neptune said. "This probably hurts."

"Everything hurts. I'll live."

"You have a lot of scars." She reached for a bandage.

"I fight a lot of monsters," Harmony said.

"I keep looking at that...thing." Neptune shot a glance at the mermaid's corpse. "It shouldn't exist."

"Can't argue with that."

"No." Neptune's eyes flashed as she looked back to Harmony. "I mean, anatomically. Look, marine biology is my life. This is my field. I know how animals fit their habitats, how they evolve...that thing isn't biologically *possible*."

The Greek coin thrummed on its chain, an insistent hummingbird under the knot of Harmony's tie.

"It's not from here," she said.

"Where, then?"

Harmony listened to the silent phone line, waiting for Kevin to come back with results. Minutes were slipping by while Dominguez got farther and farther away. Then there was Neptune. She was in this now, too deep to turn back.

"This isn't the only Earth," Harmony told her. "There are...there are a *lot* of Earths, okay? Parallel worlds. Some look just like ours, and some are...different. And a lot of them are dangerous."

"So how does a mermaid from a parallel world end up in Judah Cranston's basement?" Neptune folded her arms. "*Why* does she end up in his basement? What was he doing with her?"

"Those are all excellent questions, and I plan on asking him in person."

Kevin came back on the line. "I'm in. Back-doored myself into their network, and we've got full access."

"Good," Harmony said. She looked to Neptune. "Which way did he go when he drove off?"

Neptune closed her eyes, pointing her finger in the air and picturing the street.

"He went…west."

"West from Parkland Estates," Harmony told Kevin. "Get on the cameras and try to spot him."

It didn't take long. Dominguez was driving reckless, and a camera had already flagged his license plate running a red light.

"Got him heading westbound on West Kennedy Boulevard."

"I'm mobile," Harmony said. She slapped a fresh magazine into her gun.

"I'll drive," Neptune said.

Harmony shook her head and reached for her jacket.

"No. I want you to go home. Go home, lock your doors, and don't talk to anyone from Nautilus Research. I'll call you as soon as—"

"Hey," Neptune said. "You need to get your friend back. I live here. I know these streets, you don't. One wrong turn and you could get lost. Trust me, I can drive."

"It's going to be dangerous."

Neptune took her hand. Harmony blinked at her.

"Did you mean what you said back there?" Neptune asked.

"What part?"

"That you fight monsters for…for people like me. To keep us safe."

"That's why I do it," Harmony said.

Neptune squeezed her hand.

"Then I guess I owed you, all this time, and never knew it. Let me pay you back. Just a little. Please."

Harmony looked into Neptune's eyes, reading her intentions, making her choice. Seconds slipped away in the silence.

"You do what I tell you, when I tell you," Harmony said, "and you stay behind me at all times. Understood?"

Neptune jangled her car keys. "Got it. Let's go."

* * *

Jessie's muscles ached, a dull throb that slowly built as her cage rocked from side to side. She felt the trunk slide on something rough, back and forth, and listened to the sounds of traffic through the air holes Dominguez had drilled for her. *Truck bed,* she thought. *Probably a pickup.* Sunlight streamed through the tiny holes.

She couldn't kick with her knees balled up to her chest and feet flat against the wood. Couldn't punch with her arms pressed to her sides. She breathed, slow, focusing on the shallow rise and fall of her chest. Losing her cool wasn't going to help anything.

When she closed her eyes, she heard her blood singing.

The wolf was always inside her. Her constant companion. It wanted to come out. It wanted to come out and take over and shove her thinking parts deep down below, like an iceberg capsizing. It wanted to rip and tear and hurt and eat until it was full and then eat more just for the taste of it. The wolf didn't like being kept in a box in her head. It didn't like the skin it wore being kept in a box either.

I know, she told it. She stroked its gray fur in her mind's eye, to keep them both calm. *But I can't get the leverage to force this crate open, and if I frenzy in here, I don't know what'll happen.*

Sometimes, rarely, the wolf spoke back. A voice of winter frost that gusted up from her pounding heart to her ears.

But you want to.

Of course she wanted to. She always wanted to.

* * *

"Okay, so he passed the intersection at West Kennedy and South Howard," Kevin said. "Another camera flagged him at South MacDill Avenue. He's been running west in a dead sprint."

They were sprinting, too. Neptune's Jetta tore down the boulevard, weaving in and out of slow-moving traffic, closing in on Dominguez's trail.

"Found him again. Another camera caught him at West Kennedy and South West Shore. He turned left. He's southbound."

Neptune flicked her turn signal, glanced over her shoulder, and then veered left, crossing two lanes of traffic as a horn wailed behind her.

"I know a shortcut," she said, hands tight on the wheel.

"What's in that area?" Harmony asked her. "What's it like?"

"Beach Park, Culbreath Bayou, Stoney Point...it's near the bay, mostly residential."

Kevin's voice cut in. "We're at the edge of the red-light camera network, boss. Those neighborhoods don't have 'em. I'm looking for police cams, helicopters, anything I can use, but no promises."

Where are you going? Harmony thought. Dominguez had a destination. A purpose.

"If he keeps going south," she said, "is there any connection to the mainland?"

Neptune's brow furrowed. "One. He could take the bridge, cross on 92, and head toward St. Petersburg."

"But if he wanted to leave the state, that's not the fastest way, right?"

"Not remotely. If he wanted to leave, he should have taken a right turn fifteen minutes ago."

"Remember," April said on the line, "Dominguez has had the same briefings as any other Vigilant agent. He knows who he's dealing with."

Meaning Nadine. Harmony put herself in the traitor's shoes, envisioning how she'd try to make this deal.

"He's not going to Nadine," she said. "He's read the threat profile. He knows there's a good chance she'll take him, too, and interrogate him for intel on Vigilant. And Nadine doesn't do soft interrogations. Even better chance she just takes Jessie, puts her hands on him, and convinces him he doesn't *want* to get paid."

"He'll demand to make the trade through intermediaries," April said. "And on neutral ground."

Harmony flicked her gaze toward Neptune. "Are there any airports around besides Clearwater?"

"TPA. It's north of here."

He wasn't going to the airport. No train lines nearby, and public transport was out of the question anyway: all Jessie had to do was start shouting and she'd draw attention. He needed private transport, isolated, where no one would hear Jessie scream.

"The water," Harmony said. "Head for the water. Nadine is sending a boat."

27.

Dominguez parked his truck at the southern edge of an old marina. Seagulls squalled in a tangerine sky, early sunset painting the waters of Old Tampa Bay in oil-paint streaks. Sailboats coasted across the gentle waves and sails crackled in the hot summer wind.

The docks were half-empty, everybody out at sea, and no civilians in sight. Just old wood and water under the glow of the dying sun. Dominguez dropped the pickup's tailgate, hauled out the hand truck, and started wrestling the steamer trunk down.

"Damn, Temple," he grunted. "Ever think about going on a diet?"

Her voice drifted from the air holes. "It's mostly muscle."

There was something off about her voice. A faint, dreamy softness he hadn't heard before.

"You breathing okay in there? You die, I don't get paid."

No response. He tipped the steamer trunk back onto the hand truck and slammed the tailgate.

"Suit yourself," he said.

The hand truck's wheels rattled on the slats of the dock. He dragged the trunk to the water's edge, checked the time, and watched the horizon. It shouldn't be long. Nadine said she had people in the area already. Dominguez idly wondered how hard it would be to get in touch with the local demonic court, and how much they'd pay for intel on Nadine's spies. If he was going to burn bridges on his way to Xanadu, he might as well burn them all.

He spotted movement on the horizon. A cigarette boat, coming in fast, churning white water in its wake. He raised his arms over his head in a slow and steady wave.

* * *

Kevin found Dominguez. Found the parked pickup, at least, a silver blur in the corner of a traffic helicopter's eye. Neptune pulled in at the opposite end of the sparse parking lot. Harmony clicked her seatbelt off.

"Stay here," Harmony said.

She threaded the slender tube of a sound suppressor onto her pistol.

"I can help—"

"Not with this," Harmony said. "Stay here, keep your head down, and keep the engine running."

There were only a handful of cars in the lot, their bug-spattered grilles catching dust in the fading sunlight. She used them for cover, crouching as she ran from one to the next, closing in on the dock up ahead. She saw the traitor, the trunk at his feet, the boat cruising in to dock.

The suppressor made her first shot sound like a slamming door. The bullet punched through the meat of Dominguez's shoulder and spat an arc of dark ruby blood out over the water. He wheeled around and dropped low as he brought his pistol up, teeth clenched against the pain. Harmony hit the pavement as a bullet blasted out a car window, another chewing a pothole in the rust-flecked steel door. She came up running, sprinting sideways, firing off another couple of rounds. They went high, carving air.

Dominguez was trapped between the gun and the deep

blue sea. The cigarette boat banked hard, kicking up water while the pilot veered and poured on speed, turning away from the docks. His pickup wasn't coming. He had less than a second to decide on his next move, all the time Harmony gave him as she lined up her next shot.

He crouched, put his good shoulder to the side of the steamer trunk, and shoved it over the edge of the dock.

* * *

Jessie felt herself falling. A short stomach-plunging drop, and then a bone-jarring splash as the trunk hit the water. She sank, drifting downward, as jets of cold water poured through the air holes, splashing her face and soaking her hair. She tucked her chin, trying to keep her face from the spray, shoving her feet against the wood. The trunk was turning, tumbling in the bay, and there was already an inch of water sloshing around her shoes.

She took deep breaths.

* * *

Dominguez broke and ran, clutching his wound while he sprinted away. He'd given Harmony a choice: take him down or save her partner.

That wasn't a choice at all. She didn't hesitate, and the cold embraced her as she hit the water in a dive. The tail of her jacket billowed behind her and the tip of her necktie caressed her cheek as she swam, pushing down against the tide. Her eyes burned. She hunted in the murky gloom until she spotted the trunk, touching down silently in a bed of silt.

Lungs searing, she puffed her cheeks and swam after it. The chest thumped, rocking, Jessie trying to fight her way out. The current tried to pull Harmony away and she grabbed hold of the padlock, hauling herself close.

Shooting underwater was risky. Guns could fail, and water stole momentum like a thief. She pulled the padlock as far from the hasp as it would stretch, put her muzzle to the thick steel, and fired. The bullet crackled like distant, muffled thunder. The padlock bent, metal warping and cratered, but held fast. Her second try snapped the shackle in half. She ripped it from the hasp and the trunk's lid gusted open. She grabbed Jessie's hand. There was light above, faint and glittering bronze, and she kicked toward it with the last of her strength.

* * *

Harmony crawled onto the shore, coughing, rolling onto her back and staring bleary-eyed at the candy-colored sunset. Jessie fell on top of her. Eyes closed, their foreheads touching, the curl of Jessie's fingers shaky against Harmony's cheek.

Jessie's hand slid down, to Harmony's throat. Feather-light, but twitching, half caress and half squeeze. Harmony could feel the chaotic energy lancing from Jessie's heart, burning in her blood. The wolf wanted to come out, wanted to hunt, wanted to kill, and she was holding it back with every scrap of energy she could muster.

"Hey," Harmony said. "Hey. It's okay. You're safe. I'm here now. You're safe."

Jessie's eyes flicked open. The turquoise faded from white-hot to a soft, subdued glow.

"I still don't know how you do that," Jessie murmured. "You're the only one who can make it go quiet."

"Dominguez got away," Harmony said.

"He won't get far. And when I find him, *his* box isn't going to have any air holes."

They fell silent, lying still, catching their breath together.

"Hey, Jessie?"

"Yeah?"

"You're lying on top of me."

Jessie blinked. Her forehead gave Harmony's a little nuzzle.

"Right. Sorry."

She groaned as she got to her feet, then helped Harmony up. They headed for the parking lot.

* * *

Kevin met them back at Cranston's house. They needed to crack the laboratory's systems, fast. The stairwell down wasn't wheelchair friendly, so they patched April in on speakerphone while he got to work.

"I'm already in contact with the home office," April said. "I presume you'll be wanting a full crew of cleaners?"

"With extra mops." Jessie's toe nudged the dead mermaid. "Well, at least we know bullets can kill these things. That's a plus."

Neptune gave her a nervous look. "There are things bullets can't kill?"

Kevin nodded as he brushed past her, headed for Cranston's terminal. "Psychotic ghost-clowns. It was only one time, though."

Harmony had her eyes on the centrifuge and the laptop beside it with a running countdown on the screen. The timer had passed the twenty-four-hour mark. Just under a day and Cranston's concoction would be ready.

"I want a surveillance team on the house," Harmony said. "Cranston's going to have to come back here to get his chemical weapon once it's done cooking. For that matter, so is Dominguez."

"Think he'll try?" Jessie asked. "He has to know we'll be here."

"I think if he knows what's good for him, he's halfway to Cuba by now. All the same, April? Keep an ear on the police band. I shot him in the shoulder. If he shows up at a hospital looking for help, they'll call it in. It's not likely; Dominguez is a trained combat medic, he can probably patch himself up, but he might be desperate."

"Done," April said. "And the weapon?"

"We need a biohazard specialist. I'm not touching this thing until we know exactly what we're dealing with."

"I still can't believe it," Neptune said. "I worked with Judah for years. He was always so...*nice*."

Harmony inspected the open case on the table. It had to be the one he'd commissioned from Prometheus Chemical. Slots nestled between a snake's nest of piping, waiting for the final concoction, ready to feed the gas to discreet vents along the sides of the device.

Neptune stood beside her. She frowned. Her index finger tapped her pursed lips.

"What did he say he was waiting for?"

Harmony pointed to the timer. "According to Dominguez, Cranston has to finish synthesizing the formula."

"And it's some kind of poison gas?"

"A bioweapon. We don't know the specifics, but this is the delivery mechanism."

Neptune shook her head. "But...that doesn't make sense."

"How so?"

Neptune loomed over the centrifuge, studying the white metal box from all sides as it rumbled and shivered.

"For starters, this is a liquid centrifuge. Centrifugation

is a process used to separate contents of a liquid, like separating blood cells from plasma. It's basic physics: fill a centrifuge with water and sand, and the denser particles—the sand—will all be pulled to the bottom by the spinning motion."

"With you so far," Harmony said.

"It doesn't change *states*. You can centrifuge a liquid forever and it's not going to magically turn into a gas. You have to induce vaporization for that. Also, to make it an aerosol, you'd have to pressurize it; there isn't any equipment here that could do that. On top of that, the centrifuge is broken."

"How do you know?" Harmony asked.

Neptune waved her around the table. She pointed to a small streak of hot-pink gloss on one corner of the white metal.

"Because it's mine. Was mine. Spilled nail polish on it. Listen: you hear that little drop in the sound it's making, every three seconds or so?"

Harmony closed her eyes. She listened to the whir of the machine, a steady mechanical thrum. Now she noticed it: every three seconds, the pitch slowed and the drone deepened for the space of a heartbeat before speeding up again.

"The motor's dying," Neptune said. "I noticed it last week. I asked for funding for a replacement, and Judah said he was going to take this one and sell it for scrap."

Harmony looked from the countdown timer to the centrifuge to the open case waiting for its payload. A perfect tableau, artfully arranged, serious as a heart attack. It made sense until it suddenly didn't. She took the pieces and scrambled them in her mind, rearranging them until they fit in a different configuration.

Her fingertip pressed against the centrifuge's rocker switch. She hesitated, just for a moment, then pressed down. The engine whirred to a grinding halt.

"Uh, Harmony?" Jessie said.

The centrifuge's lid unclasped with a hiss of compressed air. She slid a plastic canister from the belly of the machine, about the size of a prescription pill bottle, and unscrewed the cap.

"Harmony?" Jessie said, coming closer. "What happened to waiting for the experts?"

"We have an expert right here," she said.

She hoped so, because she was taking a hell of a risk, but she had to know for certain. One sniff would validate her hunch. She put the canister under her nose and inhaled. Then she went a step further. Harmony's index finger dipped inside. She scooped up a sticky fingerful of liquid, put her finger between her lips, and had a taste.

"It's maple syrup," she said.

Jessie arched an eyebrow. "Cranston's doomsday weapon is…maple syrup?"

"He's not coming back. At all. It's a scam. Either Dominguez wasn't as convincing as he thought, and Cranston saw through his act from the start, or he's just being extra careful." Harmony pointed to the timer. "He concocted this story about needing a day to finish the process, set this display up to fool Dominguez into buying it, and then he skipped town."

"So is this whole thing one big con job or…?"

"I see two possibilities." Harmony held up a pair of fingers. "We know that Bobby Diehl was paying Cranston to develop a chemical weapon for him, and that he finally called to collect. The best-case scenario is that Judah Cranston is nothing but a con artist. He's been taking

Bobby's money to fund his marine lab and stringing him along all this time."

"What's the worst-case scenario?" Neptune asked.

"Worst case is Judah *did* develop the weapon, but either he has another buyer or he's going to use it himself. It's done, it's functional, and he just fled with it. The stalling tactic, the sudden disappearance...wherever he went, it's a one-way trip. He's not planning on coming back."

"Harmony?" Kevin called out.

He was sitting at the workstation on the other side of the lab. His face had gone bloodless, pale.

"You need to see this," he said. "Right now."

28.

A host of video and text files filled a directory on the wide-screen monitor. The icons were meticulous, sorted by date, and the oldest was from four years ago. The directory had a name: *Clean Slate.*

As the others gathered around him, Kevin double-clicked the biggest video file. The film had been shot by a concealed zoom lens from a second-floor window, over a block away. As Harmony's stomach clenched, she knew exactly when and where it had been filmed. Last autumn. Talbot Cove, Michigan. Festive banners, pennants in gold and harvest orange, draped the lampposts to celebrate the town's Halloween festival.

A delivery truck had crashed into the hardware store, half-buried in the facade, shredded tires nestled in a bed of broken glass and spilled oil. A small crowd gathered on the street, pointing, curious. Judah Cranston's voice echoed over the workstation's speakers.

"Log eighty-five twenty-one. My patron is demanding a demonstration of Project Clean Slate. I've told him it's not ready, in any way, shape, or form, but he insists nonetheless. He's even chosen a target for said demonstration; apparently he's having issues with some government agency and wants to send them a message. I didn't ask for the details and, frankly, I don't care."

On the screen, a squad car roared up to the edge of the accident. Harmony watched herself jump from the passenger seat, badge high. Suddenly she was back there, living it all over again, the world lurching into slow motion as her mind went into hyperfocus. She saw the back doors of the crashed truck explode open with the white-hot pop of a flashbang grenade. Then the gas billowed out, washing over the crowd.

"Where is this?" Neptune whispered, transfixed.

"Talbot Cove," Harmony said. "My hometown. You don't need to watch this. You shouldn't watch this."

She knew what Neptune was going to see. Figures writhing in the bilious green mist, falling to their knees, contorting as their muscles tore and their bones snapped. Bodies staggered and fell, skulls deflated like basketballs as their insides turned to rubber, skin transformed to rawhide leather or serpentine scales.

"There was a thing last year," Neptune stammered. "I heard about a religious cult doing a, a suicide thing in Michigan. They said it was sarin gas—"

Harmony stared at the screen. "We covered it up. This was what really happened."

She watched as the camera zoomed in tighter, fixing on Norma, the waitress from the town diner, a woman Harmony had known since she was six years old. Norma had sprouted a porcupine coat of bone spurs, jutting from her torn and ragged skin. She fixed her feral gaze on a police officer, opened a mouth lined with barracuda teeth, and lunged for his throat.

The camera jerked as Harmony shot her in the head.

"We covered it all up," Harmony said.

"Clearly," Cranston's voice said on the recording, "this was a catastrophe. Only one of the affected subjects even survived the initial exposure. Ironically, my patron is jubilant. Diehl is a simple-minded sadist; he's satisfied with mere suffering and horror. He's increased my funding twofold, eager for more results."

Cranston paused. The footage held on the street as the mists cleared, panning across the twisted bodies left behind.

"If at all possible, I intend to make certain he's standing at ground zero when my magnum opus is revealed. It's the least I can do to thank him for his money."

The screen went black.

"What...*was* that?" Neptune whispered. She kept staring at the monitor, at the empty window, like it might yield up more secrets.

"It's a mutagen," Harmony said. "We thought Bobby Diehl made it himself. We also thought it was the finished product."

"Those people, the way they changed—"

"It's a mixture of some kind of chemical weapon along with an occult curse; they work in tandem like a one-two punch." Harmony turned to Jessie. "I knew I smelled magic on him when we met for dinner. Sorcerous residue. I just couldn't figure out what he was doing with it."

Jessie picked up the phone on the edge of the workstation. "Now we know. April? You getting all this?"

"Already sending out encrypted bursts to all teams in the field," April said over the speaker. "Locating Judah Cranston is now Vigilant's top priority."

"What he said, about ground zero—" Neptune pointed a shaky finger at the screen.

"Bobby Diehl paid him to create a weapon," Harmony said. "But he never intended to hand it over. He built it so he could use it himself. That was the plan from day one."

And now he was gone, heading off on a trip he never

planned to come home from. They needed a lead. Harmony thought back to the night of their dinner, poring over Cranston's words with a magnifying glass.

"Neptune? How much of what he told us at dinner was true?"

"All of it, as far as I know," she said. "I mean, obviously I never really knew the man, but everything he said was consistent with things he's told me for years."

"So he really came from a fishing family?"

Neptune nodded. "Somewhere in New England. The ocean has always been a big part of his life."

Harmony glanced at Jessie. "What was that thing his hired thug said? Cranston told him he was going to visit his family."

"Could have been a lie. I mean, he told Neptune he was out on business."

"It's worth following up. When people hide, they hide where they feel safe. April, pull the entire support division together and do a deep dive into Cranston's history. Education, housing, anything that could give us an address. We need to know exactly where he grew up."

"Already working on it," April replied.

"I'll call Aselia and make sure the plane's fueled up and ready to go," Jessie said. "The second we get a target, we're moving. What do you want to do about her?"

Harmony looked from Jessie to Neptune. Neptune took a hesitant step back, bumping her hip on the workstation.

"Are you going to erase my memories?" she asked. Her voice quavered.

"That's not a thing we can actually do," Harmony said. "Can you keep a secret?"

Neptune's head bobbed.

"Good. You want a job?"

"Well, apparently my boss, who was the best boss I've ever worked for until fifteen minutes ago, is actually a maniac and a terrorist. So I'm probably going to be unemployed soon."

"You'd be what we call a civilian asset," Harmony said. "A specialist on call, for when we have a case relating to your particular field."

"It's part-time and the pay sucks," Jessie added.

Neptune's eyes lingered on Harmony. "But I'd...get to see you again?"

"I'd be your primary point of contact, yes."

Jessie thumped Harmony's shoulder. She wasn't sure why.

"I'm in," Neptune said.

"A cleaning team should get here shortly," Harmony said. "That's 'cleaning' as in 'making the evidence go away.' They'll take you to a safe house. I'd like you to stay there until we apprehend Cranston."

Neptune's nerves came back in a sudden rush. "You think he'd come after me?"

"No, no reason to, but there's no reason to take any chances. Just want to make sure you're safe. Meanwhile, you can do something important for us..."

Harmony pointed to the mermaid's corpse, its blubbery flesh turning room temperature on the damp, glass-littered tile.

"Think you can autopsy this thing?"

"Me?" Neptune stared at it. "I mean, I don't know anything about magic. I didn't know magic was *real* until, well, today."

"But you know about marine life. Just treat it like you'd treat an exotic species; open it up and see if you can figure out what makes it tick. How its digestive system works, how it reproduces—anything you can figure out could be useful in the field if we ever encounter another one."

"You think there are more out there?"

"Hopefully not," Harmony said. "Not on this world, anyway, but again, better safe than sorry. We still don't know where Cranston got the thing in the first place. Or why he had it in his lab, for that matter."

"I'll do my best," Neptune said.

"That's all we ask."

Harmony started to turn, already thinking three steps ahead, tracing through a labyrinth of thoughts. Something in Neptune's look made her pause.

"Hey," Neptune said. She hesitated, wringing her hands.

"What is it?"

Neptune leaned in, quick, and planted a feather-light kiss on Harmony's cheek.

"Thanks," Neptune said, staring down at her shoes as her face turned red.

Harmony blinked. She felt her cheeks go warm. "You're, um…welcome. You're very welcome."

* * *

Judah Cranston had left a paper trail, tracing most of his life in tax returns and diplomas. He'd gotten a degree from Humboldt State University, another from Duke University, and earned his first paychecks at DuPont before striking out on his own and founding Nautilus Conservation Research with the help of a bank loan. His life, in documents, was accomplished but mundane. He paid his bills on time.

Before college his trail was sketchier, but he had never made an effort to cover his tracks. He'd simply grown up in the obscurity of a small town in Maine, in a time before always-on Internet and a world of cell phones.

“Paper records,” April said, back on the plane. Aselia was running flight checks for their departure, brushing past them with a clipboard and a pencil. “Never digitized. We had to pay someone to comb through filing cabinets and fax us his records.”

“We have a fax machine?” Jessie said.

“From there, I was able to piece together the Cranston legacy. He went to school in Bar Harbor, but in the glory days of his family, they hailed from a fishing village called Graykettle.”

“Never heard of it.”

“When the fishing dried up, the village dried up with it. It’s not entirely a ghost town, but the current population can’t be more than a few hundred people.”

“It’s fifty miles from anywhere,” Aselia told them. “I’m going to have to touch down at the closest airstrip. You can drive in from there.”

Harmony and Jessie shared a glance.

“If I was running from Bobby Diehl,” Jessie said, “after stealing the man’s money—and getting ready to unleash a bioweapon—where would I go?”

“A place fifty miles from anywhere,” Harmony said.

29.

They made plans in the air. No telling for certain if Cranston had fled to his childhood home, but it was the only lead they had.

"I can pull other operatives off mission," April said. "Do we want strike teams on standby?"

Harmony shook her head, pacing.

"We have to be careful. Even if he hasn't created the final version of the gas, we saw what it did in Talbot Cove. We can't take chances, can't let him set it off in Graykettle."

She looked to Jessie, eyes fervent, her jaw clenched.

"Not again," Harmony said.

Jessie stopped her pacing with a touch. Her hand squeezed Harmony's shoulder.

"Not again," Jessie told her. "We go in soft and quiet. If he's there, he could be hiding anywhere in town. We'll have to work the locals for intel. The nice thing about small towns is that everybody notices a new arrival."

"Which means they'll notice you too," Kevin said, hesitant.

"We can use that," Harmony said. "See if Aselia can line up a rental car for us."

"Why a rental?"

"To bolster our cover." Harmony tapped her chin, thinking. "We're tourists on a road trip, exploring the charming New England coastline. Everyone expects tourists to poke around and ask questions."

"Works for me," Jessie said.

Harmony changed the bandage on her arm, buttoned up a clean dress shirt, and reloaded her gun.

The C-130 descended over an airstrip in Maine, plunging from a sky turned stormy gray. It was the gray of a house fire, roiling and touched with the tang of distant smoke. Aselia had their car waiting: a blueberry Toyota hatchback with a Budget sticker on the back bumper, nice and forgettable.

"How are you holding up?" Jessie asked. She and Harmony walked along the edge of the tarmac together.

"My everything hurts and I'll have a new scar for the collection. I'll cope. How about you?"

"I'm feeling pretty murdery at the moment."

"Well, good." Harmony pressed a remote key fob, and the car door squawked. "Let's catch Cranston and you can indulge. And after him, Dominguez is next on the list."

"Oh, he's getting *extra* murdered."

Forty minutes of highway took them to a connecting road, and the connection ferried them along an endless winding ribbon of rocky coastline. White-capped water splashed across jumbles of salt-slick stone, in the slow, ceaseless erosion of time and the ocean. The sea stretched out beyond Harmony's vision, disappearing on a cold, bleak horizon as dark as the skies over the roadway. It started to rain, a relentless drizzle, and the car's wipers tapped out a metronome beat.

As the drive went on, the road got worse. She wove around potholes like craters on an alien moon and passed fallen road signs that lay abandoned in clumps of overgrown crabgrass. America was a big country; there were patches of land that had been forgotten, or forsaken, or just used up and thrown away. This one was all three.

The road died in Graykettle. The village wasn't much more than a tangled cluster of broken streets lined with old Victorian homes, and hand-painted wooden signs dangled from wrought-iron posts over the few stores that had stayed open. Not much in the way of tourist traps. This was a working town, the streets lined with mud-spattered pickups and rusted cargo vans, and miserly fishing boats trawled for hope out on the restless sea. It was a town held together with salt and old rope.

There was only one place in town for an outsider to stay. It was a boardinghouse called the Bird and Barb, and the water-stained slats of a sign out front advertised rooms for forty dollars a night. They parked at the curb.

A woman answered the door when they knocked. She was pinch-faced, with small eyes and a frog's mouth, and she looked at Harmony and Jessie like they were a pair of Martians.

"Ayuh?"

"Hi," Jessie said. "We're here about the rooms."

"Rooms?" she asked.

Jessie pointed back at the sign.

"The rooms to rent?"

"Oh." The woman held her ground, blocking the doorway. "Gotta pay in cash. Money up front."

"We can do that," Jessie said.

"Two rooms?"

She held up a finger. "Just one."

The woman's eyes narrowed with new suspicion. She looked from Jessie to Harmony and back again.

"Room with two beds," she said, more an assertion than a question.

"That'll be fine," Harmony told her.

Jessie handed over a pair of folded twenties and she let them inside. The boardinghouse was as Victorian on the inside as it was on the outside. Grandmotherly, and an antique dresser passed for a check-in desk in the front parlor. The innkeeper picked a brass key from the drawer, shoved it into Jessie's palm, and pointed up the hallway.

"Room two. End of the hall, door on the left. No noise after eight o'clock. You make noise, you're out."

"We'll be quiet as innocent church mice," Jessie said.

"Are we your only tenants?" Harmony asked.

The innkeeper shot her a razor-edged glare. "Why?"

"Just curious," Harmony said. "We're on a road trip, seeing the coast, and it doesn't look like a lot of tourists come this way."

"They don't. Nothin' to see. Y'oughta get yourself out to Rockport or Camden. Those are for tourists."

"We'll add them to the list," Harmony said with a smile.

Back out on the street, they strolled along the sidewalk and Harmony held up her phone to snap pictures, playing tourist. Jessie leaned close.

"You should praise me for showing amazing restraint."

"Thank you for not antagonizing the owner of the only hotel in town," Harmony said.

"You're welcome. Catch how she responded when you asked about other tenants?"

"If Cranston's staying there, we'll find out tonight when we do a room-to-room search."

"After eight," Jessie said.

"Quiet as church mice."

"*Innocent* church mice."

Jessie nodded up ahead, toward the biggest building

in town: a weathered church of gray clapboard, its bell tower pointing a finger of judgment toward the stormy sky. Rotting shingles clung to its angled rooftop like scales on a dead fish.

"Then again," Jessie said, "this is Cranston's childhood stomping grounds. If his family had property here and it never sold, he could be holing up there."

"*Lots* of these houses look empty," Harmony said. She cast her gaze across dark, dusty windows, some cracked, a few boarded over.

As she studied the street, she noticed something else. A motif. It was carved above doorframes or painted with tiny dots of color. Elsewhere, she spotted it engraved into iron railings. It was a cluster of seven points, tight but uneven, with no particular pattern. Where it was painted, six points were marked in silver while the seventh was bronze.

"You noticed it too," Jessie said. "Any idea?"

Harmony shook her head. "It's a symbol, but nothing I've ever seen before."

It even appeared in the stained-glass windows of the town church. A hand-carved sign above the closed front doors read Graykettle First Presbyterian. In one window, the seven points rode above the head of a crucified Christ, like a constellation of stars in the night sky. In the other, it nestled almost hidden at the bottom of a raging sea, created with scallops of blue glass in a dozen shades. A lone black ship sailed atop it, aiming toward a distant sun.

"Harmony," Jessie said.

"I know." She raised her phone to snap some more pictures. It gave her an excuse to linger on the sidewalk and make sure her eyes weren't fooling her.

The artist had hidden tiny figures in the stained-glass sea. Mermaids frolicked between the blue scallops.

"Feel like going to church?" Jessie asked.

They tried the doors. Locked, and a discreet sign only listed hours for services on Sundays and Wednesdays. Along the back of the church, a flimsy padlock held an old pair of storm-cellar doors closed. Jessie shot a glance over her shoulder.

"I can get that open, easy."

A dented pickup cruised by, slower than the speed limit. Harmony shook her head and snapped a random photo.

"Let's keep walking. The locals are definitely noticing us, and I don't think they're friendly. We can come back after it gets dark."

The village hall was the closest thing to a tourist attraction in town. Black and white photographs lined the wooden walls of the lobby, memorializing Graykettle in its prime. Fishermen with grizzled faces and chapped lips hoisted nets, showing off the bounty of the sea. Others lined up to punch a time clock in a cannery, under a Cranston and Sons marquee.

A map of the town drew Harmony's eye. The old cannery was down on the shoreline, alongside the town's docks and a string of boathouses. The map was dated from 1972, no telling if any of it was still right. Her gaze shifted to the waters off the coast. There were islets out there, not far from shore, with a small maze of waterways between them.

Something about the islets gnawed at her. Then she saw it.

"Jessie," she whispered, tapping the map with her

finger. "That symbol we're seeing all over town. The seven points."

Jessie squinted. There were more than seven dots on the map, if you counted the tinier ones flecking the pale ink sea.

"Seven are big enough to stand out from the rest, but the pattern's all wrong."

Harmony held up the flat of her hand, then turned it at a ninety-degree angle.

"Not if you're standing on the shoreline, facing east. From that perspective, if you draw it with east facing 'up,' it's almost a perfect match."

Jessie tilted her head as she looked at the map. Across the room, a stubborn door rattled open. A bald man with a wrinkled scalp poked his head out. He had flat eyes and a broad, thick-lipped mouth that curled in a welcoming smile. *Second local we've met,* Harmony thought, *and the second one that looks like a blood relative of Judah Cranston.*

"New faces," he said. "Don't get too many of those around here, not these days."

"We're just passing through," Jessie said. "We're on a road trip, seeing the coast. Are you the mayor?"

He gave her a folksy chuckle. "Oh, no, ma'am, just your humble public works director. Mayor's on vacation in Tulsa. Must be nice, right? So…what brings you out this way? Graykettle's a little off the beaten path."

"That's where you find the most interesting places." Harmony gestured to the photographs. "I see the name Cranston and Sons in a lot of these photos. Are they still in business?"

"No, ma'am, sad to say. Was a time when Cranston *was* this town. Every man in Graykettle owed their living to that family, one way or another."

"What happened?" she asked.

"Well, as the saying goes, the sea's like a lover. She can be generous, giving...but if you demand too much and push her too far, she'll take it all away." He jerked a thumb over his shoulder. "Commercial fishing exploded a ways up the coast. Big engines and big nets, scooping up everything that swam. Now...well, a few fishermen still get by here, but it used to be a good life, not just gettin' by."

"What happened to the Cranston family?"

She caught the glint of a warning in his eyes. Just the tiniest flicker, telling her to step lightly.

"When business dried up and blew away, family blew away with it." He tapped his chin, thinking. "Last I heard, there weren't many of 'em left. Guess one of them did real good for himself, got himself a college education and started a new business in Miami or some such. Can't say I'd be happy down there, too hot for my tastes—"

The front door blew open and a stringy-haired woman in a calico dress stormed in, hands curled at her sides. "Goddamn it, Jeb, we got a boat out on the water, outsiders from Upton pokin' around again—"

She froze in mid-sentence, staring at Harmony and Jessie with her big, flat eyes.

"Sally," the public works director said, his voice taut. "We got *company*. Tourists, on a road trip."

Her attitude shifted in a heartbeat. She put on a smile and smoothed the front of her dress.

"Well, that's...that's *nice*. We don't get a lot of visitors these days. I'm Sally Ann."

"Sally Ann runs the only diner in town," he said. "Only one we need. Genuine stick-to-your-ribs home cooking."

She clasped her hands in front of her, squeezing them

tight. "You two should swing by later on, treat yourself to some of our world-famous peach cobbler."

"We'll do that," Jessie said.

"Sally was…concerned," he added, "because sometimes boats from out of town get into trouble in our patch of water. There's a tangle of islets off the coast; bootleggers used them during Prohibition, because they're a lot trickier than they look. Lots of jagged rocks just under the surface, entire stretches that are more shallow than they look, it's easy to run into a mess out there. So we try to keep an eye out, and make sure to warn off sailors who don't know any better."

"Ayuh," Sally said. "That's right."

"Ladies, it's been a pleasure, and please feel free to stop in again anytime. Sally Ann? I'd appreciate a brief word in my office."

30.

Jessie took the lead as they circled the back of the village hall. They crouched under windows, shoes crunching on rocky soil and weeds, until they reached the right one. Sally Ann's shout was muffled by the glass.

"—we don't exactly *practice* for this shit, Jeb!"

"And that's why I've been sayin' for years we got to modernize how we do things around here," he shouted back. "We got a perfectly good alarm system. We should be using it every time an outsider shows up, not just for full-on emergencies."

Harmony pressed her back to the moldering clapboard wall. Jessie did the same on the other side of the window. She couldn't hear Sally Ann's reply, too soft to catch on the far side of Jeb's desk.

"You let me worry about the city girls," he told her. "I'm more concerned about boats poking around where they got no business pokin'. You go rally the boys, get out there right quick, and learn their intentions. We can't have any hiccups, not with the doc in town."

* * *

The rocky shoreline curved like a question mark. From the water's edge, salty spray flecking her polished shoes, Harmony could see the faint outlines of the islets in a gray mist. They were lumpen tumors rising up from the depths.

"Think he's holing up out there?" Jessie asked. They

moved side by side, scrambling along the wet rocks as the village faded at their backs.

"Cranston? Either it's him or something he doesn't want us to see. I want to know how many of the locals are in on this. They're hiding him."

"Honestly?" Jessie turned, looking over her shoulder. "From the looks of these people, I think they're all related. Real question is, do they know *why* he's hiding? Could be they think he's just a hometown boy in a jam, and they don't know what he's really up to."

They found what they were looking for at the end of the question mark. A lighthouse stood at the tip, its flame extinguished in the murky sunlight. Peeling eggshell paint clung to sagging bricks, the giant standing planted in a bed of scraggly weeds. An old and tired sentry, starting to lean. Jessie circled around back while Harmony rapped her knuckles on the rough wooden door.

No answer. Jessie popped back into sight and waved her over. She'd found what Harmony hoped would be there: a short, sagging dock and the keeper's boat. It was a drab olive ten-footer built for two, with a small outboard motor and just enough space for the daily catch and a six-pack of beer. A cheap fiberglass fishing pole and a pair of binoculars sat beside the swiveling seats.

Harmony stepped into the boat, the flimsy shell rocking uneasily under her feet, and took the back seat by the motor as Jessie untied it from the dock.

"You know how to drive this thing?" Jessie asked.

"Grew up in Michigan," Harmony said. "I can pilot a motorboat. If this engine actually works and if it's fueled up. Lots of 'ifs' in play here."

Jessie clambered in and Harmony took hold of the

outboard's handle, lowering the propeller into the water behind the boat. She checked the gearshift, set the motor to neutral, a mechanical routine drummed into her from childhood summers on the shore. Then she stopped.

"Damn it. Needs a key."

Jessie looked back at her. "Before you ask, I have no idea how to hotwire something like this."

"Might not have to." Harmony slid off her seat, crouching low, patting along the floor of the boat. "Backwater town, minimal crime, everybody knows everybody…I'm hoping this is the kind of place where people leave their spare keys in the glove compartment."

Her hand slid under her seat, peeled away a yellowed strip of index tape, and produced a tiny, tarnished key.

"Or under their seats."

Jessie rolled her eyes as Harmony slotted the key into the ignition.

"I forgot I was partnered up with a refugee from Mayberry."

Harmony pressed the ignition button. The outboard motor revved to life and the boat crawled along the water, the propeller pushing them away from shore.

"Don't knock it till you try it," Harmony said.

"Oh, I've tried it. I prefer civilization. Places with mass transit, fourteen-dollar cocktails, and a healthy sense of mutual distrust."

A curling fog rolled along the water, and the seamy, clammy mist clung to Harmony's skin as she steered them toward the islets. She kept her eyes open, ears wider as they rode in slow silence. The steady low thrum of the engine was the only sound, but the open sea magnified it, the reverberations filling the empty gulf all around them.

The islets were close now. Pale lichen, sickly-yellow

and white, clung to hills of jagged rock. No gulls squalled in the mists, no crabs scuttled along the shore. This place was dead. A graveyard without graves, or at least without stones to remember the fallen.

"Do you think—"

Jessie held up a hand, sharp, silencing her. She leaned forward in her seat, her senses picking up something Harmony's couldn't. She pointed to the islet just ahead.

"Kill the engine."

The purr of the motor faded away. In its absence, Harmony could hear what Jessie heard: another motor, louder, more powerful, somewhere ahead in the fog.

The nose of their boat bumped up against the islet's shore. Their shoes splashed in icy water as they jumped out, hauling the boat up a few feet onto the rocks so it wouldn't wash away with the tide. Harmony snatched the lighthouse keeper's binoculars from the boat before following Jessie inland, crawling up the rocky hill to get a better vantage point.

They got down on their bellies. Sharp wet spearheads of stone dug into Harmony's skin. Jessie pointed off to the northeast, her cold blue eyes softly glowing, and Harmony aimed her binoculars to follow her fingertip.

A boat was anchored out on the water, and a pair of men in bright orange vests were passing the afternoon with fishing and beer. From the open, empty cooler and the number of Pabst cans crumpled around their feet, the only thing they'd caught was a buzz. Cursive script over the outboard motor gave the boat a name, the *Aquaholic*. Another boat was closing in from behind. It was a long, flat fishing boat with a raised perch and a booth for the pilot. Four men stood out on the deck, and they wore the squat bodies, flat eyes, and frog-like mouths that marked them as Judah Cranston's kin.

Harmony couldn't hear anything but the faint motor of the engine, but she saw one of the fishermen wave and call out as the second boat approached. One of the men on deck did the same, offering a broad smile as they pulled up alongside the smaller craft.

They talked, back and forth, and Cranston's man gestured to the empty beer cooler. The fisherman gave a what-can-you-do shrug. Cranston's man smiled more broadly and pointed to a pair of big red plastic coolers on the deck behind him. He held out his hand, grabbing the man's wrist and hauling him up and on board. His buddy stayed behind and kept fishing, his line drifting in the water. Another townie opened up one of the coolers as they escorted their new friend across the bigger boat's deck.

He reached inside and took out a machete.

The smile never left his face as he punched it through the fisherman's belly and out the other side, torn intestine snaking through the gash in his back. He ripped the blade loose and kicked the twitching body to the deck.

His buddy turned, startled by the sound, and saw what was happening. The fishing pole fell from his hands. It hit the lip of the boat, bounced, and plunged into the foam. He fell to his hands and knees and scrambled on all fours toward the outboard motor, desperate to escape. One of the other townies leaped into the boat, a fillet knife in his clenched fist, and landed on his back with both feet. He yanked the fisherman's head back and sawed wildly at his throat, chewing through meat and cartilage, his hands and the motor drenched in arterial spray, until the blade rasped against bone.

"*Fuck*," Jessie breathed.

"Well, we were wondering if the locals were active conspirators," Harmony said. "There's our answer."

The killers dragged the second corpse up onto the bigger boat's deck, laying the dead bodies out side by side, and talked back and forth for a minute. The killer with the fillet knife started up the outboard engine and drove off alone, taking the dead men's boat back toward shore.

The other boat kept its nose pointed seaward, and it began to glide—slow, cautious, keeping the engines steady as it trawled through the treacherous shallows.

"Now where are you going?" Harmony murmured, keeping the binoculars trained and adjusting the focus.

Her answer, if she had reckoned the symbol seen all over the village correctly, was the special seventh islet. The one marked in a dot of bronze.

Now she saw that it wasn't just an islet. It was a full-fledged island, a mountainous blot of dead and mossy stone, and its outer arms hooked like crab pincers to form a natural cove. Beyond the cove stood the open mouth of a cavern, jagged stalactites drooping down like teeth.

"He told us this was bootlegger territory during Prohibition," Jessie said. "I bet that's where they used to hide the hooch."

"Mm-hmm." Harmony's lenses tightened on the ship's deck as they neared the mouth of the cove. "And what are they hiding there now?"

They were butchering the dead men.

It was fast work. Efficient. Not their first time. The deck was washed in pink froth as they used hacksaws and hammers and chisels, breaking down human remains into anonymous meat. They hammered out teeth, yanked fingernails, stripping off bloody clothing and shoving all the refuse into black plastic garbage sacks. Blades rhythmically sawed into bone and muscle, attacking weak joints and tearing away limbs one chunk at a time.

The boat stopped in the heart of the cove. One of the townies stood at the prow and lifted up a horn. It was made from bone, like a trumpet but too thin, too long, with a bizarre pipe-cleaner bend near its flared tip. He put it to his lips, and even at this distance, Harmony could hear the mournful cry it let out. It was the last bellow of a dying bull, heart pierced by a matador's lance.

He blew it twice more. Then the world went silent.

Another townie sauntered to the back of the boat. He carried one of the dead men's heads, its toothless mouth dangling slack on a shattered jaw, gripping it by the hair and swinging it casually at his side. He pulled his arm back and let it fly, tossing the severed head out over the waves.

The water erupted. It splashed in all directions as a mermaid soared upward, toothy face-petals wide and coppery tail glistening. She caught the head in midair with a single bite, spun with her arms graceful above her head, did a flip, and dove. The beast kicked up another spray of foam as she vanished beneath the surface with her prize.

31.

It was over as soon as it began, one swift moment of frenzied hunger, no evidence left behind but the rippling of the restless brine. It happened so fast Harmony could almost doubt her own eyes. Almost.

There were more shapes under the water. Sleek, sinuous, serpentine as they circled the boat at a safe distance.

"It's a goddamn nest," Jessie whispered. "Now we know where Cranston got his laboratory pet. Are they breeding the things?"

"They're *training* them."

Harmony stared through the binoculars. The boat began to crawl, a slow vanish into the shadows at the maw of the cave. The townie at the back of the deck sluggishly tossed body parts into the foam, leaving an uneven trail of carnage in their wake.

They watched. And waited. Half an hour later, the boat returned, emerging from the cave. The remains of the fishermen were gone. Nothing but the abattoir of the deck and the sticky red hands of the townies offered any proof that they'd ever existed at all. As they emerged, the man up front gave another three slow, long blows of his bone horn. The shapes under the water moved aside, giving the boat a wide berth. One of the townies on the deck delicately cradled a jar in his arms. It was filled with black ichor that took on a rainbow sheen in the fading light, like a spilled oil slick. Harmony remembered that same color on the floor of Cranston's lab, smeared in the wake of the dying mermaid.

"Blood," Harmony said. "They're harvesting blood."

"We need to get into that cave," Jessie said.

"We need one of those trumpet things. Could be some kind of ritual gesture, but I don't think so. It felt more like a trainer's tool. Notice how they didn't come near the boat?"

"And they do tricks." As the boat vanished into the swirling gray mists, Jessie pushed herself to her feet. "It's like SeaWorld but with dismembered bodies and monsters from another dimension. So, basically, just slightly less fun than the real thing. Whether Cranston's hiding in there or not, we are *definitely* shutting this sideshow down."

Harmony winced as she shoved herself up on the rocky plateau. Jagged wet stone left welts on her palms. She looked toward the mainland, where the murky blob of the sun slowly sank beyond the stormy clouds. Night was coming on fast.

"Let's get the boat back before anyone notices it's missing," she said. "Think we should rendezvous with the team?"

Jessie thought about it, then shook her head.

"Let's do some more recon, see if we can scare up one of those trumpets for ourselves. We'll move a lot easier in the dark. Besides, I want to get inside that church with the mermaid windows. Call me crazy, but something tells me these people are *not* actually faithful Presbyterians."

* * *

They took the boat back to the lighthouse, careful to

leave everything just the way they'd found it. One way or another, they were going to be making a return trip.

Graykettle barely acknowledged the night. One or two Victorian-styled streetlamps cast lonely puddles of light here and there, but most of the village's streets were content to nestle in the dark. No lights glowed beyond the cracked windows of its abandoned manses, and the stores closed their shutters at dusk.

Harmony and Jessie kept to the shore, moving fast and quiet, searching for signs of life. There was an old boathouse by the docks, long and tall and sagging on its worm-eaten timbers. They let themselves in through the open barn door. Moonlight filtered in from above, through a ragged gap where the ceiling timbers had caved in. Boats up on trestles and shrouded under tarps stood in long, uneven rows.

Harmony peeked under the tarps as they walked, reading names in jaunty, bubbly fonts. *My Second Mortgage* stood side by side with *Money Pit* and *Have Fish, Need Beer*. These weren't working craft, for professional fishermen. They were pleasure boats. And at the end of the line, hastily dumped under an oilcloth shroud, sat the *Aquaholic*. They hadn't even hosed the deck down yet, and the air under the tarp stank of clotted blood.

Jessie's phone glowed in the dark. "April? Pull something for me, ASAP. I need missing-persons and accidental-death statistics for this entire county and all the outlying areas. Compare them to the statewide average for the last few years."

They waited in the musty silence while April and Kevin crunched the numbers.

"Thought so. Thanks." Jessie hung up and looked to Harmony. "Want to guess?"

"Three times the statewide average?"

"Four. There are an awful lot of 'boating accidents' in the vicinity of this village." Jessie hooked her fingers to make air quotes. "The kind that end with the boat and all hands presumably lost at sea, never to be found."

Harmony gestured to the slumbering boats, rusting away in the dark.

"Think we found them. Want to hit the church?"

Jessie squinted up at the moon, a slice of bone white on the far side of the caved-in roof.

"Let's get a little closer to midnight. I'm starved, and I want to rub shoulders with the locals, see if we can get any intel out of 'em. Let's kill two birds with one stone."

"Some of that world-famous peach cobbler?"

"You read my mind," Jessie said.

* * *

Sally Ann's restaurant was a spot of soft light at the corner of a five-way intersection, close to the heart of town and a stone's throw from the spire of the church. A welcoming chime jangled as Jessie and Harmony stepped through the front door. The place had a country-kitchen vibe, old wooden tables draped in gingham and vintage clocks hanging on the yellow-painted walls. A framed needlepoint by the door read *Not Perfect, Just Blessed*. The air was warm and smelled of huckleberry with a faint chemical tang drifting from a scented candle in a jar by the cashier's station.

They weren't the only customers. Locals hunched over scattered tables in twos and threes, still dressed for work—overalls and dirty hip waders—and dug into their dinners. Mostly chowder, with a few burgers and grilled-cheese sandwiches rounding out the menu. Every face, all walleyes and broad, froggish mouths, turned their way as their conversations died.

Sally Ann was the only welcoming face in the room. She rushed up like she might give them a hug, holding out her arms and a pair of laminated menus. "Look who's here! New friends."

"You tempted us," Jessie said. "Couldn't stay away."

"And I'm darn glad. I don't get to share my cookin' with newcomers all that often. This is when I get to show off. Come here, come here, let's get you settled."

The locals apparently decided there wasn't a problem after all. They looked away, back to their meals and each other, and the bubbling thrum of mingled voices returned. Jessie listened, intent, as Sally Ann led them to a two-seater table midway into the room. From what she could pick up, nobody was discussing nefarious plots, just comparing last week's catch and debating the virtues of competing motor-oil brands. She sat down across from Harmony, and Sally Ann passed out the menus.

"How's the chowder?" Harmony asked.

Sally Ann's nose delicately wrinkled. She dropped her voice.

"Oh, it's fine, honey, but you know...most of my regulars get it because it's the cheapest thing on the menu. Cheapest, but not the best."

"What if we wanted the best?" Jessie said.

Her smile lit up the room. "Darlin', assuming you're not a vegetarian, you have got to try my beef brisket. It's my grandma's recipe, and everybody swears by it."

"I am most definitely not a vegetarian," Jessie said. "And sold."

"Same here," Harmony said.

Jessie glanced to the drink menu. No liquor license. "And I'll have a Moxie with that."

"Diet Coke, please," Harmony added.

Sally Ann took the menus and disappeared into the back, through a swinging door.

They couldn't talk about the case, not in earshot of men who might be in on Judah's plot. They stuck to their cover instead, swapping small talk about their imaginary road trip so far. The two women shared the natural rhythm of dance partners, picking up each other's leads and responding in kind; from the seed of a sidelong comment, they ended up reminiscing about a blown tire on the highway and the pervy tow-truck driver who had come to their rescue. They crafted the details and passed them back and forth as they embellished the tale. If anyone was listening in, they'd come off exactly as they intended: two long-time friends on a slightly ill-planned vacation, touring the coast with harmless, guileless glee.

Jessie's glee silently died as Sally Ann set their plates before them.

"It looks amazing," Jessie said. It really did. Perfectly cooked strips of beef brisket nestled on a gingham-patterned plate, alongside a hefty slice of cornbread. A puddle of baked beans rounded out the meal, flecked with hearty, fatty shavings of fried bacon.

"You just let me know if you need anything at all," Sally Ann said. She retreated to the cashier's station.

Harmony reached for her fork. Jessie was lost for a moment, the room rippling around her as the scent of the meal rose up on a gust of steam.

"Stop," Jessie hissed.

Harmony's eyes flicked up from her plate, uncertain.

"Buy me a second," Jessie whispered. She gave a subtle

nod to Harmony's soda. "Fumble with your straw or something."

Harmony scooped up her straw and wrestled with the paper wrapper, taking her time getting it open, while Jessie quickly sliced off a bite of the brisket. She popped it between her lips and chewed. It was perfect. Juicy, fresh, exploding with flavor on her tongue, cooked in rich spices that didn't overwhelm the natural flavor of the smoked meat.

She leaned close across the table.

"Harmony. Listen to me. Get up and go to the bathroom. Wait five, maybe ten minutes. If anyone's in there, make it sound like you're throwing up. Come back out, tell me you're sick, and we'll pay the check and go."

Harmony's brow furrowed. "What's going on?"

"This isn't beef," Jessie whispered.

Harmony's gaze slowly dropped to the meat on her plate. Jessie saw eyes turned their way in her peripheral vision. Some of the locals were watching them. Some with idiot grins on their wide mouths, others murmuring, giving their buddies elbow jabs.

It was a joke. A sick prank. Harmony looked back to Jessie. "What are you going to do while I'm in there?"

"I'm going to eat my dinner, so we don't look suspicious," Jessie said.

"You can't—"

"We're outnumbered, and if they think for one second that we're onto their game, we're as good as dead." She held her partner's gaze. "You know damn well this isn't the first time I've eaten human flesh. Don't pretend otherwise."

32.

Harmony eased her chair back. She put an unsteady wobble in her step as she headed for the bathroom door, already selling the lie.

For Jessie, forcing herself to eat wasn't the hard part. Pacing herself was. She took another bite of brisket and wanted to grab it off the plate with her bare fingers, cramming it into her mouth as fast as she could, gobbling it all down. The wolf was rolling around in the soil of her heart, tail wagging, legs kicking, enraptured. She closed her eyes and took deep breaths between bites. Her ears picked up a cruel chuckle from the edge of the room. Idiot human laughing at his own joke, thinking he was feeding her something *bad*.

"How's that brisket doing ya?" Sally Ann asked.

Jessie's eyes flicked open. The hostess was standing tableside, wearing a big self-indulgent smile.

Bite her throat out, the wolf whispered, its warm wet muzzle pressed to her ear. *Right here. Imagine the shock on their faces, so much fun. Then the one at the table three feet behind her, to the left, with the gun in his pocket. You can jump that far. Take his eyes, drop him, can't shoot without eyes, he'll keep for later. Then snap his friend's neck—*

Jessie forced a clenched-teeth smile. Her hands clung to the arms of her stiff wooden chair, squeezing, fighting not to tremble.

"I can honestly tell you," Jessie said, "that this is the best meal I've had in years."

Harmony emerged from the bathroom. Still woozy on her feet, looking drawn and pale. She stood beside Sally Ann, not sitting back down.

"I'm sorry," she said to Jessie, "I have to go lie down. I'm…not doing well. It just hit me out of nowhere."

Jessie pushed her chair back. "What's wrong? Are you sick?"

"You know that convenience-store sandwich I grabbed on the road?"

Jessie sighed. "I told you that place looked shady. I'm sorry, Sally Ann, could we grab the check?"

Sally Ann looked distressed as she glanced between Harmony and the pristine plate.

"Aw, honey, you haven't touched a bite."

"I'm sorry, I just—" Harmony rubbed her stomach, frowning. "I don't think I can. Are you open for breakfast?"

"I understand, believe me. Got some bad clams once and that was the end of me for a week. And yes we are, bright and early at seven sharp. I hope I get to see you ladies again before you leave town! Let's settle you up at the counter…"

Jessie paid cash, laid down a generous tip, and hustled Harmony out and into the dark. She could hear the snickering at her back, soft and mocking.

"Boardinghouse," she said.

Harmony walked alongside her, racing to keep up with her brisk stride. "Are you okay?"

She could smell Harmony's blood. So close, like sweet perfume. The wolf whined. It wanted to hurt her. Didn't understand why it couldn't. More meat, just as good as the brisket—no, better, *fresh*, raw and untainted by man's fire—

"No," Jessie said. "I need to get this *out* of me."

The boardinghouse was silent. Their landlady was out or already in bed, and they tiptoed down the hall to their room. Jessie buried herself behind the tiny bathroom door, knelt on a furry lime-green bathmat in front of the toilet, and shoved her fingers down her throat.

After, she washed her hands and spat in the sink until her mouth went dry. Her heart was still thudding, too fast, too wild, and the room turned in lazy drunken circles when she closed her eyes. She stood in the bathroom doorway, silhouetted by the light at her back.

"You okay?" Harmony asked.

"I am now."

"Are you—" Harmony paused. Of course Jessie was sure what the meat was. She took another tack. "Why would they *do* that?"

"From what I could hear? It was a sick joke. They thought it was funny. We've got a bigger problem. I didn't see anyone from the boating party in that room. Different pack of locals."

"They're all in on it," Harmony said. "The mermaids, whatever Cranston is planning with his mutagen—the entire village is in on it."

"One big happy cannibal mermaid death cult," Jessie said.

"And if they're on edge because Cranston is here, even if they might normally let the occasional traveler slip on through, there's no chance they're going to let us out of town alive."

* * *

The landlady was waiting up. She sat in the dark of her

parlor, knitting, frowning. She'd heard noises from the guest bedroom, an ungodly retching that went on and on. Then Sally Ann had called her, wanting to know if they'd come back, and she got the rest of the story about how one of the girls had taken sick at the restaurant.

"Oh, she's sick as a dog all right. She get the house special?"

"No," Sally Ann said, "the other one did. Ate it right up, just about licked her plate clean."

"Waste of good meat."

"Aw, come on, it's a good laugh is what it is. Besides, circle of life and all that. They abed now?"

The landlady listened, cupping a hand to her ear.

"Not a peep. Sound asleep, like as not. You gonna come and collect?"

"I got church," Sally Ann said. "I'll send a few of the boys over, get it done nice and quick."

The boys showed up on her doorstep ten minutes later. She watched the windows for their arrival, so they wouldn't make noise knocking, and they dutifully wiped their galoshes on her front mat. They carried machetes, knives. One had a pitchfork, its tines rusted and warped.

The landlady whispered as she ushered them down the hall. "Don't kill 'em here if you don't have to, understand? Last time I had to throw out my momma's best quilt."

She slid a spare key into the lock. It turned with a whisper and she stepped back, out of the killers' way.

The man in front flung the door open, charged into the room with his machete held high, and staggered to a stop.

The room was empty. On the far side of the twin beds, a night wind gusted in from the open window, making the flowered curtains ruffle in the dark.

"Damn it all to hell," the landlady sighed. "Get on the horn and sound the alarm."

* * *

Harmony and Jessie ran across an empty street, corner to corner, putting distance between them and the hunting party. Their hatchback was the first stop. An easy escape, until Harmony saw the crumpled driver's-side tire. One brisk thrust of a knife had stolen their way out of town.

They weren't alone in the dark, either. There were figures up ahead, dutifully filing through the wide-open doors of the village church, and lights blazed behind the stained-glass windows.

"Sign said they only had services on Wednesday and Sunday," Harmony pointed out.

"I'm thinking they lied." Jessie looked back over her shoulder. "We're too exposed here. We need to get off the street until we figure out our exit strategy."

Harmony pointed the way down an alley. The gap between peeling plaster walls wound a jagged path and suddenly veered hard right, as if the village's layout was intended to steer visitors to the middle of the labyrinth. No escape, with the church squatting at its diseased heart.

"Belly of the beast," Harmony murmured.

"Then let's go down there," Jessie said, "and carve our way out."

There was singing now, as they neared the back of the church. It drifted out through the open doors and up to the stormy skies, too muffled to make out the words. The congregants' voices melded into a slow, melodic but mournful drone, like a band playing their final tune as their sinking ship went down. Jessie crouched in front of the storm-cellar doors. She eyed the padlock, assessing it. Instead of reaching for her picks, she took hold of the padlock, pressed her other palm flush against the wood, and pulled.

One by one, rusted screws popped loose from the warped, flimsy wood until the entire hasp tore free, padlock still firmly attached. She tossed it over her shoulder to land in the overgrown weeds, and Harmony hauled one of the doors back on a groaning hinge.

Steps, rough-hewn and dirty, led down to the flagstone floor of a cellar. Harmony listened, cautious, then chanced lighting up her phone. A focused beam caught motes of dust as it strobed off a garage sale's worth of clutter. An old bicycle with its front tire missing, a vintage lamp, furniture under painters' tarps moldering away in the dark.

A second staircase, this one newer, made of two-by-fours and iron nails, ran up through a narrow alcove at the other end of the clutter. Jessie took point. She eased up the steps one by one, testing her weight on the wood. The door at the top opened onto shadows and more of the musty, mothball odor that clung to the cellar below.

It looked like a small study for the resident clergy, from the humble desk and the seminary diplomas on the walls, but a coat of dust on every bare surface told them this church hadn't had a regular minister for a long time. Harmony checked the name and dates on the diplomas and shot a quick text to April. *Check missing-persons reports for a minister named Liam Ess,* she wrote. *Would have been the resident at Graykettle First Presbyterian, possibly starting sometime around 1982.*

They heard the grim church-choir drone from beyond the door opposite the desk. If Harmony had the layout right in her head, that door would open onto the back end of the church, just behind and to the right of the altar.

The last somber notes faded and died. Then a muffled voice rang out, strident and firm. The thick wooden door stole the meaning of the words, but they recognized the man speaking them.

Judah Cranston had come home to Graykettle. And now he was here to address the congregation.

33.

"From the sea we came," Cranston proclaimed to his flock, "and to the sea we shall return."

He lifted his open hands, spreading them to show the webbing of flesh between his fingers, on a fluttery chorus of whispered "amens." Harmony watched his back as she crouched on one knee, staying low and peering out through a two-inch crack in the doorway. The church was packed. At least a hundred grizzled parishioners squeezed shoulder to shoulder in the weathered wooden pews, all eyes turned to Cranston like he was the second coming of Christ. Cranston's silent and sullen maid stood with him, a couple of steps back, carrying a heavy-looking satchel of cracked leather on one broad shoulder.

"Our grandfathers, and our grandfathers' fathers, sang the songs of the old world. They told us of the Ocean Behind the Ocean and the glories of the endless deep. Our home, our birthright, where we swam and danced in saltwater cathedrals. They taught us the truth: how we were exiled, cast out, stripped of our true forms and forced to live upon the land. Forced to wear a human mask and mingle with the primates of this world."

The murmurs grew. The energy of the room shifted, turning restless, as Cranston took on the fervent tone of an evangelist.

"But we still made our living upon the sea!" He pointed to the stained-glass windows and to the coast beyond.

"We prayed the prayers, we made the sacrifices, hoping that the Old Man Below would return and bring us back home. And what happened? Greed. Gluttony. The depredations of man *spoiled* our fair waters, just as they're spoiling all the oceans. Humanity is a heretic parasite, hell-bent upon its own destruction."

Cranston pushed his shoulders back, chin high, and lowered his hands to his sides.

"I say, if the human race is determined to commit suicide, so be it. But they will not take what remains of this world along with them."

Shouts sounded out from the church doorway, and the jangling of chains.

It was Dominguez. He'd been badly beaten, one eye crusted over with a black bruise, his lip split and chin caked in dried blood, and he was still fighting. Four of the townies hauled him in, manacled, leading him by lengths of chain leashed to his arms.

"Let go of me, you goddamn freaks," he seethed. They yanked him up the aisle, hunters with a trophy.

"Well, well," Cranston said. "Isn't that just what I'm talking about? A man, determined to commit suicide. Bring him up here, gentlemen. Let everybody have a good look."

They forced him toward the altar and shoved him to his knees at Cranston's feet. Dominguez turned his face up, glowering, defiant to the end.

"You could have gone anywhere in the world," Cranston said. "But you followed me here. And for what? A paycheck? A promise of money? What's money going to be worth at the end of days? Bobby might as well have promised you seashells."

"I'm your *friend,*" Dominguez insisted. "I *helped* you."

"And I believed that, at first. Then little things didn't add up. We worked Cooper over for hours, and she still went to her death insisting she didn't know what you were talking about."

"Some people don't break."

"Everybody breaks," Cranston said, his lip curling. "Then the women showed up looking for her."

"More of Bobby's assassins," Dominguez said. "I'm the only person on your side!"

That got a low, rolling chuckle from the congregation.

"They checked out," Cranston said. "I looked into their backgrounds. Ordinary, average Diehl Innovations employees, just like they claimed. Cooper checked out, too. Know who didn't check out? You. No record with the company, no civilian life I could find any trace of. You're a ghost with a Special Forces tattoo and a nice fat payment deposited in your bank account one day before you landed on my doorstep. Oh, and a sniper rifle in your hotel room."

"I can explain all of that—"

Cranston cut him off with a dismissive wave. "I decided to offer you the benefit of the doubt. Gave you the slip back in Tampa, with that ruse in my lab. Figured if you were smart, you'd take a hint and cut your losses. And yet here you are."

"I came to *help*."

Another man had followed the procession. He carried a scoped rifle in one hand, a heavy mottled-olive backpack in the other, and he stepped up to present them to Cranston. Cranston leaned in, pulling back the open flap of the pack. He took out a bar wrapped in black Mylar, about the size of a stick of butter, and held it up to show the congregation.

"I do believe this is what they call 'plastic explosive,'" Cranston said. He cast a dark eye down at Dominguez. "You mean you came here to help Bobby Diehl. By stealing my work and killing me and mine. Well. I can be a generous man. If I'm standing at the head of the church, I'd better be the forgiving type, isn't that right?"

Another wave of "amens" rippled through the musty hall, but this time carried on low laughter and malicious smiles. At Cranston's side, the maid reached into her leather satchel. She produced an anesthesiologist's tool: a clear plastic mask, designed to fit over the nose and mouth, connected to a ribbed bottle.

"I can't let you take my research back to Bobby," Cranston said, "but if you're that desperate to witness the glory of the Clean Slate…I suppose I can part with a single dose."

Dominguez saw it coming. He shook his head wildly as the maid moved in, and one of the townies grabbed him by the hair to hold him still. He scrunched up his nose and mouth as the mask went on, holding his breath, fighting until his face turned purple. Eventually, biology won; he gasped for air, inhaling, just as the maid squeezed the bottle and gave him a mouthful of bilious green gas.

"Witness!" Cranston commanded the congregation as the maid stepped back. "Witness and rejoice. For in portents and dreams, the Old Man Below has delivered unto me a remedy. A remedy that will *save* this blighted planet."

Dominguez's good eye rolled back in his head. He trembled, muscles going taut. His captors stepped back, jerking his chains tight to pull his arms out at his sides.

Then he started to scream.

His flesh molted. It went loose, sagging as if someone

had poured acid on his face and arms, spattering to the floor in soggy handfuls. Beneath, wet red muscle warred with a sudden growth of coppery scales, breaking out like a metallic rash along his cheek and jaw.

Mermaid scales, Harmony thought. She flashed back to the cave, to the fishermen's killers emerging with their dark harvest. *That's why he had one in a tank in his lab. The secret ingredient in Clean Slate. He's using their blood.*

Dominguez's bones crackled and snapped. Spines burst from his back, shredding his clothes and spitting blood that hissed and steamed on the aisle floor. More blossomed along his arms like a porcupine's armor. They erupted from his brow like horns, and as they curved up and outward, they tore away what was left of his human face. It dangled from the protrusions like a rubber mask.

"This is stage one of mutation," Cranston said to his rapt audience. "With the current formulation of Clean Slate, ninety-six percent of test subjects progress all the way to stage four, the final evolution. Not perfect, but it is the cure for an imperfect world."

Dominguez's screams had risen to howls, mixed with apelike animal grunts. His handlers dug their heels in as he thrashed at his chains. His teeth wormed their way out of his gums, one by one, plinking to the sodden church floor as vicious fangs forced themselves from his crackling jaw.

"We stand at the onset of stage two. At this point human consciousness is nearly obliterated, replaced with a primal, insatiable hunger."

The scraps of Dominguez's shirt fell loose as fresh eruptions unspooled from his belly and lower back. Slick intestine twisted, shredding itself, becoming filth-coated tentacles that sniffed at the air with wormlike heads. His pants tore and more fleshy growths spilled out between his legs. Dominguez snapped at his handlers, fighting his chains, desperate to get at them. One nearly slipped off his feet, dragged dangerously close to a mouth now overstuffed with curved and jagged teeth.

"We can't hold him much longer!" one shouted, bracing himself against the edge of a pew and holding the jangling chain tight.

Cranston just nodded to his maid. She produced a .357 pistol from her bag, stepped up behind Dominguez, and shot him in the back of the head.

A gout of black blood splashed along the aisle, sizzling into the red runner and spitting clouds of gray steam. Dominguez sagged in his chains, motionless.

Then he reared up with a roar, jaw snapping hard enough to shatter his own fangs, tentacles whipping the air. She shot him three more times. Each pull of the trigger was a cannon-fire boom that rattled the stained-glass windows. He finally went down. The maid stood over his corpse, watching, waiting.

She shot him in the back one more time, just to be certain.

Cranston waited until the last reverberations of the bullet finished echoing, the sound rising to the church rafters like a solemn prayer.

"The Clean Slate," Cranston said, "is not what our cure does to its victims. It is what its victims will do for us. As we speak, the mass production is underway. Once the final batches are complete, you, my chosen, my family, my fellow believers, will spread out far and wide. To all the tainted cities, to the empires of pollution and greed, to the enclaves of human waste. And you will deliver our blessing."

Jessie cursed under her breath. "We thought he was planning *one* attack. How many people are in there?"

"At least a hundred," Harmony whispered back.

Cranston clasped his hands before him. He bowed his head and spread his fingers, as if contemplating his webbing.

"Humanity has created an engine of consumption. A system that depends upon, that demands, constant hunger. We will teach them hunger. When the globe erupts in chaos on the day of reckoning, when fourth-stage mutations are running rampant, unstoppable, devouring all in their path—we will show them the end result of their reckless behavior." He looked up and gave the congregation a sly smile. "Call it...late-stage capitalism."

Cranston gestured behind him. Pointing to something outside the range of the cracked doorway, but whatever it was, the entire congregation bowed their heads and clasped their hands as one.

"And as the world burns, we will go out to sea. And wait. We will be safe, living off the bounty of the oceans, until the mutations burn themselves out and nothing but dust and bones remains in their wake. The old civilization will be gone and we will return to lead the way, fostering a new age of peaceful enlightenment. We won't make the same mistakes. We will—"

A trilling, chiming chorus silenced him. Every phone in the church went off at once. They buzzed and sang in a confused melody as parishioners tugged them out and stared at the screens. Cranston did the same.

"It appears," he said, "we have some wayward tourists in the village. We can't tolerate any risks, not this close to the day of reckoning. *Go*. Hunt them, find them, and kill them."

The congregation was already on their feet, pouring out the door with murder in their eyes.

34.

Cranston watched the mob go. He stood over Dominguez's mutilated corpse and put his hands on his hips.

"We'll have this cleaned up. Don't let anyone eat it. Bad meat."

The maid's head bobbed. She stared at him, unblinking, and pointed to the rifle and backpack. "And…that?"

"Take the backpack out to the lighthouse, lock it up tight, and we'll figure out a long-term solution later. Right now I just don't want it anywhere near the refinery."

She gathered up the dead man's things and headed out into the night.

Cranston stood alone in the empty church, just him and his victim. He turned, facing the thing Harmony couldn't see through the cracked doorway, and lowered himself to one knee. His head bowed in reverence.

"Thy will be done," he whispered.

In the darkness, Jessie pulled back her blazer. She flashed her gun at Harmony with a question in her eyes.

It would be easy. One bullet would buy vengeance for Agent Cooper. Harmony saw the thread of if-then-elses in her mind's eye, combinations of possibilities stretching into the distance. Cranston was a true believer, and he meant to see his insane mission through to the end. What if he had rigged a fail-safe? Some sort of system to ensure his "day of reckoning" happened with or without him?

"We can't," Harmony breathed. "Not until we find out where he's keeping the Clean Slate and if he's made any backups of the formula."

Cranston rose, turned, and strolled from the church. They could hear shouts in the darkness outside, the villagers running riot through the streets, searching for them. They waited in the dark, motionless.

Harmony needed to see what had captured Cranston's reverence. She slowly pushed the door wider and crept out into the light.

An effigy ruled over the congregation. A mummified man nailed to a cross, his preserved skin the texture and color of beef jerky. He had been decapitated. In the place of his head, someone had mounted the head of a sea bass, its flat wide eyes staring out in silent, eternal shock.

In one hand, the mummy clutched a black book, his broken fingers lashed with twine around the leather cover. In the other, the dead man held a trumpet of bone, identical to the one the townies had used to win safe passage into the mermaids' grotto.

The mermaids were a relatively small threat compared to Cranston's mad ambitions, but they still had to be dealt with. Especially if only the villagers' training was keeping them confined to that cove. If they slipped out and started breeding in the ocean…

No choice. Harmony braced herself, slinking closer to the effigy. Ten feet, nine, almost there—

"They're here!" shouted a man at the church doors, bellowing at the top of his lungs. "I see one!"

She threw herself down as a gunshot split the wooden wall. Then she sprinted toward the darkened doorway, more bullets tracing her path. She and Jessie broke for the cellar stairs. They pounded down the steps, picked their way across the clutter, and emerged through the storm doors on the opposite side.

A villager ran up, screaming, swinging a machete. Jessie's fist was a blur. She punched him in the throat and as he fell back, choking, she ripped the blade from his hand. She flipped it in her hand and reversed her grip; then she drove it like a spear into his stomach. Another villager rounded the back of the church and charged with his pitchfork held high. Harmony's pistol cleared its holster as she dropped under the thrusting tines. She pulled the trigger twice and both rounds punched through the lunatic's chin, blasting out the top of his skull.

The gunshots were as good as a church bell, drawing the faithful to the killing grounds. No time to catch their breaths. Harmony and Jessie ran, angling for the shoreline, feet pounding as they sprinted between dots of dangerous lamplight along a lonely, darkened street. Even the moon was their enemy now; they needed absolute darkness to survive.

They almost found it through the open barn doors of the old boathouse. The moon still chased them, silver light streaming down through the rupture in the sagging roof, but the straw-littered floor muffled their footsteps. Shouts split the night air, the mob on the hunt, and they heard a pair of distant gunshots as the villagers fired at phantoms.

Jessie grabbed Harmony's hand and yanked her between a pair of tarp-shrouded boats. Then down to the ground, as her heightened senses picked up a threat. They squirmed under one of the propped-up boats, Harmony's face dangerously close to its sleeping propeller, and waited.

Five men, their hands bristling with shotguns and knives, moved in a tight pack down the center aisle of the boathouse. A halogen lantern cast a slow and dazzling white beam across the rusting vessels.

"Jeb says he saw 'em over on Clamoth Street," one insisted.

"Jeb's half-blind," the man with the lantern growled. "I saw 'em run this way, swear I did."

Harmony held her breath, lying on her belly with her gun braced in her hands.

They could wait until they passed and ambush them from behind, but the noise would bring a hundred more hunters down on their heads. Jessie read her mind. Next to Harmony in the dark, she held up one hand. *Wait.*

The lantern beam crawled in their direction.

"We're wasting our time—"

The lantern jerked in the leader's irritated hand. Dipping, for one stomach-clenching moment, a few feet from Harmony's and Jessie's faces.

"You wanna kiss Jeb's ass so bad, go on then, go do it in person. We'll see who comes back empty-handed."

"Both of you, knock it off," said a third villager. "Remember why we're here."

The beam moved on. The pack walked past them, still hunting.

"I know they came through here," the man with the lantern said.

"Well, they're gone now. Let's circle back around."

Harmony and Jessie waited, frozen, until the last of the footsteps faded. Then they squirmed out from under the boat, got back on their feet, and left by the other doorway.

The sea was angry tonight. The rocks along the shore were flecked with white-spittle foam, waves slapping down like open hands as the water roared. Harmony's foot slipped on a wet clump of stone and she barely caught herself. Jessie scrambled along at her side, making it look effortless. The lighthouse up ahead was hot. Its beam carved a burning arc across the night sky, swinging its eye from the ocean to the village and back again in an endless revolution.

The keeper's boat was right where they'd left it. Behind them, not far off, more flashlights and lantern beams glowed and shook, hounding their trail. All they had to do was sail off, but Harmony's footsteps faltered. She thought about Dominguez and his lethal cargo.

Jessie looked from her to the lighthouse door. No words necessary.

No time for the sound suppressors. A search party was coming this way, and in less than two minutes an angry mob would be right on top of them. They took up positions on the low stone stoop. Jessie rapped on the door. Then again.

"All right, all right," groused a man's raspy voice on the other side. "I'm comi—"

The second he turned the knob, Jessie hit the door with a full-force kick. The door slammed back and took him with it, knocking him to the floor. She was first in, breaking right, with Harmony weaving left on her heels. Cranston's maid was already gone. Two of the locals were by the foot of the circular stairs, poking through Dominguez's backpack, while another was peering up through his rifle's sight like it was a telescope.

Jessie's heel slammed down on the fallen doorman's skull as she and Harmony opened fire. One of the men by the pack jerked backward, a stream of bullets punching into his chest. The other dropped like a rock as a precision shot tore his throat out. The rifleman was struggling to take aim with Dominguez's gun, fumbling for the safety. Harmony had already squared her sights. One bullet snapped his head back and a second sent shrapnel tearing through his heart. She raced across the room and scooped up the backpack while Jessie delivered a kill shot to the man under her foot.

They'd kicked the hornet's nest. The lights were stampeding this way, furious shouts echoing over the roar of the waves, calling the entire village to finish the hunt. Harmony and Jessie ran to the dock. Jessie untied the keeper's boat while Harmony reached under the back seat. A moment of terror hit her when her fingers touched nothing but wet vinyl. Then she found the strip of tape and ripped the spare key loose. Her hands worked their mechanical mantra—*propeller down, throttle neutral, turn key*—and pressed the ignition.

The engine revved to life and the boat skimmed on a rough wave, rising up and dropping down hard. Harmony slammed the propeller left, spinning them around. Gunshots whistled through the air. Bullets punched the foam all around them, another crackling as it dug a rent in the aluminum hull.

Then they were flying, down the coast and out to sea, the murderous village fading into the distance until not even the beam of the lighthouse could chase them down.

* * *

It was dawn when they made it back to the airstrip. Harmony and Jessie walked up the cargo ramp side by side, bone-tired and barely standing, but momentum carried them on. Jessie had called ahead, waking April up at the motel, and she'd gathered the team.

"Cranston's getting his doomsday weapon prepped and ready," Jessie said, "and after last night, he knows the clock is ticking."

Harmony took a bleary-eyed glance at her phone, checking the time.

"We mobilize at dusk," Harmony said. "In one night, we have to clear the board. Cranston, his bioweapon, his cult, and the monsters they've been keeping offshore. All of it. Which means we have…just around fourteen hours to make a plan, get the resources we need, and prepare to execute."

Jessie put her hand on Harmony's shoulder.

"Somebody put on a pot of coffee. It's going to be one hell of a long day."

35.

The belly of the plane became a tempest as everyone broke off in their own directions, tasked and focused with no time to lose. Harmony stood with April at one of the terminals, reading the fruits of her research on a screen.

"As for your wayward minister," April was saying, "I checked the records. Liam Ess was sent to Graykettle First Presbyterian in 1983. No missing-persons report was filed."

"He's not missing?"

"He wasn't *reported* missing. As far as anyone knows, he's doing just fine in his happy village home."

"But," Harmony said.

April clicked her mouse and highlighted a chunk of a fuzzy bank statement.

"But he hasn't filed income taxes since 1985. Or made a cash deposit that I can find, or paid a utility bill, or anything else to prove he didn't vanish off the face of the earth."

"A minister doesn't disappear from the only church in a small town without anybody noticing."

"Nor does the mayor, or the entire city council," April said. "And yet that's exactly what they did, right around the same time."

Harmony clasped her hands behind her back and

stared up at the screen. Aselia brushed past her, phone to her ear, her other hand clenched into an irritated fist.

"—so shake off the hangover, kick her ass out of bed, and get yours *over* here, Wexler. I'm a cash customer. Show some respect. Got a pen? Okay, first, I need a boat. Yes, I said a *boat*—"

"The 'public works director' told us the mayor was on vacation," Harmony said to April. "It was a coup. A very quiet coup."

"Cranston's people?"

Harmony kept her focus on the screens. The names, the positions, the dates, all coming together to draw a bigger picture.

"How do you keep a remote village a secret from the rest of the world? You can't, not perfectly—the number of 'missing persons' in the area is proof of that—but it helps if you can stop time. Cranston's cult took over the place. They killed outsiders, like the minister, and anyone who might want to change and modernize things, like the mayor."

"Putting the village in stasis," April said. "No residents but the cult itself, and I expect if anyone did try to move in from out of town, they'd land on the dinner menu within a week. What about the claims Cranston made at the church? This business about their ancestors and this 'Old Man Below'?"

Harmony tapped the knot of her necktie. She felt the cool hard metal of the Greek coin under her collar.

"You know my family coin? It gets weird in the presence of things from other worlds. The mermaid set it off. Cranston and his people? Nothing. I think they're as human as you and me, and Cranston's the only one who even knows any magic."

"But *they* believe it," April said.

"Right. Just a cult, but Jim Jones and the Peoples Temple was just a cult. Aum Shinrikyo was just a cult, and they unleashed sarin gas in the Tokyo Metro. You don't need magic for mass casualties; you just need highly motivated believers who aren't afraid to die. And if you can convince them that they've been persecuted, that they're good and the world is evil, so much the better."

A few feet to their left, Jessie leaned in with both hands pressed flat to the console, craning her neck to study a travel map and trace a blue line from Maryland to Maine. She turned a knob on her headset, adjusting the volume.

"No, looks like you've got a twelve-hour drive from Bethesda, so round up your team, load the SUVs, and run a convoy. That's twelve hours in a civilian ride, so hit the sirens and lights and you can shave at least a couple off. Beach Cell is flying in from Texas; they were on a recon job before we pulled them off mission. They're not carrying weapons, so I need you to crack the storage vault and bring gear for both teams. Body armor, too. Everybody is wearing a vest, no arguments."

Harmony took a step back. Her fingertip tapped her pursed lips.

"Here's our biggest unknown. Somewhere in Graykettle, Cranston is running a chemical-weapons refinery. Taking him down isn't enough: we need to erase his formula and destroy every last trace of Clean Slate. If just *one* of his followers escapes the village with a supply of that gas and a working delivery system, the casualties could be..." Harmony shook her head. "We can't let that happen."

"On it, boss." Kevin hustled over, fingers dancing on a tablet as he flicked satellite maps left and right, quarantining them to the corners of the screen. "I'm tearing the place apart, digitally speaking. Obviously, on-the-ground data is hard to come by, so I'm cross-referencing aerial imagery, shipping records, anything I can find with Graykettle's name on it. If I scrape together enough bits and pieces of stray data, with any luck it'll paint a picture for us."

"Luck won't cut it. Not today. Think big. He talked about all the attacks happening on a 'day of reckoning.' That means Cranston needs a lab large enough to process enough Clean Slate for a hundred budding terrorists."

"What about underground?" he asked. "Didn't bootleggers use those islets during Prohibition? Maybe they've got tunnels in town, too."

April swiveled her chair around. "Kevin, continue sifting through the modern records. I'll run background on the village's past lives, and we'll see if anything overlaps."

Jessie was at Harmony's elbow, carrying two mugs of steaming black coffee. She pressed one into Harmony's hand.

"Here. Fuel up."

"Cheers," Harmony said.

They clinked mugs. The coffee tasted burnt, bitter and hard at the edges, kicking her brain to keep it awake.

"I went through Dominguez's pack," Jessie told her. "Those butter sticks? Semtex. Asshole brought enough with him to level the entire village."

"Which is probably exactly what Bobby ordered him to do," Harmony said. "Crazy recognizes crazy. He didn't want Cranston or his cult coming after him down the line."

"It's not a bad plan. We could use those explosives ourselves. There's just one hitch."

Jessie held up a tiny gadget, about as big around as her thumbnail. It had two short copper plugs on one side and a nest of tangled circuitry and the miniature dome of a turned-off light on the other.

"He didn't bring conventional det cord. Near as I can tell, these are remote detonators, and I have no idea how they're triggered."

Kevin held out his hand as he passed by. "May I?"

She dropped it into his palm. April pulled her headphones on, responding to a crackle of static from her screen. She paused, listening, then looked over her shoulder. "Harmony? Dr. Joy is reporting in from the safe house."

"Patch her in," Harmony said.

One of the wall screens flickered to life. A tripod-mounted camera aimed its lens at the heart of a makeshift morgue, where the dead mermaid lay upon a stainless-steel gurney. Neptune wore a plastic visor, spattered with droplets of gore, and her scrubs and long latex gloves were soaked with dark stains. She gave a cheery wave to the camera.

"Harmony, hey. So, I dug in like you wanted—I mean literally—and I don't have a lot to share yet, and I don't know if it's useful at all—"

"Anything you can tell us," Harmony said. "We appreciate it."

"Well, okay. Turns out, insofar as I can determine, mermaids are mammals."

"What does that tell us?" Harmony asked.

"They look like the classical legends of mermaids—at least until they shed their facial camouflage—so I thought at first that they might reproduce by parthenogenesis. In other words, asexually."

"A race of nothing but mermaids."

"Exactly," Neptune said. "But I was wrong. There's an ovarian system present, a womb...mermaids give live birth. And if they can be impregnated, well..."

"Mermans," Jessie said. "Mermen?"

"Can we infer anything about the males?" Harmony asked. She decided not to mention the colony they'd found just off the coast.

"This is where we go into pure speculation. It could be that the species is like humankind, tending toward a one-to-one breeding ratio. But these structures I'm studying—" Neptune frowned at the open corpse, moving organs aside with a long-tipped steel probe. "I'm having flashbacks to my zoology classes."

"What are you seeing?"

Neptune looked up to the camera. "Cows. It reminds me of a cow. Now, when it comes to cattle, a single bull can impregnate up to fifty cows in a single season of estrus. Accordingly, you see fewer bull births, a much smaller ratio in an average herd."

It was good data. And that was all it was. Nothing they could use for the challenge at hand, nothing to help them survive tonight. All the same, she wanted to encourage Neptune as much as she could.

"This is really helpful," Harmony told her. "Please, keep going, find out anything you can."

"Just...one thing?" Neptune added. "Probably goes without saying, but if that analogy is right, and if it holds, well...bulls are a lot stronger and meaner than cows. And if you mess with a bull's harem, you'd better be ready for the fallout. Be careful out there, okay?"

* * *

Kevin was hunched over his console. One of the remote detonators had sacrificed its life for science, disassembled into tiny squiggly bits under a standing magnifying glass. Another sat nestled in a bright blue circuit board.

"This is an Arduino board," Kevin explained. "It's great for prototyping, and you can do some crazy-cool robotics stuff with 'em. Anyway, I'm using this to help test my theory."

"Theory being?" Harmony asked.

"I think Bobby set his boy up with a custom phone app. Hit the button, it transmits a detonation signal—encrypted with a hashed password, for safety. I think I can reverse-engineer these things, figure out what the transmission code was, and cobble together a duplicate app so you can use the explosives yourselves."

"You think," Jessie asked, "or you know?"

"I think. Give me two hours with no interruptions, and then I'll know."

* * *

Aselia's local contact showed up a little after one in the afternoon, driving a mud-spattered Bronco and hauling a rickety boat trailer that jolted in the rocky grass alongside the airstrip. Wexler looked like he'd been marooned in the seventies, smoothing down his untucked bowling shirt as he stepped down from the cab. He had a blond bristle-brush mustache, and his chunky white oversized sunglasses would have made Elton John envious.

"This was not easy," were the first words out of his mouth as he pointed to his cargo. A night-black inflatable boat was lashed to the trailer, a sleek two-seater with a halogen light mounted on the prow and an outboard motor.

"Not like I was asking for heavy firepower," Aselia told him.

"I brought that too. That I have on hand. Finding a Zodiac Bayrunner first thing in the morning is a taller order."

"Not exactly black-market merchandise," Aselia said. Jessie and Harmony walked down the *Imperator*'s cargo ramp to join them behind the plane.

He gave her a pained look. "'Legal' doesn't necessarily mean 'easy to get on short notice.' Anyway, what you got here is a four-twenty model."

Jessie arched an eyebrow. "Four-twenty?"

Wexler shrugged. "Hey, no idea why they chose that model number. I'm only saying that it's a very nimble, very quiet boat that's good for running shallow waters and slipping around certain authorities who might want to question you or look at your potentially shady cargo. She's inflatable, aluminum frame, fifty-horsepower engine with a twelve-and-a-half-gallon tank."

"Which you fueled up on the way here, right?" Aselia asked.

"Even got a receipt, so you can reimburse me."

He waggled a tattered printer ticket at her. She responded with a flash of green, but she kept her cash tight in hand until she saw the rest of the goods.

Wexler hauled a heavy duffel bag from the passenger side of the Bronco and laid it down on the edge of the tarmac. They clustered around as he pulled back the zipper and showed them the goods. Two onyx shotguns, with pistol grips and their modular stocks removed to shorten them down.

"If you're hunting big game, I got you covered. The Benelli M3. Removable stock gives you more maneuverability in tight quarters."

He hefted one of the shotguns, showing it off, keeping the barrel pointed to the asphalt.

"Lock the pump"—he shoved it forward, demonstrating— "and now it's in autoloader mode. Under-barrel magazine holds eight rounds of very nasty buckshot, and you can fire almost as fast as you can pull the trigger. Careful, though, recoil's a bitch. Just because you can doesn't mean you should, right?"

"But it's nice to have the option," Jessie said.

* * *

By two thirty in the afternoon, Kevin's little electronics lab at the console's edge had blossomed. Now a host of detonator plugs clustered around the circuit board, and he'd marked the tips of their tiny lights with dots of paint in three shades; some were green, some yellow, and the last few stragglers were red. He waved Harmony and Jessie over as he fiddled with his phone.

"Bobby's a technical genius, but he didn't work too hard on the safety protocols for the detonation code," Kevin said. "I cracked the transmission method and the password."

"He was probably pressed for time, after what went down in Tampa," Jessie said. "And now that Dominguez reported in, he knows we're on his trail. What do you have for us?"

Kevin showed them his screen. It was a no-frills, rush-coded app, no art or style, just static colored boxes and big command buttons. He gestured to his testing board, then tapped the *One* icon on his phone. A pop-up window demanded a confirmation tap.

The tiny dome light on the detonator flashed bright white.

"Electrical impulse triggered," Kevin said. "If that was a brick of Semtex, we'd all be dead right now."

"That's reassuring," Jessie said.

"It gets better. Figured you might need to stagger your booms, so I reconfigured the detonators." He pointed to the blobs of paint. "One, two, three is green, yellow, red. You can set them all off at once or just the particular batch of detonators you want."

"And you're certain they'll work?" Harmony asked.

"Ninety percent certain. I need to keep debugging."

Jessie crossed her arms.

"Be sure," she told him. "We're going to be ass-deep in mermaids, which is nowhere near as much fun as old-world sailors thought it would be. Less naked frolicking, more human-devouring frenzy. If this doesn't work, we aren't coming back."

"By the time you leave, it'll be perfect. Just one thing: reach is a problem on these transmitters, especially out on the water. You're going to need to be close when you set it off."

"How close?" Harmony asked.

"You might lose some eyebrow hairs. I'm going to try to code a viable-range detector, but it's got to come second to making sure the trigger code works perfectly each and every time. Let me keep working on it. I'll see what I can do."

* * *

A convoy of black SUVs rolled in with the turn of the mist-shrouded sun. Their cargo was men in dark suits and dark glasses, lugging heavy duffel bags and jet-black ballistic crates. Jessie met them down on the tarmac. A two-by-two stack of rough-sided plastic crates formed a makeshift table, and she spread out a map for the briefing. A clammy wind ruffled the map, corners held down with loaded pistol magazines.

"Beach Cell is going to be stationed here," she said, short-cropped fingernail rapping a stretch of road north of town. "Redbird, your team takes up position here on the southern road. Only other easy way out, besides the water."

Redbird's new cell leader was Roberts, a thick-jawed vet with hard eyes behind his dark-tinted Aviators. He gestured to the right half of the map, all inky blue nothing dotted with tangled islets.

"And the water?"

"We'll handle that. Agent Black and I are the advance team; taking out their docks is part of the infiltration plan. We're going in first, and we're going in quiet until we have to get loud. When we get loud, you'll know about it. This is important: no matter what you see, no matter what you hear, you hold your positions. Judah Cranston is brewing up a metric fuck-ton of doomsday gas in his secret lab, and if things go sideways, I want you and your people outside the blast zone. Your job is to intercept any runners if Cranston's cult tries to flee town."

"Rules of engagement?"

"We have to assume that everyone in Graykettle is a member of the cult. They've done a good job of killing and eating anyone who wasn't on board with Cranston's agenda. Also, at least a hundred of them have signed up to play suicide bomber for the cause, so conduct yourselves accordingly. If they try to surrender, and if it's safe in your judgment, take them into custody. Otherwise, exercise lethal force. Once Cranston and his bioweapon have been neutralized, I'll report in with further instructions."

Roberts nodded, sharp. "And if you don't report in?"

"Then presume that Agent Black and I are captured or dead," Jessie said, "and Dr. Cassidy is the acting commander of Vigilant Lock. She'll call the shots from that point on. Don't try to rescue us. Stopping Clean Slate is your one and *only* priority, and if that means turning that entire village to glass with us in it, you do it."

He snapped a salute. "Understood."

* * *

While Jessie briefed the field teams, Harmony studied the fruits of April's research. The video screens above the command console were an antiquarian's treasure trove of faded maps and sepia-toned photographs.

"Turns out Graykettle was quite the pot of sordid revelry in the nineteen twenties," April said. "Not only did bootleggers use those islets for smuggling purposes, but they also had a solid foothold in the village—which, back before the waters went sour from overfishing, was a prosperous little place. Plenty of wealthy fishermen with money to burn and thirsts to quench."

She gestured to one of the sepia photographs. A beaming, dapper man with a pocket watch dangling from his trim two-button vest stood by an oddly familiar doorway.

"Geary Chandler, acquaintance of the Boston mob, opened a thriving speakeasy near the heart of town. Despite raids by the local authorities, and even the FBI at one point, not a drop of liquor was ever found. Chandler's biographer says he bragged, in his later days, about digging out a honeycomb of tunnels beneath the streets."

"If they're still there," Harmony mused, "we could use them to move around without being seen. Of course, the cult could be using those same tunnels. Where was the speakeasy?"

Two maps sat side by side on one screen, one old and one vintage. April dragged them together with a slide of her mouse and highlighted one building in fluorescent green.

"We've been there," Harmony said. "That's Sally Ann's restaurant."

"Might be worth taking a peek downstairs. But more importantly, I took Kevin's conglomeration of data points and compared them to the historical record, trying to narrow down a likely location for Cranston's lab. There are only a few buildings in town large enough to hold an operation like that, and you've been inside most of them. One standout is the old cannery, which used to rely on the fishing fleet—when there was a fleet. It's fallen into disuse, and it's stocked with industrial-size tanks, making it perfect for repurposing. There's one problem."

She brought up a satellite view of the village. Even with the grainy, black-and-white resolution, Harmony spotted what she meant.

"There's no roof."

"Apparently caved in from a storm, and no one's bothered to repair it. Not a good spot for clandestine activity. Now here's the interesting thing: Kevin found a host of shipping records going back three or four years. Construction equipment, heavy machinery, all of it delivered to the cannery's address."

Harmony pointed to the satellite-eye view. The gaping roof, the shell of the old cannery, and dry, rusted tanks. "But there's nothing there."

"Nothing we can see. Those old bootlegger tunnels, plus the proximity of the docks, suggest old Geary Chandler kept his secret liquor warehouse somewhere in the vicinity. A warehouse that would require a sizable underground construction, one that could easily be converted into a hidden laboratory. You want to look *under* the cannery."

Harmony almost jumped as Jessie's fingers curled on her shoulder.

"Sorry," Harmony said. "Nerves."

"More like you're exhausted. I already took a catnap. Your turn." Jessie pointed to the long row of jump seats on the far side of the plane. "We've got a couple of hours before go time. Get some shut-eye."

"I don't need sleep. I can keep working."

"Hey," Jessie said. She tugged Harmony's shoulder, turning her around. "I need my partner at her best tonight. And you know I hate pulling rank, but I'm making an exception. Go. Rest. That's an order."

* * *

Stretched out on the stiff, springy seats, Harmony chased sleep. It danced just ahead of her fingertips, out of reach, leading her though a dark abyss. And on the edges of the abyss, the first icy crackling of dark hungers, beginning their slow and relentless creep across the borders of her mind.

A gentle hand shook her arm. Her eyes flickered open. Jessie crouched over her. Behind her, the loading bay ramp was down, and the sky beyond was cold and dark. She'd slept through the sunset.

"Ready to kick some ass?" Jessie asked.

"Ready," Harmony said. Her cheeks tightened as she

pushed herself up, a stab of muscle pain shooting down her arm.

"Figured we'd go save the world, then maybe stop for ice cream on the way back," Jessie said. "I mean, I don't have anything better to do tonight. How about you?"

Everyone, Harmony had learned, wore their own style of mask. Hers was cold and hard, a shield against the world. She'd been confused by her partner's casual, flippant attitude when they started working together, until she realized that Jessie had a mask of her own. Her own style of coping with the evils they faced, like a cop cracking jokes at a murder scene. She could work with that.

"If we actually manage to survive this," Harmony told her, "the ice cream is on me."

36.

The Zodiac cut across the foam-flecked waves, the sea turned to choppy onyx. Bottomless and vast, with mist clinging to the horizon like the shreds of a mourner's funeral gown. The eye of Graykettle's lighthouse turned, rhythmic, sending slow slices of light across the water. They rode in the shadows between, turning hard along the coast, closing in on the target.

They'd reloaded their pistols, sound suppressors on, HUSH rounds in the magazines for added stealth. The loud option, their Benelli shotguns, dangled from nylon straps on their shoulders. The rest of their mission gear, the Semtex blocks and color-coded detonators, had been divvied up between a pair of slim bike-messenger backpacks. As they rode in, the perimeter teams were getting in place out on the roads, but their only job was catching the stragglers and stopping anyone from fleeing with the Clean Slate formula.

The rest was on Harmony and Jessie. They had to get it all. The bioweapon, the records of how it was made, and the mind that created it.

They docked at the lighthouse, dragging the Zodiac up onto the wet rocks, and made their way inland. Fast, low, silent, navigating the streets by memory and following the route they'd agreed upon. A winding, circular path that avoided the occasional streetlamps and clung to the alleys. A few times they had to freeze, pressing their backs to crumbling, damp walls and holding their breaths as villagers ambled past, but it didn't look like anyone was hunting for outsiders tonight. As long as they managed to keep things quiet, it would hopefully stay that way.

They reached Sally Ann's restaurant right on time. Closing time. Sally Ann was coming out the back, turned toward the door and fumbling with a heavy ring of keys. The muzzle of a sound suppressor pressed to her temple, and Jessie's hand clamped down over her mouth.

"You scream, you die. You fight me, you die. You do anything I don't explicitly tell you to do, you die. Nod if you understand me."

Her head wriggled up and down, as much as Jessie's hand allowed it.

"Good," Jessie said. "Let's go inside, have us a little chat."

They marched her back into the restaurant. Harmony found a stairwell behind the kitchen, leading to a cluttered cellar and the steel slab of a meat-locker door. Shelves of canned goods lined the musty shadows. From the rancid smell in the air, half of them—mostly open and shrouded with sheets of plastic wrap—were well past their prime. Jessie shoved Sally Ann to her knees and strolled in a slow circle, keeping her gun trained on her.

"Damn it all to hell," Sally Ann seethed. "They said you wouldn't dare come back around, not after the welcoming party you got last night. I knew better. I told them I knew better."

"Understand this," Harmony told her. "You are only valuable to us as a source of information. We're going to ask you questions. Some of those questions we already know the answers to. You won't know which ones, so it's a good idea to answer them all truthfully."

"I got nothing to say to you, heretic."

Jessie moved in, one brisk step, and pressed her muzzle between Sally Ann's eyes hard enough to force the woman's head back.

"Fine. Then you're useless. Harmony? Any objections?"

There's a difference between a believer and a true zealot, someone willing to die for their cause without hesitation. In Sally Ann's eyes, in the flicker of terror that betrayed her, Harmony knew what she was before she even opened her mouth.

"Wait," Sally Ann stammered. Her gaze flicked to Harmony, latching on to the woman who could grant a stay of execution. "What do you want to know?"

"The old bootlegger tunnels. We know that Cranston's lab is under the old cannery. We also know those tunnels honeycomb the entire village. How do we get there from here?"

In reality, Harmony didn't know any of those things, not for certain. Old interrogation trick: go where the evidence points and speak with authority. Nine times out of ten, if you were wrong, human nature would push the subject into babbling out the right answer. If you were right, they'd confirm it without ever realizing they were helping you.

"You can't. Not from here." The muzzle of Jessie's gun dug in deeper, and Sally Ann's hands fluttered at her sides, frantic. "You can't, I swear it! Swear it on the water and all beneath! You could back in the day. There was a cave-in, in the early nineties, cut the whole tunnel system in half. We were afraid trying to dig it out would make it worse, so we just let it be."

"Can you get to the church basement from here?" Harmony asked.

Sally Ann hesitated, but only for the space of a breath, before she pointed a trembling finger.

"Second shelf on the left, the empty one."

Jessie covered the prisoner while Harmony studied the shelf. She grabbed hold of the metal and strained, hauling it back. Inch by inch, a chunk of painted drywall peeled away with it. Beyond was the yawning, jagged mouth of a rough-hewn tunnel, a cord of dirty intestine winding through the bowels of the village. Musty, stale air rustled from the darkness.

"Good news," Harmony said. "Your odds of surviving this have just improved considerably. Let's keep it going. If we can't get there through the tunnels, how do we get into Cranston's lab?"

Sally Ann bit her bottom lip.

"I won't be doing you any favors telling you that," she said. "Think he's down there all by his lonesome? He ain't. You'll die down there."

"We'll take our chances," Jessie said.

"The old cannery. There's a storage tank still standing. Empty. Hatch on the side is fake, it's not really welded shut, and there's a ladder down like a silo. Door's at the bottom. And there's a small army of local boys with guns, standing right on the other side to greet anybody coming through. They've been on standby since last night, working in shifts, making sure nobody interrupts the doctor while he finishes his work. Second you open that door, they'll turn you into Swiss cheese."

"Like I said," Jessie told her, "we'll take our chances. Now tell us about the mermaids."

Something new rose in Sally Ann's eyes, a glimmer of fervor as her voice dropped low.

"You mean the priestesses," she said.

"Where did they come from?"

"The Ocean Behind the Ocean. *Far,* far away. They came to teach us. To show us the light. You couldn't understand. You don't have the blood in you. If you did, you'd hear them singing." Sally Ann's flat eyes went glassy and distant. "I hear them, when I lie down to sleep at night. They send me dreams of the Old Man Below. Of his driftwood palaces and the glories to come."

Jessie glanced at Harmony. Harmony responded with a tiny shake of her head. This line of questioning wasn't getting them anywhere. They needed hard facts; all Sally Ann had to offer was mythology and the faith she'd been taught.

"We saw your people toss their victims to the...priestesses," Harmony said, "so they could go into the cave. Where do you keep the bodies of the people you kill? The meat locker?"

Bringing up the mermaids had been a misstep. Sally Ann had found mental refuge in her religion and bristled with a streak of fresh defiance. The gun against her forehead wasn't scaring her now, not with visions of her deep-water god dancing through her imagination. Sometimes the difference between a believer and a zealot was just a little bit of encouragement. She looked to Jessie, and her lips pursed in a cruel, tight smile.

"Why? You hungry for seconds? Betcha didn't know what was in that brisket we fed you. Oh, you just gobbled it down. Came from the left thigh of a hiker who made a wrong turn."

Harmony figured Sally Ann expected shock. Horror. Denial. Her look of glee faltered as Jessie responded with a deadpan stare, no reaction at all. Harmony kept Sally Ann covered with her pistol as Jessie took a step back and holstered her weapon. She delicately plucked the amber contact lenses from her eyes.

Their true color, inhumanly turquoise and glowing with inner fire, blazed in the shadows. Sally Ann cringed as her bravado cracked at the edges.

"What...what *are* you?" she whispered.

"I'm the kind of monster you can only pretend to be," Jessie told her. "By the way? The brisket was good, but it needed more chili powder. Human meat is naturally gamy; you have to adjust your spices to compensate."

Sally Ann turned to Harmony, wordlessly begging for intercession.

"Body storage," Harmony said. "Where?"

"There ain't none right now. There—there ain't, and that's the truth. The rest of the hiker went to feed the priestesses. Only other body we ain't used up was that outsider, the one we caught poking around last night."

"Dominguez," Jessie said.

"The doctor had us burn the body. Said it was tainted meat, it'd make us sick, and it wasn't a good sacrifice neither."

"Well," Jessie said. "That's a damn shame."

She walked in a slow circle around the kneeling woman, coming to a stop behind her back.

"I mean, damn shame for you, since we need a fresh corpse."

Sally Ann opened her mouth, inhaled deep, about to scream for help. She never got a chance. Her neck snapped like a fistful of twigs and her body pitched to the floor, dying with a spasmodic kick of her powder-blue shoes.

"We could have taken someone closer to the shoreline,"

Harmony pointed out. "Would have made for an easier trip."

Jessie crouched down, grabbed Sally Ann's body under the shoulders, and heaved up, lifting from the knees. She slung the dead weight over her shoulders like a firefighter.

"Wasn't like we were going to let her live anyway. I don't mind the exercise."

"We've got the offering," Harmony said with a nod to the tunnel mouth. "Now we need the trumpet. Unless there's something we missed—and that's a big, *big* 'unless'—the two combined should get us into that cave."

"Let's split up. I'll drop off our dead restaurateur by the boat and spread a little love—in the form of plastic explosives—down by the docks and the boathouse. You hit the church, grab the trumpet, and meet me in…let's say twenty minutes."

"Make it twenty-five," Harmony said, shouldering her courier pack. "I want to leave a few care packages behind."

37.

Harmony made her way through the bootleggers' tunnel, guided by the glow of her phone. The walls were uneven, bearing the scars of countless pickax strikes, carved from the earth with sweat and muscle and held up with rugged wooden struts. Faint grooves marred the tilted floor, marking the paths of wheeled carts as they moved their contraband cargo beneath the watchful eyes of the law.

Her underground road ended at a blank wall, another loose patch of drywall shoved up to conceal the exit. No way to tell what was on the other side, and when she leaned close, all she heard was the faint rustle of rats. She pocketed her phone, braced her shotgun, and put her shoulder to the concealed door. It jolted open, just a few inches, with a squeal of metal on stone. She waited and listened. There was no commotion, nothing to indicate she'd been overheard.

Harmony chanced one more shove, one more high-pitched squeal, widening the gap far enough to squeeze through.

She was in the church basement. The storm-cellar doors still hung open from the night before, letting in soft moonlight to guide her footsteps. She made her way through the garage-sale clutter, over to the stairway on the far side, and up to the dead minister's office. Dust caught in her throat and she fought the urge to cough.

She crossed the office and cracked the door leading to the gallery.

Empty. The lights were off, the pews abandoned. The front doors were wide open, though—maybe anticipating another assembly where Cranston could preach to the faithful—and a couple of townies were guarding the entrance. They had their backs to her, eyes on the street, but either one could turn and catch her in a heartbeat.

She didn't want a fight here. A fight meant noise, and noise meant a repeat of last night's pursuit. Silence was their best ally right now. She slowly emerged from the doorway, head ducked and breath held, creeping as fast as she could toward the fish-headed effigy and the bone trumpet in its mummified hand.

As she stepped close, the wood under the thin red carpet groaned. She froze.

They hadn't noticed. They stood side by side with hunting shotguns propped casually on their shoulders, watching the empty road.

Her fingers curled around the trumpet. The bone was oddly cold to the touch. It felt wet, as if dipped in sea foam. She tugged and the mummy's fingers clung to it, obstinate. She tugged harder.

The hand snapped off at its crucified wrist. Harmony grimaced as she turned, slinking back to the doorway with her prize, heart pounding.

She waited until she was back in the minister's office, in the safety of darkness, before wrestling the fingers free and tossing the empty hand to the floor. Blasphemy was going to be the least of her sins tonight. She checked the time. Fifteen minutes left before the rendezvous. She unslung her courier pack as she made for the cellar stairs, looking for a few good spots to plant an explosive surprise along the way.

* * *

Jessie was already on the shore in the shadow of the lighthouse, with Sally Ann's body lying limp in the belly of the Zodiac. Harmony jogged up, showed her the bone trumpet, and they shoved the inflatable off the rocks. They splashed in the shallows, icy water soaking their feet, and clambered on board.

They waited for the sweep of the lighthouse beam to pass them by. The engine purred, and Harmony steered them out to sea.

Away from the village, the ocean was a blotchy morass, the islets becoming the looming, shaggy heads of aquatic giants. Jessie switched on the halogen beam. She aimed it to chart their course, keeping an eye on the jagged rocks below the surface as Harmony piloted them into the maze. The cove was just ahead.

"You ready for this?" Jessie whispered.

"No," Harmony said. "But let's do it anyway."

She steeled herself as she turned the motor, steering toward the mouth of the cove. As they neared the crab-pincer outcroppings that marked the mermaids' territory, she killed the engine.

They drifted in. The halogen beam caught shapes under the water. Sinuous, circling. Hungry. Harmony's coin fluttered against her skin, beating out a hummingbird warning.

Harmony put the bone trumpet to her lips. She blew, a long and mournful bellow like a whale's mating call. Then a second time, and a third, mimicking the villagers.

The last reverberation echoed off the rocks. Jessie took hold of Sally Ann's body, lifted her by the shoulders, and shoved her overboard. Salty foam splashed across their faces as she hit the water and sank.

The shadows lurched. They dove for the treat, and the beam caught flashes of piranha frenzy as the mermaids tore her corpse to pieces. Harmony started the engine and they sailed on, under dangling stalactite teeth and into the bootleggers' cave.

Most of the cave was inky water under a twenty-foot overhang, encircled by a broad ledge of rock and thick with the tang of salt. The old rumrunners had built a miniature warehouse for their contraband: on the far edge of the cave, wooden scaffolding on rusted struts formed ramps and platforms, two levels between the rough rock floor and the top of the cave. Empty now, but Harmony could picture it full of barrels and booze crates, ready for delivery to the mainland. She cut the engine again, steering toward the platform and letting momentum carry them the rest of the way, until they bumped against the stone outcropping.

"Don't know how much of a grace period we've got," Jessie said. "Let's plant the charges and get the hell out of here."

They climbed out of the boat and went in opposite directions, aiming to cover as much of the inner wall as they could. They left the halogen lamp on for light, tilting it toward the heart of the cavern. Jessie slapped a Semtex brick against the stone, pressing it tight until she was sure the adhesive would hold. Then she slid the prongs of an electronic detonator, marked with a dot of green paint, into the heart of the brick.

Harmony rushed along the curve of stone, fast as she dared on the slick rock. She saw shapes in the water, curious, bobbing close to the surface. Not attacking, not yet, but one wrong move could send her sliding right over the edge of the outcropping.

There was a break in the stone. Another tunnel, sloping downward at an angle and ending in a rounded pool. She wasn't sure if it was just another rupture in the cave floor, but something about the water seemed different. Murkier. Dirtier. She pressed a brick of explosive near the opening and moved on, aiming to cover the far end of the cave and work her way inward, meeting Jessie back at the boat.

Two bricks up and the mermaids were agitated. They knew something was wrong. Their forms twisted and twirled in the brine, tails slapping.

"Jessie," Harmony called out, "we have to go."

Jessie was climbing the scaffolding, angling for the top of the bootleggers' platform.

"Almost there," she called back. "Want to make sure we bring the whole damn roof down."

A sound caught Harmony's ear. Bubbling, burbling, like stones tumbling into water. She hustled back and peered down the tunnel.

The pool was roiling. Shadows rippled below, like a nest of water moccasins all wide awake and slithering. And as they neared the surface she realized it wasn't a nest. It was a single shadow. She fell back, shouting a warning as the pool erupted.

The bull was here.

He shot up the tunnel and into the halogen glow, amphibious, fast, *angry*, emerging with a squeal in eight different pitches from eight different mouths. He was taller than Harmony, wide as a truck, a squirming bulk that defied any rational form. He was a living tumbleweed of tentacles and knots of blubber, his surface erupting with shark-fanged maws that blossomed from his body at will, snapping in the direction of food as he reformed and reshaped his body in fluid motion. The bull careened toward the light and hit the scaffolding with a brutal slam. Jessie was up on her toes, fixing the last brick into place, and she nearly pitched off the edge. She caught herself, dropping to her hands and knees, clinging to the scaffold as the antique metal groaned.

It's defending the mermaids, Harmony realized. She moved on instinct. To save Jessie, she needed to become a bigger threat.

Earth, air, water, fire, she thought, evoking her mnemonic trigger. *Garb me in your raiment. Arm me with your weapons.*

She dropped to her knees at the outcropping's edge, her body turned to an elemental forge, and thrust her open palms toward the water. The latent energy in the air around her became heat, amplified and focused by the bellows of her heart, and then fire. Fire that blasted out in a flamethrower torrent and made the water boil.

The boil spread and the mermaids screamed. She heard their voices now, shrill and terrified and bouncing off the cavern walls as they struggled to escape the killing heat. The bull rolled on its tentacles, sensing the danger, and charged toward her in an enraged, shrieking stampede.

Harmony's guts churned, stabbing cramps setting in, her body demanding that she pay in pain for siphoning that much power. She had to fight through it. She forced herself to her feet and swung up the shotgun.

The Benelli roared. Blast after blast of concentrated buckshot tore into the creature's bulk. Black rainbow blood spattered the superheated water and ignited like ribbon trails of gasoline. The bull kept coming. She walked backward as she pulled the trigger, buying room, until her heel almost slipped on the farthest edge of the outcropping.

She spent her last shell. Nowhere to go but the mouths of the bull or dive and take her chances with the mermaids below.

Then Jessie loomed up behind him, shotgun braced. Harmony dropped low and clear as she opened fire. The bull shrieked, whirling around on his tentacles but pitching off-balance as he tried to focus on Jessie. He caterwauled and teetered on the slick stone. With a final roar of the shotgun, the bull slipped and plunged into the water with a cannonball splash. They watched him kick away, diving deep, leaving shimmering blood trails behind as he fled.

They ran along the rocky curve and piled into the Zodiac. The engine grumbled to life. Harmony steered, pointing the nose outward, blowing the bone trumpet as they wove around patches of burning blood on the restless, churning water. It didn't help. A mermaid lunged, maw-petals wide and aiming to chomp a hole in the inflatable boat. Harmony juked hard, yanking the wheel, and slid out of the way. The boat bounced as the propeller chopped into blubber and bone.

The second they cleared the mouth of the cave, Jessie triggered the Semtex.

The world went white. Harmony's vision blurred out and a thunderclap deafened her ears. She felt the water swell under the boat, a shock wave that picked them up and flung them like a child's toy, shooting them between the crab-pincer rocks of the cove on a burst of summer heat. They splashed down hard and skidded in the water. She had a white-knuckle grip on the wheel, leaning back as she wrestled with momentum and brought the boat under control.

They plowed through the shallows, sleek and fast, aiming their sights for the village.

38.

Graykettle loomed in the distance, and the beam of the lighthouse chopped across the dark water.

Jessie killed the halogen beam. They rode dark, watching for distant lights. There was movement on the docks, frantic, boat lights powering up. The villagers had seen the explosion from the shore.

"Round two?" Harmony asked.

"Wait for it," Jessie murmured. "Want to make sure we get as many as we can. Let 'em rally and..."

She counted to three. Then she punched the activation button for the yellow-paint detonators.

The night lit up like high noon.

The docks and the old boathouses detonated in a pair of blazing fireballs, smoke rising to lick the overcast sky, setting off chain-reaction explosions as boats and fuel tanks went up in the onslaught. The stained-glass windows of the church exploded, worm-eaten clapboard flying like shrapnel as its walls buckled and its steeple toppled and fell. A natural gas pipeline, snaking through the heart of the village, caught fire and erupted. The ruptured pipeline drew a jagged red sigil along the village map, like a curse-spell writ large and washing the streets with purifying flame.

They ran the boat aground and jumped out, moving fast and on foot, winding their way through the chaos. The air was thick with distant screams, the roaring of the flames, the occasional metallic *crump* of a gas tank bursting or the slow agonized groan of a moldering wall caving in. Graykettle was dying. To finish it off, they had to drive a sword through the heart of the beast.

The old cannery was empty, bathing in moonlight under its caved-in roof. Hazy moonlight, blotted out by torrents of black smoke that smelled like hickory. The tank was right where Sally Ann said it was, and the side hatch, by all appearances welded shut, popped right open under Jessie's fingertips. The welding seams were nothing but rough putty, painted dull silver. A ladder ran to the base of the hollow tank, down below the village street.

It ended at a reinforced steel door. A slim bolt-hole at eye level was securely locked. So was the imposing doorknob, with a stout vintage keyhole.

Harmony had left her empty shotgun in the boat. Now she braced her pistol, taking deep breaths to prepare herself, and locked eyes with Jessie.

"You know what I need to do, right?" Jessie asked her.

She knew. "No friendlies on the other side of that door. Let it out."

Jessie took a couple of steps back. She grinned hungrily at the steel, looking at it like a birthday present, and she was about to tear the wrapper open. When she spoke, eyes blazing in the color of winter ice, she spoke with another woman's voice.

"About goddamn time."

* * *

The bootleggers' fortress was a warren of storage rooms and pleasure dens, long abandoned by time. It had made a fine enough base of operations, Cranston reasoned. Crude compared to his Tampa operation, but effective. And secure, until now. Until the ceiling shook, dust raining down from the old splintered rafters, and all of his security-camera feeds capturing the surface world went blank.

All but one. The one showing the two women—*Bobby's* women, he was quite sure, following on the heels of their missing associate—making their way into the false tank at the cannery. He didn't understand how he'd judged the situation so wrongly. No matter. This was the end of their journey.

Cranston marched through the chaos, barking orders. The old fortress was built like a cross. A long, pillar-lined hallway marked the entrance, ending at the steel door on one side and a crossroads on the other. To the left of the main gallery, assembly tables for the delivery devices, row after row of briefcase bombs complete and ready to receive their blessed payload. On the other side, laboratory equipment and workstations lined the walls.

And at the tip of the cross, his life's work. His life's purpose. Four towering glass tanks, sealed and under pressure, joined by fat and winding hoses. Cables snaked along the pale stone floor to the consoles in the lab, monitoring heat, particle density, every aspect of the cooking process down to the tiniest detail.

Gas, the color of mold on a rotten bone, billowed inside the chambers. The Clean Slate, almost ready to be gifted unto a corrupt and undeserving world.

"You." Cranston snapped his fingers. "Run down the southern tunnel to the old cave-in. I don't know what the hell they did up there, but we might need an alternate exit."

"We decided not to blast it open. It was too fragile—"

"Then start *digging*, damn it. We can't be trapped down

here. You, get on the monitors, try to bring some of those dead cameras back online. I need information. And as for the rest of you..."

He stood before the gathered sentinels. Eight men, armed to the teeth with shotguns, rifles, handguns, anything they could scrounge on short notice. All true believers in the cause, ready to die at his command. He pointed to the doorway.

"I doubt our guests are going to get that door open, not with anything short of a battering ram. But if they do? No hesitation, and no mercy. Kill them."

He turned and strode off to check the tanks.

His followers looked between one another, silent, then turned to the door.

It responded with a leaden *thud*. Something slammed it from the other side, hard enough to make it jolt in its reinforced frame.

Thud. The smarter ones raised their guns, taking aim. The rest followed suit.

Thud. They thumbed back hammers, gripping their weapons tight, executioners in a firing line.

Thud.

There was a moment of silence. Motes of soot settled to the ground in a gentle gossamer rain.

Then the thick slab of steel tore from its hinges and blasted down, slamming to the stone and kicking up a billowing cloud of dust.

The cultists opened fire. The dust cloud erupted with muzzle flashes, strobing as the gallery filled with the deafening hammering thrum of a firing range. They unleashed an endless fusillade of death that chopped the air into shreds, firing until their guns ran dry.

* * *

The dust cloud died, settling to the stone.

In its wake stood a curtain of bullets.

Hundreds of rounds hung, quivering, in a wall of air hardened to the consistency of gelatin. They strained, struggling to spend their energy, to pass through to the two women standing just inside the doorway. Harmony held one hand aloft, eyes squeezed shut and her brow slick with sweat, struggling to hold the magical shield intact.

At her side, Jessie's eyes blazed. Her hands were hooked into the impression of claws, her shoulders back and neck low, and she licked her lips as she tilted her head, sizing up the men before her.

Beyond her eyes, hot enough to glow like beacons of rage, she didn't transform. She didn't sprout fangs or fur, and the full moon had no say in when she vented her fury. But anyone who stood in Jessie Temple's path when she let loose knew one thing for certain: the legends of werewolves sprang from her bloodline. And the legends left out the bloody details.

"*Now,*" she hissed.

Harmony's arm whipped downward. The gelatinous air collapsed and brought the bullets down with it, clattering to the stone in a thunderstorm of brass. Jessie was already airborne, leaping over the falling curtain, lunging for the closest target. Her hand shot for his face—not in a punch, her fingers jamming into his mouth, thumb clamping under his chin. She twisted and tore. His jaw ripped free in a gout of blood and dangling sinew. She didn't even slow down, tossing the mangled curve of bone to the ground and leaving the man howling in her wake, clutching his mutilated face as his tongue dangled loose. Her free hand snatched an empty rifle and twisted it, yanking it from its owner's grip.

She spun it around and thrust it like a spear. The muzzle shattered his teeth and punched out through the back of his neck.

Harmony was on the move, veering right, taking cover behind the thick stone support pillars that lined the gallery. She put her back to one, braced her pistol, and came out firing with her jacket flaring behind her, lending Jessie cover. One of Cranston's men dropped his gun in the middle of reloading. His weapon and magazine fell from his hands as he dove to escape. Harmony kept moving, obeying the first rule of a gunfight, and slipped behind the second pillar before anyone could frame her in his sights.

One man tried, slapping a speed-load into his revolver and sealing the chamber with a flick of his wrist, raising it to fire. Jessie hit him from the side. She twisted his arm, shattered his wrist, and forced the barrel of the revolver up against his wide, panicked eye. Then she curled her finger over his and helped him pull the trigger.

Hard metal slammed into her back. One of the cultists, out of ammo and desperate, had turned his shotgun into a club. She snarled, wheeling around as he hit her again. The butt cracked against her shoulder and set off a starburst of pain. She caught the third swing and ripped the shotgun from his hands. Hot blood spattered Jessie's cheeks as she brought it down in both hands and smashed it against his skull hard enough to warp the black metal. He crumpled to her feet and she swung again, and again, until he didn't have a face anymore. She tossed the dented weapon aside and ground her heel down on what was left as she hunted for another target.

More of Cranston's followers thundered up the hall, ready to join the fight. Harmony dropped to her knee, held her pistol in a two-hand grip, and closed one eye. Her suppressor spat, two rounds in quick succession, and one of the cultists pitched to the floor with scarlet stains spreading across his chest. His partner saw him drop, turned with his rifle high, and her last bullet hit him between the eyes.

Cranston was on the run. He and his maid, leather satchel clunking at her side, and they broke in different directions. He angled left, darting through the laboratory and through the narrow mouth of a tunnel.

She headed straight for the tanks of Clean Slate.

A cultist's back snapped over Jessie's knee. He was still alive and screaming, but she tossed his broken body to the floor. Eyes narrow, nose twitching as she inhaled air choked with blood and piss and fear, she honed in on the danger. Her gaze snapped to Harmony. She didn't need words. They both knew who was faster. Her legs thrust out in a bounding leap and she broke into a dead sprint, racing for the tanks, while Harmony chased Cranston down.

39.

Harmony's gun was empty.

Usually she had her magic as a backup weapon. The shield of air had stolen her strength, twisted her guts into cramped knots. Couldn't do that again, not this soon. But weakness was a luxury she couldn't afford. If Cranston found a way out of this maze and escaped, he could start all over again, anywhere in the world. The laboratory, the tanks, it was all the product of his twisted mind. He had to be stopped here and now.

Besides, she'd made a promise.

She took the winding tunnel as fast as she dared, eyes sharp, hunting for traps or an ambush. All she had right now were her wits, razor-honed and ready. And in the space of a heartbeat, catching the faintest gleam in the darkness, they saved her life.

There were trip wires in the tunnel. A nest of them at ankle level, some strung straight across the path, others at a hard diagonal, all running through eyelets in the stone. She scanned the rough stone walls and then the ceiling above. That's where she saw the seams, rigged to drop slabs of killing weight.

Slow is smooth, smooth is fast. Her heart was thudding against her chest, commanding her to hurry, to stop Cranston from getting away, but she moved with deliberation and care. She picked her way through the nest of wires, stepping from flagstone to flagstone, testing her weight in case of a secondary trap. Once she slipped free, she didn't break into a run; she kept it smooth, eyes steady, hunting for more trip wires.

There were no breaks in the tunnel, no choices about where to turn. It dead-ended in a room that might have been used for liquor storage, back in the day, or a private office for the gangster in charge of the operation.

Cranston had turned it into a dojo.

It was a pale imitation of the sleek, polished one back at his mansion in Tampa. Tatami mats lined the musty stone floor, and a few paper screens here and there added some meditative flair to the dusty, dun-colored walls. His collection of practice weapons nestled in pegs on a stand of red lacquered wood. Light shone from a battery-powered lamp, mounted on a tripod in the far corner of the room.

Cranston stood just outside its circle of light, his back to her, fumbling with a stretch of bare wall. His fingers dug at the crumbling mortar, tugging at one rough chunk of stone and then another, hunting for a hidden catch.

"Running away?" Harmony asked. "What, no faith that your ocean god is going to come and save you?"

He turned. He reared up, chin high and pressing his shoulders back, like a cobra preparing to strike.

"I will not be mocked by a woman who serves the likes of Robert Diehl. At least I chose a worthy master."

"I don't work for Diehl," Harmony said. "Neither did Natalie Cooper."

He blinked. "Oh. Well. That does put a spin on things."

"I belong to an organization that deals with people like you."

"People like me?" he said. "You mean people who are trying to save the world?"

"By destroying it?"

Cranston rolled his eyes. "Please. It's a culling, as natural as any plague. That's the beauty of the Clean Slate: at stage four of mutation, subjects only survive for a day, two at most, before they go into cardiac arrest. The infected kill the uninfected, then the infected die out. What remains is a pristine, empty land. A *healing* land, for the chosen few to return to and repopulate."

His open hand clutched at the air as he slowly sidestepped, circling the mat, edging closer to the weapon rack.

"Don't you understand? The Earth is dying. Oceanic pollution, global warming—we are murdering our own habitat. Our species is reckless, insane, suicidal. Incremental solutions won't work. You can't stop mass-scale toxic dumping by pledging to recycle your aluminum cans. Someone has to step up and take drastic action. Decades, a century from now, I'll be regarded as the savior of humanity."

Something in his words caught in Harmony's ear. She tilted her head, studying him.

"'Our,'" she said.

He frowned, not following. She took a step toward him, her shoes touching down on the far edge of the tatami mat.

"'Our species.' That's what you just said. But that's not what you tell your followers, is it?"

His hand fluttered in a dismissive wave. "Figure of speech, it means nothing—"

"It means everything. See, I heard your sermon, back at the church. You've convinced these people that they're, what was it, exiles from the 'Ocean Behind the Ocean'? That they're superior beings, forced to live among the humans? And you don't even believe it yourself. It's a grift." Harmony let out a small and bitter laugh. "Makes it easier, doesn't it? Makes it easier to get these people to kill for you. After all, they're not murdering their own kind. Just us lowly human beings."

Cranston cracked a tiny smile.

"I learned something as a young man. I was bullied as a child. Teased, incessantly, for...this."

He held up his left hand, spreading his fingers as far as the webbing of flesh would allow.

"Like I said when we dined together, my mother told me I was part fish. She was trying to cheer me up. It's just syndactyly. A birth defect. But I believed it for a time, and that belief spurred my greatest passions in life. That's when I realized the motivating power of a tiny white lie." His hand fell to his side. "There are other worlds than this. You've seen the proof of it, yes?"

"I have," Harmony said.

"I've heard the songs of the sea, the words of my priestesses. The Ocean Behind the Ocean is real, and I will lead my faithful there. If I had to bend the truth to make all of this glorious work possible, I think I can be forgiven for that."

"Your crusade is over," Harmony said. "You aren't leading anyone anywhere."

He scoffed at her and offered his wrists for imaginary handcuffs.

"What are you going to do, arrest me? Tell me, do I get my day in court or just a cell in a lonely black site somewhere, far off the grid?"

Harmony thought about that.

"When people join my organization," she said, "we lay the facts on the line. It's not a fortune and glory kind of job. There's no declassification date for the work we do; fight monsters, save the world, the best you can hope for is a handshake and a cup of coffee. People like Natalie Cooper, they understand that nobody will ever know the good they did, the lives they saved, the sacrifices they made. They do the job anyway, because it needs to be done. All we can offer in return is a promise. One promise."

Cranston stared at her, uncertain now.

"The promise is that when you go on your final mission, the one you don't come home from, we'll come hunting. We'll find the person responsible. And we *will* make them pay."

The tatami mat rustled under her foot as she took a step closer.

"I'm not here to arrest you," Harmony said.

Cranston was silent for a moment, contemplative.

"I meant what I said, at dinner," he replied. "You don't really know someone until you've tested each other's skills. I...don't suppose a friendly sparring match is in order, though."

"I don't suppose it is," she said.

"I'm curious. What do you know about escrima?"

"National martial art of the Philippines." She glanced to the rack of practice gear. "Stick fighting."

"Often, often. Understandable assumption. Escrima practitioners do use a wide array of other weapons though. The *panangga*, the *barong*, the *sibat*. Personally, I'm quite fond of the *buntot pagi*."

He reached to the rack. A whip, four feet of stiff, oddly pale leather, slithered free from the pegs.

"*Buntot pagi*," he said, "meaning 'stingray tail.' Properly preserved and treated, it makes for quite the fighting tool.

The texture is akin to very coarse sandpaper. Remarkably, even dried, a stingray's tail retains traces of neurotoxin."

Harmony was back in the morgue in Tampa, studying Cooper's glassy-eyed corpse under the stark surgical lights. The endless, thin knife cuts along her back. At least she had thought they were made with a knife. She heard the medical examiner's voice, his confusion at finding stingray venom in Cooper's blood.

"That's why I'm rerunning the tests. Because looking at these results, factoring in the falloff over time…it looks to me like she was stung repeatedly, over a course of at least three hours."

Harmony's hand curled into a fist at her side. Her fingernails dug into her palms.

"I'll admit to a bit of cheating," Cranston told her. "Access to a marine biology lab has its privileges. I *soak* mine in venom now and then, just to keep it fresh. So. Your aikido against my escrima. Shall we?"

She stared in his eyes, but all she could see was Cooper's face.

Then she came at him.

* * *

The maid was running for the bioweapon tanks. Jessie was running for the maid. Closing the open floor between them, blood roaring in her ears. She tasted fear, anger, a pheromone trail leading to her prey.

The maid spun, her flat fish eyes blazing as she swung a boatman's hook. The hook whistled through the air and Jessie leaned back, its rusted tip slicing an inch from her throat. The maid waged a fighting retreat, slashing the air wildly as she darted backward, making her last stand between the four towering tanks. Green gas billowed against the glass all around them, airborne death waiting to be unleashed on a sleeping world.

Jessie took her time now. Nowhere for her prey to run. No one left standing, just the two of them in a gallery littered with the mangled and the dead.

The maid knew it, too. Her gaze shifted left and right. To the thick rubber hoses, to the tank controls. Even if she planned on a suicide bid, she'd never reach the valves before Jessie grabbed her, much less get them open.

Mutually assured destruction was still an option, though.

Her pale hand plunged into the satchel at her side. She yanked out a ribbed plastic mask with an anesthesiologist's bottle attached, the same one she'd used on Dominguez in the church. Before Jessie could stop her, she put the mask to her own face and squeezed the bottle tight.

40.

Cranston's stingray tail whip-cracked through the air and Harmony ducked low, darting in. She was half rage, half muscle memory, moving on lethal instinct. She locked up his whip hand with her curled arm and drove her other arm at his throat, hitting him with the V of her inside elbow. Cranston went down hard. He was built like an engine block but faster than he looked. As soon as his shoulders hit the tatami mat he was already rolling, springing up, rallying for his next attack.

His whip slashed at her eyes, too fast to escape. She threw up her right forearm, shielding herself, and the stingray tail carved into her. It sliced through her jacket, her shirt, her skin, spattering her blood across the woven mat.

She brought her hand down on his whip arm, slipped around him, and drove the flat of her other hand against the back of Cranston's neck. Then she twisted his wrist behind his back, trapping his weapon. It should have been a textbook move, but her cut was doing more than slowing her down: a lit trail of gasoline burned its way up her wounded arm, neurotoxin fires making her muscles twitch and cramp. Her fingers convulsed and he broke free, twisting away from her. He dropped low and kicked at her leg. She lost her balance and fell, rolling fast as he brought the whip down. It sliced into the tatami again and again, carving razor scars in the woven mat, pursuing her as she scrambled to escape.

Harmony leaped to her feet and jumped back, just ahead of another thunderclap swing of the stingray tail. Cranston was grinning, delighted, like this was nothing but a game to him. Her right arm was starting to shake. Her fingers twitched, jerking from the neurotoxin, and she realized she couldn't even make a fist.

Her left hand still could, though.

He spun the tail over his head and let it fly. She dove under the attack and drove a punch square into his gut. He staggered, doubling over, but he jogged away just out of her reach before she could follow through.

"I've studied your art," he panted. "I know your moves, know all the ways you can take me down. All I have to do is keep my distance and wait for the inevitable."

The whip flickered like a serpent's tongue and carved into Harmony's left shoulder. She gritted her teeth at the sudden rush of branding-iron heat.

Her right arm was almost useless, ravaged by the stingray toxin. In a minute or two, her left was going to join it. Cranston was right: all he had to do was avoid and outlast her. If she didn't finish this fight here and now, he was going to win.

* * *

The maid let out a shriek loud enough to shake dust from the cellar roof. Her eyes rolled back as her clothes and flesh tore, blistering with bone-quills. Curved, jagged fangs sprouted in her mouth, forcing her old teeth loose from broken and bloody gums. She brandished fingers turned into killing claws, spears of sharp scarlet bone, and charged.

Jessie hit her with an onslaught of jackhammer

punches. The maid didn't even slow down. She grabbed Jessie by the shoulders, lifted her off her feet, and hurled her into the closest tank. Jessie's shoulders slammed against it and she collapsed to the stone floor with the breath knocked out of her.

A hairline fracture ran up the glass of the tank.

Jessie came up in a running charge, hitting the maid in the stomach headfirst, driving her off her feet. The maid's belly burst open and a length of raw intestine snaked out like a tentacle, coiling around Jessie's throat. It cinched tight as a hangman's noose as they landed together, cutting off her air. They rolled on the floor in a clinch. Jessie batted away frantic swipes of the creature's bone-claws, yanking herself out of reach, the intestine coming with her. The rubbery flesh tightened and spots bloomed in her vision. Blood roared in her ears, heart galloping, and she could feel herself tumbling into the abyss.

She grabbed the intestine between her hands, and bit down.

The maid-thing howled, thrashing on the floor, as Jessie chewed her way loose. The rubbery skin stretched and snapped, tearing free, and the coil around her throat went limp. She took a deep breath as she dove, landing with both knees on the maid's chest. She was still mutating. New bone-quills erupted from her shoulders, curving to lethal points.

Jessie grabbed hold of the quills at their bloody roots, twisted her grip, and broke them off.

The maid was shrieking, bucking under her. Jessie raised both hands high, turned the quills around, and brought them plunging down. There was a wet, ripping sound, and then silence.

Jessie knelt on the corpse, panting for breath. The

world slowly slid back into focus. She felt the impression of a winter wind and gray, snow-flecked fur brushing against her face. The flick of a tail and a rumble of contentment. The wolf had fed. It was going back to sleep. Just for a little while.

A faint crinkling sound, like someone rumpling a sheet of aluminum foil, turned Jessie's head.

The hairline crack was spreading and multiplying. Fanning out, drawing frost-white lines, along the curved wall of the tank.

Harmony, she thought.

She pushed herself up onto unsteady feet and forced herself to run, hunting for her partner.

* * *

Harmony was a tactician. A one-on-one fight was battlefield strategy made personal; it was still a game of predictions and outcomes, feints and reversals.

Her right arm was almost useless, burning and twitching as the stingray venom ravaged her muscles. She could still use her left, but only for the moment: the slash along her shoulder was already starting to throb, numbness mingling with the wasp-sting agony. Her mind raced, struggling to rise above the floodwaters of pain and save her from drowning. Cranston was already making his move, and she knew she had one breath left before this fight was over. Plan on the inhale, execute on the exhale.

Cranston relied on his whip. He had the same myopia that had saved Harmony's life more than once before, going up against other armed opponents: give someone a weapon, and they forget they have half a dozen other ways to attack. She could trust that he'd lead with the whip, every time.

She had to get close to take him down. He knew it, too, and he wasn't going to let her. He danced around her, bouncing from foot to foot, keeping a safe distance and enforcing it with snaps of the stingray tail. Harmony worked the fight like a math problem and found the answer at the end of a brutal equation. *Sacrifice play.*

She watched his eyes, waiting for the telltale twitch of an impending attack. Then she forced her right arm up, feeling it shudder as she wrenched her elbow, and held it in front of her face like a shield. She charged straight at him.

He couldn't resist the easy target. Just like she planned.

She bit back a scream as the whip let out a subsonic crack and chewed into her forearm, trapping her in its white-hot grip. She kept coming. His arm was overextended and she wrenched her shoulder back, pulling him off-balance. Then she kicked up off the ground, twisting in the air, and shot out her foot.

She felt his ribs crack under her heel.

Cranston fell, groaning, rolling onto his belly. Harmony jumped onto his back and tore the stingray tail from his hand. Her right arm was bleeding, crippled, useless for anything but leverage, but she could still use her left. She took the whip and looped it around his throat. Then she yanked it taut.

He squirmed under her, pinned like a roach. His breath escaped in a rattling gasp. Then it didn't escape at all, as the stingray tail tightened around his neck. His cheeks turned purple, eyes bulging. His palm hammered the tatami mat. He was trying to tap out, like this was a sparring match. Surrendering. Begging for mercy.

Harmony pulled the noose harder.

She leaned in, put her lips to his ear, and spoke the last words he would ever hear: "This is for Natalie Cooper."

She felt the moment Judah Cranston died. His head went limp, and the frenzied drumming of his feet fell silent and still. She left him like that, down on his face with the whip coiled around his crushed throat.

Promise made. Promise kept.

41.

The last brick of Semtex slapped against a dusty pillar. The final detonator's prongs slid in like a knife through butter. Jessie had sent Harmony ahead to the silo ladder while she finished the job. The cracks were still spreading along the tank of Clean Slate, weaving a deadly spiderweb.

Harmony struggled on the rungs. Her right arm was dangling at her side, twitching uncontrollably, useless, and her left was losing strength fast. Her torn sleeves clung to her, soaked in twin streams of blood. Jessie came up behind her, scooped her up around the waist, and threw her over her shoulder. Harmony leaned against her, limp, as Jessie carried her up to the surface.

They emerged into the heart of the old cannery. And into the heart of an inferno.

The fires had spread out of control, ravaging the village. It was past midnight and bright as a summer day. Harmony almost expected to see the sun, but the sky was blotted out by roiling carpets of bitter black smoke. Both ends of the street outside the cannery were blocked off by walls of flame and fallen debris.

Jessie got on the phone. "Redbird," she said. "Mission's done but we're trapped in the village and we don't have a lot of time here. We need an immediate evac."

The team commander's voice crackled over the line on a wave of broken static. "Negative, ma'am. We can't get to you through the fire. Beach Cell reports same problem: the road on the north side of town is completely blocked."

Harmony turned on the broken pavement, slow, looking for a way out. There wasn't one.

"Aselia?" Jessie asked her, brainstorming.

"Not enough room to land the plane. We'd need a…" Her voice trailed off.

"A what?"

"A helicopter."

She fumbled with her own phone, squeezing it in her trembling left hand as she hunted for a number. The roadway flooded with the hickory tang of smoke. The fire devoured everything in its path, feeding on her oxygen, squeezing her lungs as her breath went shallow.

"We don't have a helicopter," Jessie said.

"We don't," she said. "But Bobby Diehl does."

Jessie arched an eyebrow. "What are you up to?"

"Bobby's been using the Concierge for all of his transport needs. Remember the briefing? That's how Cooper was supposed to get out of Tampa. We know now that he'd already marked her for a double agent, but it's safe to figure he made the same arrangement with Dominguez. And considering there's no way Dominguez traveled with a sniper rifle and a backpack full of Semtex on a commercial flight—"

"The Concierge flew him in," Jessie said.

"And is presumably standing ready to fly him *out*."

"I don't think either of us can mimic Dominguez's voice."

Harmony dialed the number that Bobby had given to Cooper. Her eyes were bright, almost manic, clinging to one last shred of hope as the flames closed in around them. One last gambit to play.

The phone only rang once before it clicked. The voice on the line was modulated, electronic, impossible to say if it was a man or a woman.

"Yes," said the Concierge.

"This is Natalie Cooper," Harmony said. "I'm stuck in Graykettle, near the old cannery, and I need extraction *now*."

There was a momentary silence on the other end.

"Natalie Cooper is deceased."

"The fuck I am," Harmony shouted over the roar of the flames. "I don't understand what the hell is going on here. I got the package from the meet-up at the bar, exactly like Mr. Diehl told me to. Then some lunatic named Dominguez tried to *murder* me. He stole the goods, and I chased him all the way out here to the middle of goddamn nowhere."

"Is he with you now?"

"Are you kidding me? He's dead. I killed him. And recovered the briefcase. You know why? Because I'm Mr. Diehl's number-one girl. So can you get me out of here or not? And you'd better decide fast because me and this case are about to get cooked."

"One moment."

The line went quiet. *Right about now,* Harmony thought, *he and Bobby are going back over everything Dominguez might have told them and deciding what to believe.* On one hand, he might have warned Bobby that she and Jessie were on his trail, making this an obvious trap.

On the other hand, the temptation of a bioweapon in a briefcase—and the chance to kill Cooper with his own hands—was a glittering lure in the water.

Come on, Bobby. Bite down. Take the bait.

The electronic voice returned, fast and crisp.

"Mr. Diehl is looking forward to seeing you again, Ms. Cooper. I will be there directly. Stay exactly where you are. Pickup in five."

They waited and watched the smoky sky. Harmony's face dripped with sweat, the inferno buffeting them with waves of brutal heat and gusts of breath-stealing smoke.

Then came the whir of propellers, and a spotlight's blinding beam sliced through the choking clouds. Jessie darted into cover, hiding in the shadows of the ruined cannery, while Harmony stood in the open and slowly waved her arms above her head.

Their savior descended, dressed in white paint and bearing a blue logo on its side: CBS Channel 5 News. The helicopter touched down on the broken street. Harmony ran in, ducking low under the chopping blades, and clambered into the back seat.

Jessie broke from cover, darted across the broken pavement, and jumped in on the other side. She pressed the barrel of her pistol to the back of the pilot's head.

"Fly," she told him.

The chopper lifted off, veering as it hurtled away from the inferno, rising up through the smoke and into the clear night sky.

Jessie's free hand laid her phone down on the seat between her and Harmony. Kevin's makeshift app was cued up and ready to send its final command.

"Want to do the honors?" Jessie asked.

She tried. Harmony's left hand trembled, fingers convulsing as she fought to make them obey.

Jessie took hold of her hand. Her index finger pressed down over Harmony's, and they pushed the button together.

The cannery went up in a green-tinged fireball. Debris

flew through the air like buckshot made from torn and tangled steel. The streets rippled from the shock wave, asphalt roiling like liquid. Then came a crash of thunder as the old warrens caved in. Roads and buildings collapsed in an endless rockfall, tons upon tons of broken stone. When the dust settled, there was nothing left but a burning tomb. The final resting place for Judah Cranston, his creation, and his dreams.

The helicopter arced out over the water. The sea was tranquil tonight, and a faint sliver of moonlight shone upon the gentle waves. Jessie put her arm around Harmony and pulled her closer. Harmony rested her head on Jessie's shoulder, her eyelids fluttered, and she slowly drifted to sleep.

* * *

The last survivors of Cranston's flock gathered at the point, standing in the shadow of the lighthouse. Its beacon had gone out, guttering and dying along with their home and their hopes. They watched the village burn in silence.

Not one of the dozen men and women dared voice the question they were all asking: *how did this happen?* They were the chosen. The special few. The ones who would rebuild the corrupted world and return in triumph to their home. They would be lauded as heroes in the Ocean Behind the Ocean and dance in the saltwater palace of the Old Man Below. What had gone wrong?

"It's a sign," one said.

The others turned his way, desperate for a glimmer of hope, something to cling to.

"This world was already beyond saving," he told them. "That's what this means. We weren't wrong. We were never wrong. We just…we just didn't understand it all. But now we do."

Murmurs of agreement rose above the crackling flames.

"It's time to go home," another said.

They turned to the lapping waves. Some joined hands, some stood alone. And they all, together, walked into the sea.

They took deep breaths, all the way down.

42.

A wagon train of tinted SUVs and a wall of guns were waiting at the airstrip. The pilot had barely powered down when agents hauled him out of his seat, throwing him onto the tarmac and cuffing his wrists behind his back. A team of paramedics ran in on their heels.

Harmony wasn't waking up. They lifted her limp body out, laid her on a gurney, and raced it to a waiting ambulance. Jessie ran alongside them, climbing on board.

Later that night, a storm rolled in. Water rained down like a judgment from the heavens, dousing the dwindling fires of Graykettle, leaving smoldering and soot-smeared ruins behind. The perimeter teams held their blockade on the roadway until dawn. When their lonely watch ended, they still had work to do.

Biohazard specialists donned CDC-grade chemical-resistant suits to venture into the ruins. Their backup wore the same suits, but they carried assault rifles instead of testing kits. Samples were taken, atmospheres measured. Nothing moved in the debris, and all they found along the shore were the bodies of the drowned.

Out on the water, a small fleet of commandeered fishing boats set up a perimeter along the islets. Heavy weapons were on standby as a few brave volunteers became the first into the water, scuba diving along the collapsed ruin of the cove. There were no mermaids swimming in the deep, only body parts and ragged chunks of blubber.

"We're gathering up the pieces for storage and study," said the site commander. "Only one problem."

Jessie was standing at the window in Harmony's hospital room. The morning sun was warm against her face, and she looked out over a quiet parking lot.

"What's that?" she said.

"Well, ma'am, this...creature you described, with all the tentacles and mouths? The bull? The divers haven't recovered anything that resembles it."

* * *

"Keep your guard up," Jessie said. "Call me if anything changes."

Harmony's eyes were open. Jessie lowered her phone, smiling as she moved to her bedside.

Harmony's voice was a tired rasp. Her arms, swathed in bandages, lay limp at her sides. "Did we win?"

"Well, let's see. We unraveled a death cult and stopped a literal doomsday plan, not to mention uncovering a traitor and throwing a wrench into whatever Bobby Diehl has planned. Oh, and captured the Concierge, who is not only Bobby's conduit for contraband but one of the world's most elusive smugglers. So, yeah. I'm going to call this a solid win."

Harmony's eyes went wide. "Let me question him."

"Excuse me? Harmony? You almost died last night. Seriously, the docs say it's a small medical miracle that you took that much stingray venom without having a heart attack. You need to lay your ass down in that bed."

"Come on," she said, pleading with her eyes. "This could be a breakthrough. He knows Bobby's internal operations. He knows where to find Xanadu. You know

I'm the best interrogator we have. You *have* to let me do this."

Jessie pursed her lips, thinking it over.

"Tell you what," she said. "I'll let you lead the interrogation if—and only if—I have your word that when it's done, you let me take you directly back here, you get in that bed, and you do not move a muscle until you pass a comprehensive medical exam with flying colors. No ifs, ands, or buts. Agreed?"

"I promise," Harmony said.

"All right," Jessie said. "And if you're very, very good, I might even stop off for ice cream on the way back."

* * *

Jessie stood in front of a one-way mirror, sipping stale coffee from a paper cup and enjoying the show. Kevin was at her side. He had a shell-shocked look on his face.

"She's been at it for eight hours," Jessie said.

On the other side of the glass, Harmony was circling the stainless-steel table like a shark while her victim was sobbing into a crumpled sheet of notebook paper. The rest of it, thirty pages' worth of a confession, was at his side. Harmony grabbed the top page and shoved it in his face, pointing to one line like it was a death sentence, some tiny but fatal detail he'd forgotten.

"I wouldn't wish this on anyone," Kevin murmured.

"Right? Forget waterboarding, *this* is cruel and unusual punishment."

Eventually Harmony emerged, looking pale and unsteady on her feet. She slammed the door and leaned against it for strength.

"We have to cut him loose," she said.

"What?" Jessie asked. "Why?"

"He's not the Concierge." Harmony nodded toward the

mirror. "Every detail he gave us checks out. The Concierge outsources his smuggling jobs. This guy's been his hook-up in New England for a couple of years now. It's piecework. Usually he just does his normal everyday job, flying a traffic copter for a TV station. Once every couple of months he gets a call to fly out, pick up a person or a package, and make the delivery. The next day, a cash envelope shows up in his mailbox. 'Not asking questions' is part of his job description."

"What can he tell us about his boss?" Jessie asked.

"Nothing. The Concierge never shows their face, always calls from a different burner phone and always with a voice modulator, and only pays in cash. I had him write down the details of his last eight delivery jobs. We can check them out, see if any interesting leads pop up, but I think it's a dead end."

"I'm on it," Kevin said. "Send me the data, and I'll get cracking."

"We could pass this guy off to the locals," Jessie said. "They can at least charge him with joyriding in his company helicopter."

"I've got a better idea," Harmony said. "We know the Concierge is paranoid about security. He—or she—is careful, precise, meticulous to a fault."

"Yeah?" Jessie said.

"Let's give him something to think about."

* * *

This is the luckiest day of your life, the woman in the suit and tie had told him. He couldn't disagree. Caught red-handed with a stolen helicopter, confessing to everything he could think of—from smuggling drugs to cheating on his second wife—and they'd still kicked him to the curb without so much as a speeding ticket. No charges, no consequences.

He was on his way home in the back of a cab when his phone rang. Call from a blocked number. He answered it, and an electronic voice cut him off before he could say a word.

"You were taken into custody," the Concierge said. "What happened?"

"Hey, uh, they told me—" The pilot fumbled in his pocket, tugging out a folded piece of paper. "They told me to give you a message. I'm supposed to read it word for word."

Silence. The Concierge was listening. The pilot unfolded the page and read the lines Harmony had written out in neat, tight cursive.

"'We have no interest in conventional crimes. The only reason you are on our target list, and the only reason we even know you exist, is because of Bobby Diehl. His sloppiness has put you and your entire organization in danger. And if you continue to associate with him, then as soon as we've taken him down, we're coming for you next. Walk away while you still can.'"

The only response was a slow wash of modulated static, the sound of a heavy breath.

Then a click as the line went dead.

* * *

Harmony served out her sentence in the hospital, reading field reports on a tablet in between bouts of being poked, prodded, and pinched. After a few days, they let her walk slow circuits around the ward, getting her legs and her strength back. A few days more and she browbeat the lead physician into signing her all-clear order. She suited up and went back to work.

When she stepped off the elevator, entering the subterranean warren of the Basement, Jessie was overseeing the installation of something new. It was a long rectangle of black obsidian, bolted to the bare wall by the entrance, so that anyone entering or leaving headquarters would have to see it. A torque wrench squealed as a workman drove the last bolt snug into place. Jessie waved Harmony over.

"Just in time," she said.

"What's this?" Harmony asked.

"I was thinking about all those years we were under hell's thumb without knowing it. And it was going on for decades before we came along. Every time somebody figured out the game they'd just wipe everybody out, shut it down, and start over again. Vigilant Lock was, what, the fourth or fifth version of the same scam?"

"Something like that."

"But now it's ours. And we're here to stay. We're laying down roots, marking our territory. Part of that—the new HQ, the support staff, the mission archives—that's practical." She gestured to the wall. "And part of that is honor. Our people don't get erased, not anymore. Yeah, their files and their stories have to stay locked in a vault, and the world can never know what they did, the debt we all owe, but...but *we* know. This is to make sure we don't forget."

Harmony studied the span of cold obsidian. She looked to Jessie. "It's a memorial wall."

Jessie held up a single star, five-pointed, polished gold. She pressed it to the center of the obsidian, near the top. It hung there and shone, a single bright star in an endless night.

"This one's for Cooper," Jessie said.

Down the hall, April rolled her chair to the edge of an open doorway.

"They're ready for you in the briefing room," she called out.

Harmony and Jessie shared a lingering glance.

"Three people were responsible for Cooper's murder," Harmony said. "Dominguez, Cranston, and Bobby Diehl."

"Two down, one to go," Jessie said.

Harmony turned to the briefing-room door.

"Let's get to work."

AFTERWORD

I'm writing these final lines on the morning of a new moon. I've always found new moons a reflective time, a good moment for endings and beginnings. In its way, this book marks a little of both. The transition for the Harmony Black series, moving between publishers, took place at the same moment as a seismic upheaval in Harmony's world. Nothing could ever be the same, after that. And so I took this manuscript as an opportunity and a challenge, granting me the chance to look at everything I'd done up until now, consider what worked, what didn't work, and how to come back at the series with a fresh eye.

More than anything, I hope you enjoyed coming on this adventure with me! There's more action to come, danger just ahead, and a pair of long-overdue reckonings on the horizon...

Special thanks as always to my editor Kira Rubenthaler, who gamely jumped in to take up editing duties on the series. Also thanks to James T. Egan, my cover designer, who brought a new style to the series; to Susannah Jones, whose audiobook narration never fails to bring the fire; and to my assistant, Morgan Blake.

Want to know what's coming next? Head over to http://www.craigschaeferbooks.com/mailing-list/ and hop onto my mailing list. Once-a-month newsletters, zero spam. Want to reach out? You can find me on

Facebook at http://www.facebook.com/CraigSchaeferBooks, on Twitter at @craig_schaefer, or just drop me an email at craig@craigschaeferbooks.com.

Made in the USA
San Bernardino, CA
13 January 2020

63116378R00234